Say "I do" to these four stories of wedded bliss from your favorite authors. . . .

Barbara Metzger

"A doyen of humorous, Regency-era romance writing, Metzger pens in the witty tradition of historical romance authors Marion Devon and Marion Chesney."

—*Publishers Weekly*

Connie Brockway

"[Her] work brims with warmth, wit, sensuality, and intelligence." —Amanda Quick

"Connie Brockway's powerful characters grab you by the heartstrings and pull you into their world, their hearts, and their love." —Betina Krahn

Casey Claybourne

"A writer of extraordinary talent. [She] crafts stories you'll cherish forever." —Christina Dodd

Catherine Anderson

"[She] is an amazing talent. Her love stories are tender and earthy, passionate and poignant—and always unusual." —Elizabeth Lowell

"An Anderson book is a guaranteed good read." —*Romantic Times*

The True Love Wedding Dress

Barbara Metzger

Connie Brockway

Casey Claybourne

Catherine Anderson

AN ONYX BOOK

ONYX
Published by New American Library, a division of
Penguin Group (USA) Inc., 375 Hudson Street,
New York, New York 10014, USA
Penguin Group (Canada), 90 Eglinton Avenue East, Suite 700, Toronto,
Ontario M4P 2Y3, Canada (a division of Pearson Penguin Canada Inc.)
Penguin Books Ltd., 80 Strand, London WC2R 0RL, England
Penguin Ireland, 25 St. Stephen's Green, Dublin 2,
Ireland (a division of Penguin Books Ltd.)
Penguin Group (Australia), 250 Camberwell Road, Camberwell, Victoria 3124,
Australia (a division of Pearson Australia Group Pty. Ltd.)
Penguin Books India Pvt. Ltd., 11 Community Centre, Panchsheel Park,
New Delhi - 110 017, India
Penguin Group (NZ), cnr Airborne and Rosedale Roads, Albany,
Auckland 1310, New Zealand (a division of Pearson New Zealand Ltd.)
Penguin Books (South Africa) (Pty.) Ltd., 24 Sturdee Avenue,
Rosebank, Johannesburg 2196, South Africa

Penguin Books Ltd., Registered Offices:
80 Strand, London WC2R 0RL, England

First published by Onyx, an imprint of New American Library,
a division of Penguin Group (USA) Inc.

First Printing, November 2005
10 9 8 7 6 5 4

Copyright © Penguin Group (USA) Inc., 2005
A Perfect Fit copyright © Barbara Metzger, 2005
Glad Rags copyright © Connie Brockway, 2005
Something Special copyright © Casey Mickle, 2005
Prologue, Epilogue, and *Beautiful Gifts* copyright © Adeline Catherine
   Anderson, 2005
All rights reserved

 REGISTERED TRADEMARK—MARCA REGISTRADA

Printed in the United States of America

Contents

Prologue

—◆—

Catherine Anderson

Scotland, 1790

By the flickering light of the kitchen fire, Aileanna MacEwan ran her gaze over the wedding gown that she had only just finished making. It was a glorious dress, each stitch as fine as the ivory silk and delicate lace from which it had been fashioned. It had taken her weeks to complete the garment, and normally she would have been proud of her workmanship. But now she felt only melancholy as she draped the gown over her arm and pushed wearily up from the stool that had served as her perch these last six hours.

Mayhap it was exhaustion that darkened her mood. The upstairs clock had long since chimed the midnight hour. But deep down, she knew it was more than that. Her heart had been breaking ever since she'd started the gown, and now that the task was complete, there would be no stopping the young mistress of the house from setting her wedding date.

" 'Tis not to be borne," she muttered as she swatted the wrinkles from her threadbare skirt. "The blood of a sorceress flows in my veins. Yet here I am, playing lady's maid to the spoiled, selfish daughter of an English aristocrat, a lass who wouldn't know the meaning of true love if it bit her on the arse." Aileanna pushed angrily at her dark hair, which hadn't seen a brush since early the previous morning. "Ach!" she cried. " 'Tis my wedding gown that this should be. Instead, I'll be handing it over to that haughty Bertrade so she

3

can marry the man of my dreams. She'll make his life a misery. Why can he not see that?"

Tears threatened to fill Aileanna's eyes, for even as she bridled against the injustice, she knew that her feelings for the blond and blue-eyed Halford Bainbridge would bring her naught but grief. He was a highborn English gentleman, destined to wed a woman of equal rank, not a lowborn Scottish maid with chafed hands and a patched skirt who'd been driven from her Highland home to make way for sheep and now groveled like a commoner in order to survive.

Oh, Halford had been kind to Aileanna, never failing to smile when they passed each other in the great hall, sometimes even touching a knuckle to his forehead in respectful greeting. Perhaps in another time and place he might have paid her court, but in the present situation, with the Highland Clearances at full tilt and evicted crofters scurrying to emigrate to avoid persecution, such an alliance was utterly impossible.

Never one to remain gloomy for long, Aileanna gazed thoughtfully into the fire. Perhaps nothing could be done to change her situation, but that wasn't to say nothing could be done for other young lasses who might one day find themselves in equally hopeless straits.

It had been half a decade since Aileanna had studied the art of benevolent witchcraft at her grandmother's knee, but her memory was fine. Why not cast a spell on this dress to ensure the marital happiness of any lass who ever chanced to wear it? Such an incantation wouldn't improve Aileanna's own dismal future, but perhaps, by effecting a change of heart in Bertrade, the spell would spare Halford a lifetime of woe.

Aileanna winced at the thought. Was this truly what she wanted, to cast a spell that would ensure Halford's happiness in the arms of another woman? *No,* her heart protested. But even as the thought entered her mind, she pushed it away. She was a witch, born into a mystical aristocracy, and with the gifts bestowed upon her by blood came a solemn and weighty responsibility to rise above her human frailties and selfish desires.

Warming to the idea of sparing Halford the trials of a joyless marriage, Aileanna glanced over her shoulder to make certain she was alone in the cavernous kitchen. Then she collected some water in a cup, laid out the dress on the cook's worktable, rubbed her palms together to generate warmth, and splayed her hands over the silk and lace.

Closing her eyes, she softly chanted, "I call upon the powers that be to make something more of this dress—and me." She needed all the help God could give her, and that was a fact. It wasn't easy to be selfless when her heart was fair breaking. "Lace and pearls, ruffles and skirts, let young lasses endure no more hurt."

She wrinkled her nose. Surely she could do better than *that*. She consoled herself with the thought that it was the meaning of the words that counted, not how nicely they rhymed. Dipping her fingertips into the cup, she pressed on.

"With this sprinkle of water, I call upon the forces of goodness to heed my words. Upon this dress, I cast a charm. Let no maid who possesses it come to harm."

Oh, how it rankled to say those words when she knew the first maid to possess the gown would be the selfish Bertrade. Aileanna swallowed back a rush of jealous resentment and forced herself to continue.

"Instead let her find the man of her dreams and live a life as fine as these seams, laughing and dancing, safe in his arms." Aileanna let her eyes fall closed again and smiled slightly, imagining all the young lasses in future whose lives would be transformed by the simple wearing of this gown. "O'er the mountains and across the sea, no distance too great for this dress shall be. With time, the lace shall weather well, the fabric itself a magical spell.

"Down through the years, through many hands it shall pass, moving about from lass to lass. There one moment, and gone the next, let this dress drift like a tendril of smoke, fulfilling its destiny as I have bespoke."

After falling silent, Aileanna remained motionless, her eyes still tightly closed. Ah, but it felt marvelous to use her powers again. She could have sworn she felt a tingle of warmth moving up her arms and through her body.

With a start, she realized that the tingle was real. She gasped and jerked her hands away from the dress, staring in baffled confusion at the silk and lace. Before she could collect her thoughts, a door to the kitchen banged open. Aileanna whirled to see Halford standing in the doorway, his blond hair gleaming in the firelight, his eyes as hot and blue as the base of a flame.

"We must talk, Aileanna," he said tautly.

"Howe'er did ye gain entrance? 'Tis the middle of the night."

"I bribed a servant to leave a door unlocked." He waved a hand. "How I got in isn't important. I knew you'd be working late on that dratted wedding dress, and I need to talk with you. I can't go on like this, always passing you by in the great hall as if you're invisible, pretending all the while to love another when it's you and only you who possesses my heart."

Aileanna gulped. "But, Halford, what of Bertrade? Ye've publicly announced yer betrothal to her. If ye back out now, there'll be a monstrous scandal!"

"I cannot marry Bertrade. Have you no eyes in your head? She's a bratty little witch. Nothing pleases her."

Aileanna's eyes went wide, for it was she, not Bertrade, who was a witch. She threw an appalled glance at the wedding dress, wondering if the spell she'd just cast upon it was responsible for Halford's sudden avowal of love. Had she misspoken during the incantation and gotten part of it wrong? It had been a long while since she'd practiced her craft. Mayhap her skills were a wee bit rusty.

"This cannot be," she cried, and began wringing her hands. "Ye're not thinking clearly, Halford."

"Please," he whispered. "I know it may be difficult for us."

"Difficult? Impossible, more like."

He shook his head. "Even if my father disinherits me, which he most assuredly will, I won't be entirely penniless. I have a trust from my grandmother, a paltry sum by most standards, but if we're frugal, the monthly stipend will be enough to keep us in tea and biscuits with a roof over our heads. I love you, Aileanna. I have for months, perhaps from the first instant I saw you."

"It's the dress," she tried to explain.

A heated gleam slipped into Halford's blue eyes, and he walked determinedly toward her. "It's not that awful dress you're wearing, I assure you. Marry me, Aileanna. Say you will be my wife. I know you return my love. I've seen it in your eyes. We won't be rich, but I swear, I'll garb you in fine wool, not rags, and you'll never have to pander to someone like Bertrade again. We can leave this godforsaken place and start over somewhere else, perhaps in America, as so many others are doing."

Aileanna's last thought just before Halford gathered her into his strong arms and kissed her was that this couldn't be happening. Then every bit of common sense she possessed seemed to abandon her. *Halford.* Oh, how she loved him. The kiss was everything she'd dreamed it might be and more.

When Halford finally let her breathe again, she angled her head to glance over her shoulder. To her amazement, the dress no longer lay on the work surface behind her. She wriggled from Halford's arms to peer under the table, thinking the gown might have slipped to the floor.

"Where has it gotten off to?" she muttered. "The wedding dress! 'Twas right here, and now it's gone."

Halford tried to reclaim her lips for another kiss. "Who cares where the blasted dress is?"

Aileanna cared, for it appeared to her that the gown had vanished into thin air—like a tendril of smoke.

A Perfect Fit

Barbara Metzger

Chapter One

1813, Devon, England

*T*he wedding gown was still the prettiest thing Katie
Cole had ever seen or owned. She had thought so
the first time she'd unwrapped the ivory silk and lace,
of unusual style and exquisite workmanship, when it
was delivered by mistake from her dressmaker. The
modiste had claimed it was no design of hers, so Katie
had set it aside, with regrets, to wait for the magnificent gown's rightful owner. Then the dressmaker's
shop had burned down, along with Katie's trousseau
and her own pink satin gown. With so little time before her wedding, the ivory silk would have to do.

Katie remembered feeling like a princess when she
held it up to herself, the luckiest, most beautiful bride
in all of creation. Even now, as she knelt in the dust
of the low-ceilinged attic to pull the dress from the
bottom of an old trunk, she could feel the same tingle
she'd felt before her marriage—the hope, the joy, the
certainty that her future would be filled with happiness. How could it not be, when the mysterious gown
had arrived so auspiciously and seemed to be a perfect fit?

Unfortunately, Katie never wore the gown.

Her betrothed was killed in a coaching mishap mere
days before the wedding. Her mother said she was
better off without the drunken, devil-may-care lout.
Her father said that fortune-hunting Frederick had
been driving his racing phaeton in the wrong direction,

away from London and the church, as fast as his horses would go, once he discovered that Katie's dowry was to be held in trust. Her aunt said it served Katie right for stubbornly insisting on marrying a man her family had only reluctantly approved. Her grandmother said she was too young, anyway, at seventeen, to know her own mind. Katie's old nanny said Katie was pregnant.

Papa had sent her away to Devon. He'd have sent her to Hades if he could, but her mother had insisted. Katie had a new name—heaven forbid she'd ever mention the Bainbridge one again—a wedding band, and a meager allowance, if she stayed gone.

Katie, Mrs. Katherine Cole, as she had been known for the last eighteen years, wondered again what other choice she might have made. Give up her baby? Throw herself into the Thames? Beg in the streets? No. Her little cottage was comfortable, her neighbors kind to the widow of a heroic officer in the Navy, her precious daughter the light of her life. She could afford food and firewood, a small staff, and lessons for Susannah as she grew. She could not afford elegant gowns such as the one she carefully unwrapped from its tissue.

Katie touched the covered buttons down the front of the dress, marveling again at the workmanship, and at her own stupidity in believing Feckless Frederick and his words of love. Just touching the gown, though, still made her feel that True Love truly existed and that a happily-ever-after was possible—for her little girl.

Susannah was all grown up, a sweet young lady of comely looks and genteel manners, and the same stubborn pride as her mother. Katie wished the girl would wait to marry—Katie was not ready to part with her darling, who was a curly-haired infant just yesterday, it seemed—but she knew Susannah would not wait. Katie had not, after all. So Mrs. Cole was planning the wedding, and Susannah would wear the beautiful gown.

Unfortunately, Susannah hated it.

"I am not going to wear that musty old thing, and that is final!" Susannah stamped her foot, on the trailing hem of the gown Katie held out in her daughter's bedchamber. Perhaps her darling was not quite the sweet little moppet Katie remembered. Her blue eyes were flashing, and her rosebud mouth was puckered.

"But it is a beautiful gown and—"

"It is old and dingy and out of style. The skirt is too full, the waist is too low. Whoever heard of buttons like that? I will look a fright."

To Katie's eyes the gown looked perfect, surprisingly not the least bit faded or yellowed with time. As for the style, she told her daughter, "Mrs. Peebles in the village can make alterations. Come, try it on and you shall see how becoming it is."

Susannah was becoming more adamant. "What, after spiders have been living in it for decades, if not mice?"

Katie gave the gown a good shake. "See? No spiders, no mice. Just slip it on and you'll change your mind. The gown will make you feel more beautiful than ever. Mr. Wellforde will think he is the most fortunate man in England, which he is, of course."

"Dear Gerald already thinks he is the luckiest man in the universe, because we are to wed. He will not be happy to see me wearing my mother's dowdy castoff."

"We can say it is an heirloom, passed down through the family."

"What, I should lie to dear Gerald? Or his family?"

Dear Gerald's family—his large, London-bred, sophisticated family—was the reason Katie had unearthed the gown. "You know we discussed this, Susannah. With all the guests we had to invite to the wedding breakfast, having to rent the entire Brookville Inn and extra servants, we cannot afford much more. You still need a new traveling costume, a new riding habit, and a new night rail." Heaven knew Katie could not send her little girl off on her honeymoon in faded flannel bedgowns, or with darned

stockings and paper-thin soles on her slippers. She had
been saving a portion of her meager income for Susannah's dowry since the day the precious blue-eyed baby
was born, so not much money was ever left for extrav-
agances. "We simply cannot afford that expensive blue
velvet you wanted, not even if we try to sew it our-
selves, which would never look elegant enough."

Katie had written to her mother, through Nanny, as
usual. Twice a year unsigned notes had arrived, at
Christmas and Katie's birthday, with a pound note
tucked between the folds, and she had written her
thanks to the old nursemaid, knowing the message
would reach Lady Bainbridge. Katie recently wrote of
the wedding and her additional expenses, but without
much hope. Her father was a despot, and a cheesepar-
ing miser besides. Now there was no time to wait on
her mother's courage or her thin purse.

"If we should have a few pence left over," she said,
"we really should re-cover the chairs in the parlor.
You would not wish us to appear as paupers in front
of your new in-laws, would you?" The paltry size of
that hard-gathered dowry was bad enough.

"Of course not. According to dear Gerald, the Well-
fordes are very refined people."

"Precisely. But we did have to make repairs to the
roof last winter and have the pianoforte refurbished
after the leak so I could keep giving music lessons. If
you postpone the wedding until the beginning of the
new year, when the annuity is deposited, then perhaps
we can afford such luxuries. I could sell some strawberry preserves, or advertise for more students. In the
spring we would have piglets to sell."

Susannah's pointed chin, so like her mother's, came
up. "No, I know what you are trying to do. You want
to make me feel guilty so I will delay the wedding. I
know you have made sacrifices for me, and I am
grateful."

"I never meant to imply anything of the sort. You
know that I would give everything I had to make you
happy, darling. And Mr. Wellforde will understand."

"He will understand that I am a weak child who does not know her own mind. He will go off to his new estate and forget all about me." Her lower lip started to tremble.

"Never, darling. He will wait the few months if he truly—"

"He does love me, I know it!" Susannah said with a wail. "But you still think I am too young to get married, too young to make such an important decision."

Since that was part of the truth, the honest though regrettable lack of funds being the other part, Katie could not answer. She just kept running her fingers down the lace of the gown's sleeves, feeling a warmth, a tingle, a sense that she was right. Susannah had to wear this dress; then everything would be fine.

Mr. Wellforde was an earnest, pleasant young man, Katie told herself, again, who swore he would take good care of Susannah. He had a bit of property in Hampshire he was going to turn into a horse-racing stud farm now that he was down from university, with a modest inheritance that his trustees would release to him on his marriage. The young couple would be comfortable, and perhaps able to afford trips to London where his family lived and, Katie prayed, visits home. They seemed compatible enough, both enjoying simple country pursuits. Why, they had met when he was on a walking tour through Brookville with some classmates and Susannah had given them directions. And they both liked horses. Which was, perhaps, more than Katie and Frederick had had in common. Mr. Wellforde was not half as handsome as Frederick had been, or as well spoken, but Susannah seemed to think dear Gerald was as good-looking as Adonis and as smart as Aristotle. The boy seemed just as besotted. Bacon-brained, both of them.

But what if Susannah had inherited more than her mother's pointed chin and her father's blue eyes? Then she would not wait, as her parents had not waited. So Katie had given her reluctant permission for the engagement and hoped for the best. Now Susannah was having the banns called, which was not the best, not at all.

Taking Katie's silence for an argument as only an eighteen-year-old could do, Susannah tossed her head, sending blond curls every which way. "You were younger than I when you married!"

Only Katie had *not* married. She had not listened to her parents, had not made wise choices, had not shown an ounce of maturity. No, she had threatened to run off to Gretna Green if she could not wed Frederick, threatened to ruin herself and embarrass them all. They had relented, Lord Bainbridge saying good riddance. Katie had been paying for her thickheadedness ever since. Her foolish fancy had cost her the love of her family, her place in Society, and the ability to purchase a fine wedding gown for her only daughter. Katie regretted the last most of all.

"Very well, the wedding goes on as planned. But you shall have to wear my wedding gown. Now, come, try it on so we can see what needs to be altered before we take it to Mrs. Peebles."

Susannah brushed a tear from the corner of her eye and stamped her dainty foot again—this time Katie moved the gown. Susannah was not willing to concede, not for her wedding. "I could ask dear Gerald—"

"No! You may not accept gifts from him, even if you are betrothed! His family will think you an adventuress and will never welcome you into their midst. And especially such a personal gift."

"His mama—"

Bad enough that some other woman was going to see her daughter more than Katie would after the wedding. Mrs. Wellforde would not have the dressing of Susannah before! "That would sink your chances of earning her respect. Why, she would think you were begging for handouts." The way Katie had uselessly begged her mother for money to purchase Susannah a new gown. "Besides, I see no reason for your upset. This gown is beautiful and will make your wedding day a memorable one. Try it on and you shall see."

Susannah wrinkled her straight little nose. "It smells. I just washed my hair and do not wish it fouled with that odor."

Katie held the gown closer, but all she smelled was a lingering odor of lavender that the trunk had been packed with. Spring, new hope, a fresh start—that was what she smelled. "Fine. I shall air the gown out in the sun and then you'll see."

Unfortunately, it rained for the next three days.

Chapter Two

*T*anyon Wellforde, Viscount Forde, did not like
weddings. The women were always weeping, embarrassed at their tears and their drunken menfolk.
The gentlemen were usually foxed, either in commis-
eration with the groom or in relief that they were not
the poor blighter putting on leg shackles. Afterward,
the men were less sober, and the females were more
embarrassed at the ribald comments. Foolish ritual,
the viscount thought on his way to answer his sister-
in-law's summons to her private sitting room at Wellforde House, but he supposed he had to attend his
nephew Gerald's nuptials. He also supposed that the
wedding was to be the topic of the coming conversation. It had been, endlessly, since the nodcock had
become engaged.

Forde, as he was called, wondered if the lad would
consider a private ceremony and no wedding breakfast
if the viscount doubled his wedding gift. No, the bride
likely wanted the church, the cake, the flowers, and
the fuss. They all did, plaguesome creatures. Maybe,
Forde thought with hope in his heart, he could persuade Gerald to call the whole thing off. That's what
a conscientious guardian would do. Nineteen was too
young an age for a young man to give up his freedom
and settle down with one woman for the rest of his
bound to be long, boring, strife-ridden life.

In Forde's estimation, the worst thing about weddings was that they ended with marriages. Some of his

19

friends must have happy marriages, but dashed if he could tell, meeting them at the gaming hells and bordellos of London. His own match had been an arranged one when he was but a few years older than Gerald, and it had been a disaster. He'd been young and restless; his beautiful, wealthy bride had been spoiled and moody. He'd called her immature; she'd called him cold. Forde had stayed polite; Priscilla had stayed faithful until she presented him with a son. Then she died of a fever in the arms of her current lover.

Two good things had come of the marriage. One, his wife had died before the world, and their son, could learn of her infidelities. Two, that son, Crispin. Forde had an heir of his own. No one could say he had not done his duty to king and country. He had assured the succession and taken his proper seat in Parliament. He gave to charities and let his brother go off to fight for England and die in some godforsaken place. He took good care of his dead brother's widow and children, every tenant on his estates, every servant in his employ. No, he owed no one anything, especially not another marriage.

He was forty years old, and the matchmaking hens had long given up on their chances of snabbling him for one of the silly, frilly chicks. What, wed a girl as young as his eldest flighty niece? Never. Now the biddies were pushing their sisters and cousins at him, or their own scrawny necks and sagging breasts. Give his hand—and his title and his fortune—to a social-climbing spinster or a roving-eyed widow? Hah! There were enough women of fine looks and flexible morals who were willing to enjoy a peer with deep pockets and his own teeth without expecting a wedding band. Forde kept in shape and was keeping all of his dark hair, too. Finding a willing partner for an evening or a month was no problem; staying out of parson's mousetrap was.

Viscount Forde was not giving up his freedom. He'd felt like he was drowning for the five years the marriage lasted and was not inclined to test the waters again. Poor Gerald had to marry eventually to provide heirs to his own estate. Forde did not, for which he daily thanked his dead wife.

"No, I am not going to interfere," he told his sister-in-law over the platter of tea cakes she always had nearby. "If the young cawker wants to marry some chit from the country, that is his business. I already refused to purchase him a commission in the Army on your urging. I will not play the tyrant further."

Agnes helped herself to a macaroon, then fed half to her Pekingese, who sat beside her on the brocade sofa. In Forde's opinion, his sister-in-law was looking more like her pet every day—fat, frowning, reddish hair all in a frizz. That last might have been because Agnes was nervously pulling at it—her hair, that was, not the dog—when she was not eating. Now she swallowed, moaned, and declared, "You have to stop the wedding. That Woman is a fortune hunter. She will make poor Gerald's life a misery."

Wasn't that a wife's job? Forde took a slice of poppyseed cake. "But you were the one who told me to give my blessings to the match. I said at the time I thought Gerald was too young."

"He swore he was in love. What else could I do but approve his betrothal? Besides, I never thought he would actually go through with the marriage. Young men's infatuations do not last long, you must know."

Forde did not. His heart had never been affected by any of his *amours,* not past dawn, at any rate. Young Gerald had vowed Miss Susannah Cole was the only love of his life. Who was his uncle to tell him such a notion was rubbish?

Agnes had a lemon tart in one hand and a lock of her hair in the other. Forde watched as carefully as the pop-eyed Pekingese, but his sister-in-law managed to eat, feed the dog, and muss her hair all at the same time. He was impressed, but not by her reasoning.

"I was certain that when he returned to London after his walking tour, he would forget all about the chit. He was bound to meet the perfect bride at one of the come-out balls."

"Gerald does not care much for social doings. You must know that."

If she did, she ignored it. "He would have found the ideal wife among this year's debutantes. A female of substance, not some rural hayseed. He might have wed an heiress, who knows? A fine-looking young man, if I have to say so myself, with lovely manners and an excellent education."

Which Forde had paid for. He nodded. "I am sure Gerald would be a good catch on the marriage market, but he does not need to wed for money. He has that profitable property from my grandfather and a tidy sum from my mother."

"He needs a young lady of consequence," Agnes insisted. "One who can take her place in the beau monde as a viscountess. After all, Gerald is your heir, after Crispin, of course. If anything should happen to the boy . . ."

Forde dropped the slice of cake. The dog leaped off the sofa after it. "That is my son you are speaking of, madam. Nothing is going to happen to him."

She sniffed. "The child is all of ten years old, and puny."

"He is wiry, not puny."

She sniffed again. "Who knows what kind of care he is receiving at that school you sent him to?"

Crispin attended the same academy Forde and his brother had. He was young, but the viscount had thought anything was better than leaving him to be smothered by petticoat rule here in London with Agnes and her two daughters. Still, he worried about that nagging cough the boy had all last winter. No, Cris would do. He had to. The alternative was too dreadful to contemplate.

"Gerald is not my heir. With the grace of God, he shall never be. Therefore, he is free to wed any lady he chooses."

"Any lady. Precisely. Who knows but that Miss Cole is nothing more than a dairy maid? I was certain Gerald would see reason once her pretty looks faded from his memory." Agnes needed another macaroon to continue. Raffles the Pekingese needed a lift back onto the sofa, he was so fat. "According to my son, the girl has blond hair and big blue eyes, a heart-shaped face, and a fair complexion, despite enjoying tramping through the countryside." Agnes shuddered at the thought. So did the dog in her arms.

Forde had heard all about Miss Cole's myriad attractions, endlessly, it seemed. "Gerald does not seem to have forgotten anything about the young woman."

"How could he when he keeps going back for visits to that young man with whom he was on the walking tour? A squire's son or some such, from university. I do not doubt they are in clandestine correspondence besides, Gerald and the hoyden."

"In fairness, I do not believe letters between an affianced couple are anything improper. They'd need to discuss wedding plans and—"

"There was not supposed to be a wedding! Gerald has to marry a female of good family and good connections, I tell you. It is his duty to his sisters."

Agnes had two daughters after her son, one more goosish than the other. Forde was paying for their finishing lessons, as he would pay for their presentations and their weddings. Gads, two more nuptials to suffer through. "I do not see where Gerald and his bride need concern themselves with—"

"That is all you know. Men! Gerald must have a bride who can help the girls find the bachelors with the deepest pockets, make the best connections, get invited to the best parties. Now if you had a wife . . ."

"Which I do not. Surely, as the brats'—that is, as the girls'—mother, you are best suited to see to their futures."

"Bosh. I am too weak to do all that gadding about town."

Too fat and too lazy, Forde thought but did not say. "Gerald says Miss Cole is very well mannered. I am certain she will be of assistance."

"She will not be here. The two gudgeons intend to reside at the Oaks in the country now that you have given the estate into Gerald's keeping. Worse, he intends for me and the girls to go live there, too. He says we should stop being a burden on you and your bank account." Agnes pulled a handkerchief from her sleeve and blew her nose. Crumbs flew across the room.

"Nonsense. You are not a burden and never have been." The house was large enough that Forde seldom saw his kin by marriage. And his purse was deep enough that he never truly felt the pinch of their expenses. "Gerald cannot intend you to reside in the country, not with his new wife." Forde pitied Miss Cole if such were the case and wondered about his nephew's sanity, if not his intelligence.

"Not right away, of course, but soon." She sighed, loudly. "That is what Gerald said, that you should have your house back, and your privacy."

The idea appealed to the viscount, but he knew his duty. And he did keep a discreet love nest in Kensington for such private moments. "Gerald is not of age, and I am the girls' guardian until then, so he cannot force you to leave London."

"Thank goodness, for how am I to see my gals settled advantageously, if we are stuck in the shires? Gerald says he met Miss Cole in the country, so that is good enough for his sisters." She started to sob. "He says they are not titled, so they do not need grand presentations and lavish come-out balls at your expense."

The boy sounded more mature by the moment. Lud knew, Agnes never thought of the cost of anything, or who was to pay it. Still, Forde was head of the family, and he could not let a mere boy, one just starting his own family, beggar himself to support three women. Four, if one counted the bride. "Dash it, my brother gave his life for this country. The least I can do is see his daughters well married. I'll speak with Gerald. Is he at home?"

"He is at his new home, readying the Oaks for its new mistress and his new horses."

"Then he truly cares about the girl and is acting in a responsible manner." Forde stood up, ready to leave, resigned to attending the blasted wedding.

"There is worse."

"Worse than wanting you to ruralize? Worse than not providing you with an elegant chaperone for your daughters?"

"Far worse. Rushing into this marriage will cause talk that will reflect on the entire family. Such unseemly haste casts doubts on the female's respectability, doubts that will rub off on my own darlings."

Forde sat back down, in a hurry. "Good grief, is the woman breeding, then?" He'd murder the cawker for letting his prick push him into a misalliance. They'd had an awkward talk when the boy turned sixteen, and Forde had considered his avuncular duties done. Damn. He should have repeated the warnings and the why-nots. Maybe he should start now with his own son. The boy was ten, after all. Perhaps there was time to visit Crispin at his school before the deuced wedding.

Now that she was not being exiled to the hinterlands, with her daughters' come-outs to be at the local pub like her son's wretched wedding breakfast, Agnes could be magnanimous. And she could eat again. Two biscuits—one for her and one for the dog— disappeared while Forde fumed. "No, I doubt Miss Cole is that foolish," she finally said. "Not even an innocent boy like Gerald will purchase what he can have for free. Besides, he says they are never alone, not even on those dreadful rambles of his. What I believe, however, is that this mad dash to the altar, this helter-skelter scramble off to the Oaks, means Gerald is ashamed of the girl. He knows she will never be accepted in polite society, so he is hiding her away."

"But he says her manners are perfect, her learning impressive, and her face and figure like a goddess's."

"Humph. What's all that to decent breeding or money? We know there's hardly a groat in the family. I suspect there is no Officer Cole, either. I asked Admiral Benson to look into the matter, and he could find no records of a Captain Cole or a Lieutenant Cole whatsoever. Not even an ensign. The man must have been a common seaman."

"Gerald's bride's father? The Navy chap who died a hero?"

"Such a hero that no one at the Admiralty ever heard of him. Likely he was an impressed sailor, nothing more. And the mother is an orphan, they tell me. Heaven knows where her people came from. They live in a cottage, according to Gerald, and keep chickens." She blew her nose again, this time to rid herself of the imagined stench of the henhouse. "They must be fortune hunters."

As opposed to Agnes trying to find wealthy, titled husbands for her two lambs. All women sought to better their prospects, and Forde could not fault Miss Cole for her attempts to secure a comfortable future. "Gerald's fortune is not that great."

"To widows and orphans it is. She will be moving into the Oaks before the cat can lick her ear."

"Naturally. As Gerald's wife—"

"Not the gal, the mother. I might have to live with her there when you get married and throw us out!" Agnes wailed, setting the dog to yipping.

Forde felt like tearing out his own hair. "I am not getting married. And I told you, you and the girls can stay at Wellforde House here in London as long as you wish. Or at Wellforde Grange if you want them to get used to local society before their come-outs. There is no reason for you or my nieces to live with Gerald at all, so he can invite his wife's mother and her chickens, too, if he wishes."

The dish of pastries was nearly finished. So was Agnes, except for one final complaint. "Gerald says the chit has no wedding dress. What am I to do, spend my darlings' clothing allowance on her? You'll see I am right: The forward female is only interested in poor Gerald's fortune if she is already hinting for favors and money."

Damn. This was more serious than Forde had thought. "I'll have a talk with Gerald."

"You will not change his mind. I tried. He is adamant. Besides, no gentleman backs out of an engagement. Gerald will look no-account, and no decent female will accept him as a suitor. He'll grow into a crusty old bachelor, set in his ways, like you."

Forde ignored the last bit. "Then I will have a talk with this Miss Cole and her grasping mother. If they turn out to be the parasites you think, then I will withdraw my blessings. I can hold on to Gerald's inheritance until he reaches five and twenty. I doubt the Cole harpies will want to wait that long before sinking their talons into his coffers. I wager the betrothal will end as soon as I reveal my intentions."

"Gerald will not be happy."

Forde thought of his own marriage. "Trust me, he stands a better chance of being happy as a single man."

Chapter Three

*A*ll roads are longer when the destination is undesired. Forde traveled into Devon slowly, blaming his dallying on the rainy October weather, the mired roads, the indifferent horses he was forced to hire at the posting houses. He blamed the delay on anything but his lack of enthusiasm to confront Miss Cole and her mother, and his fears of losing Gerald's regard. If the young woman was as greedy and grasping as Agnes thought, as conniving and common, then Gerald would thank them in the end . . . if he ever forgave Forde and his mother for interfering in his life. By Jupiter, Forde barely forgave his own father for saddling him with Priscilla, and they had both been dead for years.

Thinking of saddles made Forde decide to hire a horse when his coach finally reached the little village of Brookville. The incessant rain had stopped at last, and he was tired of being jostled inside the carriage. Besides, the fewer servants to speculate about his conversation with the Cole women, the better. By riding, he could leave his groom and driver and valet behind at the only inn in town, a decent enough place, it seemed, despite his sister-in-law's dire predictions of hedge taverns and drovers' pubs. The ale was good there, at any rate.

The gray gelding he hired was not of his usual caliber or pedigree, but the hostler assured him that Smoky was a goer, once he shook the fidgets out and got over his little crotchets.

"Nothing a fine gentleman like yourself cannot handle, my lord."

Forde was ready for the challenge, rather than for the ladies of Cole Cottage. Following the innkeeper's directions through the village and a mile out, he made his reluctant way there, steering the equally reluctant gelding away from rain-filled wheel ruts and fallen tree limbs. He did not dare set the horse to a gallop, not with the road in such poor condition, but they arrived at the house with no ill effects, sooner than Forde wished.

Well, the place was not a hovel, at least. Not quite a gentleman's expansive country residence, it was no thatch-roofed, dirt-floored shack, either. The grounds were tidy, with late-blooming rosebushes and still-colorful flower beds obviously well tended, ivy neatly trimmed away from the windows. The square building itself was three storeys high, made of stone with slate roof tiles. So the females were not indigent, if the house's appearance was anything to go by, and the vista must be pleasant on a clear day, with rolling fields and wooded hills.

He rode up to the front walk, but no one came out to take his horse. He saw no hitching post or nearby fence, either, and did not trust Smoky not to bolt, not when the gelding shied at every bird and waving branch in the wind. Crotchets? The horse had more quirks than mad King George.

After calling, "Halloo the house," with no response, Forde rode around the side of the building, hoping to find a gardener or the stable.

To the rear he saw chickens and goats, a barnlike structure, and a cultivated patch that was far more extensive than any kitchen garden. Mrs. Cole appeared to be augmenting her widow's portion by growing or raising her own food, or taking the surplus to market. No true lady would have kept chickens at her back door, but Forde admired the woman's spirit and drive. Naturally he would not admire her ambition to better herself if it came at Gerald's expense. One was gumption; the other was greed. He would have to wait to see for himself.

With the clouds gathering again, the wind increasing, a dampness chilling the air, and still no groom or gardener, Forde decided to see if there was room in the barn for Smoky. He had not come all this way only to return to the inn without speaking to the females and making his decision. Besides, the rain would start soon, and he had no fancy to ride back to the village in a downpour. The smoke he could see rising from the house's chimneys and its promise of hot tea and a warming fire were far more inviting.

"I know it is not what you might be accustomed to, old chap," he told the horse as he rode the gray along a mired path, "but we all have to make sacrifices for my nephew's future."

The goats and the chickens and the cow looming in the mist did not faze the gelding. The ghost did. The fearsome white wraith was billowing and blowing across the yard, making snapping, flapping noises with every gust of wind.

In the general course of things, Forde was too good a rider to become separated from his horse. This was not his horse, however, and a trail that was more a swamp than a path was not the usual thing, to say nothing of a soaring, swooping, snow white specter. Smokey shied, bucked, then reared, but his hindquarters kept sliding in the muck beneath his hooves, terrorizing the bacon-brained beast further. He swiveled. Forde did not.

Like the fine equestrian he usually was, Forde kept hold of the reins. And he caught the ghost in his other hand before he hit the ground, trapping the blasted thing and its rope tail beneath him. He used one wadded corner of it to wipe the mud off his face, once he caught his breath. Then he lay there, wondering if he would sink deeper into the quagmire, like a potato taking root. For certain his limbs wanted no part of getting up.

He gave them no choice. First it was a ghost; now

they were under attack by a banshee. A figure from hell was screeching, coming toward him with a pitch-fork, black cape flying out behind. Forde stood in a hurry then, before Smoky could trample him in his fright. He tried to wipe some more of the muck—he hoped the chickens had not used the path recently—out of his eyes so he could see his assailant and defend himself from this latest fiend.

"My wedding gown!" The devil's own creature shrieked, thankfully dropping the pitchfork.

Forde regarded the filthy, befouled length of fabric he still held in his mud-daubed hand, the clothesline lost under his feet. Then he regarded the female. He had never been knocked breathless by the sight of a woman before. Either he had been struck by one of Cupid's arrows or his ribs were broken. She was beau-tiful, but she was closer to his age than Gerald's. She also had green eyes, not blue, and honey-colored hair instead of blond. "Miss Cole?"

"I am Susannah's mother, but she was going to wear my gown for her own wedding this month. Now it is ruined."

Either the rain was starting again already or the female was crying, for her pale cheeks were definitely wet as she wrested the rag from his grasp. She was weeping over a bit of lace and cloth? No, blast it, Forde understood that he had destroyed a treasured reminder of the widow's lost love. Who knew what else she had left of her marriage—a wedding band, perhaps a lock of hair or a miniature portrait? Damn.

She was shaking out the sodden mess, as if that might restore it. Nothing would, Forde knew, espe-cially not the gelding's snorting at it. He stepped back, pulling Smoky with him. "I shall replace it, of course," he said, full knowing the impossibility of replacing an heirloom or a memory.

"No one can. It was . . . special."

"I understand your attachment, Mrs. Cole, but a skilled dressmaker can copy it. I can send it to London in the morning."

She had stopped shaking the gown and was now brushing at it with her hand, which instantly turned black with muck. "No, I cannot let you do that. It was my fault for leaving it on the line in such a wind. We have had so much rain this week that I could not air it before this."

The woman was babbling in her upset. Forde could feel her pain—or was that a wrenched shoulder from his fall? The devil take it, he would give her the money, perhaps enough for her to let Gerald out of her clutches; then no one would need the benighted wedding dress. Maybe she could save enough of it to make a handkerchief. That was the best he could do, now that he had done his worst. "But I insist on making good for my clumsiness."

His tone must have brought her out of her reverie, for now Mrs. Cole finally took notice of the trespasser in her garden. He could see her eyes shift to the pitchfork, too far away to be any protection from a marauder, then to his hand reaching for his purse—or a pistol. She took a step back, her boots squelching in the mire, but the ruined gown stayed pressed to her chest, befouling her cloak, too, which was no great loss that the viscount could tell.

"I could not accept money from a stranger."

"But I am not truly a stranger." He bowed, a gob of mud falling from his chin. "Tanyon Wellforde, at your service."

"Oh, you are one of Mr. Gerald Wellforde's relations then." She relaxed a bit, although keeping her distance and not, thankfully, offering her filthy hand for him to kiss. "The wedding is not for a few weeks, however. You are early."

"Actually, I am Viscount Forde, Gerald's uncle and guardian," he said, sounding somewhat pompous even to his own ears. He was insulted that this countrywoman in her shabby cloak would think him so skitter-witted that he did not know the time or the place. Granted he had fallen off his horse and taken down her clothesline, but he did know the date of his own nephew's wedding: It was soon, or he would not be here.

"Gerald's uncle Tanyon?" she asked, a hint of doubt in her voice. "He is always singing your praises." Gerald had always raved what a bruising rider his uncle was. His lordship would be bruised, all right, from flying over his horse's head. Gerald also claimed the viscount was a tailor's delight, with half the gentlemen in London wanting to emulate his style. He would make his tailor rich, needing a new suit. And he was as downy as they came, Gerald had claimed. Yes, those were chicken feathers in his hair.

"Gerald—Mr. Wellforde, that is—is not here."

"Yes, I know, madam." Now Forde was more aggravated that she was still treating him like an attics-to-let jackass. He was muddied and battered, but he did not have bats in his belfry. "He is in Hampshire."

She nodded, seemingly reassured that he truly was Gerald's famous uncle. "We expect him at week's end, for the next calling of the banns."

Forde had come to prevent that very thing. He could feel his face growing warm, the only part of him that was. With any luck the mud would hide the tell-tale color of his muddled misrepresentation. "I, ah, came to see you and Miss Cole."

"Why?" she asked, too bluntly for his taste. He turned and spit a feather out of his mouth.

Why? "About the, ah, settlements. That is what guardians do, you know."

"I already gave Gerald my solicitor's direction."

And she gave Forde her back, more concerned with counting the buttons on the blasted gown than the fact that he was damp to the bone and stank like a pig. Lud, did she keep pigs in this swamp of a yard, too? Instead of being invited inside for a hot drink or a warm bath, as any lady would have offered, Forde felt a cold drizzle dripping down his neck, mingling with the mud. His heart was growing colder, too. He might have felt sorry for the beautiful widow, mourning her dead husband and her gown—but his toes were growing numb, by Harry. "I thought I should meet you and Miss Cole before the ceremony."

"I see." And he thought she did, as she turned and eyed him with suspicion again, this time a lioness ready to defend her cub. She knew he was here to inspect his nephew's prospective bride, to pass judgment. She also knew he could delay the wedding, if not cancel it altogether. "My daughter is not here, either. She is at the rectory, arranging flowers for the church. She will stay there until the storm passes." As anyone with an iota of sense would do, her expression seemed to say, instead of riding across wet ground on an unfamiliar horse in a threatening storm, on the devil's own work.

Which Forde had done, proving him a skip-brain, if not a lunatic, in her too obvious estimation. She bent to pick up the pitchfork, being careful not to let the gown drag on the ground.

Hah! Now who was being blockheaded? One more handful of dirt was not going to make a ha'penny's worth of difference to that garment's demise. And Forde was not leaving yet. He had not settled his dressmaking debt, and he had not settled his mind about Gerald's nuptials.

"If your daughter is from home, perhaps I might speak with you? I shall not need much of your time."

Mrs. Cole looked at him in the same horror that Smoky had viewed the ghost. Forde could not tell if that was because she did not wish him and all his mud in her house, or merely him. "Please, until the rain passes."

She shook her head, sending droplets of dampness scattering. "I think you should call again when Susannah will be here. She will want to meet you, too, after hearing so much about you from your nephew. I can send word when she returns. You are lodging at the inn in town, I suppose? It is the only respectable place hereabouts, if you have not already taken rooms there. You really should get out of your damp clothes. At the inn," she hurried to add, "where Mr. Roundtree will fix you a hot toddy. I am sorry I cannot invite you to stay here."

She sounded as sorry as a man who had won a fortune at the racetrack. Forde raised one eyebrow in a gesture that never failed to gain him respect and instant obedience to his wishes. This time the gesture won him a drop of mud in his eye. He reached for his handkerchief, which was as sodden as the rest of him, but looked at the back of Cole Cottage, as if counting the windows, and the bedrooms. "Oh?"

"We are preparing for the wedding, naturally, refurbishing the guest rooms for Mr. Wellforde's mother and sisters. They are at sixes and sevens right now."

Forde had no intention of staying the night here. Lud, sleep at the house of a poor widow with no chaperone in sight? He was liable to wake up as ensnared as Gerald. "I do have rooms at the inn, and my valet will have a hot bath waiting, but I would rather not ride back through the coming deluge. The roads were poor enough on my way here, and the livery horse is too excitable. We could have our conversation now, and I would not need to bother you on the morrow."

"Oh, I am too busy right now. Today is my handyman's afternoon off, and I have a great many chores."

One of which seemed to be discouraging visitors. Forde was not willing to concede defeat—or to be dismissed like a lackey by a woman who kept chickens and wore a faded, moth-eaten cloak. Of course, she had been working in the barn.

He looked in that direction. "I could help. And I would like to get my horse out of the rain."

Katie was standing there, getting colder and wetter by the minute. Her beautiful wedding gown was ruined, and this pompous, pea-brained peer was worried about his mount?

"Your horse, of course, Lord, ah, Forde."

He smiled, looking not half as arrogant. "Ridiculous, isn't it? Forde will do."

She did not smile back. "I am sorry, my lord, but there is no room in the barn, either. I use it for storage, and the hens. We keep the gig and our riding mares at Squire Doddsworth's stable." She pointed to a cart track that passed behind the barn. "It is a short walk to his property."

"Young Doddsworth was my nephew's schoolmate, I believe."

"Yes, Squire's eldest son, Roland. He fancies himself a Tulip, to his father's dismay. He would adore seeing you if you choose to call there. After you see your valet, of course. Otherwise he will be sorely disappointed. And Squire will be also, to miss meeting Mr. Wellforde's uncle."

The viscount agreed he should call there, to thank them for their hospitality to Gerald, unlike other of Brookville's residents, who showed no such generosity at all. "You say that you stable your horses at Doddsworth's place?"

"Yes, in exchange for trying to teach his two younger sons their manners. A useless effort, it appears, but Squire is kind enough to pretend that it is an equal trade."

Despite her refined accent and her grand-lady hauteur, Mrs. Cole was a poor choice to give lessons in deportment, Forde thought, not offering a half-drowned, frozen fellow a cup of tea. And no man, in his experience, was simply kind to a comely female. From what he could see under the billowing, bedraggled cape, Mrs. Cole's shape was more than pleasing, and her face would be more than attractive if she managed a smile. Her green eyes were her best feature, sparkling with intelligence. No, no man did favors for a winsome widow without expecting some better return.

"Surely teaching boys proper behavior is Mrs. Squire Doddsworth's job."

"She died some five years ago."

Ah, now Forde understood Squire's "kindness." Instead of offering baubles, bracelets, or brooches, he bought Mrs. Cole's affections with stalls and straw. Damn, this was no connection Forde wanted his nephew to make. His decision was made. The wedding would not take place this month, or ever, if he had his way. "I shall take my leave, then, since you are so busy, Mrs. Cole, but I shall return tomorrow for our talk. You can count on that."

He mounted Smoky, bowed his head in farewell, and rode off into a slanting, icy rain. He wondered if the horse could keep his footing on the way back to the inn. He wondered what Mrs. Cole was hiding, that she was so desperate to see him gone and away from her house. Most of all he wondered how, when the rain was merely driving the dirt deeper into his clothing, it was rinsing that confounded white wedding gown clean?

Chapter Four

*T*he chances of Susannah's wedding gown coming clean were as good as the chances of a god falling from the sky into Katie Cole's chicken yard. Yet that was precisely what had happened, or as near as made no difference in her mind.

Even filthy and foul-tempered, Viscount Forde had to be the most handsome man Katie had seen in decades, certainly one who wore his middle age well. His wavy black hair had no gray in it, and his complexion had no red-veined, raddled splotches. His physique would have been the envy of a man half his years, as would his strength and his agility, as the viscount leaped into the saddle without a mounting block. And his smile . . . ah, his smile could warm the coldest day and melt the hardest heart, even one that had stopped feeling almost twenty years ago.

Katie chided herself. She was a widow of a certain age, with a grown daughter and a respectable standing in her neighborhood. She had no business being moonstruck by a chance-met stranger, and no business noticing his broad shoulders, his muscular thighs in the tightly fitting breeches he wore, or his trim derriere. Heavens, a lady did not acknowledge that a gentleman had that part of anatomy, much less appreciate it! And she was far better off burying those wayward, wanton thoughts, because Tanyon Wellforde, Viscount Forde, meant her no good.

Katie had caught his glance of assessment, all right,

although his lordship was more subtle than the oafs she often encountered at the local assemblies, or travelers passing through the village. She supposed in London the viscount might have taken out his quizzing glass to make the inspection, like others of his elite kind. Here his dark eyes had briefly traveled up and down her worn cloak and scuffed boots and unwinding braids at the back of her neck, with a pause for the bodice of her gown where the cloak fell open.

She had seen enough such calculating looks on enough men's faces to recognize being measured for his bed. His lordship had made it plain that Mrs. Katherine Cole was good for nothing else.

He did not approve of her tidy house, her thriving garden, or her profitable chickens, and he did not approve of his nephew marrying Susannah. That was as obvious as the mud on his handsome, chiseled face. So, no, Katie should not be feeling the slightest shiver in her smallest toe for such a man, not even if he had fallen practically at her feet. No, not even if he was rich and titled and unmarried. He was as out of her reach as if he'd truly tumbled off Mount Olympus. He would leave after their talk, or after the wedding, and Katie would be left wanting.

It was trying on the unworn wedding dress that was bringing back wicked memories of her heated courtship, reminding her of warm kisses and fevered embraces, as if her long-buried passions had come out of storage along with the gown. She had put it on that very morning to check for moth holes and stains, to see if the size and style could be altered for Susannah—and to revisit her past. The shimmery thing had once made her think that the future was rosy, that fairy tales did come true, that true love was waiting for her. It still did. The gown fit perfectly; the pipe dreams did not.

Foolish girl, foolish woman, foolish dress. Her heart's unwise feelings and her body's unwanted stirrings were simply her imagination playing tricks again. They had nothing to do with his lordship. Nothing,

Katie told herself. Touching the gown had always made her tingle, that was all.

That was not all, not by half. An unattainable aristocrat had assaulted her laundry line and lost, but Viscount Forde's visit was not so startling, considering he was Gerald's uncle and guardian. But the gown was clean, and that was far more difficult to explain.

Katie's hands were filthy, her own cloak looked and smelled like low tide despite the pouring rain, but the wedding gown was ivory white, smelling of springtime. Without soaking or scrubbing or the use of fuller's earth, not a single streak, spot, or stain remained on it by the time Katie hung the garment next to the chimney. The lace overskirt did not have one torn thread, nor did a single button dangle.

She stepped back and murmured a quick prayer, for there was definitely some power beyond her own ken behind this work. Perhaps Susannah should not wear the gown after all? Truth be told, Katie could not be entirely comfortable with a fabric that never aged and that shed soil like a duck's feathers shed water. And she had never discovered where the gown had come from or who had sewn it so meticulously for what lucky bride.

Then again, the fabric was richer than any she could purchase, and the gown was more beautiful than anything the village seamstress could create, with finer stitching. The style might be out of the current mode, but Susannah was pretty enough to set her own fashion and impress the fine London guests.

"Come, darling," she told Susannah early the next morning, "try on the gown before you dress. It is all aired and freshened." And wondrously dried overnight, considering the fire in the hearth was dampened. "So you cannot complain of any musty odors. We must give Mrs. Peebles time to make alterations if they are necessary. We have lost days as is, waiting on the weather, and she will be busy, I am sure. Every lady in the neighborhood will be ordering a new ensemble when they hear that Mr. Wellforde's uncle will be attending the wedding breakfast in your honor."

Susannah protested, as Katie knew she would. The girl's heart was set on the blue velvet at the linen-draper's, far beyond their meager budget.

"Fine," Katie told her, too busy to waste time in useless argument. "Order the new gown. Then you must tell his lordship that your dowry has diminished from negligible to naught. Or we might sell Blossom."

Susannah had raised the cow herself from an orphaned calf and was horrified at the idea. "Can you not ask the storekeepers to wait for their money?"

"Until the new year when the annuity check arrives? How shall they pay their own bills until then, pray tell me? Or what if the barn collapses this winter and I need the funds for that? I know, we can tell Mr. Roundtree at the inn to cancel our order for champagne. I cannot imagine what Mr. Wellforde's friends and relatives will think, our serving home-brewed ale as a toast to the happy couple, but if you must have that new gown instead of this one, which is free of cost except for taking in a seam or such and means so much to your own mother . . ."

Susannah put on the gown. And started crying.

"There, I told you the dress was wrong for me! I never did look good in any kind of white, you know that. My coloring is too pale. This ugly thing makes me look like I am waiting for burial, not my bride-groom," she wailed.

Katie pinched her daughter's cheeks to bring color to them, but Susannah was right. The gown was wrong. When Katie held it up to her own face, her cheeks took on a rosy glow, her green eyes sparkled, and her fair hair gleamed with golden highlights. When Susannah put it on, her complexion turned pasty, her blue eyes faded to gray, and her soft blond curls looked dirty and dingy. Oh, dear.

Then Mrs. Cole had a brilliant idea, better than butchering Blossom. "I know the perfect solution, darling! We can dye it! We can make it a pale blue to match your eyes, just what you wished. Remember how we dyed two of our old gowns when Lord Martindale passed on?"

"They looked rusty and drab."

"That was because they were black and the fabrics were already old. Besides, I had never done it before. The gown will be stunning in blue, and Cook can help to make sure we get it right. It won't be the velvet you wanted, but you will look beautiful. Don't you feel it?"

Susannah felt itchy. She snatched the dress off as soon as she could unfasten the buttons, without waiting for Katie to check the fit or the hem. "If you insist," she said with a martyr's sniff.

"I must, darling. Now hurry, do, for we have much to accomplish before tonight's dinner, especially if we need time to work on the gown. I can purchase the dye this morning when I take Cook's shopping list into the village, if you look after the chickens and then set the table."

"For how many?"

How many indeed?

Katie had decided that his lordship could wait for his private conversation—until doomsday. Once the banns were called, she believed, not even an interfering, arrogant snob like Viscount Forde would try to stop the wedding. She had, therefore, already sent a note around to the inn saying she would be regrettably too busy for his call today, with music lessons and the ladies' guild. Susannah was promised to her friends in the morning, and fittings on her trousseau in the afternoon, so she was not available either, also regrettably. But they would be delighted—the pen left an ink blot at all the lies—to have him join them for dinner. Too bad she could not put him off for another day or two, when his nephew might have returned. The viscount should see how devoted Gerald and Susannah were to each other before he condemned the match out of hand.

Meantime, she meant him to see what a well-brought-up miss her daughter was, and how suited to polite company.

She invited Squire Doddsworth and his eldest son, Roland, to join the dinner party, and the Reverend Mr. Carlson and his family. Miss Louisa Carlson was Susannah's best friend and was *au anges,* she'd sworn out of her mother's hearing, to meet a real London swell. Katie also invited the Dowager Lady Martindale, the highest-ranking female in the neighborhood and a particular favorite of both the Cole women. They listened to the lonely old countess's tales of her younger days, and in return, she let them borrow the latest novels from her extensive library.

There, a peeress, a magistrate, and a vicar were all pleased to sup at Cole Cottage. Let Lord Forde— Katie could not stifle a chuckle—lift his nose—which was slightly beaked—at that country society. And let him try to find a private moment for his inquisition.

"Oh," she added before hurrying off on her errands, "I forgot to mention yesterday that his lordship noticed the wedding gown when he came to call."

Susannah looked up from her glum contemplation of her wardrobe, hoping against hope to find a more suitable outfit. "What did he say?"

What he'd said were words her daughter should never hear. What Katie said was, "He was vastly impressed. One might even say he was knocked off his feet by it."

"Another ruse to keep me away from the place," Forde grumbled when he received another note, this one postponing the dinner and the confrontation for another night, due to a sudden illness. "Sick with fear I will put a spoke in her plans, more like."

The innkeeper was waiting to send a reply back to Cole Cottage. Mr. Roundtree shook his head. "No, they say Mrs. Tarrant what cooks and keeps house for the ladies was a-dying this afternoon. They sent for the apothecary and all. She must've lived, iffen they are holding the dinner tomorrow."

Mrs. Tarrant had been dying, all right. She'd decided to start the ivory gown in its dye bath while the joint of beef was roasting, the soup was simmering, the potatoes were baking, the pudding was setting, and the wine was chilling. Most of all, she wanted to get the job done while her mistresses were at their toilettes. That way they wouldn't be getting in her way, like they'd been doing all day. You'd think they'd never had the vicar or the squire over for supper afore. As for the viscount, well, he was just a man like the others, and he'd eat the good, honest food what Cook put in front of him or she'd send him back to London herself. Upsetting her ladies that way, setting the house on its ear and missy into the fidgets over a silly gown just wasn't right.

Neither was the dye. Mrs. Tarrant had the silk and lace colored perfectly—darker than Mrs. Cole wanted, of course, so they would lighten when they dried. Everyone knew that, everyone but Mrs. Cole, that was. Then she used a wooden broom handle to move the gown into another tub, with cold water and the setting agent. Finally she used her stick to lift the finished gown out for rinsing under the pump. But the gown needed no rinsing—the perfectly white gown.

So she did it all again, adding a bit more of this and another dash of that. Hotter water, more mordant, longer time in the dye bath, more stirring with her broom handle. The dress was still ivory-colored at the end.

This was all the fault of that fancy toff and his uppity ways. Cook being an undeclared sympathizer with the French revolutionaries, she had no use for the English aristocracy, who had so much while the rest of the country had so little. If Lord Forde and his fussy kin weren't coming to the wedding, missy could get hitched in her Sunday best, the same way Mrs. Tarrant and her daughters had done.

Cook went at that gown with her broom handle as if it were mad King George and his profligate son both. Soon her apron, her shoes, and her hands were blue, and the floor was awash. The roast was burning, the potatoes were charred, the soup had boiled away to a thick porridge, and the wine . . . well, she drank the wine. Then she passed out, right in the bowl of pudding.

Katie could only postpone the dinner and calculate how much of her egg money had been lost, and how much more she was going to have to spend tomorrow, once Cook got over her headache and her hysteria. Katie was going to have to do something about her daughter's wedding gown, too.

"No, darling, kicking at the dress will not change its color. I was afraid something like that might happen, because the fabric seems to be coated with a protective substance. You know, like an oiled cloth?"

"You want me to wear a raincovering for my wedding?"

"No, that is not what I meant. But no matter, we can trim it with ribbons and silk flowers, and make a wreath to match for you to wear in your hair. That way the ivory will be less stark against your skin. Now come, help me clean up this mess so we can plan on tomorrow's dinner for our guests."

Forde was not certain he wished to attend the next night's dinner, if he lived that long. His head was stuffed, his chest was congested, and not even the landlord's excellent mulled ale could warm him after yesterday's chill. Besides, he was certain the conniving Mrs. Cole would find another excuse to put him off. Whoever heard of canceling a dinner for three people because one's cook was having a fit of the vapors or some such? She most likely figured that he would grow bored soon enough in this little village and leave her to her devious plotting.

He had a good mind to ride—no, he would take the carriage this time—over to her house right then and have it out with the wily widow. Except he felt as if he had a fever. He'd wait for the next day, then. Yes, and he would bring flowers, as if he truly believed there was illness in the house. That way she would not suspect his intentions and bar her door.

"Have you seen Mrs. Cole's garden?" the innkeeper asked when Forde inquired as to a flower seller the next morning, after sleeping late and awakening in somewhat better condition, except for a few sneezes.

"It was, ahem, raining." And a sore throat.

"She grows the finest roses in the neighborhood, she does, barring Lady Martindale, a'course, who has four gardeners. Asides, Mrs. Cole's already come and gone from the village while you were sleeping, and she's off to give music lessons in Little Brookville, then it's trying to drum manners into the squire's boys. She'd appreciate a fine ham better'n flowers anyway, iffen you were hoping to turn the lady up sweet."

This backwater innkeeper was playing matchmaker? Now Forde had a headache. Roundtree's words reinforced the conclusion that the Cole women were pockets-to-let, though. Or dallying with the nearby landowner.

Either way, Forde had no desire to turn Mrs. Cole into anything but a former acquaintance. He went back to bed.

Chapter Five

*W*hy, that scheming shrew! This was no intimate dinner between strangers who were about to be related, or for combatants at daggers drawn. Mrs. Cole had invited half the countryside, it seemed to Forde, to avoid speaking with him. Every seat in her narrow parlor was taken when he arrived, as if that would keep anyone from noticing the threadbare upholstery.

Deuce take that innkeeper, and deuce take the female for letting him make a fool of himself, walking into a formal dinner party with a ham in his hand. Then an older woman in an apron, most likely that Mrs. Tarrant who had been ill, reached to take the thing, and Forde stopped worrying what Mrs. Cole's other guests were thinking of him. If they were not flummoxed by a blue-handed housekeeper, a peer with a pork could not matter.

Mrs. Cole stepped forward to welcome him. She looked different tonight, naturally. She was not wet, for one, or wearing a shabby cloak with her hair scraped back in a braided bun. Tonight she wore a dark blue gown that, while not in the height of fashion or the depth of daring, still managed to show her lush, mature figure to wondrous advantage. The flesh that rose above the neckline was creamy and soft and inviting and—

She coughed. She must have caught the same congestion from the rain. Forde raised the hand she offered, and his eyes. *Her* eyes were a more vivid green than he recalled, with fascinating blue glimmers. Her fair hair was done up on top of her head, with long, honey-colored tendrils trailing down smooth, sun-kissed cheeks. She was no dasher, but damn if the widow was not one fine-looking woman, the equal to any London lady. In fact, she looked vaguely familiar.

"Have we ever met?" he asked when she took her hand back.

Katie noticed his heightened color—and his finely tailored Bath superfine coat, his biscuit trousers and his intricately tied neckcloth, and what was filling them to perfection. She could feel warmth come to her own cheeks. "Are you feeling quite the thing, my lord? We met the day before yesterday, you know."

"I do know that. I mean before. For a moment I thought—"

"Impossible," Katie replied before the viscount could say anything else. "Unless you have traveled through Brookville in the past. I have not been out of Devon since before Susannah's birth."

Forde's brows were lowered, as if he were trying to dredge forth a distant memory. "No, I have never—"

"And here is Susannah now," Katie quickly said, pulling her daughter over to be introduced to her prospective uncle-by-marriage.

The girl was not what Forde had been expecting, although Gerald would never have fallen for the painted doxy he'd been picturing. Well, he might have fallen, but he was wise enough despite his years to know one did not marry a light skirt. Miss Cole was a pretty young chit with blond curls and blue eyes, a pale complexion, and her mother's determined chin. She had some of her mother's poise, too, not simpering or blushing shyly as so many of the debutantes did. There was no mistaking her rosebud innocence, however, in sprigged muslin with ribbons in her hair. She was a bit shorter than Mrs. Cole, and daintier, like a china shepherdess.

Gerald had said she liked long walks, and the girl

must help with the livestock and the gardens and the cottage if the family was as hard-pressed as it appeared, with so few servants. So Miss Susannah Cole was no hothouse bloom, either. He could see where the combination of delicacy and vigor might fascinate a man, especially a young, idealistic, untried fellow like Gerald.

"Susannah," Mrs. Cole was saying, "why do you not take his lordship to meet the other guests while I see about dinner?"

The girl made the introductions as properly as any miss fresh from finishing school. He doubted his nieces could do as well, for all their years of governesses and expensive lessons. She offered him a glass of Madeira before leaving him with the squire while she went to pour one for Lady Martindale.

Squire Doddsworth was older than Forde, hefty, hearty, and hunt-mad. He would chase down anything furred, feathered, or finned, it seemed, and expound at length on the challenges of each. His eldest son, the only one ready for polite company, was a rangy youth dressed in yellow pantaloons and shirt collars so high they almost, but not quite, hid his protuberant ears. He stared at Forde's neckcloth with such intensity, trying to memorize the folds, that the viscount took pity. He offered to let his valet teach Roland how to tie the knot, which earned him a fervent prayer of gratitude.

"Lud, I hope he outgrows it soon," the squire muttered after the young man hurried off to boast to Miss Louisa Carlson, the vicar's daughter, of his promised treat.

"What, the lad's propensity toward dandyism, or his obvious attraction to Miss Carlson?"

"Oh, the nonsense about becoming a man-milliner. My eldest son ought to be studying agriculture, not how to be a fashionable fribble."

Forde cleared his throat, not due to the congestion.

"Gads, I'm not implying any insult to yourself, needless to say, or your valet's skill. That neckcloth of yours is a work of art the likes of which are seldom seen in our corner of the world. My fool of a son would have the cows laughing at him if he dressed so fine. As for Louisa, they've known each other since the cradle. Never looked at anyone else, either of them. A June wedding it'll be."

Now that was a match made in heaven, Forde thought. The two youngsters had everything in common, including a long-standing friendship, as opposed to Gerald and Miss Cole, who came from different social classes, different upbringings, and a handful of months' association. Here, too, both families seemed to approve wholeheartedly. The vicar and his wife were smiling indulgently at Doddsworth's heir, as if he were already part of their family.

The Reverend Mr. Carlson's passion, he soon told Forde, besides the Church and the wife and daughter he left with young Doddsworth, was cricket. Despite his playing the Tulip, Roland played a mean game. Did his lordship enjoy the sport?

"Not since my university days, I fear," Forde said, watching the door for Mrs. Cole's return. The squire was watching, too, he noted. Doddsworth seemed more interested in her announcement that dinner was served than he was in rushing to her side to escort her to the table. That favor was extended to the vicar, while Roland took in the two young ladies. Doddsworth escorted the vicar's wife, and Forde was delegated to help old Lady Martindale into the dining room, along with her shawls and cane and reticule and fan.

He was given the place of honor at the head of the table, as far away from Mrs. Cole as possible. The dowager was at his right hand and kept him busy answering questions about mutual acquaintances in Town and the latest *on dits*. Mrs. Vicar Carlson on his left was frowning, so Forde could not relate some of the more scandalous tidbits, and he tried to direct the conversation elsewhere, such as to their hostess.

The table was not very long—the whole room could have fit into the entry hall of Wellforde House—but Mrs. Cole might have been miles away, separated from his sight, even, by a large urn filled with autumn blooms.

Both of his dinner companions sang her praises, her good sense, her generosity, and her efficient capability, making do with her chickens and music lessons. She served the community just as a good neighbor should, teaching Sunday school, conducting the church choir, and visiting the sick. She did all this while raising a child, and never a hint of scandal about her, the vicar's wife added, in subtle reprimand to Lady Martindale for indulging in gossip.

A veritable paragon, Mrs. Cole was, Forde learned.

And a thrifty housewife. Dinner consisted of a tasty chicken broth with herbs, followed by chicken fricassee and vegetables. The sweet was an egg custard.

The innkeeper had been right. Forde should have brought the ham over earlier. He could have had his talk with the women, and a more varied dinner menu.

After the meal, the ladies, and Roland, retired to the parlor, leaving the vicar, the squire, and the viscount to their port and cigars. But Forde did not smoke, and much preferred brandy. Besides, what did he, a man about town, have in common with a man of God and a man of the earth? Not much. Forde thought of suggesting they join the ladies, but Mr. Carlson placed his hands together and closed his eyes. The viscount worried they were all supposed to be praying—lud knew he had enough bad habits to ask forgiveness for—but then Mr. Carlson started to snore.

The squire was filling his pipe with tobacco from a pouch. Once he got the thing going, he puffed and probed at the same time. "You aren't here"—puff—"to stop the wedding, are you?"

Forde sipped at his glass of port, not answering.

"The reason I ask is that you'll be disappointing

half the county, and disrupting my own plans, too. I mean to make the widow an offer, once the chit's future is settled and she is out of the house."

"Offer?" Forde thought the squire already had the bargain made.

"Aye, I've been biding my time, but it won't do for Mrs. Cole to be out here all alone. And I want the property for my boy Roland when he weds. Not right that newlyweds should share a house with the groom's old man and rapscallion brothers."

"Ah, that kind of offer. You wish to buy Cole Cottage?"

"Buy it?" Puff. "No, I'll count it as her dowry. Can't expect much else, and I'd wager whatever widow's portion she gets will end with the marriage."

"Marriage?" The glass fell from Forde's fingers, but luckily it was nearly empty. Even though he did not like the stuff, he wished for more. "You mean to offer Mrs. Cole a ring?"

"Can't wed without one, can I? I've been thinking about it for a while now, what with my wife gone these five years and more. A house needs a woman's touch, don't you know, and so does a man. A fellow gets lonely, and the gals at the inn . . . well, you can't bring them home with you, not without causing a stir in the neighborhood. Bad example for my sons, besides, don't you know. The boys all adore Mrs. Cole, and they listen to her, too. And she is a fine-looking woman, what?"

What, indeed? Mrs. Cole was more than fine, for a nearly middle-aged mistress. "She is an attractive female," he agreed, thinking of her green eyes and creamy skin, "but a wife?"

"You ain't thinking of anything disrespectful, are you?" Doddsworth set down his pipe and scowled through the smoky haze.

"Heavens, no." And Forde hoped the vicar was not listening or he'd rot in hell for the lie. "She is a devilishly attractive woman, as you say. I am just surprised. A man your age, a woman her age . . ."

"I don't need any more heirs, if that is what you

are thinking. Got three already," the squire bragged, making Forde feel less of a man for producing only the one son. "Although that's not to say it couldn't happen, with Mrs. Cole not yet forty. She suits me to a cow's thumb. And she is a real lady," he added, in case Forde still harbored doubts.

He relit the pipe, then noticed Forde's raised eyebrows. "Oh, I know the dead sailor had no title. But I met Mrs. Cole when she first came here almost twenty summers ago. Adjoining properties, and all that. My wife took pity on her, alone and breeding, without kin or friends in sight, don't you know. We saw a good deal of her, introducing her around, showing her the sights. We wouldn't have done so much if she weren't a real lady. Both the missus and I knew right away that the widow was a gentlewoman, with her London gowns and fine manners and hands that had never held a broom or a mixing spoon. She came from a good family, I'd swear, although she won't speak of them."

The vicar woke up and added his opinion. "But she never put on airs, our Mrs. Cole, not at all. We were happy to have such an upstanding young woman come among us, to help with the choir and the children. She always gives to the poor box, even though she has to raise chickens to put food on her own table."

"That is admirable, I am sure." Forde was not sure of anything anymore. If Katherine Cole was not the squire's ladybird, a fallen woman, then just maybe she was a lady fallen on hard times, and maybe he had no cause to stop the wedding. For a poor, virtuous widow, Mrs. Cole had done well for herself, and raised a lovely daughter, by all estimates. Her neighbors universally admired her, so she must not be the greedy, grasping female Gerald's mother suspected. Gerald was still too young, and his bride was still too poor, but those were not sufficient reasons for the viscount to go back on his word. He had already given his approval of the match, albeit grudgingly. He could leave on the morrow and come back for the ceremony.

Still, doubts nagged at him. There was something smoky about the widow, or else she would have spoken to him sooner, alone. Her green eyes nagged at him, too. If this had been a cozy dinner for the two of them, who knew what could happen after?

Nothing. He was forgetting about the daughter, Gerald's betrothed. He couldn't go making advances to his nephew's prospective mother-in-law, could he? No, not with the girl in the house. Squire was right: Mrs. Cole might be more amenable to an offer after the wedding. An offer of carte blanche, that was.

When the men reentered the parlor, Mrs. Cole stopped playing the pianoforte and stood up from the bench.

"No, no, please continue," the vicar insisted. "Your playing is far more soothing to the digestion than cigars or spirits."

She resumed playing, and excellently, Forde realized. She had to have studied with a master, so, yes, Doddsworth's opinion of her gentility was not farfetched. And yet she grew turnips and kept goats.

After a long, difficult piece, played to perfection, Mrs. Cole switched to popular songs. Roland and Louisa sang a duet to her accompaniment, not for the first time, it sounded. Then Susannah raised her clear voice in a lovely rendition of "Greensleeves." Forde applauded with the others, genuinely appreciative of the picture the sweet young woman made—and her mother, leaning over the keys so her gown fell a bit lower, with a touching look of pride on her face.

He missed his boy. And a woman.

The same female servant, Mrs. Tarrant, wheeled in a tea cart. Mrs. Cole got up to pour, while Susannah handed the cups around and carried plates of biscuits.

When she reached his chair, Forde casually said, "I was wondering what ship your father was sailing on when he perished."

The teapot thumped as Mrs. Cole set it down. "I do not like to speak of my dead husband, and Susannah was too young to know him."

"Your pardon, ma'am. I merely thought I might know some of the men who served with him. Susannah might like to meet them, to hear their recollections."

"I doubt it. That is, she has never asked." Before the girl could, Katie said, "Here, Susannah, take the platter of raspberry tarts around again. You know they are Lady Martindale's favorite."

Forde carried his cup closer to where the widow sat, so the others would not overhear. "I am sorry if I upset you."

"I find it difficult to speak of Mr. Cole."

"John."

"George," she corrected.

"Ah. Did you meet him in London? Or at your home in . . .?"

She pushed the teapot away. "Please, this is too painful."

"Odd. I have no trouble discussing my late wife, and she has not been gone nearly as long. You must have loved James very much."

"George. I did. And I cherish his memory to this day." Katie clasped her hands together to keep them from trembling.

"Yet you do not share your memories with your daughter—his daughter. What of her grandparents? If they are sending funds, as Gerald told me, surely she has met them?"

"A bank handles the matter. They are both deceased."

"What of your own family, then? The reason I ask such personal questions is that I wonder why Susannah has not been brought to London. Brookville offers a solitary kind of life for a young lady, especially a beautiful, talented one like your daughter. She could do far better than Gerald if someone were to present her to Society."

"She has never been interested in the city or the beau monde. And, no, I have no family, either. Would you like more tea? A biscuit?"

She might not have spoken. "Ah, you were born

under a cabbage leaf? Left for the fairies to raise? Your musical ability was not learned at any orphanage."

He was not going to stop. "Very well, since you insist on bringing up distressing topics, my family is dead. The Brownes." Which was the most common last name in all of Britain. "And we moved around a lot when I was a child, so, no, you will not know our home. My mother was an accomplished performer who taught me what little I know." She got to her feet. "Now I must bring Lady Martindale a fresh cup of tea."

"Let me."

"You are too kind," she said through thinned, lying lips. "May I offer you another cup also?"

Forde declined. He wouldn't be surprised if there was rat poison in it. And he wouldn't be surprised if her story had more holes in it than a fishnet. Devil take it, he had to find out the truth about this woman. For Gerald's sake.

Chapter Six

Everyone was leaving, except the one guest Katie wished gone the most. Susannah was helping Cook clear the tea things in the parlor, but he was waiting by the front door. Gerald's uncle appeared strong and confident and determined to stay the night unless he had answers to his questions. Fiend seize the man. Here he was, looking every inch the gentleman and acting like a cad. No one else had ever shown such disregard for her widow's grief or disrespect for her privacy. She supposed he was looking out for his nephew, which was admirable in a guardian but unnerving in a dinner guest. To be honest, the man rattled her no matter what. To be entirely honest, she was not honest, and feared him as much as she was fascinated by him.

He was too good-looking, too well built, and too . . . virile. His brown-eyed gaze was too penetrating, and his smile too boyishly apologetic and appealing when she caught him looking at her bosom. Why did he have to be so blatantly manly, and why did he, of all men, make her feel like an attractive woman again?

She knew she should not have shown so much of her anatomy tonight, but her best gown was an old one, she might have gained a bit of weight, she had no matching shawl—and she wanted to show his lofty lordship that she was not simply a dowdy rustic widow. Botheration! She had only increased his curiosity. If she had dressed in one of her faded, shapeless gowns, he might not have shown such interest in her physical being or her past, a past she was not about to reveal.

"Good night, my lord." Katie covered her mouth with her hand, as if she were hiding a yawn, a not-so-subtle hint.

With the servant and the daughter cleaning up just out of sight, Forde could not press his investigation. He nodded acceptance of his dismissal and stepped closer to the door. He politely thanked her for the meal and the chance to meet her neighbors, and then announced his intention of calling on her the next day.

"Oh, but I have—"

A hundred excuses not to be there. Devil take it, Forde wanted to know, tonight, if Mrs. Cole was a real lady, or open to other invitations. He could set her up in a cozy love nest in Town, with pretty gowns and a carriage of her own. Why should she raise chickens when she was raising his temperature just by standing near?

Susannah and the servant were carrying trays toward the rear of the house, laughing together, ignoring the front hall.

Forde took a step back, closer to Mrs. Cole, and leaned forward. He liked how she was tall enough that he did not have to crick his neck, and he liked the rosewater scent she wore. He liked how her cheeks flushed with color when she realized his intention, and that she did not run away. He lowered his lips to hers, softly, tentatively, just to satisfy his wondering about her reaction, he told himself. His own reaction was an instant surge of desire, a stronger surge than he had been feeling all night, that was.

She kissed him back! So he was right, and she was not all prim and proper, the beautiful, beloved widow of Brookville. Elated and aroused, he stopped thinking altogether, except how well they fit together, as he pulled her closer.

Good grief, Katie thought. *First an inquisition, then a seduction.* The man was the very devil, and she was no saint, either, to permit such liberties. It felt so good to have a gentleman desire her, though, and then to have him hold her, that she allowed the kiss to continue. She'd forgotten how thrilling a man's embrace could be, to be surrounded by strength and sinew. She pressed closer, reveling in her first kiss in almost two decades.

Then Katie remembered where her last kisses had taken her.

"No," she murmured.

"Oh, yes," he purred, sending sparks down her spine with his knowing hands.

But no. Katie was a lady, not a strumpet, and she would not forget, even if his lordship did. She might have given herself to Susannah's father, but they were engaged and in love, or so she thought. She knew better now.

Forde was another rake and a rogue, taking his pleasure wherever he found it. Katie had learned to take pleasure in her simple life, her daughter, her spotless reputation. She would not destroy all that now, not for a brief dalliance, no matter how expert Forde's kisses. He was Gerald Wellforde's uncle, for heaven's sake!

She drew her arm back and slapped him. "I said no."

Forde rubbed his cheek. "You could have said it a bit more forcefully, and sooner."

"I should have. I beg your pardon. It was the wine and the lateness of the hour. I was surprised. I thought—" Katie stopped making excuses for herself. *He* was the one who had stepped beyond the line of what was permitted. She opened the front door. "That is, I do not believe we have anything more to say to each other, my lord. Now or tomorrow. Good night."

Forde could not decide if he was more confused that the widow had kissed him or that she had slapped him. Either way, he now had more questions than before.

"Oh, I think we do, madam. Have more to say, that is." He raised her hand to his lips. Why not? The

night had already been full of ham-handedness, blue
hands, and a very efficient openhanded slap. He could
not go back and face his sister-in-law empty-handed,
either. He had to stay at least until Gerald returned,
to discuss his concerns with his nephew. There, that
was a good enough excuse to prolong his stay in
Brookville, although he'd been soundly dismissed
from Cole Cottage.

He'd also been soundly smacked and still wore the
red outline of Mrs. Cole's palm on his cheek. No matter, Forde went back to the inn whistling.

Katie did not have to wake up early the next morning to be at her chores; she'd hardly slept. The plaguey
peer had destroyed her rest, strolling confidently
through her troubled mind. She had no doubt he'd be
walking across her doorstep, just as sure of himself,
before this day was over. She could not let him tempt
her again, or destroy her daughter's chance for a secure future. So she could not be home again.

Katie knew she could not put his lordship off forever, but Gerald had to arrive soon. Surely Lord
Forde would see how well suited the young people
were, and how much they deserved their chance at
happiness. Just as surely, he would not act the liber-
tine in front of his own nephew.

"Come, Susannah, here is your chocolate, so wake
up."

"It is barely light out," her daughter said, rolling
over and pulling the covers over her eyes.

"But we have much to do. We have to find the right
ribbons for your wedding gown, and the silk flowers
to match. Then we really have to bring it to Mrs.
Peebles for a fitting so she might finish it in time."

"Can you not simply take one of my old gowns and
measure from that? I told Lady Martindale I would
read to her this morning. I want to know how that
novel ends. The handsome knight is just about to res-
cue the damsel from the tower where her wicked uncle
locked her."

"He saves her and they live happily ever after. They always do." In novels, Katie thought. Real life was unfortunately not as predictable, or as assured of a happy ending. It was up to her, as a mother, to take what precautions she could for her daughter. Wicked uncles, indeed.

"You have to try on the gown so Mrs. Peebles can pin the trimmings where you wish them. You can stop in at Lady Martindale's afterward, while I try to teach the vintner's two daughters their scales, for a discount on the champagne. We will still be in time for tea at the vicarage, so you can listen to Louisa enthuse about Roland's latest sartorial efforts. And remember that tonight is choir practice."

There. That ought to keep them out of harm's way until bedtime.

First they had to stop at Squire Doddsworth's to pick up the gig and to thank him for the leg of mutton that had been delivered earlier.

Viscount Forde was breaking his fast with Mr. Doddsworth and his sons, before going shooting with them. Drat!

Luckily Squire was more eager to be on his way than he was in pursuing his courtship. "What, no breakfast? You are off to purchase fripperies? Good, good, Mrs. Cole. You go on to the village. We'll catch dinner for you, my dear, see if we don't."

The viscount was everything polite, and more appetizing than the steak-and-kidney pie or kippers and eggs, in his doeskin breeches and hunting coat. Katie hurried Susannah away.

"Gerald's uncle is very handsome, do you not think?" Susannah asked as they drove into the village.

"Very."

"Far more good-looking than Mr. Doddsworth."

Katie had to laugh. Comparing the squire to the viscount was like comparing a plowhorse to a Thoroughbred.

"But he is not as handsome as Gerald."

"Oh, never." Gerald was a green colt. His nose was not as prominent as his uncle's, thank goodness for

Katie's hoped-for grandsons and daughters, but Gerald did not have Forde's air of dignity, authority, and elegance. Only age could bring that to a man, Katie thought, although the viscount might have had that aura of assurance even as a youth.

"He is a bit haughty."

"Gerald?"

"Do not be silly, Mother. I mean his uncle, of course."

"Oh, his lordship's arrogance is merely part of being a wealthy titled gentleman. People have been toadying to him his entire life, I'd assume."

"Have you known many peers, then? He is my second, after Lord Martindale."

"I have known enough. Do you think we should select the silk flowers first or the ribbons?"

Susannah was not to be diverted. "He is not condescending, though. We had a nice conversation about music."

"Did you, darling? How nice, since he is Gerald's trustee."

"His manners are pleasing."

Toward everyone else, it seemed. He had no manners where Katie was concerned, but she would not disturb Susannah with her worries. "He is a gentleman. I should hope he knows how to act. Squire's younger sons might learn more from him in a morning than I have been able to teach them in months."

"Gerald says the ladies of the *ton* have given up pursuing him."

Katie flicked the whip over her mare's ear, to hurry her along. "I doubt his lordship runs far or fast from a willing woman."

Now Susannah laughed. "Unless she is seeking marriage. Gerald thinks his uncle is waiting for someone as beautiful as his first wife."

What with all the belles in London over the years, Lady Forde must have been a Diamond beyond measure. Katie suddenly felt ugly and old. "It is not polite to gossip about your relative-to-be."

Susannah looked over at her mother and studied

Katie's profile. "You know, you looked quite lovely last night, with your hair up like that. You should wear it that way more often."

"What, to feed the chickens?"

"To attract a certain gen—"

"Here we are!"

Susannah threw herself into the selection of trimmings for the wedding gown and her hair, thank goodness, instead of matchmaking. Then she complained how scratchy the gown was, when she had to try it on for the seamstress to pin.

"That is impossible, when the gown has the finest fabric and the neatest seams in creation."

Now the dressmaker was in a taking that Mrs. Cole was praising another modiste's workmanship over hers. Mrs. Peebles wanted to refuse the commission to shorten the hem, narrow the skirt, tuck up the bodice, and add the trimmings; heaven knew she could not match those perfect stitches. She had gained much commerce from the coming wedding, however, and hoped for more from the Cole ladies. She would start right in on the fancy garment, she promised. Right after she had a bit of wine to steady her hand.

Clouds had covered the sun by the time the fitting was over, and Susannah's mood was just as black. Katie offered the treat of a luncheon at the Brookville Inn, rather than go home only to drive back in the coming rain for tea at the vicarage.

Viscount Forde had left the shooting party rather than suffer another drenching and was eating his own meal . . . at the Brookville Inn.

He was also invited to the Reverend Mr. Carlson's house for tea.

Thank goodness for choir practice, Katie thought. He wouldn't be there.

Thank goodness for choir practice, Forde thought. She wouldn't be home. He knocked on the door, pretending surprise when the cook/housekeeper told him the ladies were away.

"I'll wait, if I may, and if you have any of those raspberry tarts from last night's tea. I need to speak to Mrs. Cole about the wedding, and I have been away from my own home far too long to delay. I promise I shall not keep your mistress up too late."

Mrs. Tarrant was highly susceptible to handsome smiles, pretty compliments, and gold coins. She tucked one of the last into her apron pocket and left his lordship alone in the library. For two gold coins he could have waited in Mrs. Cole's bedchamber—or Mrs. Tarrant's own. Forde asked to be shown to the library so he could find a book to read to wile away the time.

The small room was more an office than a library, filled with old ledgers and new agricultural journals. After a cup of tea and an excellent pastry, Forde let his curiosity overcome his manners. He opened the topmost ledger, justifying his shameful intrusion by telling himself that as a conscientious guardian he had to know what Gerald was getting into. The lad would feel obliged to help his wife's mother if the need arose, wouldn't he? Forde might as well be hung for a wolf as for a sheep, so he read Mrs. Cole's bank statements, too. He was amazed that two women could live on the income from that annuity. His sister-in-law could not have paid her dressmaker's bills with that amount, much less fed and clothed her daughters. Now he felt guilty not only for trespassing but also for not sending over another ham.

In remorse, or so he almost convinced himself, Forde picked up Mrs. Cole's Bible, the one inscribed to her, or the name she was born with, anyway, the name she used on her graduation from Mrs. Meadow's Select Academy for Gentlewomen.

Chapter Seven

*T*he first inkling that the following day would not be one of Katie's favorites came with the morning post. Gerald was delayed, he wrote, due to a promising mare. He would try to arrive in Brookville on Saturday, in time for the last reading of the banns on Sunday. And, he added, he had a wonderful surprise: He'd be bringing his mother and two younger sisters. They were eager to meet their new relation. Wasn't that a delightful treat?

Three houseguests, used to a lavish London lifestyle, a week early? Lovely.

Katie was in a frenzy and Susannah was in tears, that dear Gerald cared more about his horses than her. That was before the wedding gown was delivered from the dressmaker. As Katie unwrapped the parcel, she knew she'd been right to urge her daughter to wear it. The gown was even more stunning with the blue ribbons and the circlet of blue forget-me-nots tacked to the neckline and at the hem. Just holding it made her certain her daughter's marriage would be a happy one, and to the devil with anyone—any viscount—who thought otherwise.

Then Susannah tried it on, to make sure the alterations were correct.

The hem that had been too long, fitting Katie's taller height, was now too short. Susannah's ankles showed. The skirt that had been too full for fashion was now so narrow that Susannah could not take any but the smallest steps. The bodice that had been too loose was now so tight the gown would not close. The silk flowers fell off in the struggle to fasten the buttons, and the trailing ribbons tripped Susannah so she fell against the standing mirror, putting a crack in it.

"It's this awful gown! It's bringing bad luck! Gerald is late and his mother is early and now the mirror is broken!"

Could it be? Katie's own wedding gown had burned in a fire; then, when she was about to wear this one, her fiancé died. And yet, when she picked the gown up from the floor where her daughter had thrown it, Katie felt lucky and hopeful and full of love.

"No, my pet, it is not the gown. It is Mrs. Peebles, the seamstress. We always knew she tippled. I will make the alterations myself and sew the flowers back on. The mirror is not shattered, which might have meant bad luck. It is only slightly cracked at the corner. As for the unexpected company, I am certain Squire Doddsworth and the Carlsons will help us entertain them. And we do have that leg of mutton, the brace of partridges, and the ham Gerald's uncle brought us. You will have nothing to be ashamed of in front of Mr. Wellforde's family."

Which was not what Viscount Forde thought.

He'd left before confronting Mrs. Cole last night, needing to ponder his discovery. He also wanted to consult with his valet. Campbell knew everything about fashion—and a great deal about fashionable society, past and present. He had his Debrett's *Peerage* memorized, as well as more old gossip than any ten sharp-tongued spinsters.

He confirmed Forde's conclusion.

Mrs. Tarrant let him into Cole Cottage without hesitation, and without waiting for a coin, she was that busy. "Young miss is upstairs crying her eyes out because her beau is late, the mistress is ruining her eyes in the library because Mrs. Peebles is a tosspot, and I am supposed to fix a fancy supper on Saturday, with one day's notice. I suppose you'll be coming, too?"

Not if he had any choice. He'd be long gone by Saturday. Forde said he could show himself into the library, where he stood outside the opened door, wondering what Mrs. Cole was reading by dim light on this overcast day. Instead he saw that she was bent over a pile of sheets, not surprising if company was coming, he supposed. But no, the stuff in her lap was that infernal gown from the clothesline, as pale as a dove now. Mrs. Cole seemed to be trying to affix flowers and ribbons to it, but her thread kept breaking, and she kept pricking her fingers. Instead of cursing, the peculiar woman just smiled, as if she knew a joke no one else heard.

Her smile should have made the sun shine. She looked like a saint, with a halo of light from the nearby lamp, although Forde knew far differently. Her hair was loose, pulled back with a ribbon—which she accidentally sewed to the gown. She laughed. Perhaps she was a bedlamite, besides a liar and an imposter and a fallen woman.

"Mrs. Cole? Or should I say Miss Katherine Bainbridge?"

She dropped her needle, her scissors, and her good humor. Her complexion turned whiter than the gown. She lurched up, the ivory fabric and flowers falling at her feet, like a spring garden in the last snowfall of winter.

"How . . . ?" She did not try to deny her former identity. Nor did she invite him to be seated.

Forde stepped toward her desk and lifted the Bible. "I read the inscription, then remembered why you seemed familiar. My cousin attended Miss Meadow's Academy. I must have met you at one of their functions for senior girls, or perhaps you were at Elaine's come-out. Elaine Montmorency."

"Yes, she was a particular friend of mine, but I did not know you were related. I do not recall meeting you."

"How could you, when you had eyes for no one but that scapegrace Nevins, who died on the eve of your wedding? They said Lady Katherine Bainbridge died of a broken heart somewhere in the country, never to be heard from again."

"She never was."

"Ah, but Katie Cole arrived at the same time in Brookville. I know, because I consulted with the innkeeper. And I know the date of your proposed marriage, because that was the week my father passed away. Nevins's death was all anyone spoke of at the funeral. I also checked the church registry here. Your daughter was born seven months later."

Katie sank back into her seat and picked up the gown, looking for that feeling of well-being it usually lent her. She rubbed the soft fabric, not even marveling that the marks from where she had picked out the hem were already gone and the loose button was firmly attached. The flowers were not.

"My father gave me the choice," she said. "I could give up my infant and return to London, or I could disappear forever."

His own wife would easily have forsaken her son for a new lover or another party. "What about now, now that she is grown?"

"My father has obviously not changed his mind. My daughter is about to change her name, though. No one need ever suspect what came before."

"But she is to change her name to mine, and I know she was born out of wedlock."

Katie looked up from the gown, her hands clutching the fabric, her eyes troubled, beseeching. "Will you tell?"

"I am not a bastard."

"Yet my daughter is. Will you ruin her life?"

They both knew the girl's future would be destroyed by the stigma of illegitimacy. Susannah's friends would desert her, the villagers would shun her. As for Mrs. Cole, she would be ostracized in her own community, only because stoning had gone out of use. Let a woman no better than she ought to be teach music to their innocent daughters? Have a fallen woman sing with the angels in the choir? Purchase her morally tainted eggs? Yes, he could shatter both women's lives, but no, he would not. He did not have to tell Mrs. Cole that, however. "I think you should cancel the wedding."

It sounded like extortion to both their ears. Forde winced. Mrs. Cole gasped, seeing everything she had worked for, sacrificed for, gone up in smoke.

"Why? What is it to you if Susannah's birth was irregular? You have seen for yourself that she is a perfectly behaved young lady, with no blot on her name or character."

"But that stain is there, and we both know it. Others might find out."

"How could they? And why should anyone care enough to look?"

He set the Bible down and leaned against the desk, close enough to reach over and smooth the errant honey blond curls away from her cheeks, if he did not fear she would stab him with her scissors. "What if someone recognizes you?"

"That is unlikely. I do not go anywhere, and strangers do not come here. Besides, I am not the same girl you met almost twenty years ago."

"Yet I thought you looked familiar. Your green eyes are distinctive with those blue flecks in them." He did not mention that he'd been staring, fascinated. "And so is your chin."

Katie's hands flew to her face to see if her chin had sprouted a wart or a beard. It seemed the same as usual. "I could wear glasses to disguise my appearance. And my hair will turn gray. Furthermore, no one will look that hard, my lord. No one has in all these years."

"My sister-in-law might. My cousin might, if she comes to the wedding."

Now Katie looked down, at the fabric in her lap. "Her name was on Gerald's list, but we could not accommodate everyone at such a small wedding breakfast."

"Or she was not invited due to your fears of being unmasked. So you will be safe from discovery for now, but what of your daughter? We both know the old tabbies in Town will want to know her ancestors for the last ten generations. They will poke and pry: Who are her people, where are they from, what families are they related to? You know the gabble grinders who make a sport and a skill out of destroying reputations."

"Susannah and Gerald are going to take up life in the country, not among the so-called polite world. She need not be exposed to the gossipmongers."

"What, you think there are no nosy neighbors near Gerald's estate? I thought you knew small towns better than that. No matter, Miss Cole will face enough scandal broth in London."

"Your nephew says he hates city life."

"But his mother adores it. He cannot ignore her, or his sisters. He must come to Town for the girls' come-out parties and presentations, at the very least. Gerald's wife ought to be presented at court too, for their own children's sakes, if nothing else. How can Mrs. Gerald Wellforde be announced to the queen or the prince under an assumed name? Sired by a father who never existed? I doubt my sister-in-law would be pleased to sponsor a girl of questionable birth. The blemish could color her own daughters' chances of making decent matches."

"My daughter did nothing wrong!" Katie insisted. "She deserves her happy day and her bright future."

"I agree that Miss Cole is an innocent. But that does not change anything. She is not a suitable bride for my nephew."

"He loves her."

"He is young. He will get over it."

"Spoken like one who has never loved. How old were you when you wed, my lord?"

"My age makes no difference, since my marriage

was neither a love match nor a success. Neither was your, ah, girlish infatuation. Your experience alone ought to persuade you of that."

"I was younger than Susannah, yes. But," she quickly added, "I have no regrets. I have my daughter. And I did beg her to wait, to be certain of Mr. Wellforde's constancy."

"But she did not listen, I suppose, just as Gerald did not heed his own mother's admonitions."

Katie shrugged. "A daughter's tears can melt the hardest heart."

He looked at the gown she was laboring over, recalling that the bride was crying in her bedroom. "You have spoiled her."

Katie raised her chin. "I did not hear about you refusing permission for Gerald to become engaged. You were the one with the power to delay the betrothal, since you hold the purse strings."

"I had no reason then. But tell me, madam, did you think they would be happy, with such a difference in their stations, aside from the question of Miss Cole's parentage or why her lofty grandparents do not recognize her?"

"Susannah has no grandparents. My father disowned me, as I said. And yes, I thought she would be happy with her young man. We are not ignorant, illiterate peasants. Susannah has a fine education and gentle manners. She has a dowry to bring to the marriage, too."

"The innkeeper's daughter has a dowry, he told me. That does not make her a suitable bride for my nephew."

"Your nephew wishes to become a horse breeder. Susannah will grace his table, manage his home, keep to a budget. She will be a good mother to his children. Further, she and Mr. Wellforde have much in common: their love of music and the outdoors. My daughter is at home in the saddle, and in the country, where she was the belle of local assemblies. So, yes, I think she will make Gerald an excellent wife, and he swears to make her a loyal husband. No one has to know of her birth. I will not be in London to invite speculation when she goes to Town, so she can be accepted there, too, especially if Gerald's mother smooths her way into Society."

"You do not know Agnes. She was hoping your daughter had enough social standing to take charge of her girls. The daughter of an unknown Navy man and an obscure Miss Browne has no standing whatsoever. And what shall your daughter answer when people ask why her mother does not visit?"

Katie waved her hand, as if to clear the air. "You are making too much of this. She can say I am an invalid or a recluse. It matters not."

"You would ask your own daughter to lie? I assume she does not know the truth."

"Of course not. A small child could not understand the ramifications of her situation. Later, there was no need to disillusion Susannah about her heroic father. He gave her little enough without stealing that, too."

Forde could hear her bitterness and wanted to wipe away her cares, but he could not. "Mrs. Cole, I sympathize with your desire to see your child well settled in life. I wish the same for my boy, too. But that changes nothing. Think on it. Heaven forbid something should happen to my son, Gerald will be my heir. His wife will be viscountess, with a place in Society whether she wishes it or not."

"Nothing will happen to your son."

He nodded his appreciation of her confidence. "If I were the one to die, then, Gerald would be the boy's guardian. I could have broken my neck in your chicken run, no thanks to that gown. Or look at what happened to your own fiancé, cut down in his prime. Gerald would have to be in London part of the year to manage my assets and investments for Crispin. Again, his wife must be—"

Katie had heard enough. She carefully draped the gown over an arm of her chair and stood. "Let me understand, my lord. You would ruin my daughter's life—and your nephew's—now, on the chance that he needs to fill your shoes in ten years?"

"Hopefully more than ten. I am only forty, and barring skittish horses and bad roads, I intend to make it to sixty or seventy at least."

"At which time your son will need no trustee. No, my lord, your arguments are absurd. You have met Susannah and seen what a lovely girl she is," Katie said with a mother's pride. She waited for Forde to nod his head in acknowledgment.

"And you have said that you do not hold her illegitimacy against her. Therefore you are basing your disapproval on your own interests, not Gerald's. It seems to me that assuring the succession to your title and properties is your responsibility, not his. If you are worried that your son will be left without guidance, select trustees now. If you fear your son might not survive to succeed you—as you say, heaven forbid—then do something about that, too. You are forty, surely capable of begetting another heir, the proverbial spare."

Forde was not about to discuss his abilities to procreate. He did not get the chance, either, for the widow was going on with her tirade. "According to Gerald, you could have your pick of titled, wealthy, perfectly delightful young ladies. Go marry one and let Gerald marry where he wants, you selfish, thick-skulled man!"

Forde clenched his teeth to keep from shouting. "You are insolent and impertinent, madam." He paced the small room, kicking her scissors and a spool of thread out of his way. "And perhaps you are correct. I should not lay my burden on my nephew. Nor will I act the tyrant and forbid his marriage. I shall ask him if he wishes to marry into a family of liars and cheaters and—"

"Whores? Go on, say it. It is nothing my own father did not say."

"I was going to say chicken farmers."

"Then you are going to tell him?"

"He has a right to know . . . unless the wedding is canceled."

"With half the banns already spoken? You know it cannot be called off. My daughter will be labeled a jilt, your nephew a here-and-thereian. If he cries off, people will ask why and assume the worst."

"Nonsense. You can postpone the wedding on some pretense—an illness in the family or something. You were not above lying two minutes ago. Then, in a few months, you can drop a hint that the youngsters have decided they will not suit. No one will question the change of heart, given their ages."

"Impossible."

"Gerald is a wealthy young man by most standards. If you are worried about losing the money, I am prepared to—"

Katie would have thrown something at Forde, except the nearest thing to hand was the wedding gown. She was more determined than ever that Susannah would wear it, and on schedule. Instead she threw him a look of such disdain that Forde's spine—and lower attachments—should have shriveled.

"Delay the wedding in a quiet, convenient manner? How, I ask, am I supposed to do that, you featherheaded fool? Even if Susannah were willing, which, I assure you, she is not, it would be impossible, my lord."

"Anything is possible."

"No, my lord, not at any price, not with your sister-in-law and her daughters arriving for the happy occasion. Tomorrow."

Chapter Eight

*T*anyon Wellforde, Viscount Forde, was a gentleman born and bred. The tenets of honor and duty
were the building blocks of his very essence. A gentleman did not lie or cheat or steal. He defended the
weak and protected those who were dependent on
him. He kept his house, his assets, and his family safe
and without scandal.

So what did he do now?

He could not let Gerald live a lie, marrying a woman
whose very name was a fabrication. The truth was
bound to come out sometime, when the first rush of
infatuation was faded. Then the young man would
have a lifetime of regret ahead of him. Nor could
Forde betray a woman who had given up her way of
life to protect that lie and her own family. Besides, he
liked Mrs. Katie Cole.

He had to respect what she had done, with courage,
by all accounts, raising chickens and a baby when she
ought to have been raising her fan to call a beau to
her side at some ball or other. Few other pampered
daughters of the polite world could have done as much
with so little, all on her own. No other fallen woman
would have sold her musical skills and her eggs instead
of her body, her lush and lovely womanly body.

He also admired the fact that she had not lost her
spirit when she lost her family, wealth, and prospects.
Every inch an earl's daughter, she would not bow
down to the demands of a mere viscount, even though

he could rend apart her world the way she cracked
one of her eggs. She had bottom, did Katie Cole, and
a nice one it was, too. Her top was not bad, either,
Forde reflected over a glass of cognac back at the inn.
He liked her ample breasts and the way they filled
her gown, the way they would fill a man's hands
when he—

He wouldn't. But he'd have one hell of hard time
sleeping tonight while he tried to decide what to do
about the wedding.

He was still trying to decide when his sister-in-law
arrived at the inn the next day.

She commandeered the second-best suite of rooms,
which were reserved for Gerald, which meant Gerald
would be sharing Forde's chambers. Then she demanded the viscount's presence in her private parlor,
where maids and footmen were busy carrying in bags
and trunks, jewel cases and hatboxes, enough for a
small army, much less one woman and two daughters.
Before he could greet her—actually, he was going to
ask after Gerald, so he could wring the young man's
neck—she began shouting at him from the chaise
longue where she reclined, one hand on her dog, the
other clutching a vinaigrette.

"My stars, Forde, what kind of uncaring uncle are
you? I thought you were going to do something about
this awful idea of Gerald's. You must! He cannot be
permitted to marry into that family. Why, the woman
is—"

"She told you, then?"

"She told me to leave, and in the rudest way possible."

"Mrs. Cole?" Forde could not imagine the widow
being so impolite to a stranger, and her daughter's
future mother-in-law at that. She had been rude to
him, but he deserved it. "She was happily preparing
for your arrival when I saw her last." Actually, she
was holding that blasted dress to her bosom when he
left. She was furious and frightened, and he wanted
nothing more than to take her into his arms and tell

her everything would be fine. But everything would not be all rosy and romantic, because the world was the way it was, cruel and unforgiving. That was unfortunate, but not likely to change, especially if she had insulted Agnes at the first meeting. He did his best to smooth those waters. "You did arrive a week early, you know."

"That is as may be, but she said she had no room for my dresser, the girls' maid, and the governess. Or time for anyone's megrims." She sniffed. "As if I were wont to suffer the vapors. All I requested was a cup of tea, some lavender water for my brow, perhaps a posset, and a bit of steak for Ruffles. She claimed my darling barked at her chickens so they would not lay, then she said she had no time, not with a sick child in the house."

Forde stopped his pacing around the parlor. "What, has one of the girls taken ill? And you left her for Mrs. Cole to tend?"

"My daughters are fine, and in their own chambers here at this tawdry inn, resting. There is nothing niminy-piminy about them, I'll have you know."

On the contrary, Forde recalled his nieces whining and wailing at each minor scrape or sniffle. "Did Miss Cole contract a fever, then? She was in perfect health yesterday."

"If you must know, it is Crispin, your son."

Forde almost snatched the vinaigrette out of Agnes's plump hand. "My son is ailing? And you waited until now to tell me? And . . . Crispin is here, not at his school?" Forde was already halfway out of the door and calling for a horse.

"Oh, sit down, do. Gerald's dilemma is far more serious. Crispin is not about to stick his spoon in the wall. He was begging to be permitted to feed the chickens when we left. That woman keeps chickens, Forde. Did you know that?"

"Yes, and goats, too. Piglets in the spring. What is wrong with my son, dash it?"

"Oh, a piddly measles outbreak at his school, if you

must know. The headmaster wrote to inform you, but you were gone, weren't you? I could not leave the poor boy at that dreadful place, could I?"

"Instead you dragged him halfway across England? You put a sick child in a carriage and drove for days to get here, where I doubt there is a competent physician in miles?"

"Pish tosh. I told you, he is not ill. Besides, my girls both had the measles and did not require anything but an apothecary."

And the services of a nanny, two nursemaids, and a score of other servants.

"Furthermore, Crispin did not ride in the carriage, not past the first change, that is. He is a poor traveler, don't you know. I had forgotten. Gerald took him up with him on his horse, or had him sit by the driver. He rode with the servants in the baggage cart the rest of the time."

"Great gods, ma'am, if he was not ailing before, he would be now."

"Nonsense. He begged to be given the reins."

Forde looked long and hard at the woman his brother had wed, wondering if she could be evil enough to wish Crispin ill so that her own son would be next in line to the viscountcy. Deuce take it, he was suspecting everyone's motives these days. No, Agnes was lazy, not malicious.

She seemed to shrink under his glare. "Crispin wished to see his cousin Gerald married, and he looked so small and lonely, with half the school in hospital. And I could not recall if he had the measles before. My girls did, or I would not have exposed them, naturally. That Cole woman took it into her head that he had to stay at her poor excuse for a cottage, rather than here with you at the inn, which had been my intention. She said that if the boy is not sick himself, he might carry the disease to the village children."

"And she was right. But if he did come down with

the contagion, who did you think was going to nurse him. You?"

"Me? You know my nerves are too delicate for that. Why, I had to take the waters at Bath when my poor girls came down with the disease at the same time. So disfiguring, don't you know. And Nanny took another position when poor Crispin was sent to school, so she was not available to look after him. I supposed your valet could play nursemaid."

They had had the same argument for two years now, about sending Crispin to school. "*Poor* Crispin adores his school and his friends there, where he would have received adequate medical care. Damn, now Mrs. Cole has to take care of my son as well as prepare for the wedding." And now he was in her debt.

"I thought we decided that you were going to stop that nonsense about my son marrying a nobody. That was why you came here. And why I came early, to make certain you did."

"I came to look into the matter, that was all. After weighing the facts I have decided . . ."

"Yes?"

"To speak with Gerald. If he is old enough to marry, he is old enough to make his own decisions."

The dog yelped at being squeezed so hard and jumped down off the chaise, growling at Forde. Agnes did, too. "What? Gerald is a mere child! His bride is a dowd."

"You mean she is so pretty she will put your daughters in the shade."

"Bosh. Her looks are nothing out of the ordinary. Another blue-eyed blond chit, that is all. Short and thin as a rail, to boot." Agnes's own daughters were in her younger image: ginger-haired and plump. "She is nothing, I say, a nobody. They are poor, Forde. Why, they do not have room for servants, even if they could afford them."

"That is not a crime, not that I know of."

"It is not fitting for a Wellforde."

Agnes was not born a Wellforde, and the viscount resented her setting herself up as the family's arbiter. "Did you get a chance to speak with Miss Cole? I found her charming and well mannered, besides a comely lass."

"Hmph. How could she be well mannered, coming from such a creature as that Cole woman?"

Agnes did not know the half of it.

"If Mrs. Cole was rude," Forde said, "I can only assume it was out of worry for Crispin. And her house truly is small, adequate enough for two women and a guest or two, I'd suppose, but that is all. She undoubtedly felt you would be better served at the inn."

Agnes wrinkled her nose, looking more like the Pekingese than ever. "I can see she has won you over."

"No such thing," Forde insisted.

Agnes ignored his disclaimer. "I must say I am disappointed. I was certain a man of your experience and intelligence would have seen through her mock ladylike manner. I thought you would have convinced her to withdraw her daughter from the engagement the day you arrived."

The day he arrived he was flat in the mud. He had not fared much better with Mrs. Cole since, either. "How was I to do that, Agnes?"

"How should I know? You manage to intimidate everyone else."

"I do? Then why are you—? That is, Mrs. Cole is not easily swayed."

"Then you could have bought her off or seduced her."

He had tried both, unsuccessfully. "Mrs. Cole is not the mercenary adventuress you take her for. Nor is she open to a gentleman's advances."

"Aha! You did try, then."

"I assure you, I am not in the habit of forcing myself upon virtuous ladies."

"Which means she turned you down. The woman is a fool, besides being a pauper. The daughter must have feathers for brains, too. Or else they are looking toward Gerald to pull them out of poverty."

"I do believe Miss Cole is sincerely attached to the lad."

"You see, you do consider Gerald a boy!"

"That was a figure of speech only. He is man enough to choose his own bride. I did not, and that was a mistake."

"A mistake? Your wife brought you a fortune and gave you a son. That was no mistake. Miss Cole is. You must talk to Gerald tonight. Make him see reason, not merely her big blue eyes. With the last banns not yet called he can cry off gracefully. No one in London needs to know the particulars."

"Miss Cole lives here. She would be shamed if her groom decamped a week before the wedding."

"You care more about that woman's daughter than your own nephew?"

"Right now I care about my son. Good day, Agnes."

First he checked the boy for spots, then for fever. Then he picked him up and hugged him close, even though Crispin felt he was too old for that. Forde could have lost his boy, though, and needed to hold him tight.

"I am fine, Father. I already had the measles, remember?"

Forde did not, and was embarrassed. "Of course I remember," he lied—it was against his principles, but so was letting his son think he was a care-for-naught—"but you might have suffered on the journey."

"Oh, no, I do not get the carriage sickness anymore. I did not want to sit with Aunt Agnes and the girls, though. All they talked about was bonnets and beaux. Jem Coachman says I will make as good a whip as you when I get bigger."

"I am sure you will, but you should not have worried your aunt, or Mrs. Cole."

"Oh, Mrs. Cole is great guns. She knew I wasn't sick, but she said she'd rather have me as a guest than my aunt. Promise you won't tell Aunt Agnes, though? I swore I wouldn't peach on Susannah's mother."

"Then you mustn't. And I would not think of telling."

"She says I can feed the chickens tomorrow, and she will show me how to gather the eggs."

The future Viscount Forde mucking in a henhouse? The current viscount almost scooped the boy up again, to get him out of such common surroundings. But Crispin looked happier than he'd seen him in ages, babbling about the goats, and how there was a stream next door at the squire's, and could they go fishing there? Gerald's friend Doddsworth had two younger brothers, and they went all the time with their father.

Forde had never been fishing with his son. The boy spent summers in the country with his grandparents, his mother's family.

"I'll ask Squire Doddsworth, shall I?"

"Mrs. Cole said she would. He is coming to supper tonight, but Aunt Agnes insisted I am to have my meal on a tray upstairs. Mrs. Cole asked the cook to make strawberry tarts 'cause they are my favorites."

"Are they?" He had not known. "Mine, too."

"And she found me some books that used to belong to Miss Susannah so I won't be bored. But tomorrow we are all invited to dinner at Doddsworth Manor after church. Me, too. Isn't that capital, Father?"

Forde had never sat to a formal supper with his son, either.

"Susannah says the squire has hounds, lots of them. And the biggest boar in the county. That's a boy pig, you know. And she says I can come visit her and Gerald in Hampshire next summer, if I don't have to spend the whole holiday with Grandmother. I like her, don't you?"

"Your grandmother?" Forde had not seen the woman since his wife's funeral. "Of course."

"No, Father. Miss Susannah."

"Oh. She is a very charming young lady."

"But not as nice as Mrs. Cole."

"Where is Mrs. Cole?"

"Sewing on the wedding dress. It is the prettiest gown I have ever seen. Do you know, when you touch it, your fingers get all fluttery? Miss Susannah hates it and says that is all fustian nonsense. She and Cousin Gerald are arguing in the parlor, so I came outside to wait for you. Mrs. Cole said you would be here soon, and she was right."

"She is very wise." And very confident that he would do the right thing, which made Forde surprisingly proud, as if her good opinion of him as a father mattered one whit.

"May I stay here, Father? May I?"

Katie Cole had already shown the halfling more attention than Crispin's own mother had, and more care than his aunt. "If you behave and do not cause her any headaches."

"I would not. Mrs. Cole says she will chop me up and feed me to the chickens otherwise. She's a prime 'un, isn't she? That's what Jem Coachman says, anyway."

"I do not think you should be using the head groom's vocabulary, but, yes, Mrs. Cole is top drawer."

"You like her, don't you?"

She was kind to his motherless son. "Yes, I like her. Very much."

Chapter Nine

*V*iscount Forde embodied masculinity from the top of his windblown hair to the bottom of his shiny boots. He was charm incarnate when he wished to be, flashing that smile. And he was seductive, an attraction that had been missing in Katie's life for so many years she was surprised she could recognize it, like an elephant. She had never seen one of those creatures, but was certain she would know it when she did. And then there was another quality that his lordship possessed, one that made the others pale in comparison.

A woman might observe a gentleman flirting, or dancing, or riding his horse, and find herself moonstruck. But seeing a man hug his son—his filthy little boy who'd been playing tag with the goats—that was something else altogether. That was heart, a pure, rare commodity in this world. Any number of men had courage and honor and physical attraction, but heart—now there was a treasure to fight for, to grasp, to keep forever.

Katie stepped back from the window where she'd been watching the reunion, curious at how the viscount would treat his heir. Her own father had been distant and cool, while the squire was oblivious to his sons. The blacksmith often cuffed his boys, and many of the farmers considered their offspring nothing but unpaid help. Forde loved his son.

Why that should bring tears to her eyes was a mys-

tery to Katie, but it did. She wanted to despise Forde
for bringing chaos into her life. She should resent him
because he had the power to wreak havoc over her,
and no female could admire her persecutor.

Katie did not hate him, though.

She doubted he would make her secrets public, despite his unspoken threats. If he had spoken to Mrs.
Wellforde about Susannah's birth, that overfed vixen
would have been here with a pistol, reclaiming her
precious cub. No, Forde was too much the gentleman
to heap unearned dishonor on an innocent girl. He
merely wanted to protect his family, the same way
Katie had lied to protect her daughter.

She could not hate him. Not at all, to her regret.

Gerald rushed past his uncle without a greeting. "I
am staying at Doddsworth's place, where there are no
females to natter and nag," he called over his shoulder.

"I need to speak to you."

"I need to hear about something other than dowries
and dresses. Squire and his horses do not care if a
chap is a few days late, or brings his mama. Or wants
to wed a poor girl."

"Will you be here at dinner?" Forde called to his
nephew's receding back, although it sounded as if Gerald already had enough trouble on his plate.

Susannah was crying again, angry at Gerald, his
mother, her mother, and the wedding gown. "This is
supposed to be the happiest time of my life!" she
wailed on her way to her bedchamber to throw herself
into a satisfying spate of woeful tears and worse temper. Forde could hear a door slam above when he
entered the library.

"I am sorry. Am I calling at an awkward time?"

What could be awkward about having twelve people
for dinner unexpectedly, a daughter suffering bridal
nerves, a dirty-faced cherub she had nearly kidnapped
from his overbearing family, and the most devastat-
ingly attractive gentleman ready to denounce her over
the dinner table? Oh, there was the matter of a gown

whose hem would not stay turned and whose seams would not gather for Susannah's narrow torso. No, nothing awkward about that at all. She set the gown aside for another try later.

"Welcome, and I do hope you will permit Crispin to stay on with us here. He has been a big help."

It rankled Forde that she could not afford maids, when his own family was demanding service—and his son was being pressed into a footman's role. He knew she would not take money from him, so he did not offer. "I could speak to the innkeeper about sending a few of his girls."

"Thank you, but that is not necessary. Mrs. Tarrant's nieces are already at work in the kitchens and will help serve. Crispin is going to make out the place cards for the table, aren't you?"

"Mrs. Cole says my handwriting is perfect for the job, Father."

"Excellent, my boy. Why do you not go practice? That is, somewhere else. I wish to speak to Mrs. Cole privately."

Crispin stuck his jaw out, looking mulish. Or like his father. "You said I could stay."

"As long as you behaved. Now go. We will be done shortly."

How shortly? Katie wondered. Saying that the wedding was canceled would take no time at all. Mending Susannah's broken heart might take forever, if it were possible. After all, the wedding gown seemed impossible to fix. Why not a heart?

The viscount was pacing the small room, lifting a book here, moving a paper there, until he was certain they were alone. Then he told Katie, "I have decided that I have to speak to Gerald. If he found out later, and it mattered to him that his wife could not be comfortable in London, or might be exposed as an imposter anytime, then he would never forgive me. I would never forgive myself."

Katie nodded, not wanting to look at him. "And I could never forgive myself for letting my daughter wed a man to whom such an insignificant thing would matter. If he loves her, it is for herself, not for what name she bears, or does not. We shall tell both of them, together. If your nephew cries off, Susannah must know the reason, lest she think herself to blame."

"After dinner?"

"Definitely not before! Or during."

Dinner was more formal than the last one at Cole Cottage, mainly due to the presence of Gerald's disapproving mother. Gerald spoke to young Doddsworth about horses, his sisters batted their eyelashes at the younger Doddsworth boys hard enough to cool the soup, and the squire and Agnes Wellforde seemed to be competing over who could eat more.

With ham, mutton, beef, and chicken on the menu, there was nothing parsimonious about this evening's offering. Katie felt proud of her table, glad that no one could complain about the simply cooked but ample meal, not even the dog. Gerald's mother took hearty portions of everything, then fed some to her pet.

Katie wanted to throw a dish at the woman, but they were her good plates. Young Crispin was deemed too unmannerly to sit with the adults, but the Pekingese had a place on Agnes's ample lap? Besides, the dog was gobbling down food that could have fed the Cole Cottage residents for another day, at least.

But she stayed smiling, the perfect hostess, and led the ladies out of the dining parlor when the meal was finally over. Susannah and the Wellforde girls—Katie had not learned which was which yet—were giggling over something, and Mrs. Wellforde was napping after her huge repast. Katie took her place at the pianoforte, hoping to ease her nerves with her beloved music.

Forde hurried the gentlemen through their port, fearful of what offensive remarks Agnes might make. Half of the gentlemen were mere boys, besides, so they did not need to smoke or drink, in his opinion.

With so little to offer, and no cards likely, either, Dodds-worth decided to leave. The two families that were about to unite ought to have some private time to-gether, he declared. Besides, he and his boys were planning a foray after fish early in the morning before church. Forde and his son were invited.

Dawn was not a part of the day Forde usually saw from the bright side, but he said he would consider the invitation, for Crispin's sake. After the manor party left, Forde took a seat next to Mrs. Cole on the pianoforte bench, thinking that he might never tire of her proficient playing, or her rapt expression as she gave herself to the music. For that matter, he might never tire of the small, rare smile she gave him when he praised her performance between pieces. She was wearing the same dark-colored gown, which he *would* grow bored with, even if it did reveal more of her bosom than the sacklike frocks she wore during the day. He would dress her in green velvet, as soft as her skin, as sultry as moonlight. Then he would undress her, caress her, make her beautiful body—

"Sing?" He coughed. "You want me to sing with you?"

She looked at him oddly. "That is what I asked. Your nephew said you had a fine voice, and I would not wish to bore your sister-in-law with my contin-ued playing."

Agnes was already sleeping off her dinner in the most comfortable chair in the room. Susannah and Gerald were whispering in the corner, as usual.

Without waiting for his reply, Katie opened a new score sheet and began to play. Thank heavens he knew the words, for Forde did not know himself anymore. He had never been so attracted to any woman, had never been so often or so awkwardly aroused over a virtuous female. Botheration.

"I believe that is 'both a robin and a sparrow.' Shall we begin again?"

They did, and this time he paid attention to the music,

not just his companion on the bench. Their voices melded as if they had practiced together for weeks—a perfect fit.

Katie could forget her worries for a brief time in the pleasure of having Forde sitting next to her, near enough that she could smell his cologne, feel his thigh pressed against hers, his sleeve brush her shoulder as he reached to turn the pages. Best of all, he seemed to share the simple pleasure she took in playing and singing. Not many men of her acquaintance, limited though their number was, would endure an evening of music, but the viscount seemed to relish it, to find the same quiet joy she found. When they sang, he showed none of Gerald's embarrassment, or Roland Doddsworth's affectations. Instead his rich baritone was steady and sure, like the man himself.

His nieces, however, had no patience with the entertainment. The young Wellforde girls had their set pieces to perform in public, as all well-bred females were taught to do, but that was the extent of their interest in music. Since their mama was asleep and so could not push them into drawing attention to their nonexistent talent, they refused Katie's polite invitation to take a turn at the instrument. As for singing, the girls claimed that their voices were more suitable for calling cows home than creating a pleasant ambiance in the drawing room. Besides, they declared, earning a scowl from their uncle, such tame pursuits were rustic and backward. All agog about the wedding, they wanted to see their new sister's dress instead.

With a backward look of regret—for the viscount's closeness as much as for the music— Katie took them to the library, where she'd left the gown. Susannah stayed behind with Gerald, in earnest discussion, it seemed. She told Katie, "Go ahead, please. I do not wish to see that gown any more than I need to."

Awakened by the fervent words, Agnes bestirred herself. Curious, she set the dog down from her lap, hauled herself to her feet, and followed. Her daughters were oohing and aahing, but Agnes thought the gleaming ivory gown outrageous, overelaborate and unfashionable. The garment was not what befitted the bride of a viscount's heir. It was more spectacular than anything she or her daughters had ever owned, also.

Then she touched it.

"Ah." The fabric was softer than the finest silk, the lace like the most delicate spiderweb. Just touching the gown made Agnes's fingers feel like a young woman's again, not thick and gnarly. Suddenly she felt that she was not so old, after all. Why, she might just take Squire Doddsworth up on his offer to stay at his manor house rather than at that sorry excuse for an inn. The man was a rustic, of course, but he obviously set a good table, judging from his girth. Her girls could practice their wiles on his younger boys, and she could save the expense of the inn—save Forde, that was, for Agnes had no intention of paying the bill. Who knew but that the squire might be convinced to visit London now and again? And give up all that hunting. And get a new wardrobe. The world was full of wonders.

The dog was making odd sounds that Agnes, lost in her delightful daydreams, did not hear. Never having had a dog, Katie thought Ruffles was growling as she carefully folded the gown over the arm of the chair, to finish tomorrow.

The Pekingese was not growling. He had been fed too much, nearly enough for two women for a week, and so he did what overfed dogs often do. Only no one let him out, so he did it on the hem of the gown.

One of the Wellforde girls ran shrieking from the room, the other fled to hide her giggles. Their mother took her usual escape: She swooned, but onto a chair where her limbs would not be exposed and her feathered turban could not be dislodged.

Gerald and Katie came running, Forde close on their heels.

"Mama!" young Wellforde cried, falling to his knees beside his mother's chair.

Susannah took one look at the gown and refused to wear it, ever.

Forde offered to purchase a new one, again.

"No," Katie said, "the gown will be fine." She was already carrying it—at a distance—to the kitchen, and to the devil with her company. Forde followed, carrying the dog at an equal distance until he could toss the creature out the back door.

When he returned, Katie was already sponging the skirt clean. "You see? This gown can withstand much."

He doubted Miss Susannah Cole could. "I think your daughter would prefer—"

"No. The gown is a symbol, I feel, of what a good marriage should be: beautiful on the surface but lasting and true beneath, able to outlast adversity and overcome any difficulty life might toss a young couple's way. Perhaps it is an omen, too. I truly believe it will bring joy and happiness to the bride."

Forde was dubious of such an unfounded superstition. "You did not derive much joy or happiness from it."

"Ah, but I never got to wear it. Susannah will."

Chapter Ten

*A*gnes insisted that she required both Forde and Gerald to escort her, her daughters, and her poor sick doggy back to the inn. The viscount insisted that Gerald join him in the private parlor before heading to Doddsworth Manor.

"I wish to speak to you about the wedding."

"Good. I wish to speak about it also."

Over the landlord's excellent cognac, Forde broached the delicate subject. With much deliberation and careful choice of words, trying not to cast the smallest aspersion on Susannah or her mother, he urged Gerald to reconsider.

His efforts at diplomacy were in vain, but not for the reason he'd supposed.

"Her parentage? I've known all about that for an age. It matters not. Besides, we have decided to postpone the wedding anyway."

Forde needed another drink. And two to loosen Gerald's tongue enough for an explanation. The young couple had decided to wait, it seemed. They loved each other—Gerald was adamant on that score—but he needed to give all of his attention to establishing his horse-breeding program right then. Reading between the lines, and between Gerald's increasingly outspoken complaints, Forde deduced that Susannah was not the perfect angel of Gerald's initial infatuation. She was not the sweet and docile countrywoman he'd assumed. Rather, she was spoiled and demanding, jealous of his time and his mother, of all things! She was stubborn to a fault and frivolous besides, fretting herself to flinders over a silly dress. His beloved would outgrow such unappealing traits, Gerald was sure, and he would wait. She was too young to marry, he concluded, and his uncle had been right all along: A chap should not marry until he had to.

Forde was both relieved and upset. His nephew was not rushing toward disaster, but Mrs. Cole would blame him for Gerald's defection. And now he would not have an excuse to stay in Devon, or to see the woman again.

"Are you sure?"

Katie was having a similar discussion, only this one was in her kitchen, over tea.

"My father? Oh, I know all about that."

Katie wished she could swoon on demand like Agnes Wellforde. "How . . .?"

The answer was simple: Her daughter was intelligent, and the village children were cruel. When Susannah had no portrait to show of her hero father, no ceremonial sword, medal, or ribbon, not a scrap of a letter or a lock of his hair, the local bullies started to taunt her that he never existed. Her mother refused to speak of Mr. Cole, so Susannah took her questions, and the name in Katie's Bible, to Lady Martindale, who knew everything about everyone who ever lived.

"Do you blame me?" Katie asked, her voice trembling.

"How could I, Mama? I would not be here if you had not done what you did. Gerald did not care, either."

"You . . . told him?"

"Of course. Someone else might have, you know, and I could not be less than honest with the man I would marry. But that makes no difference. We have decided to postpone the wedding for other reasons."

Gerald, it seemed, was not quite the perfect beau. On closer examination, and longer acquaintance, he was immature, horse-mad, domineering, and entirely too devoted to his mama.

"Do you know that he actually wants her to come live with us?"

And the dog? That would be enough reason for Katie to call off the engagement altogether, but she merely took another sip of her tea and listened.

He was also stuffy and staid. Just because he had lived in London and did not care for it, Gerald felt Susannah did not need to go traveling, not to Bath, Brighton, or anywhere but his new estate, secluded in the countryside where she would have no friends, no parties, no dances. He, meanwhile, would be visiting horse fairs and race meets across the kingdom. He thought she would be too busy with babies to care!

"As if that is all I am good for, to bear him sons."

Gerald's worst fault, however, according to his beloved, was that he was condescending. He thought Susannah ought to be pleased with whatever he decided about their future, because it was bound to be better than what she had now.

"But he is right, darling, I am sorry to say. Not that you should wed for the material advantages a good match can bring, but I cannot take you to London or any of the fashionable resorts, either. We are well established in our own community, with its dinners and assemblies, but your friends will be marrying soon, and you do not care for any of the local young men. Few eligible bachelors pass through Brookville, few who can afford a bride with such a small dowry, and fewer who will ignore a blot on the family escutcheon. I worry about your future without Mr. Wellforde."

"Oh, I fully intend to marry Gerald when he grows up a little, just not yet. And you do not have to worry about me. I wrote to Grandmother."

Katie found the last dregs of the dinner wine. "You do not have a grandmother."

"Your mother, Lady Bainbridge. I invited her and

Grandfather to the wedding. Gerald brought back her reply. She thinks we are too young to choose, as you were. She promised me a Season in Town if I postponed the wedding."

"Good grief, and you are choosing parties and such over Gerald?"

"Oh, no. Grandmother said that I should see a bit of the world before settling down, to make sure I do not regret it later. Gerald had to agree, because he has been to Town and university and visiting all over England, but all I have ever known is Brookville."

"And London is what you want?"

Susannah reached for her mother's hand, which was clutching her fortified teacup. "Please do not think I have been unhappy here. I have not. I just think there must be more to life than the chickens. And Lady Bainbridge—should I call her Grandmother or Countess?—says that no one will question my birth, not if she and the earl accept me as their long-lost kin. I would not care if no one invites me to their balls, for I do love Gerald, despite his faults. But if I go to London, you see, we will be more equal. He cannot take me for granted then, or treat me as a charity case."

Perhaps her daughter was wise after all. "I shall miss you," was all Katie could say. She would have missed her when she went off with her husband, too, but then Susannah would be moving to another county, not another world where Katie could not visit.

After a flurry of notes in the morning, both families decided that the last of the banns should be announced at church, to show there had been no falling-out. The wedding was to be delayed, that was all, while Susannah attended her grandmother and Gerald readied his stud farm. They even went together to midday dinner at Squire Doddsworth's, who was no happier than Katie.

His fishing expedition had been canceled, and now his plans for both widows, too. Mrs. Cole was still encumbered, and Mrs. Wellforde was leaving for London tomorrow, putting paid to any hopes of a bit of dalliance while she was under his roof. Ah, well, there was always Sukey in the village.

To smother any sparks of scandal, Susannah was to travel to London with Gerald's sisters and his suddenly accommodating mother. The granddaughter of a wealthy earl, sponsored by an influential countess? Why, dear Gerald could not have found a more lovely bride if Agnes had selected her herself.

Crispin was staying on at Cole Cottage. He had a measle, he swore, a headache, and perhaps a fever. He was definitely too ill for the long journey. Katie was glad to have the imp so she would not have to face the emptiness of the house without Susannah.

His father stayed on at the inn. How could Forde leave when he'd promised Crispin a fishing trip? The boy was not too ill for that, or hiking around the countryside, playing with the goats, or helping with the chickens.

They kept Katie so busy, insisting they needed her company since she was familiar with the countryside, that she hardly had time to miss her daughter, away from her side for the first time in eighteen years. She also had her house and gardens and animals, plus choir practice and music lessons, with Crispin added so his education was not entirely forsaken. He took a great deal of her time, thankfully. His father took a great deal of her thoughts.

Forde could take the boy to his own estate until school resumed, taking him fishing in his own streams. He could buy Crispin a pony, rather than teach him to ride Susannah's ancient mare. He could be attending the opera, not singing duets with a country widow. Instead, he was sitting at Katie's fireside listening to her play, at her dinner table talking about books and poetry and the news from the papers. He was at church and at Squire's, taking Susannah's place reading to Lady Martindale, and going along on Katie's errands. Mostly, he was in her dreams.

As much as she missed her daughter, somehow

Forde's inevitable leaving would be more painful. Susannah would always be her flesh and blood; the viscount would be a stranger again, once he was back to his glittering London life. Katie did not know how she would manage. Perhaps she would have to get a dog for a friend, like Gerald's mother.

When a week had passed, a magical week full of laughter and rosy cheeks and a companionship no dog nor daughter could provide, Forde asked to see her privately. He was leaving, she knew, and he must not see her cry. So she took up her mending, the same wedding gown she had tried to sew so often. Susannah had refused to take it with her, but Katie hoped she would reconsider after she'd had her time in London, if she still wanted to marry Gerald.

That was another silly dream, because Susannah would have an entire new wardrobe before then. The Earl of Bainbridge might be a miser, but he would be too proud to let a kinswoman of his be seen in rags. The beautiful gown would never be worn.

A tear splashed on it, in her lap.

"If you miss her so much," Forde asked, "why don't you go to London, too?"

"My father has never forgiven me. And I would only hurt Susannah's chances of being accepted into Society. Too many questions would be asked if I appeared after so long."

"You could wear your gown." He took it from her lap and held it up. "Such a pretty thing. Why don't you try it on for me?"

"What, now?"

"Why not? I have seen the blasted—that is, the blessed thing constantly, and heard about it, but I have never seen it on a woman."

"It has been altered for Susannah."

"It looks too large for such a little dab of a thing," he said with a connoisseur's knowledge. "Please, put it on."

It still fit perfectly. Katie could not imagine how, looking at herself in the mirror in her bedroom. It had never been altered for her, neither for her wedding nor recently, but the gown might have been sewn to her measure. If this was the last time Forde would see her, she decided, let him have a perfect memory. She pulled her hair up and threaded her pearls through it. She bit her lips to bring color, and pinched her cheeks. In spite of her years, Katie thought she had never looked better, nor felt more alive. She could almost imagine that she was a bride, going to meet the man of her dreams. She would not think about tomorrow.

"Beautiful," he whispered, almost in awe, as she returned to her book room.

"I told Susannah everyone would think the dress was magnificent."

"The dress? Oh, that is all right, too. Katie, you have to come to London. You will be an Incomparable, a Toast, a Diamond."

"I will be an outcast."

"Not if I am at your side."

She stepped away, her pleasure at his compliments fading. "I will not be your mistress."

"I am not asking you to be my mistress."

"Then . . . ?"

"Then I am asking you to be my life's companion."

"Ah, I see. Crispin wants me for a mother."

"I want you."

"You cannot. Your position, your place in the government, even your friendships would be in jeopardy."

"I say not. Come to London with me and let me prove what a viscount can do, especially with the backing of an earl and his countess. For once, a title and a fortune will be of some use. Be brave, my Katie, and come with me. Anything is possible, you'll see."

"No, that is just the gown talking."

He raised one eyebrow. "Strange, my garments have never spoken to me."

"No, you do not understand. I barely do. The gown is so pretty, it makes you think of fairy princesses and happy endings. Life is not like that."

He brushed away a shimmering teardrop from her

cheek. "It can be, my Katie, it can be. I need you to make me a whole man, to make my son the man I want him to be. I need you to bring the music to my soul."

She shook her head. "I cannot be your lover."

"Who said anything about being lovers? Although that is part of the bargain, saints be praised." He kissed her, to prove his eagerness. Both of them felt the warmth spread until their bodies flowed together of their own volition, a perfect fit. His hands stroked, his tongue explored, his voice whispered words of encouragement.

Katie would have followed him anywhere, even to a love nest in Richmond or Kensington.

He only led her to the sofa. His kiss turned into a caress, an embrace, an eternity. The roar of blood in their ears was deafening, the pounding of their hearts—the shouts of "Unhand my daughter, you cad!"

Eighteen years had gone by. The angry gentleman was thinner, grayer, with lines etched in his face. He was still tall and proud.

"Papa?"

"I was invited to a wedding, and by Zeus, I mean to have one. Not a moment too soon, either, from what Lady Martindale wrote your mother."

"Lady Martindale wrote to Mama? But Susannah is in London. Surely you have seen her. The wedding has been postponed."

"Faugh." He waved her concerns aside, with the pistol in his hand. "The chit is well enough. She'll do. Can't hold a candle to you for looks, not even after all these years, but I'd say she has a wiser head on her shoulders. And take yours off Forde's, dammit!"

Katie's legs could barely hold her, but she did move away from Forde's sheltering arms.

"At least you've picked a better man this time, so I suppose you ain't an entire ninnyhammer. And button your gown." He waved the gun in Forde's direction. "As for you, sir, I demand to know your intentions. Of course, your choices after this bit of work are a ring on my girl's finger or a pistol ball between your legs."

"Papa! You cannot threaten a viscount. Besides, I am too old to worry about my reputation, which was destroyed ages ago any—"

Forde stopped her with a finger laid gently across her lips, which were red and swollen from his kisses. He told the earl, "I was just trying to convince your daughter to make me the happiest of men."

"You were trying to seduce me!"

He shrugged. "That, too. I intend to be very happy in this marriage."

"Good," Lord Bainbridge said. "I'll send for the special license. And your mother and daughter. And the rest of those connections of yours, Forde, who are underfoot at my house. But hear me, both of you. I am not taking any chances this time. I am not going to take my eyes off you until the deed is done."

Katie stamped her foot. "The deed will not be done! No one has said they love me!"

"Deuce take it, girl, why else would I fly halfway across the country to make sure you get hitched all right and tight this time?"

Forde smiled. "I do not think she means you, my lord."

"What, the gal is half out of her wedding gown, and you haven't said you love her?"

"I was getting to it."

Katie looked over at him. "You were?"

"And will if we can have some privacy. That means you, too, Crispin, so you do not have to hide in the hall. Take Lord Bainbridge to see the chickens, the ones his daughter raises to make ends meet."

"Ten minutes," the earl said, ignoring the slur. He took an ecstatic Crispin by the collar and led him out, too. "Come on, boy. I always wanted a grandson, you know. I say, do you play chess?"

"Father has been teaching me this week."

"Good. That means I can still win."

When the door shut behind them, Forde took Katie

back into his arms, but not to kiss her, only to look
into her eyes and swear, "I love you, my Katie. And
I will love you forever and ever, and have since I fell
at your feet."

"And I love you, and have since you landed in
the mud."

Now he kissed her. "There, do you hear the music
of our hearts beating together? It is a symphony. And
do not say it's the gown."

No, it was the goats. It was feeding time.

Chapter Eleven

The Brookville wedding took place a mere month late. Everyone agreed the bride was the most beautiful they had ever seen. Susannah got to wear blue velvet, but all eyes, especially the groom's, were on Katie in her ivory lace and silk. Later the villagers agreed she glowed with happiness like they'd never seen, but then the viscount did, too.

And later that day, on their way to his country seat for their honeymoon, Lord and Lady Forde finally had the privacy to express that happiness. Her father was not watching, and Crispin was on his way back to school. With the shades of the carriage windows pulled across and the driver pretending deafness, they consecrated their love in perfect harmony, sealing their vows for all time.

So rapt were they that they never noticed when a trunk fell off the back of the coach . . . the trunk with her finally and finely worn, perfectly fitting, wedding gown.

The author of more than two dozen Regency romances, **Barbara Metzger** is the proud recipient of a RITA and two *Romantic Times* Career Achievement Awards for Regencies. When not writing Regencies or reading them, she paints, gardens, volunteers at the local library, and goes beachcombing on the beautiful Long Island shore with her little dog, Hero. She loves to hear from her readers, care of Signet or through her Web site, www.BarbaraMetzger.com.

Glad Rags

Connie Brockway

Chapter One

St. John's Wood, ten miles outside of London
The Height of the Season, June 1856

"*E*ven if you did win your wager, how in God's name do you expect me to fulfill the requirements?" Alexander, Viscount Thorpe, asked in disgust.

"My great-aunt's attic is a warren filled to overflowing with my ancestors' detritus." Across the gaming table Hugh St. James lifted eyes as dark blue as his sister's to meet Alex's. Hugh was drunk, disastrously drunk, yet he still managed to invest his slurred words with a jeer. "I'm sure we'll find something suitable."

Marcus Penworthy and Tom Davidson, having long since bowed out of the current game, traded anxious glances. Even the servant, whose sole duty was to keep their glasses filled with their host's best claret, could not keep the concern from his expression.

This was not going to end well. The viscount had always been constitutionally incapable of backing down from a challenge, and Hugh St. James kept hurling taunts at him.

It was a shame, as not long ago these two men had been boon companions, raised on neighboring estates. They had even gone to Oxford together. It was there Penworthy had met and befriended both.

"What will it be, Thorpe?" asked Hugh. Once, the handsome young man had been as well known for his easygoing nature as his boldness. Though he was no longer so easygoing, he was still bold, though the word "foolish" came more easily to mind this night.

Certainly it was foolish to bait someone as formidable as the viscount Thorpe. All six feet four inches of his powerful frame vibrated with rigidity, and the scar he'd won in the Battle of Balaklava showed red against his lean cheek before snaking beneath the hard angle of a square jaw.

No one had ever accused Alexander Thorpe of being easygoing, but he had been capable of laughter. Now his expression was always stern, his wide mouth having forgotten what it was to smile. Though he had always been frank, now his manner was blunt to the point of rudeness.

Some thought the Crimean War had made Alex aloof and abrupt. But Penworthy thought the same thing that divided Alex from St. James was also responsible for his stern, unyielding demeanor—St. James's sister, Lucy.

"Bless me, I can scarce countenance it! The great, the mighty, the infallible Viscount Thorpe is *uncertain*?" Hugh asked as the moment grew longer and Alex still hadn't answered. "I swear, what next? Are the heavens to fall?"

The viscount drummed his well-manicured fingertips against his overturned cards. They hadn't come here with a mind to gamble, but upon entering the ballroom Penworthy had noted the moment Alex's gaze had found Lucy's on the dance floor below. He'd nodded in curt acknowledgment, and she had angled up a dark brow in mocking reply.

They should have left then. And, indeed, for half a minute Alex had hesitated at the top of the stairs before swinging around and gruffly stating his intention of finding himself a game of cards. Penworthy, who'd been rather looking forward to dancing with a few of the Season's beauties, had reluctantly followed.

Unfortunately, an hour later her brother had found the same companions. And *still* Alex hadn't taken

Fate's prodigious hint and departed. No, he must stay and play and drink.

They had been at this table for nearly three hours, during which time ten thousand pounds had found its way into St. James's pockets. It should have ended there, with St. James smugly and righteously victorious, but it hadn't. It had come to this. St. James, flush with the mistaken notion of his luck's infallibility, had insisted on one last foolhardy bet that all but guaranteed Alex would recoup every last penny he'd lost this evening and then some.

There was a catch, of course. There was always a catch. Thorpe must first agree to St. James's ridiculous terms should he lose.

Not that he was going to lose. St. James hadn't a hope in hell of winning.

St. James would need to draw to an inside royal flush in order to beat the ten high straight that had become Alex's hand on the last flip of the card. The probability of its happening was essentially nonexistent. Even the unnatural luck that had attached itself to St. James all evening could not hold out against such overwhelming odds.

"Well, Thorpe, what's it to be? Do you accept?"

"Don't be a fool, Hugh. You only make yourself ridiculous," Alex answered.

The room went utterly silent except for the susurration of the gaslight in the sconces, hissing like a scold. Davidson's eyes widened, and Penworthy shook his head. Must Alex always say exactly what he meant?

"Ridiculous?" Hugh's eyes narrowed. "Too late. You've already seen to that."

At Alex's stony silence, Hugh's smile thinned. "Or is it only the *females* in my family you bother making ridiculous?"

Alex did not answer, but his scar grew pale against the darkening hue of his face.

"Indeed, I would think you would relish an excuse to continue," Hugh went on, ignoring Penworthy's silently mouthed admonitions. "Start with my sister, work your way up through me . . . who knows? Next year the opportunity may present itself to make a fool of my great-aunt Sophie."

"Bring me a piece of paper and a pen," Alex abruptly barked, lifting his hand and gesturing sharply toward the attendant hovering near the doorway. "I shall give you my vowels for the amount on the table, St. James."

St. James leaned over the green felt, arms braced on either side of his four upturned cards. A lock of dark auburn hair fell across his forehead. "I don't want your bloody *vowels,* Alex."

"Are you suggesting that my note is not good?" Alex asked in a carefully neutral voice.

At that St. James scoffed. "Good God, man! Do I look ready to shuffle off my mortal coil? No. I am certain your note is worth as much as your name. It is just that I do not want your *money,* Thorpe. I *want* you brought low. I want to deal a blow to that over-weening pride of yours. I want you to know what it feels like. What Lucy felt like. And I want these gentlemen"—he gestured blindly toward Penworthy and Davidson—"to bear witness."

"This is absurd," Alex said, his jaw bunching. It would take a great deal to push him into accepting a wager he could not lose from a man who could not afford the loss. Especially one as drunk as St. James. The amount on the table was formidable even to a man as rich as Alex. To one less wealthy, like St. James, it would represent half a year's income.

But Alex Thorpe could be pushed too hard.

"In or out?" St. James demanded.

"I refuse to accept such a wager," Alex answered.

"Coward." The word echoed in the silent room.

"Hugh!" Penworthy whispered urgently, putting his hand on his friend's shoulder. "Desist!"

St. James shook him off angrily. "Who else but a coward would refuse to allow his victim a chance to settle the score?"

"You are and never were my victim, Hugh," Alex said tightly.

"I beg to disagree. It was *my* sister whom you publicly insulted and thus, by extension, myself."

"It was not well done of me. I concede that now," Alex ground out, amazing Penworthy. In the two years since it had happened, Alex had never referred to that night.

"No, it was not well done," Hugh agreed, his face darkening.

"But she danced three times with Desmond Fitzgerald. Three times when it was understood by everyone that . . . that she was my . . ." *His betrothed,* Penworthy silently finished when Alex's lips pressed together, refusing to allow another betraying syllable to escape.

Yet . . . Lucy St. James had not been his betrothed. Nor had she ever been. Not officially. Whatever understanding existed between Alex and Lucy had been of a private nature. *If* it had existed at all. Except that everyone, apparently including Alex, had thought it did. And certainly for several years and through several Seasons before the "incident" Lucy had acted as if it was understood, as well.

During their years of . . . courtship? dalliance? association? she had danced many more than three times with Thorpe in a single evening. She had gone driving in the park with him. She had visited his townhouse. On several occasions, she'd been seen dining with him at London's finest restaurants. And she had done all these things without a chaperone, without apology, flaunting Society's rules, tweaking their collective noses.

Lucy St. James was as spirited and independent as her brother was hot-tempered and bold. It had seemed to all of them that Alex had admired those qualities. But then, it would appear that they had all been wrong about *that,* too. He certainly had not been appreciative of her independence two years ago.

"And that wasn't the worst of it. Not in the least. My God, what she put me through!" Alex's voice was raised, his eyes flashing. The rare display of emotion from so famously a self-controlled man caused David-son, who did not know either gentleman as well as Penworthy did, to grow slack-jawed with wonder.

"You were jealous," Hugh sneered.

Alex made a dismissive and impatient sound. "You don't understand."

"Not jealous?" Hugh asked bitterly. "Then your pride was offended. An excellent reason to insult a lady."

Alex ground his teeth together, an involuntary muscle lifting his upper lip in a snarl.

"She had spent the entire Season flirting and dancing and playing the coquette," Alex said in a cold, terse voice. "She was making a fool of me. You yourself noted it. You even commented on it. You said, 'Best beware, Alex, she intends to lead you a merry dance'!"

Hugh bolted to his feet and leaned over the table, his knuckles braced against the surface. "And you *drawled* back, 'Yes. A telling flaw, that. Lucy must *always* lead, and I find that I no longer have a taste for following.' "

"You could not have found a more public venue for your statement—nor more avid ears to hear it than in the crowd gathered that evening. I can still hear their titters! And then, not to leave any doubt as to your opinion of the lady everyone assumed you would make your wife, you left her to find her own way home."

"So I did!" Alex shouted back. His hands clenched into fists on the tabletop, as though recalling how they'd wanted to clench about Fitzhugh's neck. Or had it been Lucy's neck he had imagined wringing? Penworthy wasn't certain he could guess.

"She told me you left her there without so much as bidding her a good evening," St. James thundered.

"I am surprised she mentioned it to you. How kind of her to have noted my leaving," Alex bit out. "I recall hearing later that she stayed until four in the morning and danced twice more with Fitzhugh."

For a long moment the two men's gazes locked, their

jaws tight. Then, as though realizing how close he stood to violence, Alex took a deep breath, exhaling through his nose. He spread his palms flat on the table, staring at them as he pushed himself back in his seat.

"You are not the only one with a surplus of pride, Thorpe." St. James, too, seemed to realize how close they'd come to blows. He sank back down in his chair, his mouth twisting. "What else could she do to save face?"

"Ah, I see. And that accounts for the next day, too, when she was at Carleton House until dawn, and the day after that, when she danced so long at the Monforts' that she needed to be carried from the room by two 'strapping footmen'?" His laughter held no amusement. "I fear you took our separation a good deal harder than your sister did, Hugh."

"How would you know?" St. James asked, upending the rest of his wine into his mouth. "You left for the Crimea within a fortnight. Without even calling on her."

"I didn't want to interfere with her social activities."

"Ever the gentleman. And it was that same gentlemanly restraint that kept you from coming to call when you returned home?"

"Yes."

No, Penworthy thought. Whether or not Alex wanted the world to think his relationship with Lucy St. James had faded to indifference, Penworthy knew better. He had been there the first time Alex had seen Lucy St. James after his return from Russia. He had heard him catch his breath when she appeared on the other side of the coffee shop where they'd been drinking. He had seen the expression in Alex's eyes, lost and dazed, when he'd murmured, without taking his eyes from her, "Penworthy, please. No one has written me such, but I find I . . . I really must know. Before I . . . before I speak to her. Did she marry Fitzhugh?"

"No, Alex," he'd said gently. "Miss St. James is unwed."

He hadn't needed to see the relief flood Alex's eyes. He'd seen it in the way Alex's entire body had relaxed. Alex had risen and made his way through the crowded little inn to her table. There, he had bowed over her hand and greeted her with some mild triviality. She had responded in kind. And just as easily as that, they'd agreed to act as if nothing had ever been between them. For the sake of their pride.

Since then Alex had never asked another question regarding Lucy St. James, nor, indeed, had he ever mentioned her name.

Now, if only Hugh had been as civil as his sister. Unfortunately Hugh made it clear to all and sundry that he laid the blame for his sister's ongoing spinsterhood firmly at Alex's door. Because "who would wed a woman whose onetime fiancé found her so unfeminine and forward that he must make a public declaration of such?"

Such a mess, Penworthy thought unhappily.

"There was no reason to bother her," Alex was saying in reply to St. James's last accusation.

St. James's lip curled. "So you were a coward then, too. Lucy is well shut of you."

"Damn you, Hugh," Alex said, his palm slamming into the tabletop, sending the piles of coins skittering and jumping across the felt.

"Really, Alex. Shouldn't you be saving your insults for my sister? Or is there some other unfortunate girl dangling along after you waiting for *her* public dismissal?"

"That is hardly fair, Hugh!" Penworthy protested.

"Now you've gone too far, Hugh," Alex said coldly. "Since you insist on your own ruin, far be it from me to dissuade you. I'll take your wager and revel in your loss. Don't think I won't."

"As will I! Deal the last card, Penworthy!"

"But—"

"Do it!" Alex barked.

Reluctantly, Penworthy reached into the box, slid the top card out onto the green table, and flipped it over.

Hugh St. James smiled.

Chapter Two

"**D**id you *see* the way he looked at her?" Elizabeth Roberts breathed from behind the safety of her ostrich feather fan.

Mary Penworthy's round head of blond ringlets bobbed eagerly. "If a man looked at me like that, I should *swoon*."

"I should swoon, too," the third of their little coterie, Theresa Vane, agreed, "but I would wait until I was close enough to him so that when I sank gracefully to the floor he would have to catch me."

"Shame on you, Terry," Lady Mary scolded.

"Oh, don't be a mud lark, Mary. You know you find him just as delicious as any other young lady of the *ton* does."

"I don't," Elizabeth announced somberly. "He frightens me."

"Of course he does," Theresa said with a little puff of exasperation. "He frightens all the young ladies and a good many young men, too, I should warrant. That's part of his fascination, don't you see? All those dark, grim good looks and that powerful physique and that nasty, nasty scar. He received it during the Russian War. It gives me shivers just to think on it."

"When he looks at you, you have no idea what is going on behind that cold expression," Elizabeth avowed. "He looks as ready to carve you up as to say a civil word."

"Oh, he's always civil," said Lady Mary, whose

brother was one of Thorpe's confidants and thus had
personal knowledge that the others—much to their
dismay—lacked. "None more so. Frightfully correct."

"If only one could win an occasional smile from
him," Theresa sighed.

Marcus says that he smiles sometimes."

"Blue moons happen with greater frequency," Elizabeth said significantly.

Mary ignored her. "Indeed. Marcus says that he
once smiled a good deal before . . . the war."

"Before Lucy St. James, you mean," Theresa said.
All three young ladies turned from where they stood
clustered at the end of the ballroom and looked across
the dance floor at the object of their speculation.

Lucy St. James was speaking to her host and great-
uncle by marriage, the Marquis of Carroll. The elderly
gentleman's spine had become so twisted with age that
he was obliged to angle his head sideways to peer up
at his companion. His affliction had made him more
and more self-conscious, yet whatever Lucy had said
had caused his face to light with a smile and his faded
eyes to sparkle.

"She must be telling him off-color jokes," Theresa
murmured.

"Don't be absurd," Lady Mary said. "She's being . . .
Lucy."

Lucy St. James was no longer a girl, not even by
the kindest estimation. Yet here she was, the belle of
the Season. As she had been the belle of last Season
and the belle of the Season before that and for the
four preceding those.

And, tiresome as it was, it looked like her ascen-
dancy was far from over. With skin as pale as cream,
eyes so dark blue they looked indigo, and hair of a
deep, rich auburn hue, she looked like something one
ought to find dancing amongst the standing stones on
a moonlit night, a slender and delicate and ethereal
creature. Even her features were fine wrought. But
this waiflike frailty was belied by a vibrant, even willful, personality.

The three young ladies regarded her wistfully.

"She's even wearing a crinoline," Mary murmured appreciatively. Not one of them had yet convinced doting parents to let them purchase the new contraption.

As always, Lucy St. James stood in the vanguard of fashion. Her low-cut white organdy bodice was attached to a billowing tulle skirt at the cinched waist. The gossamer overskirt was patterned with faint golden stars and draped in swags over a petticoat comprising no fewer than fourteen layers of fragile lace flounces edged in gold. When she moved, the crinoline swung out gracefully, allowing just the smallest glimpse of white kid slippers with gold heels.

With little sighs of admiration, the three girls turned back and regarded one another morosely. Lucy St. James was as lovely at twenty-five as she'd been at twenty-two. And, as none of the young ladies collected in the trio had been "out" before that, they could only depend on myriad assurances from others that she'd been just as lovely when she'd come out at seventeen, too. And even then the object of Alexander, Lord Thorpe's affections.

Not that any of them were at all certain that "affections" was the appropriate term for the emotion she currently called up from the cold corridors of Thorpe's heart. But there could be no doubt that whatever feeling she evoked from him, it was strong. Rumor had it that Thorpe was even now getting monstrously drunk in some anteroom. But then, rumor had also had it that he had vowed never again to accept an invitation to a party that included Lucy St. James.

"I wonder why he came, knowing that she would be here?" Liz asked.

"Don't be a widgeon, Liz," Theresa said. "The marchioness is Thorpe's godmother as well as Lucy St. James's great-aunt, and this *is* her eightieth birthday. He couldn't possibly refuse."

"Why . . ." Liz's eyes widened. "It was at the marchioness's *seventy-eighth* birthday that he . . . that Lucy

St. James . . . that . . . Oh my! How awful. I *thought* she blanched when he looked upon her so terribly. I *thought* her lips quivered. I *thought*—"

"And you thought you'd seen a fairy in the end of your garden last year, too," Mary broke in dryly. "Lucy St. James looks as pampered and lighthearted as ever. Not a whit of color left her cheeks, and her lips were trembling on the cusp of a smile, nothing more." Lucy St. James was rather a heroine of the young lady's.

"Doubtless you are right, Mary. It is only that . . . Whatever is the matter with you?" Theresa asked abruptly as she noted that both Mary and Liz were no longer attending her but instead were staring behind her with eyes as round as saucers.

"What do you see, Liz?" Theresa whispered urgently, loath to do anything so uncouth as to turn around. "Never say that old Lord Menglerott has brought his doxy? Mother said he swore he would, but I—Mary? What *is* going on?"

Whatever it was, nothing could account for such appallingly bad manners. But then, *no one* in the room was attending to manners. Voices all around had fallen silent, movement had come to a standstill, and every head had turned in the direction of the grand staircase. She might as well look too—

Theresa turned, and her mouth promptly fell open along with everyone else's.

For standing at the very top of the staircase, brilliantly and brazenly lit by the glare of the marquis's newly installed gaslight sconces, stood Alexander, Viscount Thorpe.

In a dress.

No one moved. For a full moment, no one even breathed. They stood like sheep in a chute.

The thing was, the dress—and bedamned if it didn't look like a *wedding* dress—fit all six feet four inches of Lord Thorpe's manifestly male figure like it had been made for him. The white lace overdress stretched across his broad shoulders without a wrinkle. The seams on the delicate lace sleeves did not strain a bit over the bulging triceps and biceps muscles in Thorpe's brawny arms. And the narrow band collar did not appear any tighter than a well-tied cravat about his wide neck. Even the white satin beneath the lace molded to the planed contours of his hard, corrugated belly and trim hips like a second skin.

No one knew quite what to do. Under any circumstances Thorpe was intimidating enough, but standing there in that huge, white bride's dress, his big hands dark and hairy below the delicate lace-trimmed sleeves, his expression as coolly displeased as if he'd just come in from a walk to find unwanted guests in his home—well . . . one didn't know how to react.

With one notable exception.

The silence broke on the sound of a single female's throaty laughter. There was a slight shift of the guests at the far side of the ballroom, and from their midst emerged a fairylike creature, as pretty in her white tulle as Thorpe was monstrous in his white lace.

"My poor Thorpe," Lucy St. James said, gliding slowly across the ballroom to the bottom of the grand staircase. Her deep blue eyes sparkled wickedly, and her mouth trembled on the verge of a grin. "I hate to be the one to have to tell you this, but white is simply not your color."

Chapter Three

*H*is skin tingled, his muscles contracted, his heart thundered, and the whole room seemed to dissolve into a haze of indistinct colors and shapes, indistinct except for *her*. *Her* he could see with almost supernatural clarity. Her form, her face, her arms and throat, and every stitch of her gossamer-light gown were as crystalline as if he'd put her under a magnifying glass. He could see the pulse beating in the hollow at the base of her neck, the fine sheen of powder glistening on the silky swell of her bosom, the way her spiky dark lashes entangled with one another at the corners of her sapphire blue eyes.

And he could almost *smell* her, that delectable fragrance that was hers alone. It hung just beneath the surface of his conscious, like autumn mornings and spiced tea and sun-warmed skin.

The tingling in his skin grew more accentuated. The strange, nearly electric sensation strengthened and deepened, reaching into the very core of him and burning away at anger, consuming his bitterness, releasing the despair he would not even acknowledge. Something inside broke, as though he'd been holding his breath for two years and now suddenly could exhale.

Well, there it was, he thought vaguely. He was still in love with her. Madly, impossibly, angrily but apparently also eternally. Why now? Why, when he was standing in front of the *ton* dressed in a white wedding dress? Because Love was not yet done making a fool of him, and, Lord help him, he was once more a willing victim. The only question remaining was what the bloody hell was he going to do about it?

She was sashaying up the staircase, the absurd contraption she wore swaying, lifting the hooped skirts to allow a peek of the satin laces crossing her delicate ankles and above that, silk embroidered stockings.

She stopped a few steps below him, and let her gaze travel slowly from the hem to the top of the dress he'd found in Lady Carroll's attic. "I could lend you something green. Perhaps something to match your skin tone?"

She was entirely adorable, winsome and devilish and appealing. How he had missed her flashing eyes, her impertinence, her refusal to take his consequence seriously. She'd made him laugh, sometimes even at himself. Looking down at her now, feeling his mouth twitch irresistibly at the corners, he realized how bereft his life had been without her.

"Could you?" he replied.

"Well"—her lids slipped with feigned bashfulness over her bright eyes—"I would lend it to you, but I'm afraid you'd only be able to use it as a chemise." She peeked up at him. "But it is, of course, yours for the asking. Shall I have it sent round?" She batted her eyelashes.

The wretch! He took a step forward, but she didn't back down, not his Lucy. She didn't even appear to notice that he was being intimidating. Instead she bent forward and with an oddly elegant little gesture flattened her crinoline at her knees so that the whole of the peculiar device canted up a little in the back, held there by her hand, a bell on the cusp of gonging. Then, with every appearance of a woman dreading what she might uncover, she gingerly lifted the hem of his skirt with the tip of her fan, revealing a pair of crisply pressed charcoal gray trousers and well-polished black boots.

"Thank God," she said devoutly, and around them a ripple of titters erupted, only to be at once contained when Thorpe raised his pale eyes and glared. For a few minutes, he'd forgotten they were not alone. But then, why should anyone leave when the entertainment proved so titillating? He scowled at them. A few had the grace to flush. Most simply avoided his gaze.

Alexander Thorpe disliked being an object of derision.

But the alternative, to stomp out of the room and leave her here, laughing at him—oh, hell and damnation. He was tired of lying to himself. The idea of leaving her anywhere, in any state, was anathema.

"What were you expecting to find?" he asked coolly.

"I was *fearing* pantaloons," she said.

More laughter.

Once, a lifetime ago, he would have known exactly how to handle her audacity; he would have kissed the boldness from her lips. Old habits died hard. Her mouth looked the same as it had two years ago after she made some saucy remark, ripe and unrepentant. Her face was raised in just the same attitude as it would have been then, eagerly waiting for him to crush her in his embrace and rain kisses on her mouth in order to keep her from further impertinences. It was only one of a million reasons he loved her.

Now, his arms ached to gather her to him. Instead, he forced himself to look past her at all the riveted faces turned toward them. If only everyone would just *go,* just continue on with whatever the hell they'd been doing before he arrived, he might have a chance to . . . say something . . . something of a private nature . . . something that would make her—he didn't know what! All he knew was that he felt like a circus performer. Notably, a clown.

Lucy bit down on her lower lip, obviously trying not to giggle. "Tell me, Thorpe. Wherever did you find a seamstress who could accomplish something like this?" She wiggled her fingertips at him. "All that lace must have kept an entire abbey full of Belgian nuns in work for a year."

"What?" he started in confusion and then the impact of her words hit him. "Are you suggesting this *thing* is mine?"

"Isn't it?" she returned innocently. "It's just that it fits you so very, very well, and you must admit that you are a very, very unusual size for a bride. And, well, when one takes into account both particulars, how can one conclude other than . . . what one concludes?" she concluded apologetically.

His mouth fell open and snapped shut. So, she was still angry, after all, and not willing to stop short of drawing a little blood in order to get some of her own back. He could appreciate that. She wouldn't be Lucy if she meekly forgave the sort of insult he'd dealt her in this very room two years ago. But then . . . he wouldn't be Alexander Thorpe if he timidly tolerated her provocations. And she could be *exceedingly* provocative.

"I didn't have it made," he replied. "I found it in your great-aunt's attic. By which *particular* one can only *conclude* that there must be some truly amazing antecedents lurking in the branches of your family tree, Miss St. James."

"Doubtless from the Carroll side of the family," she replied with a dismissive sniff. "No blood relation to me. We St. Jameses are a fine-boned people. But that does rather beg the question of what on earth you were doing in my great-aunt's attic looking for a wedding dress to don."

One side of his mouth crept up before the other followed. Once, she'd liked his lopsided smile. She called it wicked and kissed the corner that got left behind, saying it deserved encouragement. Still, he couldn't help but savor the moment. Lucy St. James was one of the few women he knew who could match him in pride. And his answer was going to deal it a sharp little sting. No, she wasn't going to like this. Not at all.

"I'm afraid you'll have to ask your brother for the answer to that."

"Hugh?" For the first time, she looked a little nonplussed. Her straight dark brows dipped in consternation. "What the devil has Hugh to do with this?"

"I suggest you ask him." He stood aside, and Lucy peered into the gloom of the corridor where her nefarious sibling lurked, or at least had been lurking ten minutes ago. Lurking and sniggering. Though in all fairness the sniggering had probably been Davidson—Hugh had been too righteously triumphant to be amused.

"Hugh?" There was an odd note in Lucy's voice. Embarrassment, one might have been tempted to say. Or hoped to say, he amended truthfully.

Alex turned, wondering how Hugh would answer his sister. But as soon as he saw his onetime schoolmate he realized that Hugh might not be answering at all—for St. James was slumped against the far wall, his eyelids drooping over his blue eyes, his chin nestled tenderly amongst the folds of his snowy cravat. He'd passed out. Yet, half sentient though he undoubtably was, the triumphant grin plastered on his face still managed to irk Alex.

After winning the bet, Hugh had insisted they all celebrate his great good fortune—and by tacit implication Alex's misfortune—with rounds of port. One round had turned into two and then three before the bottle was finished. If Hugh had been drunk before, he was well and truly blistered by the time he'd stumbled down the staircase from the attic in the wake of Alex's lace and satin train. Now, the only thing keeping him from sinking to the floor was Penworthy and Davidson, who stood, one on either side, propping him up.

Poor Hugh, Alex thought. He'd set up the hunt, loosed the hounds, loaded the gun, fired the shot, and here the poor bastard wasn't even in on the kill. Alex felt a little sorry for him. Until he looked down and realized that some of his chest hairs was poking through the lace bodice.

"Hugh!" With an angry swoosh of her belling skirts, Lucy charged into the hall. Davidson, deciding discretion would be his best course, dropped Hugh's arm and fled. Wise man.

At the sharp sound of Lucy's voice, Hugh roused himself enough to open his eyes and stare at her groggily. "Wha—Hm? Tha' you, Lucy, old girl?"

"Hugh!" Her lips pursed, and a small pointed toe peeped out from under her flounced hem to commence an angry tapping. "Hugh, what have you done? Why is Alex Thorpe dressed in that ridiculous manner? More importantly, what has it to do with you?"

His foolish grin faded, replaced by a sharper rendition, as he struggled to push himself off the wall. Penworthy, the disloyal dog, helped him. "I have recovered the family honor."

"What family honor? What the blazes are you talking about, Hugh?" Lucy asked, but from the slight paling of her smooth cheeks it was clear to Alex that she at least had a suspicion of what was afoot.

Hugh's unfocused blue gaze wandered around the crowd choking the entrance to the ballroom until it fell on Alex. "Him! In the dress! He intuned—" He realized his mispronunciation at once and broke off, screwing his face up and studying the ceiling thoughtfully for a full ten seconds. "No, that ain't right. He *impugned* your honor. Cast aspirin. Aspirations. No, that ain't right, either."

He shook his head mournfully. "Damn it, Lucy, me words won't come out proper." He grinned winsomely at his baby sister. She glowered. "Oh, Luce. Come on now . . ." His face suddenly lit with inspiration. "*Aspersions!* He cast *aspersions* on your womanhood!" he crowed.

"I'm delighted you're delighted," Lucy said dryly, taking hold of his forearm and pulling him away from

Penworthy's support. "Now, enough of this non-sense—"

"No!" Hugh shook her from his arm and stumbled back into Penworthy's waiting arms. "You don't understand. I have repaid the insult he gave you."

"Thank you," Lucy said, looking anything but grateful. "I don't suppose it ever occurred to you that by involving yourself in any manner with him you do far more to ensure that the rumor mill keeps grinding merrily away than simply ignoring him would have done?"

"Is that what you've been doing?" Alex could not help but ask. She was talking as if he were absent, not five feet away and dressed in a bloody bridal gown. "Ignoring me?"

She glanced at him over her shoulder and turned back to her brother, who was regarding her with wounded eyes. "Can't ignore an insult such as he gave," Hugh said sullenly. "Especially what with all the repercussions of his infamy."

By God, Alex realized, Hugh, drunk as a lord and belligerent as an owl at high noon, was ignoring him, too! He was unused to being ignored. It was unsettling.

"And what repercussions do you think those are, dear brother?" Lucy asked in a silky voice.

Alex knew that voice. It brooked no good for whomever it was addressed to.

Apparently Hugh, even in his drunken state, was not unfamiliar with that tone, either. He reached over, and snagged a cup of spiked punch from the nearest goggle-eyed spectator, and drained it. He replaced the empty cup in its stunned owner's hand and faced his sister.

"Well, Hugh?"

"Don't think I don't know why you ain't married with a passel of brats clinging to your skirts, Lucy."

"I wouldn't begin to doubt your discernment. But, just out of curiosity, exactly why *do* you think I dwell in my current pitiable unwed and childless state?"

"Him." Hugh flung a hand out, pointing blindly in the general direction of where Alex stood, apparently no longer an integral part of this little drama. Though how anyone over six feet tall dressed as he was could be overlooked was something of a miracle. A miracle that owed much to the fascination the inimitable and lovely Lucy St. James held over Society.

When Lucy did not reply, Hugh seized yet another nearby cup of courage and finished that off, too. Then, squaring his shoulders, he blinked and plowed on. Poor fool.

"He said that wretched thing about you always having to lead in every dance and him not dancing to your tune anymore and now every likely male in Society thinks you're some sort of termagant who will strip them of their masculinity if they wed you." Alex shifted uneasily, not for the first time in the evening uncomfortably aware of the justice of the charges laid at his door.

The poor girl. The poor valiant, dashing girl, he thought wretchedly. He would do right by her. Indeed, it was long past time—

Lucy burst into laughter. Thereby effectively quenching the impulse Alex had been about to heed.

"I see," she finally managed between bouts of laughter. "Seeing how Alex refused to marry me thereby denying me the pleasure of henpecking him"—another stifled giggle—"you decided to strip him of his masculinity for me?"

Hugh, uncertain why but cannily intuiting that he had just dodged a bullet, grinned delightedly.

"Just so," he said and toppled forward, unconscious.

Chapter Four

"*H*ugh did not *convince* me to put on a dress," Alex explained stiffly. "We were playing poker. He wagered an enormous sum of money on his hand, but as he had already cleaned me out, I was unable to match it. I offered to write an IOU, but he did not want my money. He wanted my word that should I lose I would put on a dress and appear in public in it."

Lucy regarded him stonily.

"It was a wager. An enormous sum of money, and the way the cards stood on the table, I couldn't lose."

"Huge," Penworthy confirmed, his hitherto divided loyalties no longer pulling him apart, since one of those commanding them was presently snoozing it off in the Carrolls' morning room. "He couldn't lose."

"But you did."

"As if I needed anything besides this," Alex lifted a fold of lace, "to remind me."

The marchioness of Carroll having finally emerged from the drawing room, made her way across the ballroom to find out what held her guests so riveted. Upon seeing her favorite godson garbed in such a remarkable manner and receiving not a whit of explanation from him at the same time as her great-niece began making loud disclaimers of having nothing to do with it, (and being a St. James and thus knowing this to be highly improbable), she at once insisted that all those involved retire to the library to "sort things out."

Then, with a loudly intoned, "You disappoint me, Thorpe, you really do," she had turned and clapped her hands. Once. And because she was as autocratic a lady as ever had been bred, as well as one of the few who still knew how to set a table, the company obeyed her unvoiced command at once and returned to their dancing, leaving Alex, Lucy, and Penworthy to follow her orders.

So they had arrived here, and here is where Lucy had demanded to know how her brother had convinced Alex to don a dress.

"The odds against Hugh winning were staggering," Penworthy avowed.

"I see. So you colluded to take advantage of my brother when he was so foxed he could not make an informed decision."

Alex felt his jaw muscles bunch. The entire evening had been a nightmare of reliving his past culpabilities, and she had just added another dollop of guilt to the heap he'd been carrying. One would think that wearing a dress in public ought to buy a little expiation for one's sins. He knew he *shouldn't* have made that bet. It was just that Hugh had made him so damn mad!

"It wasn't like that at all, Miss Lucy," Penworthy said.

"How was it, then?"

"Hugh *goaded* Alex into accepting his bet."

Oh, God.

"Go and check on Hugh, Penworthy," Alex suggested. "If you don't roll him over he's like to suffocate under all his self-satisfaction."

"Huh?"

"Go!"

"Oh. Oh! Right!" Without further prompting, Penworthy sprang to his feet and hurried out of the room, leaving Lucy standing in front of Alex, regarding him with unfriendly eyes.

"So, Hugh *goaded* you into accepting his wager, did he?" she asked.

He nodded. He should be able to handle one fey-looking female. He was a mature adult male, a captain of the cavalry, battle seasoned and capable of cool thought under the most extenuating circumstance. "Don't you believe me?"

"Of course I do. Just as I am sure you put up a manful resistance to his overwhelming provocation. What did Hugh do that finally tipped you over the edge, shattering your self-restraint?"

Silently, he recited to himself all the names of the battlefields upon which he'd led his men with cool-headed deliberation. *Balaklava . . . Sevastopol . . . Inkerman . . .*

"Call you naughty names?"

No battleground in the Crimea had ever had Lucy St. James on it. If it had, he would have been lost. He seized her arms and dragged her close to him.

"Yes! I accepted his bloody wager!" he admitted furiously. "Hugh got under my skin. It seems that the St. Jameses have a veritable talent for it!"

Her eyes went wide in surprise, more, he suspected, at the sight of him losing his temper than out of fear. Then he was trapped in her gaze, reliving the past— moments of laughter, heated arguments spiked with passionate rejoinders, the sweet hours of accord, the quality and intensity of *being alive* that came with being with Lucy. How could he remember and let her go?

But he had to. His fingers were still wrapped around her slender upper arms. She'd made him forget himself, take hold of her person without her leave. Aye, she'd always had the knack for that, too.

He dropped his hands and stepped back. "Forgive me. That was unnecessary. Unworthy of my name."

A carmine stain rode high in her cheeks, and her gaze slewed sideways, avoiding his. She turned away . . . Disconcerted? Distracted? Had he offended her so greatly? Once she would have laughed at him and told him he thought too much of his name.

"It's all right," she said in an oddly flustered voice. He ached to turn her around so that he could read her expression, but he had forfeited that right. No, he had never had it. He'd never laid claim to any rights regarding her, fool that he was!

"No, it's not," he said softly. After this evening, everything between them would revert to cool, rife nothingness. Words unspoken, accusations never made, a future left to fade like morning mist. He could barely tolerate the thought.

"Well, you've fulfilled your part of the bargain," she said in that strained, uneasy tone, "and I know that you must be eager to get out of that dress." Her gaze darted toward him, a hint of her former humor finding its way back into the dark blue eyes. "Fetching as it is."

She looked away again, her hand uncharacteristically busy pleating and unpleating one of the tulle flounces. "I'm sorry."

Lord. She'd trumped him as neatly as her brother. He was the one who should be apologizing. He should be on his bloody knees. Begging her forgiveness for how he'd treated her and for whatever ways that treatment had adversely affected her matrimonial prospects. But if he apologized now she would only suspect he did so to reciprocate her good manners. So, instead, he said, "That must have been painful."

Again, the minx in her made a brief appearance. She grinned. "You have no idea." Her expression grew remote. "Just as you have no idea how humiliating I find this."

"I might have some small notion," he answered, with a telling glance down at the bride's dress.

At that she laughed. "Well, perhaps we march in step in that matter," she allowed. "Now, do get out of it. The human eye can withstand only so much dazzling."

And that was when it came to him, full blown, a battle plan designed to secure once again the lost territory known as Lucy St. James.

"Would that I could," he said. "Unfortunately, I haven't yet finished paying my debt."

Chapter Five

She wasn't really paying his words much attention; she was too busy filling her eyes with the sight of him. She hadn't been this close to him since he'd greeted her in that coffee shop five months ago.

Her heart had stopped in her throat when he'd approached. It was probably just as well. She'd been torn between throwing herself into his arms to kiss his hard, unsmiling mouth and weeping for all the pain he'd suffered in Russia, pain attested to by the terrible scar he bore. Instead, she sat as still as a statue, a gargoyle-like smile frozen on her face as she answered his brief queries as to her health and the health of her brother.

And after he'd bowed and left, her friend had placed a glass of water in her shaking hands and applauded her for her aplomb and clucked her tongue over Alexander Thorpe's audacity. Mary hadn't any idea. No one did. She'd carefully maintained the manufactured fiction that she was heart-free and footloose.

She had her pride, after all. Oh, yes. The one thing she had without question was pride.

As did Alex.

But now . . . pleasure filled her, and gratitude for the opportunity simply to look at him. His mouth was just as unyielding, the well-shaped features a little sharper, the bones beneath the skin more apparent. His sable-colored hair was as thick, but a few silvery threads wove through its luxuriant darkness. And though his eyes were still that clear, compelling gray, somehow their color now seemed oblique, a little less translucent, as if some of the color had been robbed from shadows. He was only twenty-eight years old.

Had the war done that?

She longed to ask him. She longed to run her fingers through his hair, to cup his hard, beard-rough cheeks between her palms and press her mouth to his, to feel the moment when his restraint cracked a little and his arms pulled her to him and he opened his mouth over hers . . .

Only she had forfeited any chance of that happening.

He was leaner, too, but more muscled. She could see the carved quality in his arms whenever he moved, shifting and bunching in his forearms and across his chest. She glanced away, feeling a little warmth stealing into her cheeks as she suppressed a cynical smile. There were not many men who could rouse a heated response from a woman while wearing a dress.

Not that Alexander Thorpe seemed to be aware of the anomaly. He'd probably forgotten he was even wearing the dratted thing. She would have been tempted to say he was taking her brother's ill-fated attempt to humiliate him like a good sport, but being a good sport didn't really enter the equation. Alexander Thorpe couldn't be humiliated by being made to don a dress. He was so supremely certain of himself, it would never occur to him that anyone would doubt his masculinity.

Poor Hugh, thinking that something as inconsequential as a dress was going to bring Alexander Thorpe low.

"Lucy?"

What had he been saying? She must pay better attention to his words instead of staring like some moonstruck girl every time he smiled. She couldn't remember seeing him smile since his return. And she had watched for his smiles across the crowds during those concerts and public outings they both attended,

where they both assiduously avoided one another. She
had watched to see if any woman received the smiles
that he had once so effortlessly given her.

She had been more relieved than she had any right
to be to discover that none did. At least, not yet. But
tonight, she'd won a few smiles from him—grudging,
perhaps, but honest.

She missed making Alex smile. Truth be told, she
missed a great deal about Alex. Everything, in fact.

If only they could go back in time and she could
undue all those stupid dances with Walter Fitzhugh
and in the process undue her even stupider ploys to
make Alex so jealous he would finally bend his knee
and ask her to marry him. She should have asked him
to wed herself since she was so determined they do
so before he left for the Russian War. But then, that
would have meant unbending her own pride.

Two years ago that had mattered. She could no
longer remember why.

"Lucy." His voice was low, concerned. "Are you
feeling quite the thing? You look a little strange."

"*I* look a little strange, Alex?" she asked, forcing
herself to attend to the present. "I must find you a
mirror."

"Please don't."

"I was thinking of something else, hard as that
might be to believe of someone faced with such a
fashion plate as yourself. Now, say again—why is it
you are still in that abomination?"

"I haven't yet fulfilled my part of the bargain."

"And what might that be?" she asked.

"I am to walk down Pall Mall at the stroke of midnight when there is likely to be a goodly number of
upstanding citizens on the boulevard." Pall Mall was
close to the center of one of London's most fashionable neighborhoods, where her brother, Hugh, had
his townhouse.

"Good God," she said, growing even more annoyed
with Hugh. "Pall Mall is all the way back into the city.
That's ridiculous."

"I agree. But there it is. I lost the wager, and now I must pay the penalty. And you, I am afraid, must come with me," he said.

"Me? Oh, no. Not me. I had no part of this, nor do I want any part of it."

"Whether you want to be involved or not, you are," he returned calmly. "And as my two former aides-de-camp, Davidson and Penworthy, have bolted and your brother is in no condition to be able to successfully gauge whether I have fulfilled my part of the bargain, I insist you stand in as his witness."

"You don't need to bring your own witness," she said. "I am certain there will be any number of people willing to attest to your appearance in Pall Mall. I shouldn't be surprised if it makes the morning papers."

"I beg to disagree." He shook his head, a tutor attempting to practice patience with a dull-witted student. "Your brother holds a rather substantial grudge against me. Had you not noted it? If there is the smallest chance he can call me to task, he will take it. What he will not take is my word that I did as I promised. Nor will he be satisfied with a few reports, especially if they cannot verify the fact that I walked the entire length of the street. No, I will need a witness."

He had her there. Hugh did bear Alex a great deal of antipathy, thinking Alex had betrayed not only her but their friendship. She'd tried to tell her brother that she had been complicit in the events of that fateful night, but he would have none of it. As far as he was concerned, Alex Thorpe should have just taken her out of that ballroom and told her that he'd had enough of her foolishness and married her.

She sighed. That had been exactly what she'd wanted.

They were siblings, all right. Perhaps they shared one mind. That might explain the half-witted plan she had thought would force Alex's hand. She should have known better. But she'd been desperate.

He'd been due to leave for Russia within a few weeks.

She had told him that it mattered not a whit if he

should come back whole or in pieces. So long as the pieces were breathing and labeled "Alexander Thorpe," she would be happy. It was as close to a proposal as she could make, and he understood it as that, too. He'd been most apologetic, very tender, but in the end too damned proud to allow the possibility that he would bind her to him only to make her a widow or, worse, return to her as a cripple.

So, desperate, angry, passionately aware of the clock ticking away, she had reverted to the time-honored ploy of trying to make him jealous. Instead, she'd only disgusted him.

Yes, she'd had a role bringing about that final scene. But Alexander Thorpe had not been entirely blameless, either. He had publicly denounced her as unfeminine and manipulative.

"Besides, Lucy, as you are the injured party and the bet was made on your behalf, you really ought to be there to enjoy it." A flash of flint in the slate-colored eyes. Apparently, he held a similar thought about her accountability for that night. Hm.

On second thought, she wasn't entirely sure she was ready to forgive all, either. Besides, there were now other insults to consider.

In laying the blame for her continued maidenhood on Alex, her wretched brother had gotten it all wrong. Just because he assumed that since Alexander Thorpe deemed her unfit to wed no one would have her didn't make it so. *Plenty* of men would have been willing to wed her. She'd had three proposals this season alone. It was *she* who wouldn't have *them*.

But this great towering giant in a dress, looming over her and studying her face with such wolfish intensity, didn't realize that. Oh, no. She had read it in his guilt-stricken face. He actually thought her unwed state was a result of his comments. The vanity of the man! The hubris!

And right at that moment she decided she did indeed want to go along and watch him stride down Pall Mall in his wedding dress. Not that she had much hope it would damage his enormous ego, but a few well-placed rotten tomatoes hurled by some jeering guttersnipes might make a pleasing sound hitting him upside the head. She might even bring a few herself, to hand out to the crowd.

"All right, Alex. I will go along as your witness."

"Thank you."

"But I don't know who we shall ask to play chaperone . . ." She felt ridiculous as she realized she was blushing.

She hadn't wanted a chaperone to tend her since her twentieth birthday. She and Alex had always somehow circumvented the rules and done as they pleased, without much concern for Society's displeasure. But then, she had always assumed that she and Alex would wed. Now, her reputation was a bit more important to her.

"You're jesting," he said with a flat look of disbelief.

"Not at all," she said in an unnaturally prim voice. "I know a woman of my advanced years must seem not to have much to protect, but I would have you know—"

"Don't be an idiot, Lucy. It isn't your desirability I doubt. It is my, or any man's, ability to reach you across that contraption you are wearing. Believe me, my dear, that thing was invented by a suspicious father."

She had never thought of her crinoline as a chaperone, but now that Alex mentioned it, she could not remember any man ever making any, er, untoward advances when she wore one, and that *was* odd. Perhaps they needn't drag some poor woman with them just to appease a few gossips . . .

"All right, Alex, we'll go, just the two of us. But we will take my coach."

And her heart, for two years so still, pattered impatiently.

Chapter Six

*T*he mist had grown heavier and the air cool by the time the coachman pulled the brougham carriage to the front of Carroll House. Already it was impossible to see more than a hundred yards down the street; closer to the river it would be thicker still. Not that Alex was disappointed. The fewer people who witnessed his little stroll down Pall Mall the better.

"How in God's name do you travel in that thing?" Alex demanded as, with a great deal of fussing and maneuvering, Lucy finally managed to get herself and her crinoline inside the carriage. He ducked inside and took the seat opposite her as the coachman— Owen, Alex believed—shoved the block under the seat and, donning a slicker, retreated to his seat atop the carriage.

"I generally kneel in the center, between the seats," she explained, collapsing the back of her crinoline against the rear wall and settling down beneath the resultant arch. She blew away a flounce hanging down over her face.

"That can't be very comfortable."

"Who expects comfort from their fashion?" A little dimple appeared in one of her cheeks. She'd never had that dimple before. But two years had pared the last remnants of girlhood from her face, leaving behind the cleaner and more refined beauty of womanhood. He regretted he'd not been there to see the birth of that small, telling indentation.

She turned up the flickering wick on the small interior lantern, flooding the carriage with soft light. It was a new carriage. Far more sumptuously appointed than the predecessor Alex recalled. The well-padded seats were deeper, upholstered in buttery-soft leather, the floor covered with a dense carpet. Polished brass fittings trimmed the mahogany wood paneling. Heavy doeskin-colored velvet drapes hung over the small glass windows.

With the manner of any good hostess, Lucy flipped up the lid on a box built into the corner, reached in, and withdrew a cut crystal traveling decanter. "Port?"

A nice stiff drink sounded like just the thing. "Please."

With a gracious smile, she reached back into the box for a matching glass, poured him two fingers' worth of liquor, and handed it to him. As soon as he'd accepted the drink she reached up and rapped on the ceiling. At once, a little trapdoor opened and Owen's damp face appeared, pale and moonlike, in the rectangle of dark sky.

"Pall Mall, Owen, and hurry."

"Yes, miss." The trapdoor shut, and the carriage lurched as it pulled away from the curb.

She turned her attention to him. "Best get this done and over with, eh?" she said. "Like that bad-tasting elixir my nurse used to give me when I was a little girl."

Outside, the mist had turned to a light but steady rain. Condensation gathered on the small windows in the chill. She took a deep breath. "I really feel I ought to apologize."

"For what?"

"For my brother. I admit I can see Hugh's making you appear in Great-aunt Sophie's ballroom, but this does seem a little excessive, even for Hugh. But then," she continued blithely on, "he took your public humiliation of me most poorly."

He choked on the mouthful of port he'd just swallowed. "Humil—I did *not* humiliate you!"

Another smile, but this time the dimple did not appear. "Really? How strange that I have been so deceived. I could have sworn otherwise. Doubtless you know best."

He waited, and just when he had begun to relax, thinking she would let the matter drop, she said, "Perhaps you would allow me to say, 'Before you publicly disengaged yourself from me'?"

She was doing it too brown. Yes, he had a lot to answer for. Yes, he had been stupid. But he had not been *wrong*. She *had* been leading him a merry dance and he had been trying—and valiantly, he might add—to do the right thing by her.

"For someone who endured public humiliation," he said, "you took it quite well."

She tipped her head inquiringly. "Why is it I do not feel this is a compliment?"

"Oh, but it is," he said. "You were magnificent. Your brother, emotional and overfond creature that he is, nearly called me out on your account. Your great-uncle did call me out . . . on the carpet. And a blistering interview that was, until Lady Carroll intervened and set forth the conjecture, ludicrous though your great-uncle found it, that perhaps I might not be entirely to blame for what happened."

She flushed slightly. Good. He went on. "My mother swore to disown me and only relented a few days before I set sail for the Crimea. There was some talk of blackballing me from my club. Indeed, everyone was most upset."

He smiled blandly. She shifted uneasily, avoiding meeting his gaze as a rumble of thunder broke in the distance, like some ancient god-child throwing a celestial tantrum. He could commiserate. The memory of her driving gaily in the park or sauntering past him in the street, meeting his gaze with no more than a haughtily raised brow or a silent laugh, still grated.

"But not you," he said with dark admiration. "In fact, you seemed to get over your disappointment with unparalleled speed. Why, just four days later, you had only smiles for me when you arrived at the opera on Lord Benford's arm. In fact, if one did not know otherwise, one might say you evinced nothing short of *relief* at your 'humiliation.'

"But one *does* know otherwise, doesn't one?" He leaned forward and had the satisfaction of seeing her shrink back. "Or does one?"

The thought that she might have wanted him to break off with her and had actively conspired at it had never occurred to him before. Because two years ago, no matter what else he knew, he'd thought he knew Lucy. She'd loved him. Hadn't she? Yes. *Yes.* Damn it!

He started to cross his legs but got all tangled up in the yards of satin and lace. No bloody skirt was going to stop him from crossing his legs! With a growl, he jerked one leg over the other and with immense satisfaction heard the unmistakable sound of ripping seams. He folded his hands lightly on the trousered knee the rent exposed and eyed her expectantly.

"What was I to do?" she asked, rather than answer his question directly. "Spend the evening frowning at poor Benford? Please recall that I am a gentlewoman, Alex, not the martinet you named me."

He scoffed at that. "Do not try to pass off your lack of feeling and obvious indifference as a virtue."

"Indifference?" Her voice quivered.

Unfortunately, he was beyond being able to heed the warning flash in her narrowed blue eyes. The poisonous little suggestion he'd fed himself would not be gainsaid. "When Miss Lillian Trent felt herself wronged by Sir Newburton, she did not show herself in public for the rest of the Season," he announced stiffly, conveniently shoving aside the memory of telling his mother that Miss Lillian Trent deserved her poor treatment if the best she could do in answer to an insult was hide on her family's estate for a year.

"Oh. I see." Soft, patient, *cool*. She'd never had the gift of being able to pretend coolness toward him before. She'd always been a creature of fire: heated replies, scalding remonstrations, burning ardor, and scorching kisses. Sometimes cold, yes, but with an iciness so intense it burned. Never simple coolness.

He hated it.

"I was suppose to spend the evening frowning at *you*," she went on as another clap of thunder broke, closer this time. The rain grew harder. "But, my dear Alex, that would have only given you an overblown sense of your importance to me. As well as Lord Benford."

He wanted to wring Lord Benford's neck. And who the hell was Benford anyway? Some jumped-up duke's grandson.

"Added to which," she continued, "I was even then well aware of the approach of my spinsterhood. I did not feel I had the time to waste making a point regarding my abused feelings that the *jeunne fille* Miss Trent had."

"Spinsterhood?" And there it was, instead of shouting like he'd been on the verge of doing, he found himself laughing.

She always made the same mistake in every argument. For as far back as he could recall, whenever she wanted to win a point—which was all the time—she finished her diatribe with some statement that was such a gross exaggeration of the truth that he ended up laughing. As he was now.

She was not laughing. That little crystal-studded toe was tapping out a warning on the carpeted floor.

"Good God, Lucy," he said. "You are hardly an ape leader."

Her eyes widened at his laughter, but he thought she was not altogether displeased. She tried a little imperious sniff. She wasn't going to back off. But then, when had she *ever* backed off?

"I beg to differ," she said in a frosted voice. "I am well on the shelf and collecting more dust all the time. Why, any honest member of Polite Society would agree that I was already on my last leg, as it were, when you finished dallying with my affections."

"Dallying with your—" he sputtered.

"Affections," she finished for him loudly. "*Affections* that you dallied with since I came out at seventeen. Which means that you dallied with them for . . ." She tilted her head and went silent for a few seconds. "Why, six years! I was twenty-three when you decided we did not suit. I am twenty five now."

He took a deep breath. "First, you are not at all . . . dusty."

"How kind of you to say so." Her eyes dropped to her lap with every appearance of being modestly flattered, except that she had no modesty and she wasn't flattered. Who would be at such a backhanded compliment? Damn. Now he had the disadvantage not only of sounding irritable but also of being gauche as well.

This was no way to go about winning her back. Why must she make everything so bloody difficult? Why must he find it so exhilarating?

He would *not* let her do this to him. "Second of all, I did *not* dally with your affections, and well you know it."

She lifted her gaze to his, and for a fleeting second he saw the impish light before she donned a vastly wounded expression and sniffed back a nonexistent tear. Her lower lip trembled—possibly with laughter, though he had the feeling she'd meant to simulate distress.

"Do not say you were"—another sniff, a little gulp—"*amusing* yourself."

God help him. He would dearly love to throttle her. Or kiss her. And he couldn't do either.

"Yes, yes, I admit it," he said, spreading his hands wide in a symbol of surrender. "Diabolical fiend that I am, I spent six years trailing after you, trapping you in the dark snare of my irresistibility, with but one thought—how could I maneuver you into making a fool of me at Lady Carroll's birthday party? And waiting eagerly for you to do so again."

Rather than the amusement he'd expected, the pertness faded from her expression, and she frowned. "Is that how you see it?"

"What?"

"That I made a fool of you?"

His ire faded. "Lucy," he said, with a twisted smile, "*look* at me."

She did so and had the grace to look uncomfortable.

"And you, Lucy. Do you really think I amused myself with you?"

"No," she answered softly. "I just . . . It is just that I never realized that anyone thought I hadn't married because of . . . of what you said. And when Hugh claimed that I was a spinster because no one would have me . . . Rather than have you think that I was the only one whose reputation had suffered—which it hasn't," she hastily added, "I wanted you to think that you, too, had lost some of your desirability as a potential suitor."

"Which I haven't?" he asked with a crooked smile.

She blushed at that. He watched in fascination as the color swept over her shoulders and the snowy column of her throat. Would it warm her flesh? Would the curves and vales exposed by her bodice know different temperatures, would the crest be cool and the shadows warm? Would her pulse beat closer to the surface at her wrist, beneath her ear, at the base of her throat? He looked up into her eyes.

Her hand rose and dropped in a quixotic little gesture of exasperation. "Pride. Between the two of us, we have rather cornered the market, haven't we?"

"Yes," he said softly, liking this newfound candor, the tacit admission of shared accountability.

They had been so young. So certain they could have their way if only they persisted. War had taught him differently. What had taught her the same lesson, he wondered.

Her smile grew gruff. "I may still have too much."

The carriage suddenly turned a corner, the wheel skittering on the wet cobbles, banging into the curb. It lurched, tipping sideways, and Lucy, perched precar-

iously as she was, fell forward. Alex reached out and
caught her, pulling her into his embrace and cushion-
ing her fall.

"Oh!"

The carriage righted itself, and the hatch flew open,
water streaming in. "Everyone all right?" the driver
asked.

"Owen," Lucy started angrily, glaring up from
where she rested in his arms, "you'd better take—"

The hatch slammed shut, and the coach continued
on.

Her lips pursed with frustration. She lowered her
face and only then seemed to realize how very close
he held her, her crinoline spread out behind and
above her like the tail of some albino peacock. The
soft mounds of her breasts, pushed tightly against him,
swelled with each breath she drew. And she was drawing many, rapidly.

He looked down into eyes grown darker, the exact
shade of blue that hangs above the horizon when dusk
becomes night. In the amber-colored lantern light, her
skin gleamed as though she'd been dipped in honey.
And she was warm. The heat from her soaked through
the thin bodice of . . . both their gowns.

Bloody hell! There was no possible way he was
going to pull off a seduction while he wore a dress.

He eased her and her crinoline back into the seat
opposite him.

"What were you going to say?" he asked irritably.

"What?" She blinked as though coming out of a
light sleep.

"You were saying something about pride and wanting my desirability as a suitor to suffer and that because of Hugh's assumption that you are currently
unwed because of . . ." He raised his brow
questioningly.

"Oh, yes." She nodded. "I could not stand to have
you think no man would marry me because you
wouldn't have me—"

"Wouldn't have you?" Once more she'd caught him completely off guard.

He had put himself through hell not *having* her. Even now, just looking at her, with nothing more than a scant few moments of having her in his arms, his body had grown heavy with want, his heartbeat quickening with awakening desire. A hundred visceral memories filled him, thickening the blood in his veins, making his muscles contract painfully in anticipation.

How often and how near they'd come to making love: in the library, under the trees at his country estate, in the darkness of the walled garden behind her brother's townhouse. But they never had. Because he'd loved her.

God. He closed his eyes. Wouldn't *have* her? He'd had her a thousand times in his dreams, in his cot on the battlefield at night, and in the army's hospital tent after the charge at Balaklava. "My *dear* girl, I have had—"

The carriage abruptly rolled to a stop, and the hatch swung up, releasing a torrent of cold rain on them. Lucy shrank back as Owen's sodden form filled the opening.

"Pall Mall, Miss St. James!" he shouted above the thunder and slammed it back shut.

Thank God.

Lucy regarded Alex owlishly. "You don't really mean to go out in this?"

"On the contrary." A good cold shower sounded perfect. "Pick me up at the end of the street, if you please."

Chapter Seven

*L*ucy pressed her nose against the glass window and squinted out into the lashing rainstorm. All she could see of Alex was a large white figure striding alongside the carriage with torn skirts flapping wildly about his trousers.

She'd ordered Owen to keep the carriage pacing Alex in case he came to his senses and wanted to jump back into the cozy interior. Even Owen, dressed in his slicker and top hat, hands properly gloved and trousers tucked into his high, rubberized boots, was grumbling about the weather. Alex would be soaked by the time he made it to the end of the street and chilled to the bone.

The only good thing about the rain was that it had kept everyone inside. Those who would have been leaving parties had decided to remain sensibly at their hosts' homes until the worst of the storm passed. Consequently, Pall Mall was deserted.

She wiped at the condensation collecting on the inside of the window with one of her skirt flounces and peered outside again. He was moving right along, like a sodden bridal ghost from a mariner's nightmare, imperious, bold, undaunted.

He was being an awfully good sport.

Either that, or he was awfully angry. She couldn't decide which.

For a moment there, when the carriage had tilted and he had snatched her up in his arms, she had thought she read something in his eyes, something familiar, dark, and urgent, something that had kindled an answering breathlessness in her chest and set her pulse racing. But then the moment had passed, an expression of disgust had crossed his face, and he set her aside as if he could hardly wait to remove his hands from her.

Perhaps he wanted nothing to do with her other than what he'd claimed, that she should bear witness to his keeping his word.

But then when she'd said something about his not wanting to marry her . . .

What *had* that all been about? He'd looked frightfully angry. He'd pressed his lips so tightly together they disappeared, and he'd had to force his last few words out between clenched teeth. Whatever had she said to so provoke him?

Could it be that she did not know Alex as well as she once did? The thought filled her with melancholy. She had known Alexander Thorpe all her life. Orphaned early, she and Hugh had been raised at her great-aunt Sophie's country estate, which shared a border with the Thorpes' property. It had been Alex who'd secretly taught her to ride astride, and she had taught him to dance the polonaise. She'd loved him for as long as she could remember.

They had been young, so green and untested. No longer. There was nothing green about the man she'd faced tonight. The years had changed him, matured him. But, she thought wistfully, his smile was still as devastating.

What did this new Alex want from his life? she wondered as she watched him marching along, the mud climbing up the ripped skirt, his stride long and easy even in the driving wind. And could it still include her?

Yes. She was still the only woman for him. She knew it. Absolutely and without doubt. During every moment they had spent together tonight she had felt more alive, more vital, more *awake* than during all the hours she had spent without him over the past two years.

They were meant to be together, and these two years had been nothing but a detour in the path their lives together must take.

Now she had only to convince him of it.

She was so lost in her thoughts that she did not realize they had come to the end of the street until she saw Alex approaching the carriage. The door swung open. He did not get in. He stood in the light from the lantern, water streaming down his face, shielding his eyes with his hand as he called to her over the wind. "I'll ride up top with Owen!"

"You'll do no such thing!" This couldn't be the end of their time together. There was so much more she needed to say, and she would not risk losing this opportunity. She'd taken that risk two years ago and lost.

He only shook his head, the water flying off his dark curls. "I'm drenched, Lucy. I'll ruin your nice new coach."

She saw by the stubborn tilt of his jaw that he wouldn't be bullied.

"If you insist. But it's not my coach. It's Hugh's nice new coach," she said in a carefully neutral voice.

He tilted his head, squinting at her through the rivulets of water streaming down his face. "Hugh's, eh?" he repeated thoughtfully.

"Yes."

"Well, then . . ." Without further protest he swung himself up and into the carriage, pulling the door shut after him. He was indeed soaked through.

So was the dress.

Water had rendered the material nearly transparent, plastering it to his body like a second skin, leaving nothing to the imagination. Every muscle, every sinew, every rib, and every whorl of dark hair across his magnificently planed chest was delineated in breathtaking detail under the wet, clinging fabric. Even the goose-flesh rising on his chilled skin could be seen.

Oh, my. He had always had a fine physique, or so

she had concluded from the times she'd managed to pull his shirt from his trousers and smooth her hands beneath the linen, exploring his body like a blind woman. But the years and an arduous military life had made him a near perfect specimen—

"Miss?"

"Lucy?"

Alex was regarding her strangely. With a start, she realized that the hatch was again open and rain was falling on her head. "Miss St. James?" Owen said in a tone that made it clear he was repeating himself.

"What?" she said, drawing herself up.

"Where to now?"

Where to, indeed. Two years back, please, and no delay.

She glanced at Alexander. He had tipped his head and was squeezing water from a fistful of black hair. He would catch a cold if he didn't—

"My brother's house, Owen."

At Alex's startled look, she went on with a confidence she was far from feeling. "You've fulfilled your part of the wager. There's no reason you should make yourself ill by traveling all the way back to my great-aunt's house in that wet dress when my brother's house and decent dry clothing are only a few short blocks away."

"Well . . ." he said doubtfully. He really had changed. He was willing to be reasonable.

"I insist," she said.

"If you insist." He shrugged, giving in with a little less graciousness than he might have, but giving in nonetheless.

She rewarded him with a brilliant smile.

Chapter Eight

*L*ucy tipped over the flowerpot beside the door and revealed a key. "Good old Hugh."

"Where is everyone?" Alex asked as he helped Lucy alight from the carriage under the porte cochere on the side of Hugh's elegant townhouse. He then sent Owen to the stable to see to the horses.

"Oh, Hugh doesn't keep much of a staff. Since he planned to spend the weekend with Great-aunt Sophie he probably let them have the night off."

She fit the key into the lock and opened a door into the side foyer, turning up the gaslight inside and motioning for Alex to follow. He stepped in after her, cursing as he kicked off his ruined half boots, hopping first on one leg and then the other as he dragged off his soaking-wet socks. He dropped them with a splat to the tiled floor. "That's better."

"Now, where to find you something to wear . . ." she muttered, eyeing him. "I'm afraid Hugh's shirts will be too tight and his trousers too short."

"Believe me," Alex said, lifting his muddy, dripping skirt, "I shall welcome anything you choose to offer with extreme gratitude."

She grinned. "Right. Follow me."

She led the way toward the front of the house and up the stairs to the first floor. At the top she paused and spent a few seconds rummaging in a shallow closet, then turned and tossed a towel to him. He caught it one-handed and began mopping his head and face as he trailed after her.

"In here." She opened a door and reached inside, turning up the light. Alex moved past her into the center of what was clearly Hugh's bedchamber. His personal effects covered the surface of a chest topped with a swivel mirror. A book lay open on the seat of the deep leather chair placed beside a small table that held a nearly empty decanter and glass on a silver tray. Across the room waited a neatly made bed next to a door leading into a small closet.

"You'll find some clothing in there, I should think," she said, aware of the silence of the house, the fact that they were quite, quite alone.

"Excellent."

She smiled, looking around and finding her courage fading fast. It had seemed such a perfect idea in the carriage. After all, she wasn't going to do anything she hadn't been prepared to do two years ago. But now that she was here, and the moment at hand, she understood all too well that the man she'd wanted so desperately to share her life, her heart, and her body with two years ago was not this man.

This man had done and seen things she could only imagine. In many ways—in many *real* ways—he was a stranger. She couldn't possibly seduce him. What had she been thinking?

She felt embarrassed and nervous and a little frightened at how close she'd come to making a disastrous decision. *Another* disastrous decision.

Besides, what if he'd refused her? And *of course* he would refuse her. He'd refused her two years ago, and then he had wanted her with all the urgency a virile and red-blooded young man desires a woman. Why would she think this cool-eyed warrior with his well-controlled temper—well, mostly well-controlled temper—would throw away his honor and moral integrity now?

Good God, the more she thought of it, the more insane she realized the impulse had been. Thank heavens she had come to her senses!

"I'll just wait downstairs, shall I?" she said, smiling nervously, her hand on the door handle.

He continued rubbing at his hair. "Sorry. 'Fraid you can't do that. I need you."

"N-need me?"

He stopped rubbing his hair and turned his head to look at her sideways. "Yes. I'm afraid you'll have to play lady's maid for me. I've tried to undo these blasted buttons, but my hand . . . the damn fingers get stiff when they're cold and . . . don't work so well then." His face closed with embarrassment, and he made a sharp, impatient gesture toward the row of pearl buttons beginning at his neck.

"Oh." His right hand, she recalled, had become entangled in his livery during the frantic moments of a charge against enemy lines. Three fingers had been dislocated. She felt instantly ashamed of her nascent suspicions.

He only needed her to undo his buttons. She couldn't refuse such a reasonable request—though there hadn't been a lot of "request" about it, now that she thought of it. Still, she couldn't refuse. It had been her suggestion that he come here and change. "All right."

She eased tentatively into the room, her hands clasped uncertainly behind her back. She hadn't touched him in two years. She recalled the last time vividly—the smoothness of his skin, the soft-crisp hair on his forearms . . .

"Whatever is the matter with you, Lucy?" He'd straightened and was regarding her with just a hint of impatience.

"Nothing," she denied. She could be as impersonal as he. It was just a row of buttons, after all. "Face me."

He obliged, presenting her with an extremely wide pair of shoulders well above her eye level and an extremely long row of buttons. There had to be more than a hundred of them, marching down from his strong throat over his equally strong chest. This was going to take some time. She wiggled her fingers experimentally.

"Well?" he said.

"Yes. Right." Gingerly she reached up and brushed the damp black hair away from the band collar. A single curl coiled around her finger as she worked, as though willing her to remember what it had felt like to comb her fingers through the rest of those thick black locks.

She did. She shouldn't. It hurt too much.

She glanced up. His eyes were half closed and relaxed, his expression thoughtful and interested. The only sound was the rain lashing against the window as she struggled with the little buttons. She bit her lip, trying to think of something to say while performing this far too intimate task. "It's a pity about the dress, really."

"Excuse me?"

"The dress. It's amazing. You should see how fine the stitches are on each of these tiny lace-covered eyelet buttons. The craftsmanship is exquisite."

"I'm sorry I've ruined it."

"Yes," she said, feeling a little wistful, her fingers moving down to the second, then the third and fourth buttons. "I wonder what the bride was like."

"She must have been a bloody Amazon."

"I wonder if she was beautiful."

"Not if she was as flat-chested and broad-shouldered as the way it fits me suggests she was."

She laughed and looked up, meeting his amused gaze. "Haven't you a single romantic bone in your body?"

His eyes seemed to smile, but there was gravity in their smoky depths, too. And memories. Memories she did not share. "One learns to be pragmatic."

"Where," she asked softly, unbuttoning more of the little buttons. "In Russia? How does it help?"

He didn't answer at once. Then, "It helps compartmentalize your emotions, set aside your anger or your fear or your sorrow to deal with later, when there is time and opportunity."

Her fingers stilled. "And did you . . . find a compartment for me?"

"You?" he laughed. "You got an entire room, my dear."

"And did you ever find the time or opportunity to deal with me?"

"Good God, no," he answered in honest amusement. "I locked the door and threw away the key."

She flushed and went back to work on the buttons. So that was that, then.

She still had a place in his heart, all right—in its dungeon. For long minutes she worked unbuttoning him from the dress until she had finally managed to undo the top six inches. But then the buttons started getting all caught in the lace overdress, and in annoyance she peeled the fabric back.

Her breath caught in her throat.

She'd found the end of the scar that started on his cheek and followed his jaw, disappearing beneath the collar. It angled across the base of his neck to the top of his pectoral muscle.

Without realizing it, she reached up and brushed her fingers gently across the pale rope of scar tissue. "Dear Lord, Alex, how did you survive this?" she whispered.

His whole body tensed at her touch, his shoulders pulling back as if he were a marionette jerked to attention by unseen strings. She barely noticed. All she could think of was how close he'd come to death, how close she had come to losing him forever. With infinite tenderness, she traced the scar, as though by doing so she could somehow erase it, erase the pain it must have caused, and the war it had occurred in.

"It happened in Balaklava," he said stiffly.

"During the Charge of Heavy Brigade." She nodded. Her fingers returned to the buttons, and now they flew from their eyelets as though by magic. The lace fell away, revealing the smooth, sculptured muscles of his chest, the dark, silky hair that grew across the dense surface, the curving ramparts of his ribs. She found another mark, not a scar but a knot beneath the flesh low on his side.

"Sevastopol," she whispered, touching it reverently. "You fell from your horse and broke three ribs. One hasn't healed properly."

He didn't answer. He had gone very still.

She reached up and stripped the material from his shoulders, letting the dress drop into the puddle of water at his feet. She needed to see it all now, the visual evidence of how near to death he'd marched, all the wounds, the scars, the mementos of war, the evidence of a life barely saved.

"Sevastopol," she murmured again as she found the crescent-shaped mark on his left triceps where a bayonet had pierced his uniform. She edged closer, fingers trailing lightly, testingly, on his torso, her gaze searching for the . . . there, on his left breast beside his arm, a dime-sized puckered piece of flesh. A pistol shot, fired from too far away to do more than "be an annoyance."

"Inkerman," she murmured, blinking away the brilliance suddenly threatening her vision. Without conscious volition, she leaned forward, brushing a fleeting kiss across the ruined flesh as though she could somehow soothe the old wound and heal it anew. He inhaled sharply.

And these were only the ones she knew about. There were other marks, too, though all fainter and smaller. Marks that would eventually fade away as though they had never been. But she would remember. Every single one.

She looked up and found him looking down into her eyes, his dark brows drawn together at the bridge of his nose.

"How do you . . ." He shook his head. "You read the dispatches."

"No," she said. "Your mother. She let me read your letters."

"She never told me."

"I made her promise not to. When you were over there I didn't want you . . . I didn't want to distract you. After you returned and you never came . . ." She tried to smile. "I believe I have already mentioned my overabundance of pride?"

"I didn't know."

This time she managed the smile. "It's all right."

"No." Abruptly, she became aware of his half-naked state. "It's not all right."

His chest gleamed in the saffron light of the gas globe, rising and falling deeply with each breath he took. The whorls of dark hair covering it thickened into a dark line that followed a riverbed between the muscles flanking either side of his flat belly and disappeared beneath the waistband of his trousers. She looked down. Even his feet, long and naked, were masculine.

She fell back a step, but he reached out and caught her by the upper arms, his touch gentle but firm, his eyes questioning and compelling. "It hasn't been right for two years."

"Alex."

"Lucy. All you ever said to me was yes. Don't start saying no now."

"All you ever said to me was no."

He lifted one hand, sweeping the hair back from her temple, and in doing so releasing a cascade of glittering pins and combs. The heavy mass of auburn hair fell about her shoulders. A small sound of pleasure rumbled from his throat. "Never again."

His fingers curled around, cupping the back of her head, holding her still. Slowly he pulled her to him, crushing the crinoline skirt between them as he looked down into her face. His pale gray eyes glittered with the unspoken question, his face stark and hungry in the shadows.

She hesitated for a heartbeat, no more, and then she was pulling his head down and he was crushing her in his embrace, his mouth falling hungrily on hers. There was nothing of gentleness or sweet lassitude in his ardency. Hunger, rampant and ungovernable, exploded between them, seeking an outlet for all the weeks and months of denial.

His kisses were rough, wanton, his tongue sweeping inside her mouth, plundering and fierce, a little brutal, a little punishing. Mouths melded together, he reached between them, wrenching at the tabs and ribbons holding her crinoline in place, finally pulling the last of the bands free. The crinoline slipped from her waist and held, imprisoned between their bodies. With a harsh sound, he caught her as her knees buckled, lifting her lightly as she shed the heavy crinoline and skirts like a butterfly emerging from its cocoon. He straightened, his gaze scouring the room.

"Not here." He strode out of the bedroom and down the hall, stopping at the next door. "Whose?"

"Mine," she managed to breathe.

He did not answer. He kicked the door open with his bare foot and backed into the room, his gaze scouring the shadowed interior. The curtains were drawn back from the huge single window on the far wall, letting in the soft, diffuse light from the street-lamp outside. Rain sparkled and shimmered as it fell against the panes. The bed was pristine and virginal-looking in the semidarkness, the counterpane cool and white, the pillow smooth and unmarked. In the corner stood a folding screen behind which he could make out a water pitcher and basin.

Without a word, he bent and ripped the coverlet away. The wooden slats beneath the mattress creaked as his knee sank into it. He eased her onto the bed and leaned over her, bridging her body on straight arms as he looked down.

There was nothing familiar in his expression. No sweet, fevered frustration, nothing tested and tender. His expression was certain, unfaltering, resolute.

"I dreamt of this. Of you," he murmured, his gaze moving over her like a caress, making her flush. "Some of the other men found ease in the beds of the camp followers or some women in the towns we passed through. But I . . . I would rather have had what my imagination could conjure than any poor substitute of flesh and bone."

His gaze trapped hers, holding her with him in the past. His smile was a little crooked, a little self-effacing, but when he settled himself beside her hip and reached down, there was nothing hesitant or uncertain in his actions. He unfastened the front of her bodice and, with the delicacy of a man unwrapping a fragile relic, parted the satin and folded the edges back, revealing the sheer little chemise beneath. His gaze fell on the sight of her breasts rising and falling with passionate anticipation. Her body felt afire, awash with sensation, abraded by frustration and longing.

"In my dreams I touched you. Every measure of your body. I taste every portion of your flesh." His voice was smoky, languid.

She reached up, holding her arms out. His hand slipped beneath her head, sinking into her hair and angling her face toward his as he bent and kissed her mouth. She opened her lips eagerly for him, meeting his tongue with her own.

For long moments their kisses grew hotter, more urgent. Then his lips slid down the side of her neck, along her collarbone. Impatiently, he brushed the chemise down to her waist and filled a hand with her small breast, curving beneath the soft mound and lifting it to his lips.

She gasped as he drew her nipple deep into his mouth. He had never . . . It was more wicked than anything . . . It was . . .

Her back arched off the bed as he stroked her nipple with his tongue, suckling softly. The pleasure was exquisite, overwhelming . . . and carnal . . . erotic. She reached down, clutching handfuls of sheet and twisting the material to keep from raking his back with her nails. His free hand slipped beneath her, arching her up even farther, the stubble on his jaw rasping across her tender flesh. It was a delicate pain that she relished.

"You drove me mad," he whispered as he savored her breasts and shoulders and throat. He lifted his dark head. "How many years did I spend hanging by the barest thread of control?"

She swallowed, transfixed by his crooked smile, the damning gentleness, uncertain if he meant to teach her pleasure or retribution. He eased her back, his gentleness at odds with the dark promise in his smoldering eyes.

She lifted her arms beseechingly. "Alex?"

His eyes closed at the sound of his whispered name. His lips parted a little, and then he was turning away from her and reaching down, stripping the belt from his waist and pulling off his trousers and smallclothes.

He did not wait for her approval or consent. Instead, he turned back, clasping her wrists and pulling her arms over her head. Naked, hard, and heavy, he rolled his big body over hers, keeping her hands captive above them.

She felt his erection, swollen and hot, pressed against the skin bared at the top of her pantaloons, but then his mouth found hers in a slow, searing kiss, and she forgot everything but the sensations he roused so effortlessly from her, the fire he'd started in her muscles and joints and tingling flesh. He moved his tongue in and out of her mouth, sweeping against the sleek lining of her cheeks, drawing her own tongue into his mouth and gently sucking the tip of it.

Desire pooled in her breast and between her legs. She twisted, trying to find some means of alleviating the growing want. He released her mouth, pressing his damp forehead against her shoulder.

He breathed a sound like a curse as she tried to twist her hands free to comb her fingers through his hair, to return his mouth to hers. "Slow." He sounded out of breath, his chest moving like a bellows. "Slow."

"Please."

He let go of her hands and rolled on his hip to the side, his hand falling in a long, slow caress down her arm, her side, to her hip, and forward. He pulled the ribbon holding her pantaloons in place free and peeled back the fabric before returning his fingertips to their sensual trip down her body to the vee at the apex of her thighs. She clutched his arms, shivering as he made a small circle with the tip of his finger at the very top of the folds that hid the entrance to her body. Her thighs fell slightly apart and her hips lifted against his hand.

She heard him suck in a sharp breath before he rocked the heel of his hand against her mound. Her fingers dug into the hard muscles of his shoulders, and her head pushed back into the pillow as she gasped with amazed pleasure.

And now his mouth was on her breast as his hand was on her mons, his fingers slipping through the sleekness, stroking, moving, playing with the fold of hooded flesh, making her tremble and pant, making her hips jerk involuntarily with every little tug and pull. And when she thought she would surely die from the pleasure of it, from the promise of it, he moved back on top of her, pushing his legs between her knees. Gently, he wrapped a hand around her thigh and notched her knee above his hip.

She had never felt more vulnerable, more defenseless, more eager. His gaze locked with hers as his hips rolled forward and she felt his cock pushing inside of her. *Inside of her.* Stretching her, easing inside of her . . . Except there was nothing easy about it. He *filled* her.

She shrank away, trying to pull free of his possession.

No. No. She was supposed to find a release to the building sensations, fulfill that intense need. She wanted to sob. "I . . . don't think this is going to . . . work!"

He froze. She raised her face to his, expecting to see pity, understanding, perhaps frustration, but certainly acquiescence.

She didn't. He was breathing heavily. His mouth opened to release lungfuls of air in short, harsh bursts. His eyes glowed, pale and intent, and his expression was ironical. Nothing more; nothing less.

"All these years she nearly killed me with yeses, nearly drove me mad with yeses, and now she says no." He pinned her with his gaze, inimical, commanding. "Lucy, you aren't leading anymore. You are going to have to trust me. Do you understand? You *have* to trust me."

He wasn't going to roll off her and comfort her with soothing words and sweet kisses. He wasn't even going to push her away and stride from the room, cursing her and himself and everything in between.

He was going to make love to her.

She stiffened as he shifted forward, his erection pushing deeper inside of her. His lips touched her tense face and moved gently against her temple. "Relax. I swear I am made no different from other men, and I swear you are made no different from other women."

"How do you know?" She tried not to whimper. She wasn't certain she succeeded.

She felt him smile against her skin. "I know. Trust. Remember?" His arms shook as he spoke. He pulled back, and she nearly sighed with relief that he had come to his senses and realized that they were not—He pushed inside, deeper this time.

Her betrayed gaze flew to his. His expression was strained, intent, a fine sheen of perspiration glistening on his forehead. He pushed himself up, bracing himself on rigid arms above her, and rocked forward.

She waited for another, sharper pain. None happened. Instead, the movement dragged the root of his erection against the nerve-rich kernel of flesh he'd teased, sending little flutters of gratification shivering through her. He pulled back, his eyes fixed on her face, reading every little moue of discomfort, every start of surprise, every shiver of excitement.

Slowly he sank into her again, inciting a rush of pleasure. Intense pleasure. Her eyes widened, and this time when he withdrew, her hips lifted to follow his retreat, brokering a grim smile from him. He watched her as he thrust into her. The last remnants of discomfort dissolved as a rush of excitement took root and bloomed within her. Her palms slipped from his arms, smoothed over his heaving chest, and linked behind his neck.

"Do you want me to stop?' His tone was lightly mocking, but his expression was almost tender.

"No," she whispered. "No!"

"Every time you left me, you left me in the state you are now in. Every time you bid me stay I had to fight against the pull that you feel. Unspent passion makes a very special sort of hell, don't you think?"

She captured his face between her hands and pulled his mouth down to hers. "No. No. You mustn't. You can't."

"No. I won't. I can't." He lowered himself to her, sliding his hands beneath her buttocks and lifting her, taking her deeper this time. Her reaction was immediate and instinctive. She dug her heels into the mattress, clinging to him as she tilted her hips up.

It was beyond intimate. Alex possessed her. She drowned in him, in pleasure so intense that tears slipped from the corners of her eyes and washed down the sides of her face. Her heart pounded faster and stronger with each second, each muscle in her body contracting.

Again and again she met his thrust, the pressure inside building, spiraling toward some indiscernible summit. It was so close. So . . . close. She sobbed with the effort. Her back arched off the mattress, and her shoulders bowed back and toward each other, her legs straightened, her toes pointing, her feet arching. Every point of her body rose, giving itself to him, to the place they joined. The walls inside her body contracted, eliciting a shudder from Alex.

"Yes," she panted. "Yes . . . yes!"

Her breath caught in her chest. Her eyes squeezed shut. Wave after wave of pleasure lifted her and held her for one glorious eternity on an apex of sensation. And then she was falling, a tumble of ecstasy and relief, echoes of pleasure throbbing in her.

Above, she heard a sound both masculine and exultant. Her body lifted again, raised by strong hands. One powerful thrust and Alex held her there, his body straining as shivers rippled through his big body. With a low sound replete with satisfaction, he sank down on her. His breath beat harsh and heated against her neck. His heart thundered against her.

For a long moment they did not move. Then, without warning, he rolled her over so that she sprawled on top of him. He pushed the mass of auburn hair from her face and traced her lower lip with his finger. She felt oddly shy then, and uncertain. But he smiled and she felt her heart flop in her chest like a green girl with her first beau.

And he had been her first, her last, her only beau. She smiled back, pleased with herself. She had no regrets. Her plan had worked out perfectly. *Finally.*

"Well, Alex," she said, stopping when she discovered she could not resist dropping a light kiss against his mouth. He tried to follow her when she lifted her head, but she only laughed and pushed his shoulders back against the mattress. Beneath her, he was hard and warm and dense, a wonderful bed.

"Well, Alex," she repeated pertly, her confidence growing with each passing moment, "now that I have finally managed to seduce you, will you at last do the right thing by me and make me your wife?"

Chapter Nine

$\mathcal{F}$or a few moments he had been so captivated by the reality of a gloriously naked Lucy sprawled indecently across his body that he hadn't understood what she'd said. She could have sworn he was a green giant and he would have agreed. But then her words began penetrating his besotted brain, and he laughed. "*You* seduced *me*?"

She nodded. "Yes, and a good thing I did, too, otherwise we might have ended up wasting another two years."

He pressed her face between his hands. She was so delicately formed, so ethereal, and yet there was nothing insubstantial about the manner of her lovemaking. It had been fierce and passionate. "I hate to disturb this little fantasy," he said, pulling her down for an all too brief kiss, "but you did not seduce me. I seduced you."

She pushed herself upright in order to better glower down at him, in the process digging her elbows into his stomach. "Really, Alex. You don't have to play the gentleman for me. I am perfectly willing to admit to being the instrument of your downfall."

"Instrument of my *downfall*?" he echoed incredulously. "Pray, where did I fall from?"

Only Lucy St, James could have said something outrageous enough to distract him from the feel of the warm feminine curves spread in the most intimate manner against him. Thigh to thigh, belly to belly, her small, perfectly formed breasts jiggling deliciously in her indignation, the nipples brushing his chest . . .

"—pedestal of moral superiority you live on!"

"Hm?" He was growing hard again.

"Are you ignoring me?" she asked, her eyes narrowing suspiciously.

"No. Never."

"Yes, you are," she accused. "You'd never let me get away with saying that if you weren't lost in some . . . some lecherous fantasy, I suppose!"

What the deuce *had* she said, anyway? Not that he particularly cared. Her eyes were flashing with the intense blue at the heart of a flame, and her lower lip was thrust out in a manner designed to make a man forget his name, let alone the words in a conversation.

"Guilty," he said. He reached behind her and trailed the backs of his fingers down the valley made by her spine and had the satisfaction of feeling her shiver. "Care to join me?"

"No!" She swatted his hand away. "Why can't you just admit that I seduced you?"

"Because you didn't." He let his head drop back against the pillow, linking his hands behind his neck. "Actually I'm a little surprised you haven't figured it out yet."

"Figured what out?"

"Lucy. I'm a captain in the cavalry. My men's lives depended on my ability to judge the weather and when it would arrive. I knew there was a rainstorm coming."

"So?" She sounded a little less certain, and the hands resting with such thought-destroying languor on his chest had begun plucking nervously at the hair there, which at least had the effect of keeping him in the moment.

"And Pall Mall. Why do you think that of all the fashionable streets in London your brother chose that particular one to send me to?"

"That's easy enough. Because it is near his townhouse and he would be able to savor the tales of your bridal walk from his neighbors for years to come."

"True." He smiled. She relaxed a little. "It makes perfect sense. But it would also be the most logical place to go if a man were to assume that he would soon be soaking wet yet knew that he could depend on the kindheartedness of a certain young lady not to return him to the scene of his humiliation soaking wet when dry clothing was so near at hand."

"But I suggested it."

"Bless you. But if you hadn't, I would have. Come, Lucy, even you kept making comments about how surprised you were your brother was willing to go so far for revenge. Well, he didn't. Doesn't that make you feel better about him?"

He expected her to laugh then, because Lucy was not a poor sport. At least he expected her to smile and lower her lips to his and reward him for his clever seduction. He did not expect her to scramble off of him, dragging the top sheet with her and holding it in front of her.

He sat up, frowning as he sought to read her expression. But the light from the window behind her that curved over her shoulders and set a nimbus of fire around her auburn hair also steeped her face in darkness.

"Lucy."

She moved quickly, dipping down and gathering some of her clothing before hastening away, her bare feet soundless as she fled behind the screen. He heard the splash of water in the basin. He looked down and saw a dark stain on his body. He'd forgotten there would be blood.

He stood up. "Lucy." He took a step forward.

"Stay there, you—you—" Her voice was low and angry.

What the devil had he said? Was she angry that he'd taken responsibility for their lovemaking? Would she not let him play the gentleman in *any* instance? What the hell was wrong with the girl?

"What the hell is wrong with you?" he demanded, confused and irritated as he jammed first one leg, then the other into his trousers.

"You *manipulated* me." Her voice shook with indignation.

His hands tightened into fists. He forced himself to count to three very . . . very . . . slowly and then, in the most cool and reasonable tones, said, "How is it that what you do is seduction, but the same from me is manipulation? I am afraid even you cannot have it both ways, Lucy."

"I *never* manipulated you," she breathed in horrified tones from behind the screen.

He laughed. "All those blatant attempts to get me to bed before I left for the Crimea—I suppose you would call those just good old friendly persuasion?"

"You are now being ungentlemanly."

"I thought *that's* what you wanted. It is certainly what you wanted two years ago."

"No!"

"Yes! Let's have this out once and for all, shall we? Why do you think I left you at the marquis's house two years ago?"

He heard the sound of a wet cloth splatting against something solid—like a wall. The screen snapped back, and she stood in front of him dressed in pantaloons and chemise, her hands on her hips, the bodice of her gown half undone to the waist.

"You were angry at me for flirting. You were jealous."

"I was going mad!"

She started to turn away from him with a sound of scorn, but he clasped her arm and wheeled her back around to face him.

"Do you really think a *flirtation* could make me so crazy? I didn't care who you danced with or how many times. I knew you were mine," which was mostly true, "but I could not tolerate the frustration you were daily heaping on my head. I thought to give you a taste of what you put me through earlier. Shall I repeat the lesson?"

She flushed, and he dragged her into his arms, kissing her roughly before pushing her away, holding her at arm's length.

"I loved you, Lucy. More than . . . God." He released her, raking his hair back with his hand. "I tried to tell you why, to explain that I could not marry you when the possibility of returning to you crippled or disabled was so real. But you would not listen.

"You wanted me to bed you, wed you, and abandon you with nothing more than a faint hope that I would return to you in one piece. You didn't want me to act ungentlemanly, you wanted me to act the complete blackguard. Well, I am sorry that I had to disappoint you."

She bit down hard on her lips, and he saw the glitter of tears in her eyes. He reached out and she backed away. No. Not again.

"No. Don't touch me. I shouldn't want you to compromise your values for me!"

"You are deliberately misunderstanding."

"I understand perfectly well." Her voice shook, squeezing the very soul from him. "You meant what you said at Great-aunt Sophie's birthday party. I am too strong-willed, too leading for you."

"Bloody hell, Lucy. You *are* strong-willed. You're a veritable termagant. You're wrongheaded and impetuous—"

The sound of the door banging open cut off his words. A second later a loud but indistinct baritone rumbled up from the main floor, singing a very ribald and very popular tavern song. Lucy's gaze met his.

"It's Hugh!"

"Grand," Alex muttered. "Have him up and we'll make a party of it. How the hell did he get here, anyway?""

"Marcus Penworthy probably brought him home. Oh, Lord! He'll kill you if—"

"No one is going to kill me, Lucy."

"He mustn't find us!" she said, ignoring his reassurances. Her eyes were wide and her face pale. "Please, Alex."

"All right." He capitulated in frustration. "We'll just stay in here and remain quiet until he passes out, which, judging from the butchery he's doing on those lyrics, shouldn't be long. But come tomorrow we go and—"

"The dress!"

"What dress?"

"The bride's dress you wore," she whispered urgently. "I have to get it before he goes to his room. And he is bound to go to his room!"

Before he could react, she darted past him and was through the door.

With a heavy sigh, he followed her to Hugh's room, entering to find her spinning around, her hair flying like a mane about her slight shoulders. "It's not here."

"What do you mean? It has to be."

"Well, it's not. Look!" She pointed at the pool of muddy water standing in the center of room. She was right. The dress was gone. He strode over to the bed and lifted the coverlet, bending over to peer beneath. It wasn't there, either. He straightened, puzzled and frowning.

"The closet room," he suggested.

With a look of relief, she flew to the door, Alex trailing behind.

"Her name was RITA—" Hugh bellowed from just beyond the door.

"And nothing was SWEETER—"

"In here!" Lucy yelped, and grabbing his wrist, yanked him into the closet with surprising strength for such a fey-looking lass.

Inside the small closet it was pitch-black. A few pieces of clothing hanging from hooks cushioned the walls, muffling the sound of their breathing.

"Than what she had under her SKIRTS!"

Lucy giggled. And Alex fell in love all over again.

She still held his wrist, and he could feel her grip tighten at the sound of Hugh's approaching footsteps. Luckily they shuffled past the closet door without stopping. But they could still hear his slurred voice.

"Damn." Hugh said. "Forgot how much I liked that bastard. First of his class. Capital officer. Awful card player." He chuckled and then trailed off. "Did Luce a bad turn. Said so 'imself."

They heard the decanter strike the lip of the glass. A long pause. "Still . . . fellow can only hold a grudge so long. And Penworthy said she left with the bastard. Poor old dear, poor old Luce, still in love with the great oaf," he moaned in a ripe, maudlin tone.

In the dark, closed quarters, Alex felt the heat of embarrassment rise from Lucy's skin like perfume. Hugh sighed deeply.

"Nope," he muttered thickly. "Nothing for it but he must marry her. Or I'll have to kill him. Should hate to kill him—where'd all the whiskey go? Damn! Where was I? Oh, yes . . . killing Thorpe. Only choice I'll have if he don't come up to scratch."

With a choked sputter, Lucy reached for the door handle, but Alex caught her arm and spun her around, pulling her shoulders into his chest and covering her mouth with his hand. "Quiet!" he whispered, unable to keep from smiling. Lucy was not smiling. The curve of her lips against his palm was turned decidedly downward.

"Maybe there's another way," Hugh was musing doubtfully. "Fellow would need another drink to rouse the old brain cells, though. 'Nother drink. That's the thing!'"

And with that his footsteps stumbled out of the room.

Lucy's hand slipped from Alex's wrist. "I think we can go."

"Better wait a bit. You never know with Hugh. He might be sitting on the top step even as we speak, gearing up for his next concert."

She laughed again before she recalled her embarrassment, and then he could almost picture the way her lips snapped together. He longed to tease them apart, to make them soft with amusement . . . or pleasure.

"A few minutes longer, then," she agreed and turned. The movement sent her hand swinging gently against his fly. She froze. He could feel the realization that he was still mostly naked, and mostly aroused, wash through her.

She made a nervous little sound, and he heard the clothing shift as she pressed herself tight against the wall. "How much longer, do you think?"

A man can stand only so much.

"Long enough for me to do this." His found her without effort, pulling her into his embrace as he bent down and his mouth opened over hers. She did not kiss him back.

"Kiss me, Lucy," he whispered against her lips. "And I might let you go before Hugh comes back."

"That's extortion."

"Yes. You're very good at it. So am I." He trailed a series of nibbles across her mouth and over her smooth cheek, pausing beneath her earlobe to nip the tender flesh there. "Kiss me."

In the darkness, in the blackness, her head slowly turned and her mouth, as chaste and cool as a nun's, brushed over his. She disliked not being in control.

"Use your tongue and I might let you go even faster," he suggested.

"No." She didn't sound as certain as the word implied.

His hands marked a lingering trail down her arms to her hips. He clasped the delicate bones in his palms and held her there, just a few inches away from his body. He dipped his head and traced a line from her chin to the valley between her breasts with the tip of his tongue. Her breath caught on a little hitch of excitement.

"I was in love with you." He bumped his hips, his erection, lightly against her. She swallowed but did not move. "And in lust. It was all I could do not to throw you over my shoulder and carry you off to some rotting pile in Scotland. But I wasn't going to roll over and do what you wanted and be less than the man I wanted to be. I had obligations. Not the least of which were to you, Lucy."

He pulled her hips tight to his.

"You made me crazy that day. Do you remember? You had my shirt all but off and you were lying in the field behind the stables, flowers in your hair and your skirts about your thighs. I had to leave.

"And then, that night, you wouldn't even talk to me. You just flirted with Fitzhugh." He couldn't help it. The heat was rising between them like an aphrodisiac. He found her mouth again, this time open and willing. He plundered it softly with his tongue, finally breaking off and holding her back.

"I was furious. You'd pushed me past every bit of endurance I had left. I never intended to hurt you. It all . . . happened, and then I didn't know how to undo it and you didn't seem to care."

"I cared." And in those few words he heard all the sorrow and tears and pain she had never shown the world. Too proud. Both of them.

"But tonight, when I saw you, it suddenly didn't matter what the last two years had been, who you danced with or how many times. I didn't even care if you'd fallen in love with another and even now were waiting for him to declare himself. I love you. I have always loved you and I always will.

"You're mine, Lucy. You always have been." With infinite gentleness, he wrapped his arms around her and pulled her to him. She slid her arms around his back and rested her head against his chest. "Nothing can keep me from you except pride. And that, I vow, is not going to stand in the way. Not this time."

"You . . ."

"What?"

He felt her silky head shake against his chest. He cupped the back of it and brushed a kiss against her temple. "I thought you didn't want to marry me," she said.

"What? Why?"

"Because when I asked you to marry me, all you said in reply was that you had seduced me."

"Wait." He held her away from him, trying and failing to see her in the dark closet. "You asked me to *marry* you?"

He felt her nod.

"When?"

"After we . . . made love. I said that now that I had seduced you, you would have to marry me."

He laughed, and she started to squirm, trying to break out of his arms, angry again. Such passionate creatures are faeries. "My darling, my beloved, my . . . sweet fool. Men are simple, basic organisms, especially after they have just engaged in the most physically intense experience imaginable. Their senses come back slowly, like sand dribbling in an hourglass. First we are able to breathe again, then see, then, slowly, hear, and even slower still, understand what we are hearing, and finally, think."

And just to make sure she understood, he added in a very clear, firm voice. "I didn't hear you. If I had, we should be at the church right now making preparations."

For a long moment she was quiet. Then, "Really?"

"Really."

"It's amazing men ever engage in . . . well, you know."

The darling prude. Who'd have thought it?

"I mean, it makes you so *vulnerable*."

"Oh, my dear, you have no idea."

"Ha." She gave a little sigh. A very happy little sigh. "And you do want to marry me?"

"No, no. This will not do. I refuse to have you throw this in my face every time we have a fight, and, God help us, Lucy, we will have many fights."

"But we will also have many reconciliations," she said cheerfully.

"Be that as it may . . ." He dropped to his knees in the black closet, grabbing her hands and clasping them tightly. "Marry me, Lucy St. James. Please marry me."

Her hand reached down and brushed against his face. "Yes, Alex."

He turned her hand over and pressed a warm kiss in the center of her palm.

"But *I* get to wear the bride's dress."

He rose, catching her up in his arms. "Hussy. Is that why you pitched that bloody dress somewhere? So you won't be shone down?"

She started laughing. "I swear, I have no idea where it is!"

"Thank God," he muttered, his head bending for a kiss as he reached for the door. It swung open, letting the light in.

Finally.

Praised for her sophisticated romances, Connie Brockway has twice received coveted *Publishers Weekly* starred reviews as well as unqualified recommendations from *Booklist,* which also named her novel *My Seduction* one of 2004's top ten romances. A seven-time finalist for Romance Writers of America's prestigious RITA Award, Brockway has twice been its recipient, first in 2000 for *My Dearest Enemy* and again in 2002 for *The Bridal Season.*

Today Brockway lives in Minnesota with her husband, David, a family physician, and their dogs. A regular speaker at national and local writing conventions and workshops, Brockway also enjoys cooking, gardening, tennis, and working for her favorite charitable organization, the Wildlife Rehabilitation Center of Minnesota.

Something Special

Casey Claybourne

Prologue

Seattle, 1864

"*R*ain."

A small leather boot kicked listlessly at a dust ball, as the boot's owner, eleven-year-old Eliza Cooper, peered out the attic window to the sodden fields below.

Having passed nearly half of her life in the Washington Territory, Eliza was certainly no stranger to inclement weather. Today, however, the dark skies proved especially annoying, for not only had she been unable to take her journal up to University Hill as she'd planned, but her search through the attic's cobwebbed corners had yielded little to amuse her this long, wet afternoon.

Expectantly, she pushed her freckled nose up against the sooty square of glass and searched the distant horizon. Habit compelled her to look north, even though she knew that her father would not be home for many weeks yet. Joshua Cooper's logging business forced him to travel for extended periods of time, which meant that Eliza was left to her own devices and to the questionable care of their housekeeper, Seamus Macgorrie, a taciturn, one-legged Irishman who didn't much relish his role of reluctant nanny.

"If only . . ." Eliza whispered, the plea as nebulous and unformed as her puff of breath that frosted the tiny pane.

With a sigh, she gave one more lackluster kick to

the dust ball, when suddenly a stray beam of sunshine fought its way through the dense clouds to shoot past her into the garret. The unexpected ray, bright and golden, shone like a lance as it sliced across the room to fall squarely upon the brass latch of a large, weathered trunk. Eliza's fair brows beetled together. *Odd.* How had she failed to notice that unfamiliar chest during her foraging minutes ago?

She scooted forward and quickly scanned the trunk, finding no clues as to its ownership. Where had it come from? Her father could not have brought it home, as she was certain he'd not been up to the attic in months. And Macgorrie most assuredly could not have hauled such a weighty piece up the stairs unassisted. Curiosity astir, Eliza lifted the lid.

"Goodness me."

She had not known that fabric could be this rich, this lustrous. Why, it was like a moonbeam. A satiny moonbeam. Slowly she reached down and pulled it from the trunk, stretching her thin arms in front of her to better study her discovery.

She had found a gown.

A beautiful white gown.

Beneath her chilled fingers, the silken folds rustled softly.

Eliza blinked, then stared in wonder at the gown. As if from nowhere, an idea had popped into her head. An idea so wonderful, so amazingly perfect, she could not understand why she'd not thought of it before.

"Of course," she said aloud. "Of course." The answer to everything . . .

Chapter One

A few months later . . .

"Quee-Queen. Of the . . ." Penelope Martin squinted hard at the letters. "Fai-Fai-Fairies."

With a satisfied nod, she closed the moldy volume of Shakespearean works in her lap and gave the cover a hearty slap. Having just completed *Much Ado About Nothing,* Eliza had announced her wish to play Titania this afternoon, and Penny, hoping to surprise her, was determined to find one or two simple costumes to add to their playacting. Now what might she use for a fairy queen?

Last month, if anyone had told Penny that someday she'd be looking forward to an afternoon of Shakespeare with an eleven-year-old child, she would have accused that person of tipping one too many whiskeys. But Eliza loved acting out the plays, and her youthful enthusiasm was infectious. In fact, Eliza's portrayal of Dogberry yesterday had made Penny laugh so hard, she'd actually split open the seams of her threadbare corset.

As she set the book aside, Penny glanced at her valise, left empty in the corner of the bedroom. It was difficult to believe that a mere three weeks earlier she had carried that valise off the steamer after a fifty-seven-day journey across two oceans.

The wind had been sharp that morning when she first set foot on the dock, her gaze sweeping over her

new home. Her survey took less than two seconds.
Although she'd assumed that Seattle would be small,
she was still amazed that anyone might describe a
smattering of clapboard houses as an honest-to-
goodness city. Why, to her mind, it looked to be no
more than a village. And a teeny little village at that.

Perhaps three or four dozen buildings dotted the
landscape, their square silhouettes holding back the
forest that hovered just beyond the hills. Sawmills
lined the edge of the bay and, instead of paved streets,
muddy paths smelling of ocean salt climbed up from
the many wooden piers fronting the water. A buggy
or two rattled through the mud, and a handful of riders on horses clustered at the end of the wharf, yet it
was still quiet enough for Penny to hear the gentle
slap of waves against the shore.

"Well . . ." She squared her shoulders with determi-
nation, then gave her satchel a reassuring jiggle.
"Whatever it is, at least it ain't Boston."

A group of dockworkers lumbered past carrying a
pallet of crates, and Penny hurried to step aside. As
she did so, her attention was caught by two people
approaching from the other end of the dock. The pair
presented a curious picture: the elderly, peg-legged
man wearing a harsh scowl as he thumped down the
gangway and, at his side, a wisp of a girl skipping
along, her grin as wide as the Pacific. Although the
man sported a shabby tartan tam, the girl was bare-
headed, her mass of curly blond hair unlike anything
Penny had seen before. Resembling an enormous
cloud of white spun cotton, the child's hair swirled
about her head, looking almost as if it were something
alive, separate from the girl herself.

So taken was she by the two that Penny did not
notice until the last moment that they were stopping
directly in front of her.

"Miss Martin?" the child asked in a tone that reminded Penny of a librarian, although, in truth, she'd
never actually known a librarian.

"Yes?"

"How do you do?" The child thrust her hand forward, forcing Penny to drop her valise so that she could return the greeting. The girl's handshake was as self-assured as her manner.

"I am Eliza Cooper and this"—she gestured with her thumb to the man standing a pace back—"this is Macgorrie."

The old gentleman bobbed his chin.

Penny nodded cautiously and smoothed her auburn hair with nerve-twittery fingers. Since she herself had not known which steamer she'd be taking from Port Townsend, she had not expected to be met, and she certainly had not expected to be met by this peculiar welcoming committee. After all, it had been a Mrs. Cooper who had written, offering a teaching position, and the same Mrs. Cooper had wired money to pay for the traveling expenses of train and ship. . . . So then, had Mrs. Cooper sent one of her children to fetch the new schoolteacher from the docks?

"If you can point out your trunks," the girl prompted, waving again in her regal fashion to where the workers were setting out the freight, "Macgorrie will arrange for their delivery, and we can be on our way."

"Ah." Penny cast a quick glance first to the pile of trunks and then to the valise at her feet. "I brung only this."

"Just that?" The girl blinked once, her eyes the color of wild violets, before shrugging away her surprise. "Very well. Off we go, then."

Once settled inside the carriage—where Penny had to force herself not to stare at the luxuries of an honest-to-goodness closed carriage—a silence fell. After a lifetime spent amid the constant sound of chatter, Penny could not tolerate the quiet, particularly not when she was so nervous that her gloves were growing damp.

"I reckon Mrs. Cooper is your mother?"

Her question seemed to echo in the coach's confines as Eliza's lips pursed, in either deliberation or disapproval. Penny could not say which.

"Your aunt?" Penny offered.

"Mmm." Now not only her mouth, but Eliza's entire face, as thin and white as parchment, scrunched up. "There is something I need to tell you, Miss Martin, and since I can see no benefit in delaying the telling of it—"

Penny's breath caught. These last weeks, she had often wondered as she leaned against the steamer's railing, gazing out to sea, if it all had been too good to be true. She had told herself not to fret, that her luck had finally turned. She had vowed to make this opportunity work one way or the other, convincing herself that it had been nothing short of heaven-sent. But now . . .

"My mother is dead."

The breath Penny had been holding released in short, jagged bursts. *Sweet Mary . . .*

"I am sorry," she managed, even as she sensed that Eliza's matter-of-fact declaration seemed wrong. Unnatural. Where were the grief, the tears, the evidence of loss?

"To tell you the truth, Miss Martin, my mother has been dead these past six years."

Six years? Penny felt as if she were back aboard ship, fighting to keep her balance during rough seas.

"I-I don't understand."

"Allow me to explain, although it's rather a long story. You see, Mr. Asa Mercer, who is a very important man in these parts, recently brought a group of ladies from Massachusetts to be schoolteachers here in Seattle. They arrived and everyone was delighted, since there are scarcely enough women to be teachers or to be anything, really." Eliza's speech came faster and faster as she spoke, her words tumbling together so that Penny had to concentrate to make sense of what she was hearing. "Well, Mr. Mercer's idea struck me as a very fine notion indeed, so I wrote to a Mr. Shakely, who is a Boston relation of my friend the widow Murphy, and since I could not advertise for a teacher as eleven-year-old Eliza Cooper, I had to pretend to be someone older, don't you see?"

"*You* sent the letter?" Penny bit her lower lip. "And the money?"

"Well, of course I did have some help. You needn't worry, however," Eliza continued. "The money I sent you was rightfully mine to send, and I would not have brought you all this way without good cause. A teaching opportunity does await you, although perhaps it is not precisely the sort of employment you were expecting." At this point, the child delicately cleared her throat. "The position I am offering you, Miss Martin, is that of personal governess. To me."

Penny sank back against the banquette, undecided as to whether she was more cross than she was relieved, or more relieved than she was cross. How in the name of the saints had this wee thing, who couldn't weigh even four stone, arranged to bring her here from a continent away? Why, the fact that the child had accomplished such a feat was remarkable. Unsettling, even.

Nevertheless, Penny knew she wasn't in any position to be persnickety about gainful employment. Not when the most valuable item in her coin purse was the dried remains of a four-leaf clover. The truth was she'd simply had to get out of Boston, and this child had managed to make that happen. And at least the job would provide her with steady employment and room and board. Besides, she could scarcely start pointing fingers and preaching to the child about honesty and the like. Not when she herself had been less than forthcoming in this affair. As Lewis had always said, "Desperate times call for desperate measures." And Penny was desperate, no question about it.

Even so, to work as a nanny for this little girl who gave every indication of being ten times too intelligent and a hundred times too clever for the likes of one Penelope Colleen Martin?

Yet . . . what choice did she have?

*   *   *

"What choice indeed?" Penny asked herself, as she rose from the chair, rubbing lightly at her forehead as though to wipe away the confusion of that day. Because once she had thought about it, she'd realized that she'd had no choice. There was nothing for her in Boston. Nothing but trouble. And she'd spent nearly two months sailing from one part of the world to the other so that she could start anew. So what else was there to do? If she could pretend to be a teacher, she could just as easily pretend to be a governess. . . . Couldn't she?

Luckily—and Penny fervently believed in luck—she and Eliza had gotten along right from the start. Eliza had explained that because of his business, her father only visited from time to time, having placed the taciturn Macgorrie in charge of keeping the house. Eliza never did explain who was in charge of keeping her. Yet if Penny considered it an odd arrangement, she wasn't about to say so. She didn't know much about how rich folk lived, and it was evident that the Cooper family, with their grand house, lace curtains and Oriental rugs, were the wealthiest she'd ever met.

As a result, Penny and Eliza had arrived at an unspoken agreement over the last few weeks. They didn't talk about the past. They didn't ask each other many questions, instead choosing to pass the time picking blueberries, poring over catalogues, washing each other's hair, and acting out Eliza's beloved plays. Even when Penny's lack of education became obvious during the first few days, Eliza made no mention of her governess's apparent shortcomings. For this, Penny was grateful. Enormously grateful. As far as she was concerned, she had put Boston behind her, and she wasn't looking back.

A half-hour later, after rummaging through wardrobes and closets and finding nothing suitable for Titania, Penny decided to have a look in the attic. Upon her arrival at the Cooper home, Macgorrie, who had since avoided Penny like the plague or a bothersome tax collector, had suggested that she could sleep in the garret; Eliza had overruled him and instead had moved Penny into a large, comfortable bedroom on the second floor.

Entering the attic, Penny smiled and mouthed a silent "thank you" to Eliza. Although she had inhabited less inviting quarters in her day, she was still very glad not to be sleeping among the attic's spiders and dust.

An old rocking chair, a bassinet, a rolled-up carpet, half a dozen lanterns, a row of trunks, and various piles of crates nearly filled the drafty space. The faintest scent of rose water laced the musty dampness. Feeling like a child let loose in a candy store, Penny was wondering where to begin her search when she was drawn to one particular trunk. It was slightly more battered than the others, its leather dark with age, but its brass lock gleamed like a freshly minted coin.

As she walked toward the trunk, her pulse began beating faster. Even stranger, her fingers trembled as she unlatched the clasp. She hesitated, not sure what had caused her to pause. From her memory came the awareness that, months earlier, she had experienced this same sense of premonition when old Mr. Shakely, one of her oldest and dearest customers back in Boston, had pulled from his pocket the well-traveled letter.

Slowly, she pushed up the lid.

"Oh, my," she whispered. "Oh, my."

Inside the trunk was a gown. A gown made for a princess, a creation so beautiful that Penny felt the surprising prick of tears at the corners of her eyes. Like frothy mounds of freshly whipped cream, yards and yards of satin billowed and swelled, shimmering in the softest of ivory hues. Adorning the satin was lace as delicate and intricate as any that Penny might ever have imagined, much less seen.

She could not help herself. An inexplicable compulsion came over her, and she had to know what it felt like to wear such a gown. She did not question whose it might be. She did not worry that she might tear or soil it. She simply had to put it on.

With no concern for the cold, she stripped off her brown linsey dress, and pulled the ivory gown over her chemise. To her amazement, even though she wore no stays—her only corset had split yesterday—the dress fit her to absolute perfection. The skirt hung to the perfect length. The waist fit her exactly. And the décolletage molded to her bosom as though a seamstress had crafted it to her precise measurements.

So thrilled was she that she actually tingled from head to toe. She felt beautiful, wonderful, marvelous. Every girlhood dream of happily-ever-after felt possible when wearing such a gown.

Humming softly, she danced around the attic, dipping and swaying, careful to dodge the ceiling beams. If later asked, she would not have been able to say how long she pirouetted back and forth, savoring the melodious *swish-swish* of the silk, but it seemed scarcely a moment—yet also an eternity. Nevertheless, at some point she recognized that she could not dally in the attic all afternoon. Nor could she demean such loveliness by making use of the gown as a costume for a child's play. With a deep sense of regret, she told herself that she must put it away. She must. She could not wear it forever. Even if it did feel like something purely magical. . . .

Chapter Two

*J*oshua Cooper needed a hot bath, a warm bed, and a willing woman. And not necessarily in that order. He'd been riding since well before sunrise, which meant that this was the third day in a row he'd spent fourteen hours in the saddle. On top of that, his shoulder ached like the devil, thanks to his horse having shied and tossed him earlier that morning after a run-in with an ornery trio of skunks. Although he was pretty sure he'd not broken any bones, Josh was less than pleased with the tumble he'd taken. Already sore to the bone and filthy to the core, he had been in a foul enough humor before that unforeseen roll in the mud. Now he was downright cranky.

Grimacing, he spat, the taste of dirt still clinging to his mouth and beard. This last trip, he decided, had been too long. Either that or maybe he was getting too old for this work. Sleeping on the cold, wet ground, living on moldy hardtack, and riding halfway across the Territory and back every few months were taking a toll on his body and his sanity. And what the hell for?

God knew he had enough money stashed away to live like a king for the rest of his days. So why did he keep pushing himself? By all rights, his foremen, competent and trustworthy men all, should be managing the day-to-day operations. There was certainly no need for him to be personally overseeing each facet of his business from Walla Walla to Portland. But old habits died hard, and Josh had been running full steam ahead for twelve years now. Did he know how to slow down? Did he want to?

As he crested the hill, his property came into view, and a sense of pride pulled him a bit taller in the saddle. One of the largest houses in Seattle, it sat on the town's outskirts on a sizable piece of land. It wasn't overly fancy like some he'd visited in San Francisco, but it was a proper house, complete with stables, a white picket fence, and a fireplace in nearly every room. It was the kind of house that said the man who owned it was a success.

Josh rode into the stables, hopeful that Eliza had spied him from a window and begun preparations for his bath. But after rubbing down his tired mount, he limped into the back door to find the house disappointingly quiet. Macgorrie wasn't in his room off the kitchen, and there were no kettles boiling in anticipation of a hot soak, although the lingering aroma of bacon stirred his empty stomach. His daughter, the troublesome imp, was nowhere to be found.

Feeling even more out of sorts because he was going to have to see to his own bath, Josh was kicking off his mud-caked boots when he heard the fall of footsteps from above. He turned his face skyward, realizing that the noise came not from the second floor but from the attic.

"That girl," he muttered, scratching at his beard. Josh figured if he lived to be a hundred, he'd never understand what Eliza found so interesting about poking through piles of old junk no one had thought about in years.

Stifling a sigh, he headed up the stairs, his steps slow with fatigue, his stomach grumbling with hunger. As he approached, the sound of light footsteps was replaced by a quiet humming. At the back of his mind, Josh wondered if Eliza was suffering from a sore throat—he remembered her voice as being pleasant and musical, not this scratchy, off-tune warbling.

His daughter's name was poised on his lips as he crossed the attic threshold—

And then he went still.

Silhouetted before the garret's lone window stood a woman. A woman half clothed.

Her thin white chemise, backlit by the summer sunshine, appeared nearly transparent, displaying firm legs and bountiful curves in agonizing detail. Agonizing to Josh, that is, since he'd not had a woman in more than three months, and his body's swift response to such a vision bordered on painful.

She was in the process of removing a gown, and thus was slightly bent forward, revealing more creamy flesh than any sane man dared dream about while living alone on the trail as long as Josh had done. A handful of bright coppery-red curls teased her neck, and her expression was soft and dreamy.

Soft and dreamy, however, proved to be all too short-lived. In the next instant, a piercing shriek nearly shredded his eardrums, causing Josh to rear back in surprise and smack the back of his head on an exposed rafter.

As he cussed richly and soundly, he reached for the knot already swelling on his skull, noticing how the woman's green eyes grew wide. For less than a second, a hint of guilt came over him as he worried that he'd frightened her, but then the trespassing miss boldly ordered, "Out!"

Out?

Frantically, she set about dragging the dress over her pale limbs, as Josh felt an annoyed scowl dig into his forehead. Goddammit, what was going on here? Who was this woman who thought she could order him out of his own home? And what in the name of Moses was she doing practically naked in his garret?

"Shoo!" she yelled again, waving him off as one would a stray dog.

That disdainful "shoo"—coupled with his throbbing

scalp, shoulder, and groin—pushed Josh from being merely annoyed to feeling full-blown anger.

"Just who the hell are you?" he growled, perhaps more loudly than he had intended.

To his astonishment, the woman straightened to her full height, which wasn't all that impressive, and shoved her fists onto her hips. The gown, a pretty white frothy thing, clung to every inch of her.

"And just who the hell are *you*?" she retorted, challenging him with a defiant thrust of her chin. Her accent, an odd blend of the deep South and something vaguely Irish, surprised Josh almost as much as the ease with which she swore at him.

"I," he replied slowly, each word clipped, "am the owner of this house."

Uncertainty flickered across her face—a lovely face, Josh decided—as she looked him over from the top of his aching head to the tips of his stockinged feet.

"You're Eliza's pa?"

Josh would have sworn that her nose actually wrinkled and, while he realized that he probably wasn't looking his best, he didn't much appreciate the way she was studying him as if he were a slug on her dinner plate.

Before he could answer, however, or demand the name of the nose-wrinkling intruder, Eliza's high-pitched voice drifted up from the staircase, calling out, "Hello? Penny, are you up here?"

The woman started.

"I thought," Eliza continued to call out as she rounded the landing, "we could begin *Midsummer Night's*—"

In ordinary circumstances, Josh might have laughed at the comical sequence of emotions that played across his daughter's face. Initially, her eyes lit with delight to see him, and she made a movement to rush into his arms. But just as quickly that light faded to visible trepidation, and she pulled up short, her gaze darting to the woman Josh now assumed to be "Penny."

"Papa."

"Eliza."

He could almost see the wheels spinning in that brain of hers. Her tongue darted nervously to the corner of her mouth as she tugged at a stray leaf caught in her hair. But in typical Eliza-like fashion, she did not long remain at a loss for words, recovering her composure with a forced smile.

"I see you've met Penny." The smile grew yet brighter.

Josh did not answer. Although his anger still bubbled just below the surface, years of experience had taught him to proceed with caution where his daughter was concerned. From the day she had uttered her first word at the precocious age of six months, the child had thoroughly befuddled him. She had a gift whereby she could talk anyone into anything, and by the time she had reached her second birthday Josh had known himself to be completely outwitted. More than once Macgorrie had claimed that Eliza must be a descendent of the fairy folk, a theory that Josh dismissed as superstitious nonsense. Nonetheless, there was no denying that there was something different about the child. Something that caused one to question whether a young person should be so clever.

"Eliza, I'd like to speak to you in the parlor."

Josh had endeavored to sound calm, yet even to his own ears, he'd failed.

Eliza opened her mouth to argue, but he stopped her with a brusque, upraised palm.

"Now," he added, before she could set off on one of her long-winded explanations.

Without looking back at the woman, Josh headed for the stairs, his jaw clenched with an unsettling combination of irritation and desire. In his mind's eye, he was still reluctantly savoring the picture the redhead had made when first he'd entered the attic. God help him, he couldn't remember the last time he'd run into anything so tempting. Worse yet, he couldn't decide at which point she had looked more appealing to him. Clad only in a flimsy chemise, she had presented a mouthwatering eyeful by any man's standards. But then in that ivory dress. . . . He couldn't quite explain it, but just as he was thinking how pretty she was, she had pulled on the gown and had suddenly gone from pretty to out-and-out beautiful. Of course, it must have been the sun at her back, but he had felt as if there had been a glow about her.

"Fercrissake," he muttered. "A glow?" He really had been out on the trail too long. He gave himself a shake, then immediately regretted the sharp movement, for his head had begun a steady pounding.

Marching into the parlor, he decided to settle this business with haste, since he'd not yet achieved even the first of his homecoming goals: bed, bath, or bawd. And he was itching to get to at least one of them.

Eliza scurried in right behind him, her manner lacking its customary confidence. Josh folded his arms over his chest, leaned back against the fireplace mantel, and took a deep, calming breath.

"Papa, I—"

"In ten words or less."

"But—"

"Ten words, Eliza."

She rolled her right foot onto its side. "Penny is my new governess."

Josh hid his reaction behind a scratch of a sideburn.

"*New* governess?" he questioned dryly. "Has there been a previous one?"

"Oh, no." Blond curls flew upward as if taking flight. "Penny is the first. The only one."

"I see. And just how long has she been serving as your governess?"

"Three weeks. She lives with us."

Josh nodded, convinced that his daughter had to be some heavenly retribution for his youthful days of drinking, womanizing, and general carousing.

"She's wonderful, Papa," Eliza rushed to assure him. "You're simply going to adore her."

Wonderful, indeed, Josh thought to himself, picturing the woman unclothed in front of the attic window.

With a deliberate effort, he pushed the distracting vision from his mind.

"Eliza, I doubt that I will have an opportunity to 'adore' her, since, as of today, her employment is terminated."

Eliza answered with a gasp. "But, Papa, you can't!"

"What I cannot do, Eliza, is have a young woman living here in my house. It's not—" He struggled to find the appropriate words. "It's not . . . proper."

"But she will have nowhere to go."

"She can go back to where she came from."

"All the way back to Massachusetts?"

Josh clutched the top of his head, his voice rising, "What in the name—"

He saw a telltale glistening on the tips of Eliza's lashes.

"She came from Massachusetts?" he managed to say.

"That's right." She fought back her tears with a sudden show of bravado. "From Boston. I had her shipped here!"

Dear God. The Big Man Above was definitely getting even.

"Look here, Eliza Jane." He tried to adopt a tone of reason. "You can't go ordering up a governess like you order books or a winter coat. And what do you need a governess for in the first place?"

Eliza's lips pushed out into a small, quivery pout. "I need a governess. I do."

"Why? For Pete's sake, you're probably more educated than anybody teaching up at the university." He thrust a finger in the general direction of the hill. "Are you trying to tell me that this Penny is more qualified than any of them?

"I don't know. But I needed her."

Josh studied her for a long moment. "Needed her for what?"

Sighing, Eliza closed her eyes and rubbed them hard with the heels of her palms. "I don't know," she said, her words slow. "I guess it seemed to me that every-

thing was working out so well for the ladies that Mr.
Mercer had brought that I thought maybe . . .''

Josh snapped to attention. The Mercer girls? Asa
Mercer claimed those women came to Seattle to be
schoolteachers, but everyone from San Francisco to
the Yukon knew they'd been brought here to marry
the local bachelors.

Then the realization hit him head-on with the force
of a falling sequoia.

"Good God, Eliza, you brought that woman here
to marry me?"

"Marry?"
Penny, who'd been eavesdropping just outside the
doorway, did not bother to conceal herself or her
alarm. She stepped into the parlor, mouth agape.

"Is your pa speakin' the truth?"

Eliza's woeful expression revealed her guilt in no
uncertain terms, and for a split second, Penny came
close to feeling sorry for the child, especially when she
read the silent pleading in her gaze. Then Penny
caught a whiff of Joshua Cooper, and any sympathy
she had been feeling evaporated like smoke.

"No. Uh-uh."
Penny shook her head back and forth, all the while
keeping a cautious eye on the man on the other side
of the parlor. Heaven knew she had run across plenty
of rough-and-tumble men in her day—men so down
on their luck that they'd been living in the Boston
alleys for months without the benefit of clean clothes
or a decent bath. Men who'd suffered the ravages of
war so deeply that comfort could only be found in a
bottle or in the arms of a stranger.

But never had Penny seen any man as frightening
as this one. Not only was his dark brown hair matted
with dirt and long enough to reach his shoulders, but
he was also twice the height and girth of an ordinary
person. He wore a filthy buckskin coat that Penny
would have sworn he'd used to mop up mud puddles,
and his right cheek was crusted with dried blood. Why,

when she'd first seen him in the attic she'd genuinely feared that a bear or some other forest creature had wandered into the house.

"I'm sorry, Eliza," she said, still shaking her head, "but I ain't looking to get married."

Josh Cooper released a short, sarcastic laugh. "You don't have to worry, 'cause I *ain't* asking!"

Although Eliza had taught her that "ain't" wasn't correct English—and Penny was trying her best not to use it—the word still slipped out from time to time, but that didn't give him, Penny told herself, the right to poke fun.

"Well, it wouldn't do you any good to ask," Penny retorted, stung by his mockery. "I didn't come all this way to get tied to a fellow who smells like he's got somethin' dead in his pockets."

"No?" He leaned forward as though to get a better look at her, or to bring his stench closer, and Penny noticed that his eyes were the color of Elliott Bay, a dark, flinty gray blue. "What did you come for, then?"

"Now, Papa." Eliza tried to jump between them, but he moved her to his side with one large hand. Standing together, the father and daughter did not look as if they could be even remotely related, Penny thought. Eliza was so pale and delicate, while he was all burly and dark and gruff. And hairy.

Penny met his taunting gaze, and wondered how much he already knew. What had Eliza told him while she'd been upstairs hurriedly buttoning herself back into her old brown linsey? She concluded the safest course was to answer with as much honesty as she could.

"I came west probably for the same reason most folks do: I wanted a fresh start."

Something flickered at the back of his eyes. Could it have been understanding?

"That's all well and good." He cleared his throat and stepped back a pace. "But I don't need a wife and Eliza doesn't need a governess."

"But Pa—"

Joshua silenced his daughter with a single stony glance. "Eliza, I am not going to discuss it, nor am I going to stand here and listen to your arguments. You've gone too far this time, and you damn well know it. You're lucky I don't tan your hide."

Eliza's chin dropped to her chest, and Penny thought his expression softened a smidge as he looked down on the tiny bent head. Then he turned back to Penny, and his jaw hardened beneath his thick beard.

"I'll pay for your passage back to Boston, and since you're not to blame for my daughter's folly, you'll have two months' salary as severance pay. I should be able to get you on the *Mary Woodruff* next week."

Eliza muttered something unintelligible into the front of her pinafore, but her father ignored her.

"Now I am going to find Macgorrie, have myself a bath, and get some sleep." He tugged at the bottom of his leather coat, as if to signal the conclusion of their business, then headed for the parlor door.

"Oh, Papa."

He paused, but did not turn around. Penny saw his massive shoulders rise and fall in what might have been a silent sigh.

"I, uh . . ." Eliza scrunched up her face in that funny way she did when she had something unpleasant to say. "I put Penny in your room."

Oh, golly. She should have figured as much when she found the men's clothes in the armoire. "I'll move my things," she hastily offered.

"No."

"Truly, I—"

"No," he repeated, half turning to spear her with his gaze. "I'll bed down in the study until you leave."

Penny would have protested, but she had seen something in his regard that she dared not provoke. "Thank you," she said quietly.

With a curt nod, he left the room.

Before Penny could take another breath, Eliza's thin arms were wrapped around her waist, and she was talking as fast as it was humanly possible to speak.

"Oh, Penny, I'm sorry. Please don't be angry with me. I'm sure he doesn't mean it, because once he comes to know you, he'll love you the way I do, and then you'll stay and everything will be perfect, and we'll become a family exactly as I had imagined."

Become a family. Penny's heart twisted at the words because, like Eliza, she understood what it was like to be an orphan hungering for family. But she also knew the dangers of clinging to false hope. Her touch gentle, she loosened Eliza's hold, drawing her backward so that she could see her face.

"Eliza, did you honestly think that your father and I would agree to get married?"

The child's smile was sweetly desperate. "He will grow to like you. He will. I mean, you are so very kind and so very fun."

Penny wanted to reply, "And he is so very cranky and so very hairy," but she refrained.

Instead she said, "Sweetheart, I think you could keep ordering governesses 'til there wasn't a single woman left in all of Boston, but I don't think you're going to get what you're looking for. Your pa doesn't seem keen on the idea of marriage."

"But that's only because he's never been in love."

Penny frowned. "Oh, now don't say that. I'm sure he loved your mother very much."

"No, he didn't." Eliza's eyes drew wide with conviction. "Mrs. Murphy told me the whole story. He married my mother because it was my grandfather's last wish and he couldn't say 'No' to his dying friend. You see, Papa barely knew my mother, but he knew my grandfather, and when my grandfather suddenly fell ill, he begged Papa to take care of his daughter, Madeline. So Papa did as my grandfather asked and married her." Eliza's voice fell to a near whisper as if she were sharing a secret. "But the widow Murphy said that they were never happy together. Never. Because they didn't love each other."

Penny smoothed a curl on the child's forehead. "Come now, you don't know if that's true." Even though many children weren't conceived in loving marriages, for some reason Penny didn't want Eliza to believe that about her own birth.

"It is," Eliza insisted. "Mrs. Murphy says that back then it was hard enough for anyone to make a life in the West, much less someone as sickly as my mother. So Papa had no choice but to marry her."

"Hmm." Penny found it difficult to believe that the crusty mountain of a man she had just met would wed a woman as a favor to a friend.

"Well, from what I can tell, your pa isn't someone who's right now looking to fall in love or get married. And neither am I."

Although as the words left her mouth, she remembered the girlish dreams she had entertained as she'd danced around the attic in that breathtaking gown. An odd pang shot through her as she wondered whether she had been wearing Madeline Cooper's wedding dress.

"Eliza." She hesitated, almost embarrassed to ask. But at the same time, she needed to know. Crazy as it was, Penny felt as if that gown had been made for her and her alone, and she couldn't bear the thought that it may have been worn by Eliza's mother. "I happened to be in the attic, and I, um, stumbled onto an old trunk with a pretty dress—"

"You found it?" Eliza's expression brightened.

"The ivory gown?"

"Yes, isn't it lovely?"

"Yes, it is," Penny reluctantly agreed. "But I was wondering . . . did it belong to your mother?"

"Oh, no. I have no idea where it came from, but I am certain it wasn't my mother's. Mrs. Murphy said that when she died, the physician ordered that all Mother's clothing be burned for fear of the fever spreading."

"Oh." A sense of relief washed over her, which made her feel silly, yet inexplicably glad.

Eliza tugged her back to the present. "You aren't really going to leave me, are you?"

Penny steeled herself to answer, wondering how she had grown so fond of the girl so quickly. But then, staring into Eliza's angelic face, she knew the answer. They had both been searching for someone to love, and through luck or fate or whatever one might call it, they had found each other.

"If your father wants me to leave, Eliza, then I must go."

"But—"

Penny hushed her with a finger across the lips. "No more talk of this," she said, summoning a determined smile. "Not now. Besides, you can't forget that you promised me a Titania this afternoon."

Chapter Three

"What the devil were you thinking?" Josh demanded, as Macgorrie poured another kettle of boiling water into the tub, which was barely large enough to hold Josh's frame. "Did you not know what she was planning?"

"And what makes ye think I can control the lass any better than ye can?" Macgorrie answered, letting the last few scalding drops fall onto Josh's bare knees.

"Ouch!" Josh narrowed his eyes, but the Irishman took no notice.

"By the time I got wind of what she'd planned, 'twas done. The widow Murphy and she had arranged it all, and as I told ye before, I can't be held responsible for that girl's mischief."

Not to mention that Macgorrie spent many a chilly evening in the widow's warm company. If the widow Murphy and Eliza had been up to no good, Macgorrie had likely turned a blind eye rather than risk his relationship with the friendly seamstress.

Josh sat back in the tub, letting the hot water soothe his tired muscles. "What am I going to do with that girl?" Closing his eyes, he snorted quietly. "Can you believe she actually thought that I would consider wedding the woman?"

Macgorrie clumped over to the tub, then dropped a clean towel on a nearby chair. "From what I've seen, ye could do a lot worse."

Josh cocked open one eye. "What are you saying?"

Macgorrie shrugged, the corners of his mouth turning down. "I'm only saying that Liza sure has taken a fancy to her and the lass isn't all that bad to look at."

"Hmph." Josh shut his eyes, irritated. "That may be, but I'm not looking for a wife. And even if I were looking, I doubt the woman has the right qualifications. I mean, can she sew? Cook?" He gestured to the cast-iron stove in the corner of the kitchen. "I mean, if you ask me, she doesn't even seem to be much of a governess."

"Aye, and I'm not much of a nanny or housekeeper, but ye know as well as anyone ye hafta play the cards ye're dealt."

Josh couldn't argue that point. He himself had been forced to play many unexpected hands over the years, and not always with the happiest results. From marrying Eliza's mother to becoming a widower with a child, he had experienced his fair share of adversity and had muddled through as best he could. Not that he harbored regrets. And certainly none about having Eliza. In his heart, he feared that his greatest failing had been that he hadn't known how to be a better father to her.

Yet, he wanted to believe that he hadn't made an utter mess of it. She was an intelligent, lively child and, to judge from the noise coming from the parlor, he hadn't crushed her spirit during this most recent confrontation. In truth, he'd been soaking in the tub for the last twenty minutes or so, listening to Eliza's childish giggles interspersed with a woman's warm laughter. And he did like the sound of the redhead's laugh. It was a throaty, yet feminine sound that was really most pleasant . . .

"And just what are ye grinning about?" Macgorrie demanded.

Josh's eyes flew open. Had he been smiling?

"I was thinking about a drink," he lied. "How about you earn your wage and run over to Gem's for his best bottle of whiskey?"

"Lah-dee-dah, aren't we the lord of the manor today?" Macgorrie replied, although he obediently hobbled out the back door.

Josh had almost dozed off when a cool draft and a slight noise stirred him awake again. Inside the kitchen doorway stood Penny, looking almost as startled as she had when he'd come upon her in the attic.

"I'm sorry." Her cheeks were flushed a bright rosy color. "I didn't know . . ."

Josh quirked an eyebrow, surprised that she didn't immediately race from the room in maidenly horror. On the contrary, the woman was staring at him. Practically gawking.

His body started to respond to her appraisal, and he drew his knees closer to his chest, the water sloshing. Although annoyed by his reaction, he wouldn't have been a man if he hadn't been flattered by the attention.

"Can I help you?" he asked, as he pulled the towel from the chair and draped it strategically across the copper tub.

"I—" She swallowed and at last averted her gaze. "I beg your pardon. Eliza wanted a cup of cocoa," she weakly offered, "and I, uh, did not recognize you."

Josh rubbed his freshly shorn chin. "I shaved."

"Yes . . . I see."

Yet still she did not leave, continuing to sneak glances in his direction as if he wasn't supposed to notice. But he did notice. And he told himself he'd damned well better get himself over to Rose's place real soon or he might be in danger of doing something stupid with a certain auburn-haired governess.

"Perhaps the cocoa could wait until I finish my bath?" he finally prompted.

Her eyes widened yet further, as she must have realized that she'd been standing there too long. "Yes, of course."

She was nearly out the door when, to his surprise, and without any intention of doing so, Josh called out in a gravelly voice, "How old are you, anyway?"

She twisted back toward him, but did not meet his eyes. "I was twenty in March." Then she was gone.

Huffing a loud sigh, Josh let his head fall back against the tub as he looked up at the ceiling. *Twenty*. That made him a full dozen years older than she—

He sat straight up, flinging soapy droplets onto the wood floor. Good Lord, what was he bothering with the math for? In one swift movement, he pushed aside the towel, leaned forward, and submerged his entire head underwater.

Josh didn't make it to Rose's place that night. Or the following night, either. The first evening, Eliza had insisted that they all dine together to celebrate his return; on the second night, she had pointed out that he'd been away for her birthday, and announced that her celebration couldn't be put off any longer.

"Not even one more day, Papa."

Unfortunately, Josh, as happy as he was to see his daughter, was starting to become irritable. Irritable approaching ornery. Normally, after a long trip, he wasted no time in reacquainting himself with one of the girls at Rose's, since he made it a practice while traveling not to dally under unfamiliar skirts. Of course, this meant that he sometimes went months without a woman, which made the trip to Rose's a rather important part of his homecoming ritual.

Now, while Josh might not have expected a day or two to make much difference, the current delay had turned out to be difficult. Some men might even have called it torture. The presence of one young, attractive redhead—who happened to be sleeping in his bed— was beginning to wreak havoc with Josh's state of mind. And his state of body.

So when he entered the kitchen that evening to find Penny hunched over the stove, he tried to make a quick retreat before she'd seen him.

No such luck.

"Hell," he whispered, as she greeted him with, "Hello," her eyes wide. For one insane moment, Josh entertained the fanciful notion that her eyes were the color of spring moss, a thought that further convinced him he had to get out of the house. And soon.

Despite the fact that the two of them had spent the last twenty-four hours avoiding each other and pretending that they'd not seen each other nearly naked the first day of their meeting—a pretense that had been difficult, to say the least—she seemed not displeased to see him.

She wiped her hands across the front of her apron, eyeing him cautiously as if she wanted to speak to him but didn't know whether or not she should. She even opened her mouth, but then seemed to think better of it.

He found himself equally frozen with indecision, pretty sure she wanted to say something, yet thinking he'd do better to turn and run.

"I, uh . . ." She was clearly struggling.

He wasn't of a mind to ease her struggles.

Finally, she appeared to screw up her courage. "I, um, don't wish to be a bother, but do you think you could help me?"

Josh curled his toes until they ached inside his boots. "With what?" he asked warily, not liking the way he had already warmed to the sight of her wavy auburn hair piled in a sloppy knot atop her head.

"Well, Mrs. Murphy gave me a receipt for blancmange," she said, waving a scrap of paper in her hand, "which is supposed to be Eliza's favorite. Unfortunately . . ." She let her voice trail off.

Josh glanced at the stove, where a pot of milk was bubbling over, then across to the kitchen table, where mounds of sugar and flour spilled onto the floor like snowdrifts. Amid the powdery mess a broken bowl lay in shards.

"Unfortunately?" he prompted, his earlier suspicions about the woman's cooking abilities confirmed.

"Well . . ." With her teeth, she softly worried her bottom lip. "I guess if I am to leave next week, there is no use in being proud or silly." She reluctantly handed him the sheet of paper covered with Mrs. Murphy's handwriting. "Could you tell me: What *is* that word?"

She pointed to a group of letters penned in the widow's flowery hand. Puzzled, Josh glanced at the word, which clearly read, "S-c-a-l-d." What was this? Was she playing at some game?

Only that very morning he had happened upon her and Eliza in the midst of taming Shakespeare's shrewish Kate. He hadn't intended to spy on them, but, concealed behind the open door, he had been unable to tear himself away. Eliza had been directing Penny's performance as the governess read a scene involving a fiery temper tantrum, complete with stomping feet and windmilling arms. Although Eliza's cheery face had first caught his attention, he had lingered to watch Penny. She had attacked the role with vigor, her voice animated and strong. When she'd stumbled over the lines, she had laughed at herself; when she'd stumbled over the footstool, falling backward onto the chair, she'd laughed even harder.

As reluctant as Josh was to admit it, he found the woman intriguing. There was something about her . . . She wasn't truly beautiful, and she lacked the refinements one would expect from a real lady. She dressed shabbily, swore when she didn't think anyone was listening, and more often than not her hair was in the process of falling from its pins. But she had a certain spirit. A certain something that kept drawing him to her, when common sense was telling him to keep a safe distance.

"The word is 'scald,' " he told her. " 'Have a care not to scald the milk.' "

"Ah." She reached to take the piece of paper from his fingers, but he held fast to it, causing her to lift her face to his.

"I don't understand. What about Kate?" he asked. "The 'shrew' from this morning?"

She seemed confused for a moment, then breathed an airy, embarrassed sound. "Oh, that. Well, thanks to your daughter, I might not be very good at reading receipts, but my Shakespeare is coming along quite nicely.

"You see, acting out the plays was Eliza's idea," she explained after a short hesitation when she looked to be debating how much to reveal. "I think she figured out that very first day coming home from the wharf that I was not as educated as a proper governess or schoolteacher should be."

She ignored the sarcastic lifting of his eyebrows.

"Anyway, it took me a while to realize what she was doing—I'm not as quick as she is, that's for sure—but then I saw how she had turned the tables on me. She was the one doing the teaching, using the plays as a way for me to improve my reading."

Her mouth quirked in a half smile, and he saw that she had a dimple in her left cheek.

"But you don't have to worry about me trying to swindle you out of a governess's salary," she said, with a sudden flash of vehemence. "I'm not planning to take any of your money, Mr. Cooper. Not any of it. I may have been a bit dishonest in order to get out here, but I ain't—" She quickly corrected herself. "I am not a cheat."

Josh studied her with no pretense of doing otherwise, noting the defiance in her cocked chin and the way the color was rising up her neck.

"So you came west to teach when you yourself could not read?"

"I could read. Some." She swallowed, her throat working. "Not that it mattered really one way or the other, because I would have gotten on that ship even if I had never held a book in my hands. The way I saw it, fate handed me an opportunity and I had to take it."

Josh nodded, recognizing in her the same fighting instinct that had kept him going these past dozen years. Madeline, regrettably, had lacked that instinct. Already physically frail, she hadn't been strong enough to withstand life's everyday struggles, much less the additional hardships of frontier living. But Penny—

Josh blinked. What the devil was he doing, comparing his wife to this woman?

He gave himself a sharp mental kick, thrust the receipt into Penny's hand, and headed for the kitchen's back door. At his back, he could sense Penny's astonished stare.

With his fingers on the doorknob and one foot across the threshold, he shouted in a particularly gruff voice, "Tell Liza I'll be home in time for her dinner."

Chapter Four

$\mathcal{P}$enny studied herself in the mirror, turning first left, then right. She tweaked the satin bow at her waist and fluffed her forest green skirts.

"Well, it isn't gray or brown," she said approvingly, as she reached for another pin to tame her hair.

Mrs. Murphy, having learned that Penny owned only two dresses, had insisted on cutting down one of her old gowns, claiming that such a young girl shouldn't be dressed, as the widow described it, "in the color of spit or mud." Penny had been reluctant to accept the widow's charity, but Eliza's wheedling had ultimately melted her resolve.

Having made a final adjustment to the bow, Penny was feeling very glad that she had accepted the dress in spite of her misgivings. Except for those magical moments dancing through the attic in the ivory gown, Penny had never felt so feminine. So pretty.

She knew there was no reason to be making a fuss over her appearance. In fact, it would have been far wiser to have worn her old brown linsey and left her hair in its slipshod topknot. But since yesterday she'd been feeling as though she wanted to take a bit more care with her toilet and had been attempting to convince herself that this impulse had nothing to do with her reaction to seeing Eliza's father in the bathtub.

Truth be told, she had been stunned. Stunned speechless. Breathless.

In the first place, she had not expected to find anyone in the kitchen, so to have discovered a man bathing had been sufficiently shocking. But then, after realizing that the filthy, hairy beast she had identified as Josh Cooper had transformed into someone young and handsome with muscled arms and sleek, dark hair . . .

Penny frowned at her reflection and gave her cheeks a robust pinch, which was done more as a reprimand than to bring color to her complexion.

"Gracious, aren't you ridiculous?" she chided herself. "Why, he doesn't even want you here, you ninny."

Besides, a bath and a shave only changed a man so much. Josh Cooper was still Josh Cooper, and from the little she knew of him, she suspected that he must be a hard man. After all, what kind of father left his daughter alone for weeks at a time with no one but Macgorrie for companionship?

Holding fast to that question, and to her resolve not to behave foolishly, Penny went to see about dinner. She hadn't gone more than two paces down the hall, however, before she stopped. She sniffed.

Smoke?

By the time she reached the dining room, her hair had already begun to tumble from its carefully wrought coiffure, and her lovely bow had come loose.

"Oh, dammit," she murmured, glancing upward to where smoke drifted into the ceiling's corners, appearing very much like the ribbons of fog that regularly drifted above Elliott Bay. She supposed this was her comeuppance for being overly ambitious. She ought to have begun simply, as the widow had counseled, with just the blancmange.

"Don't worry," Josh said, coming up from behind her so that she nearly jumped from her skin. "Macgorrie saved your roast."

"How?"

"I believe that he has cut off the crusty black parts and put the rest into a stew."

Penny covered her eyes, undecided if she wanted

to laugh at her ineptitude or shed a grateful tear for Macgorrie's assistance.

"All right, I've learned my lesson. From now on, I'll leave the cooking to those who know what they are doing."

"Nah." Josh sidled a step closer, bringing with him a faint odor of spirits. "Everyone has to begin somewhere. You'll do better with practice."

Penny inched backward. "Maybe."

"Trust me."

However, at that particular moment, Josh Cooper appeared a million miles away from trustworthy. In fact, he looked to her to be positively dangerous, the way his slate blue eyes glinted, and with the half smile that lurked at the corners of his mouth. Standing so close, Penny was struck again by his height as he loomed over her, his shoulders nearly as wide as the doorway behind him.

"I, um—" She felt her mouth go dry.

Luckily, Eliza bounced into the room at that moment, her cloud of curls unusually buoyant.

"I think it's going to rain," the child announced. "Look," she invited, pointing to her head. Eliza held to the theory that she could predict wet weather by her hair's degree of unruliness.

"My," Penny agreed, glad for the distraction as she walked over to peek out the window. "If those curls are any indication, a monstrous storm must be brewing."

Despite the lingering smell of burnt beef, the birthday dinner proved to be a success, thanks to Macgorrie's quick thinking and the almost edible blancmange. Josh poured blackberry wine liberally, while Eliza steered the conversation time and again to any trivial commonality shared between Josh and Penny.

"Isn't it interesting, Papa," Eliza commented, "that you and Penny both like to play hazard?"

Or, "Did you know, Penny, that Papa's birthday is in March, just like yours?"

One particularly frivolous observation concerning a

shared fondness for asparagus caused Josh and Penny to exchange knowing glances across the table. However, as soon as their eyes had met, Penny wished she had not looked in his direction, for there was more in his regard than merely amusement. She nervously cast her gaze to her fingers twined together in her lap.

She, better than most women, recognized the effects of drink on men; she understood why Josh's mood continued to improve in direct relation to the amount of wine he'd consumed. Still, she felt strange and uncomfortable as she sat there, examining her tattered fingernails, his gaze upon her.

Although Penny had years of experience in deflecting the interest of drunken men—and was admittedly skilled at it, having mastered all sorts of tricks involving bony elbows, hot drinks, and broom handles—never had she found herself in a situation where she felt attracted to any of those same tipsy men. But she had a niggling suspicion, even a growing fear, that she might be attracted to Josh Cooper. How else might she explain her cotton-dry mouth, her restless hands, her uneasy stomach?

Well, to be fair, the blancmange might have had something to do with her unsettled stomach. But what about the rest of it?

He wasn't at all the kind of man she had imagined she would be attracted to. In her fantasies, she had pictured a princely gentleman, fair-haired and charming, who spoke French. Or maybe Italian. He would be poetic and suave, with big, brown, expressive eyes. She snuck a peek across the table. He wasn't supposed to have cobalt eyes flecked with shards of silver that seemed to cut right through her as if she were made of warm butter.

She took a breath, thinking that her insides rather felt like warm butter. Soft and pliant. Perhaps she had had a wee bit too much wine herself.

"Well, if you'll excuse me." She stood, suddenly eager to retire. "It's been a lovely party and a very long day, so I'll bid you all a pleasant good night."

"So early?" Eliza asked, her disappointment plain.

"It's not that early," Penny said. "In fact, I think it's close to your bedtime, as well."

As she pushed back from her chair, thunder cracked overhead, followed by the gentle ping of the storm's first raindrops. Eliza proudly announced, "I told you so" to no one in particular, while Penny popped her head into the kitchen to thank Macgorrie for washing the dishes, although he had grumpily informed her several times that she shouldn't be thanking him for doing what he was paid to do.

Eliza was pleading with her father to let her stay awake another hour when Penny quietly slipped away to her room.

She did not know how long she'd been sleeping when she abruptly sat up in bed. The house was dark, the wind like a mournful dirge through the trees. She listened, uncertain as to what sound had awoken her. Had it been Eliza, frightened by the storm? Or had it been the thunder and wind?

Knowing she wouldn't be able to fall back to sleep without checking, she threw her shawl over her shoulders and tiptoed down the chilly hall. The parlor's grandfather clock chimed two o'clock. The child's bedroom door stood ajar. She stole a quick look through the narrow opening and saw that Eliza lay as peacefully as a veritable angel, her white-blond hair spread across her pillow. Penny was about to withdraw when a flash of lightning cast a glow into the room, illuminating a figure in the chair beside the bed. Her breath caught before she recognized Josh Cooper.

She inched backward, careful not to draw his notice. But his attention was fixed on the sleeping child, as he sat there simply staring at his daughter. Curious, Penny hung back, watching him watch Eliza. What was he doing here at this time of night?

She probably stood there a minute or two, until another burst of lightning flickered through the room, allowing her a fleeting glimpse of Josh's face. The ghostly light threw into relief the sharp planes of his cheekbones, the strong line of his jaw. But what caused her heart to turn over was the raw emotion she read in his expression. She would not have believed she knew the man well enough to see all that she saw in his face, yet she could not deny what she had witnessed. And what she felt.

She backed away, strangely moved by the tenderness in his expression. But it had been more than tenderness; she had also sensed vulnerability and yearning. As if he were a man desperate for something that would forever elude him.

Her thoughts heavy, she wrapped the woolen shawl more tightly around her and headed back down the shadowy hallway.

Josh wasn't a praying man, but sometimes he wished he was, because he damned sure could have used some divine guidance from time to time. Like now.

Leaning forward, he pulled the blanket up to Eliza's shoulders to ward off the chill night.

God, just look at her. She was so beautiful. So perfect. How could anything so delicate and precious have come from him?

Her hand lay outstretched on the satin counterpane, her lips slightly open, parted by shallow breaths. She lay in the darkness, so trusting. Trusting that he would take care of her. Trusting that he would make the right decisions for her.

If only he knew how.

At eleven years old, she seemed to know a lot better than he did what she needed.

After watching Eliza and Penny these last couple of days, Josh had gained a much clearer picture of what had caused Eliza to hatch her harebrained scheme in the first place. Apparently, a young girl needed giggling and petting and cooing. The feminine fussing over colored ribbons, and the messy dipping of cookies in milk, and the gentle humming while brushing out wet hair.

He didn't know how to give Eliza all of that. He didn't know how to be a mother.

But perhaps . . .

Perhaps he could *give* her one.

He dropped his head into his hands, laughing softly at himself.

Hell, who was he kidding? He was merely looking for excuses, wasn't he? Was his greatest concern really finding a mother for Eliza? Or, could he be honest for once and admit that he wanted that redhead for himself?

He squeezed his temples until he could feel the blood pounding beneath his fingertips.

Stop it, he told himself. Just because a man got an itch in his pants didn't mean he married a woman he barely knew. Particularly not after managing to dodge every other matrimony-minded miss who had crossed his path these last six years. Then again, he had married Madeline when he'd known her not at all. And he sure as hell hadn't been itching in his pants for her.

Josh felt a pang of regret, thinking of Madeline, aware that he hadn't been much of a husband to her. He had wanted to love her—he'd tried. And she had been a fine, decent woman in many ways. She just hadn't been his woman.

No, he needed someone fiery and sassy and earthy. A woman who was strong enough not to be intimidated by him or his wealth or by the challenge of frontier living. Someone with curvy hips and long legs and a mouth that was made for—

"Christ."

Josh burst out of the chair. *Enough.* He didn't care if it was the middle of the night, he was going to run over to Rose's and take care of business even if he had to knock down the damned door.

In his rush, he didn't see the figure at the other end of the hallway until he'd nearly walked into her. She wore a plain cotton night rail and a shawl.

"What are you doing awake?" he asked in a hoarse

whisper, irritated that he'd not seen her, and even more irritated that he hadn't the sense to march away that very instant.

"I thought I heard Eliza."

She was too close. She smelled too good.

"You should go to bed."

"I will."

Yet she did not move. What was the matter with her? Couldn't she tell that he was as randy as the proverbial goat? That he was seconds away from doing something insane that he couldn't blame on whiskey and wine?

As a test—of himself or of her?—he placed his hand on her elbow. "Go to bed. It's cold. You'll catch a chill."

But where his fingers wrapped around her arm, there was nothing but heat. Heat spreading up into his shoulder, across his chest, everywhere.

Still she did not pull away.

Slowly he bent toward her, waiting for her to wrench free of his grasp. He came closer, his gaze fixed on her mouth, giving her plain notice of his intent and ample time in which to say no. Her lips trembled, but she merely let her lashes flutter closed as she leaned into him.

A voice inside warned him that he was playing with fire, flirting with madness. By God, he was supposed to put the woman on a steamer next week. All the same, since the moment he had seen her in the attic, a radiant vision in white satin, he had scarcely been able to think of anything else.

Anything . . . but this.

His lips settled softly on hers, not asking too much, a delicate caress. But what began as gentle and questioning flamed into a kiss that had her pulled hard against him, his hand cupping the back of her head, her fingers gripping his shoulders.

He backed her against the wall, feeling as if he wanted to devour her. He kissed her ear, her neck, the hollow of her throat. She moaned breathlessly as his palm skimmed her waist, then moved higher to explore her breast's ripe fullness.

His knee pushed between her legs and he could hear his heart hammering above the crash of thunder. Nuzzling her neck, he took a deep breath, doubtful that any perfume could have matched the scent of her warm skin. As he tried to shove the night rail from her shoulder, he felt her body go stiff beneath his.

"Josh," she whispered, her voice tremulous and uncertain.

Suddenly he realized just how far he had fallen. He was minutes away from taking her right there in the hallway of his house.

"I—" An apology stalled in his throat. How could he apologize when he would have bartered his very soul to finish what they had begun?

"Penny."

He had hoped to explain himself. Instead, he turned away, strode down the stairs, then through the front door and out into the stormy night.

Chapter Five

*P*enny did not sleep the remainder of the night, but lay in bed, listening for Josh's return. After daybreak, Eliza awoke, and they ate sugared toast, then played draughts before the parlor fire. The day stretched on while the storm grew yet more violent, trees bending in the wind and rain pummeling the earth with torrential force. When it came time to sit down for the evening meal and still there was no Josh, Penny quietly took Macgorrie aside.

"I'm worried," she said. "What should I say to Eliza?"

The older man shrugged. "Ye don't have to say anything. The girl is used to his comings and goings. He's more likely than not seeing to business affairs."

So Penny and Eliza ate their dinner and then read for an hour before Penny tucked the child into bed.

By the following morning, Penny's concern was enough to send Macgorrie out to check some of Josh's favorite haunts. Fortunately, the weather had finally begun to turn, the rain reduced to occasional showers and a hint of summer warmth returning to the air.

Macgorrie had been gone less than an hour when a forceful pounding sent Penny racing to open the door, Eliza hard on her heels.

"Oh, sweet Mary." With one hand, Penny clutched the doorframe to steady herself, while with the other hand she held Eliza back from looking onto the porch.

Two burly men whom Penny recognized from the

general store were carrying Josh on a canvas stretcher. Macgorrie, stumping behind as fast as he could, was barking orders like a Union general.

"Take him straight on in," he told the men, his accent heavier than usual. Then he instructed Penny to "put the kettle on and have Liza pack a rucksack."

"Pack?" Penny questioned.

As the men approached her with their burden, Penny saw that Josh, muddied and wet, lay unconscious. Blood oozed a thick crimson ribbon along his hairline. Behind her, Eliza strained to look past, but Penny held her back.

"Aye," Macgorrie explained as he hobbled onto the porch. "He's runnin' a fever, and we'd best take no chances with the lass catchin' it. I already spoke to the widow, who'll keep her for a couple of days."

Fever. Penny remembered that Madeline Cooper had died of fever. Swinging around, she swiftly herded a protesting Eliza out of the room.

"What is it, Penny? Is Papa ill?"

"Yes, he is, and he wouldn't want you catching whatever he has. So you'll be going on holiday at Mrs. Murphy's for a day or two."

"Aren't you coming?"

Penny shook her head. She could hear the men grunting as they carried the litter into the bedroom she had been occupying this past month.

"No, but there's no need to fret," she told Eliza, helping the child put clean clothes into a carpetbag. "If anyone ought to be worried, it's me, since the widow will no doubt spoil you rotten and then I'll have to undo all her handiwork when you come home."

Despite Penny's playful tone, a frown still creased Eliza's forehead.

"He is going to be well again, isn't he?"

"Heavens, of course. Why, it's probably just a wee bit of a cold." Penny made no mention of the frightening head wound.

Eliza snapped the bag shut, her perplexed gaze encircling the pink-and-white room. "I never stopped to think what might become of me if something were to happen to Papa."

Penny stilled. "Nothing is going to happen to your father," she assured her, although a shiver rippled down her spine. "Hurry up now, and I'll walk you over to the widow's."

Within thirty minutes, Penny had returned from depositing Eliza at Mrs. Murphy's house on Jackson Street. She rushed upstairs, knocking softly on the bedroom door before letting herself in. Macgorrie stood at the side of the bed. He waved her back into the hallway, but not before she'd had a long look at Josh. She didn't like what she saw. Although Macgorrie had cleaned him up and managed to rid him of his sopping-wet clothes, he appeared pale. Pale to the point of gray, his brow bruised and gaping open.

Macgorrie met her in the corridor.

"What happened?"

He scratched at the top of his head, sending a few feathery hairs flapping aimlessly.

"Well, from the looks of it, lightning struck that big oak down there on the other side of the creek. Now, he may have been hit by a fallin' limb or could be he was tryin' to dodge the limb or the lightnin', and then hit his head. Either way, I found him lyin' in the creek. It's hard to say how long he'd been there, but long enough. He's damned lucky he didn't drown, if ye ask me."

"Is there a physician to call?"

"No use. With the measles goin' round, the doc's been runnin' ragged. I heard tell he was called over to Port Townsend."

Penny gnawed at the side of her thumbnail. "I don't like that gash in his head. I've seen a few of those in my day, and I think he needs to be sewn up."

"Aye, but not by me. The widow is handy with a needle. I'll go fetch her."

"No." Penny stalled him with a hand on his forearm. "I can do it."

Macgorrie's bushy white brows lifted. "Ye think so, do ye?"

Swallowing her misgivings, Penny nodded. She'd had to do it only once before, and that patient had been stone-cold drunk. With Macgorrie's help, she swiftly assembled the supplies.

The wound stretched almost two inches long above Josh's temple, a ragged tear. No matter how neatly she sewed it up, it was bound to leave a nasty reminder of the accident. But she saw that this scar would hardly be his first.

Macgorrie must have noticed her staring at the white, puckered mark that ran along the top of Josh's bare shoulder.

"Aye, that one I gave him."

"You?"

"Aye, ye could say so. We was working at the camp, and a load of logs came loose from their moorings. I lost my leg, but 'twould have been a helluva lot worse if Josh hadn't come after me."

Penny glanced again at the large blemish. So that was how Mac had become the Cooper family's caretaker.

"How long ago was this?" she asked, while threading the needle, glad to see that her hands were steady despite her nerves.

"Oh, ten years ago now, I suppose. Been here in Seattle ever since."

Penny allowed herself a hint of a smile. She had never heard Mac so talkative. Either the man was finally warming up to her or he was as anxious as she was.

"Do you think he's going to feel anything?" she asked as she perched on the edge of the mattress.

"I'd say ye're about to find out."

With a steadying breath, she pierced the loose flap of skin on one side of the wound. Behind her, she heard Macgorrie sputter a cough.

"I'll go put on the kettle," he offered, then bolted from the room.

"I guess," Penny muttered, listening to the hasty *thump-thump* of Macgorrie's retreat, "I am on my own."

One stitch. She sighed with relief. Two. Three neat little stitches.

She had just finished tying up her fourth when she all but leaped from the four-poster bed. A pair of silvery blue eyes was fixed upon her.

"You're awake."

He said nothing, only continued to stare up at her.

"Does it hurt?" She held aloft the needle and thread as though to explain the grounds for his discomfort.

He answered in a croaky rasp, "Like hell."

"I am sorry," she said, wincing with regret. "But you need at least another two or three, I do believe."

His lids closed. "Go ahead."

He did not reopen his eyes while she finished her stitching, his breathing so even that she wondered if he had lost consciousness or fallen asleep.

However, when she reared back to examine her needlework, he was again watching her.

"I'm done," she told him.

"Good."

She placed the back of her hand against his stubbled cheek. The skin burned with fever.

"You're very ill." She stood up from the side of the bed.

"Eliza?"

"She's with Mrs. Murphy." Penny, careful not to jostle his head, adjusted the pillow beneath his neck. "Do you know what happened?"

He did not answer for a few seconds, then said, "I kissed you."

Heat flowed into her cheeks, and she straightened her skirts to give herself something to do.

"After that," she prompted, feigning composure.

"Kissing you is all . . ." His voice faded as his eyes again fell closed. "All that . . . I remember."

Penny stood there, her pulse drumming. Fear crept

into her thoughts. Surely Josh was too strong to be done in by a fever and a knock to the head. Surely.

But his unusual pallor worried her. Who knew how long he had lain in the creek, pelted by the cold rain? And hadn't she seen men healthier than this suddenly succumb to mysterious illness?

When Macgorrie returned, he and Penny argued over who would assume the role of nurse. At first Mac kicked up a fuss, but he eventually conceded the argument when she pointed out that he couldn't be hobbling up and down the stairs all day, carrying pots of hot water and bowls of broth.

And as Penny pointed out, her limited experience aside, she had learned a few lessons about doctoring over the years. Keep the patient warm and out of drafts. White vinegar worked wonders for almost any ailment. And encourage liquid nourishment such as weak teas and bouillons.

Josh, however, did not wake again until late that evening, after sleeping fourteen hours straight. By that time, a frantic Penny had been ready to pull out her hair, not knowing if she ought to be worried by his lengthy sleep or to be thankful he was resting peacefully.

Earlier she had found, tucked away in the parlor's library, a dusty copy of *A Compilation of Household Receipts*. She was flipping through the yellowed pages, hoping to find some miraculous remedy, when a low groan drew her out of her chair.

"Josh?"

She touched his forehead. Was it her imagination or was he warmer than he'd been a few hours before?

He stirred awake, his gaze cloudy and unfocused.

"Is the lamp too bright? May I get you some broth? How do you feel?"

He blinked at her battery of questions. Then, slowly drawing out each syllable, he answered, "No. Yes. Utter shit."

Fighting back a relieved smile, she hurried to fetch

a cup of beef broth. Then, with some difficulty, she propped him up with another pillow before pulling her chair closer to the bed.

As she had expected, he tried to grab the spoon from her grasp, but she pushed his hand aside with ease. He was too weak to put up much protest.

She fed him close to half the broth before he croaked, "Enough."

"A little more," she coaxed.

"No." With his jaw set stubbornly, he might have been a boy Eliza's age, except for his heavily muscled arms and two days' growth of dark beard.

Acquiescing reluctantly, Penny exchanged the cup for a clean damp towel, which she used to cool his neck and forehead. As she dabbed at his brow, a shock of chestnut hair tumbled forward, and she tenderly smoothed it back.

"Who are you?"

Penny's hand froze just above his ear. Goodness, did he not remember? Had his memory been damaged? She had heard of that sort of thing happening to soldiers in the war, particularly where a head wound was involved.

"My name is Penelope Martin."

"Yes, yes, I know your name." He gave a weary sigh of annoyance. "But who are you? Where did you come from, Penelope Martin?"

"Ah." She cocked her head to one side, feeling a kink settle in her neck from sitting so long in the chair. "It's really not a very interesting story."

"Indulge me."

Penny feared that she had already indulged him too much the other night, when she had allowed him to kiss her senseless. Indeed, she had allowed him more liberties than she had ever allowed any other man.

"If you insist," she said, shrugging. "Though don't say I didn't warn you. Let's see . . . I was born outside Hampton, Virginia, where my father was a sharecropper. A pretty poor one. My mom ran off when I was still in swaddling, so it was just Pa, Lewis, and me. When my pa died, Lewis took me with him to Boston. And that's where I grew up. End of tale."

"Who was Lewis?"

Penny's lips pursed thoughtfully. "He was either a slave or a servant—I don't rightly know. But he was my closest, dearest friend."

"And what did you do in Boston?"

Penny rose from the chair. "I learned when it was time to stop answering questions," she said, moving the pillow so that Josh was in a reclining position.

He narrowed his eyes at her, but she ignored him.

"You need your rest."

He grumbled beneath his breath, but before Penny had settled back into her chair and drawn her shawl across her lap, he had fallen back to sleep.

Throughout the night, his condition grew worse, his feverish mutterings hoarse as he tossed and turned, mangling the bedclothes. His flesh was so hot that Penny would have sworn her fingers blistered when she touched him. Up and down the stairs she raced nearly every hour, fetching ice so that the towels she used to bathe him remained cold.

Just as the first rosy glimmers of dawn appeared in the east, his fever broke. Perspiration beaded his skin, and he suddenly seemed to fall into a deep, dreamless sleep.

Penny had never known such relief. During the night, she had been tormented by the question Eliza had posed. What would become of the child if something befell Josh? Would Eliza remain here in this house, to be raised by Macgorrie? Had Josh made arrangements for the girl? Did he have family to whom she could go? Penny could not bear the thought of Eliza growing up orphaned and alone. She knew too well how difficult such a life could be.

And as much as she worried about Eliza's fate, Penny couldn't pretend that she didn't harbor her own private, selfish concerns. What she had felt the other evening in Josh's arms had been indescribable, unlike anything she had felt before. To be truthful, the depth of her feelings had frightened her, the way she had responded to him without reservation. As if she were meant to be held by him, meant to be touched by him, meant to be with him.

It wasn't as if she were some green girl who had no familiarity with the opposite sex. She had worked beside men her entire life and had rebuffed a few bold characters who had succeeded in stealing a kiss in a corner. Some of the bolder ones, like young Thomas Bailey, had tried to steal more than a kiss, and he had been half the reason she'd had to flee Boston. He'd not taken kindly to the black eye she'd given him last spring.

Yet her experiences had not all been wrestling matches. Since becoming a woman, she had doled out one or two kisses of her own free will. But those encounters had been basically meaningless, particularly when compared to the emotional and physical response she had known with Josh.

A wiser woman would have made herself forget the incident in the dark hallway. In fact, throughout the night as she had tended him, she had warned herself not to make too much of it. A kiss was not a declaration of undying devotion, and she had no reason to believe that Josh Cooper was interested in anything more than a stolen moment in the moonlight. But couldn't she hope that perhaps he had felt as she had felt, that what they had shared had been something unique? Something special?

Chapter Six

"*Y*ou're not as good-looking as my other nurse, you know."

"Aye, and you don't smell as good as she does neither," Macgorrie pointed out with a disdainful sniff.

"That may be," Josh admitted, warily eyeing the bowl and cloth in Macgorrie's gnarled fingers. "But there is no way in hell that I'm letting you bathe me like I'm some kind of invalid."

"Well, what else are ye, man? Ye've not left this bloody bed for three days."

Josh pointed to the closed bedroom door, pleased to discover that he had the strength to lift his arm. Yesterday, when he had finally regained consciousness, he'd been too weak to even blow his own nose.

"It's that redheaded tyrant who's to blame. She's keeping me prisoner."

Macgorrie nodded knowingly. "She's a strong-willed one, she is."

"Do you see how she refuses to bring me even a scrap of clothing? It's unseemly, I tell you ."

"That's because yer clothes *are* in scraps. I had to cut them off ye. And she knows it's the only way to keep ye from gettin' outta bed."

Josh's glare could have singed the white whiskers from Macgorrie's chin. "You could bring me something else to wear."

"Oh, no, ye're not getting me into trouble. I'm

scared of what the lass might do. She made it perfectly clear—ye're not to get up until she gives the word."

"Well, hear these words, Seamus Macgorrie: You're not bathing me," Josh repeated, snatching the wet cloth from the man as he approached the bed.

Macgorrie waved his hand in front of his hooked nose. "Well, someone is going to have to see to it."

"I can do it myself." And Josh proved the point by wiping his bare chest with the damp towel.

"Fine. And while ye're taking care of yer stench, I'll bring in fresh linens."

"Might I at least have a pair of drawers?" Josh demanded.

"Faith, I never knew ye to be such a prude," was the Irishman's parting shot as he left the room.

Although he had to pause more than once to catch his breath, Josh did succeed in bathing himself. Afterward, despite his exertion, he actually felt better, well enough to think about food.

In timely answer to his prayers, a soft knock sounded on the door.

"Come in," he called, sitting up in anticipation. He wanted to believe he was eager for a meal, but the sudden stirring of his stomach had little to do with conventional hunger.

In came Penny, her hair piled in charming disarray, her eyes a brilliant leaf green, albeit shadowed from evident lack of sleep. On a tray, she carried the ever-present cup of broth.

"What's that?"

"Beef broth," she cheerily replied.

His brows drew together, causing him to flinch slightly as his stitches pulled. "Thanks very much, but I'm ready for some real food. Ask Macgorrie to rustle up a lamb chop, will you?"

"No solid food yet. According to the medical handbooks, you are to remain on liquids until tomorrow."

"Medical—" Josh sputtered. "Why the hell are you reading medical handbooks?"

Her smile brimmed over with unruffled tolerance. "Because I can."

Silenced for the moment, Josh could only scowl as she took a seat beside him.

"I don't want broth."

"Aren't you hungry?"

"I'm starving, for God's sake. I need food."

"Well, then." She lifted the spoon in invitation. "Here you go."

"I told you. I don't want that." He knew he was behaving like a peevish child, but he hated being so damned helpless.

"I don't think you realize just how sick you have been. A lamb chop might sound appealing, but I doubt you're ready."

"I've recovered much faster than *you* realize," he retorted, adjusting the bed linens to better disguise his body's very healthy reaction to her thigh near his. Then, wrinkling his nose, he peered into the unappetizing broth. "I'll tell you what . . . I'll make you a bargain."

One auburn brow rose speculatively.

"I'll drink that god-awful stuff if you finish your story."

"You must truly be bored."

He reached for the steaming cup.

She hesitated before handing it to him. "What do you want to know?"

"What did you do once you arrived in Boston?"

She took a long, deep breath, as though she were dusting off her memories. "Lewis found work cooking in a saloon, the Pig and Whistle. Unlike me, he knew his way around a kitchen. I washed dishes, mopped floors, ran errands. He and I shared a little room abovestairs—"

"You shared a room?" Josh interrupted.

"For heaven's sake, I was just a scrawny little thing—about eleven, I guess—so what did anyone care? At least, no one in that part of town gave it much mind. Anyway, by the time Lewis died, I was working as a serving girl, so Mr. Bailey, the owner, kept me on."

Josh sipped from the cup, his expression reflective. "I still don't see how a serving girl from the Pig and Whistle became my daughter's governess."

"Ah, that was simply good fortune. You see, Mr. Shakely, a regular customer, had at one time or another worked for the Boston Primary School Committee. He also happened to be a distant cousin of Seattle's famous widow Murphy. So when Eliza decided to advertise for a schoolteacher, Mrs. Murphy sent the letter of inquiry to Mr. Shakely."

"And he passed it on to you?"

Penny glanced to her lap. "He knew how desperately I wanted to get out of Boston."

"Why were you so desperate?" Josh asked, as she slid from the side of the bed.

"Have you been to Boston?"

Her flippant tone didn't fool Josh for an instant, but he chose not to press her. It was easy enough to imagine what challenges a young, pretty girl working and living alone above a tavern might have faced.

"Where are you going?"

She had collected the empty cup and was headed for the door.

"Well," she said slowly, casting him a teasing, sideways smile, "since you've been such an obedient patient, I thought I'd see if I might find that lamb chop for your dinner."

Josh wanted to ask her to stay, but bit his tongue as the words surfaced. What the heck was the matter with him? He was acting like a needy child . . . or a lovesick swain.

Penny was still smiling when, through the window, she saw a figure briskly approaching the house. With her hand on the knob, she opened the door as a gentleman, fortyish and heavily bearded, raised his knuckles to knock.

"Good afternoon."

"Afternoon, ma'am. Mr. Swensen here to see Mr. Cooper." He doffed his straw hat, his demeanor businesslike yet friendly. To Penny's eyes, he looked like a barrister or an accountant. Not like the typical man one found working in Seattle.

"I am sorry, Mr. Swensen, but Mr. Cooper is not able to receive guests today. May I help you?"

The man handed her an envelope. "If you'd be kind enough to see that he gets this right away. Mr. Cooper had asked me to take care of booking a passage on the *Mary Woodruff* and she's pulling out tomorrow. I meant to get this to him days ago, but my courier boy was down with the measles and I plumb forgot about it."

Penny felt her smile grow stiff as she accepted the proffered envelope. "Yes. Of course."

"Thank you, ma'am, and have yourself a nice day."

Penny murmured a faint good-bye as she shut the door. A chill raced through her. The *Mary Woodruff*.

With trembling fingers, she opened the envelope, certain what she would find there, but praying that she might be wrong. That the papers were meant for someone else. Her heart sank, and she felt as if she had taken a punch to her middle.

She was going back to Boston.

Although Josh got his lamb chop for dinner that night, he couldn't enjoy it. Macgorrie delivered the meal without volunteering information as to Penny's whereabouts, which forced an exasperated Josh to inquire outright, since he'd not seen her since midday.

"Where's my jailkeeper?" he finally asked, cutting into the juicy chop.

"She's gone over to the widow's to visit with Eliza."

"So I guess she believes I'm going to live?"

"I guess so," Macgorrie agreed, with an unconcerned shrug of his stooped shoulders.

By late evening, Josh was wondering if he was strong enough to fetch her from Mrs. Murphy's himself. Unfortunately, however, he had to discard the idea when even threats of dismemberment failed to persuade Mac to bring him clothing.

"All right, Macgorrie, I can see the woman has put the fear of God in you, but let me tell you this: If I don't have a pair of trousers waiting for me when I wake up in the morning, there's a certain son of Ireland who's going to have hell to pay."

The other man merely rolled his eyes, muttered something about "bullyin' an old cripple," and then shuffled out of the room.

Josh woke with a start. He had been dreaming about Penny, and in the dream he had felt ridiculously happy. They had been standing together in an open field. Penny had been wearing the ivory dress and had been smiling. For him. Then, beneath the bright summer sky, she had begun to remove the ivory dress. Slowly. For him.

And suddenly he had come awake, disoriented and aroused, to the heavy blackness of a cloudless night. The dream had seemed so real to him that he would have sworn he could smell the lavender water that she wore. He lay in bed for two heartbeats before he realized that it was not merely his imagination.

His hand snaked out and grabbed hold of a wrist. She gasped.

"What are you doing?" he asked huskily.

"I-I was checking on you."

"In the dark?"

"I didn't want to wake you." She gave a tentative tug, but he did not release her.

They both remained silent in the thick darkness as she stood stock-still, no doubt questioning why he insisted on holding her there. He was asking himself the same question.

"What time is it?" He could feel her pulse fluttering like the wings of a bird.

"It's after midnight."

As his eyes adjusted, he saw her turn her head away

from him, although there was nothing for her to see in the impenetrable shadows.

"Mac said you saw Eliza today?"

"Yes. She's eager to come home."

"Then let her."

Beneath his fingers, Josh felt Penny tense. What was wrong? Was she worried about Eliza? Worried he might be contagious?

Or . . . could it be that she was frightened? Could she sense what he wanted from her?

After a long moment, she asked, "Are you well enough for her to come home?"

"I'm fine."

To prove his point, he sat up, pulling her closer until she stood right against the bed. She deliberately kept her gaze averted from his bare chest.

Josh, wishing he could read her thoughts, let go of her hand.

"Well, as long as you're feeling better . . ." She turned to walk away.

"Don't go."

"Do you need something?"

He almost laughed. He needed something, all right. The question was whether or not he should take it.

Josh had spent the better part of the day trying to sort through what it was that he wanted from Penny. He desired her—that much he was sure of. In fact, right now he wanted her to the exclusion of any other woman. Why else had he walked into Rose's the other night, downed two drinks, chatted up the girls, and then left without so much as a friendly pat on the back?

He wanted to believe that once he scratched that particular itch, he'd be himself again. He'd be the same Josh Cooper he'd been two weeks ago. He wouldn't pass an entire afternoon trying to piece together the puzzle of this woman's life. He wouldn't worry if she was feeling tired or frightened or anxious. Dammit, he wouldn't think about her at all.

"If I said I felt feverish, would you stay?"

"Are you?"

"Am I?"

She stepped forward, then hesitantly placed her hand against his cheek. As she did so, he turned his head to kiss her palm. She went still. He covered her fingers with his and carefully drew her down to the side of the bed.

Then taking her hand, he placed it on his chest. His heart was pounding as though he'd swum across the bay and back. Josh himself was surprised by the force of his response.

Slowly he reached up and threaded his fingers through her hair, dislodging pins as the thick tresses fell loose around her face. Then he cupped the back of her head and drew her face to his, barely brushing his lips over hers. She tasted like mint. He deepened the kiss. Her fingers dug into his skin, holding him fast.

In one swift movement, he rolled to his side, pulling her with him, her skirts tangling until he kicked them free. He explored the curve of her hip, the dip in her lower back, the swell of her breast. His entire body throbbed, and he had to force himself to slow down even as his hands moved faster over her, wanting to know every perfumed nook and hidden freckle and silky square of skin.

At first her touch was tentative, but as he grew more demanding, she answered his need. Her fingertips, cool and velvety, slid across the muscled furrows of his stomach, causing him to clench his teeth against a hiss of delight.

"Penny," he murmured.

She answered him with a soft sound that might have been his name or might have been a sigh.

"I want this," he told her quietly, his voice almost shaking. "I want you. But—"

She, too, hesitated, turning her face into the crook of his neck, her breath a tantalizing caress against his warm skin.

"I want you, too," she whispered. "And I am not afraid."

"Are you sure?"

He felt her nod. And then, her words a sweet torment, she added, "I trust you."

Feeling like a schoolboy, Josh had to struggle to hold himself in check as she kissed the side of his neck, his name a breathless whisper on her lips. With infinite care, he unbuttoned her gown, groaning as she helped him push free the coarse wool. Her skin was a creamy white, glowing in the deep darkness, softer than he had even imagined.

Once she lay next to him, her eyes bashful, her body wanton, Josh knew there would be no turning back. Not if his life had hung in the balance would he have been able to stop himself from having this woman. Gently, reverently, he brought her to the edge of the precipice before he claimed her innocence with a decisive thrust of his hips. Her eyes flew open, but she soon met his rhythm with a passion that nearly undid him. He held strong until she cried out, burying her face in his shoulder. Then, at last, he allowed himself to join her in the lovely agony of release.

He struggled to catch his breath before realizing that he was probably crushing her with his weight. He moved to her side and lay there, one arm draped over her middle, staring blindly into the dark, asking himself what the hell had just happened. When finally he turned his head back toward her, Penny was fast asleep.

Chapter Seven

*P*enny woke up alone in the massive bed. Sore from the inside out, she knew she hadn't dreamt the events of the previous night, although a part of her wished that she had—the part of her she generally called common sense.

Sighing, she closed her eyes, wondering where and when Josh had gone. And what he was doing. And what he was thinking.

The bedroom curtains were drawn, but sunshine still seeped around their edges, causing her to wonder if she had slept later than usual. She listened carefully for any sound from belowstairs, but all was silent.

Worried that Eliza might be hoping to return that morning, Penny hurried to wash and dress, her muscles aching in places she hadn't known she had muscles.

"No use having regrets now," she muttered. She could have walked away from him. She knew it. But she had chosen not to. Deep down, she knew that she had wanted it as much as he had, and she wasn't going to pretend otherwise. She'd known what she was doing when she snuck in to peek at him. Of course, she hadn't planned on him waking. She had only wanted to look at him, to memorize each and every feature. The way his lashes curled up at the ends. The tiny scar to the right of his chin. Perhaps it had been foolish of her to fall into bed with him, but women had been doing foolish things in the name of love since before the dawn of time.

Penny had suspected that she was falling in love with Josh that first night he had been so ill. Many years ago, she had nursed Lewis during his final days. She had remembered how terrible it was to watch as death threatened someone you cared about. But during those hours tending Josh, she had felt much more than a friendly concern. She had feared that if he did not survive, the very essence of who she was would shrivel up and cease to exist.

And yet she had still not allowed herself to believe it was love until last night. His touch had confirmed what she had already known in her heart. And so she had stayed with him. And so she had known love. If only for one night.

She would have no regrets.

Her mind so occupied, Penny was lacing up her boots when the parlor clock started to chime the hour.

Six, seven . . .

Her stomach twisted with each ring that followed.

Ten o'clock.

My God, she had never slept past six in her life. The day was nearly gone. And then, Penny actually had to bend over to subdue a wave of dizziness as the realization hit her: In four hours' time, she was supposed to be climbing aboard the *Mary Woodruff.*

Holding her skirts up, she raced downstairs and darted from room to room. The house was empty. In vain, she searched for a note, while an odd sense of loneliness crept over her. Just as she was headed up the stairs, having decided that she may as well begin her packing, she heard the kitchen door creak open. A jolt of anticipation shot through her, but then she heard the familiar *plonk-plonk* of Mac's wooden leg.

"Mornin'," he offered, a bit more civilly than was his custom.

"Good morning." She fought the rush of heat to her cheeks. "Do you know where Mr. Cooper might be?"

"No, can't say that I do. Although this mornin' he rushed outta here like a bat outta hell, he did."

"Oh?" Penny lost the battle of the blush.

"Aye. Didna say where he was goin' or when he'd be back, but he mounted up and was gone like the wind."

"I . . . see." An icy tightness settled in Penny's chest. Wasn't she a foolish thing to have expected anything else? "It, um, seems that I'm to go out on the *Mary Woodruff* today."

"That so?" The old man gave a thoughtful nod. "Aye, I suppose it is time for her to come in."

"Yes." Penny lowered her head, quietly agreeing. "I suppose it is time."

After choking down a meal of biscuit and tea, Penny set to packing. She had acquired one new piece of clothing during her stay—the emerald gown gifted by Mrs. Murphy, which fit easily with her other belongings into the battered valise. Everything she owned in the world was collected and stowed away in less than twenty minutes. Then Penny began the more difficult chore of drafting a letter to Eliza. She scribbled and scratched and labored over spelling, but an hour later she had produced a note meant to express her gratitude and love, without straying too far into the realm of maudlin.

She toyed with the idea of leaving a note for Josh; however, after a few futile efforts, she concluded that it was impossible. Either her words sounded formal and cold or, worse yet, they revealed too much of her sentiments. For the briefest of moments as she held pen over paper, she wondered if she might give way to a self-pitying tear. But Penelope Martin was made of sterner stuff than that. A sniff here. A bite of the lip there. But she would not cry.

After all, why should she? She was better off than she'd been a few months ago, wasn't she? Gosh, she was a fairly decent reader now, thanks to Eliza. And she'd cured herself of "ain't," and she'd learned a little bit about cooking. Maybe she could find work in Boston or elsewhere, if not as a teacher then as a governess or housekeeper. No, she wasn't going to feel sorry for herself. Not her.

Yet, as the clock struck the hour, reminding her that her time in Seattle was almost at an end, sadness washed over her. She had felt different here in this place, in this home. Perhaps for the first time in her life, she had known what it was to hope for something more.

With her bag in hand, Penny mounted the stairs to the attic. Silly, undoubtedly, but she wanted just one more look at that dress. The one that had made her feel like a princess. Like someone beautiful and special.

The air was chilly, the dust swirling in sparkling spiral patterns as she opened the attic door. She set down her valise and walked over to the trunk. Or where the trunk should have been. She glanced to both sides of her, frowning in confusion. Where was it? She opened one or two different trunks, knowing that they weren't the one she was looking for but thinking that maybe somehow she'd forgotten what the right trunk looked like. But neither the trunk nor the gown was to be found. Could she have imagined it all?

She was brushing a cobweb from her skirt when Eliza appeared in the doorway.

"No," the little girl said, her eyes pink-rimmed and watery, her hair as chaotic a jumble of curls as Penny had ever seen.

Wordlessly, she rushed over and hugged the child close.

"It's not fair," Eliza whispered. "It's not what was supposed to have happened."

Penny squeezed shut her eyes, forcing back unwelcome tears. "I'll write to you," she said in a falsely cheerful voice. "All the time. And I expect you to do the same, you hear?"

"Are you going back to Boston?"

"I don't know. I might stop somewhere along the way if a city looks particularly interesting. But I'll let you know where I am. I promise."

"And what about Papa? Have you said good-bye?"

Penny shook her head. She didn't want to tell Eliza that her father might have left town again.

"I don't think I'll have the opportunity," she said instead. "Besides, it's just about time for me to head down to the docks. Do you want to come with me?"

Eliza's lips trembled. "No. I can't." And then she ran from the room.

Mac had proposed earlier that he take her down the hill in the coach, an offer that Penny had declined. She wanted one last look at Seattle before she left, and since the day was pleasant, she figured the walk would do her good.

She walked past the Occidental Hotel, where the Mercer girls had stayed upon their arrival to Seattle. She walked past Pinkham's store, where Eliza liked to buy licorice. At the corner of Commercial, she looked north to the university, its cupola glowing in the sunlight, its neat picket fence freshly whitewashed. In such a short period, this town had become home.

The wharf seemed unusually quiet for a summer afternoon. She recognized a handful of people, including a few dockworkers she remembered from her arrival. Since she had no luggage to attend to, she simply carried her valise onto the steamer. She was surprised to learn upon boarding that she had been assigned a private cabin, an extraordinary luxury. She appreciated the thought, yet wondered whether Josh had arranged it, or if Mr. Swensen had taken it upon himself to procure the nicer quarters.

When the steward offered to show her to her accommodations, she demurred, telling him that she preferred to stay on deck until they'd pulled away. Unrealistic as it was, she entertained the faintest hope that Josh had merely forgotten that the steamer left port today. That any minute now, having recognized his error, and having acknowledged how very much he needed her, he would come galloping up to the pier and prevent her from sailing away from him. So she stood at the railing, the salt wind pulling at her bonnet, and watched the docks. She watched the last bit of cargo being loaded onto the steamer. She watched the seamen scurry back and forth, shouting to each other, sometimes in languages unfamiliar to her. She watched the mooring ropes come loose. Then she watched the expanse of water between pier and ship begin to lengthen. Almost in a daze, she noticed how the stretch of azure ocean continued to grow larger and larger until, raising her gaze to the east, she saw that Seattle was becoming nothing more than a group of grayish-white specks against a forest green background.

A knotty lump had formed in her throat, making it nearly impossible for her to breathe. But, by God, she wasn't going to cry. She wasn't. After twenty years of hard living, she wasn't about to start feeling sorry for herself now.

With measured steps, she made her way across the deck, nodding politely when greeted, since she didn't trust herself to speak. Her cabin, one of the few private quarters, was easy enough to find, though she felt bewildered and lost as she navigated the steamer's corridors.

After the brilliant sunshine on deck, she had to stand in the open doorway a moment to adjust to the dimness of her room. An actual bed, instead of a cramped berth, claimed the center of the space and, despite her dazed condition, she was still awed by the cabin's lavish comforts. It smelled of lemon polish and cedar, and was easily thrice the size of the stale-aired communal cabin she'd shared with seven other women on her westbound journey.

Upon the bed lay a coverlet of some sort, a rich, cream-colored . . .

Penny dropped her carpet bag to the floor and took a step closer, not believing her eyes. It could not be. But it was. Spread across the bed was the magical ivory gown she had been searching for only hours earlier. She pressed her fingers against her lips, both touched and amazed. Had Josh arranged to leave it here in her cabin? And how on earth could he have known that the dress meant something special to her?

Reaching out with tremulous fingers, she ran her hand lovingly across the lustrous fabric.

"It's pretty, isn't it?"

She spun around so fast that she nearly lost her balance. Or was it the shock of seeing him that caused her to sway on her feet?

Josh steadied her, and his hand upon her elbow assured her that he was real. He was real and standing there in front of her, the top of his head almost skimming the ceiling, his expression somber. His dark chestnut hair was neatly slicked back, and he was dressed like a gentleman in a dress coat and necktie.

"Wh-what . . . ?"

She scarcely knew where to begin, with so many questions rattling around in her head. And the lump in her throat was bringing her perilously close to tears.

"I was hoping you would wear it for me again."

The timbre of his voice sent goose bumps skittering along her arms.

"The gown?" She searched his face for an explanation, although already a tiny kernel of hope had begun to blossom within her.

"Yes." He took hold of her other elbow, drawing her near. "I think it would make a lovely wedding gown, don't you?"

Joy surged up from the tips of Penny's toes, but she dared not give way to it just yet.

"Do you ask this because of Eliza? So that she can have a mother? A family?" She took a shallow, shaky breath. "Because you don't have to marry me in order to have someone look after her, you know."

Yet if Josh were to ask her to stay only as a governess, and not as his wife, how could she say yes? Would it not be torture to live in his house, loving him as she did, knowing that he did not feel the same?

A shadow of a smile played across his lips. "I won't lie to you. Eliza clearly adores you and that matters a lot to me. I haven't seen her so happy—ever, I think."

Penny dug her fingernails into her palms.

"But," he continued, his grip on her growing stronger, "as crazy as that child is about you, I doubt that her feelings could hold a candle to mine. What happened between us last night—" The look in his eyes softened, and Penny felt her knees do the same. "Honestly, it scared the hell out of me. I've never felt this way about a woman. Nothing even close. And it took me a few minutes to figure out what it was and what I wanted to do about it."

"And that's why you ran off this morning?"

"Well, that and I had to see to the honeymoon plans."

Penny's eyes widened with laughter as she reared back in his arms. "Honeymoon? You were that sure of me, were you?"

Josh lifted one shoulder, his expression both sheepish and smug. "Sweetheart, I don't mean to brag, but I've been with my fair share of women, and well . . . you pretty much showed all your cards last night."

Blushing furiously, Penny shoved at his chest. "You conceited beast! Why, I don't know that I can marry a man as bigheaded as you."

He laughed and drew her close against him, plainly showing her that his head wasn't the only sizable part of his anatomy.

"You can marry me, and you will. Wearing that white dress. And we'll honeymoon in San Francisco, and we'll work real hard at giving Eliza a little brother or sister."

Hearing Eliza's name, Penny gasped. "Oh, but Josh, we can't go to San Francisco! Eliza was so terribly upset when I left. We have to turn the boat around so that we can go back and tell her."

Josh wagged his head. "As friendly as the captain and I are, my dear, I don't think he'd take kindly to my ordering his steamer back to port. Besides, Eliza probably already knows. I left a note for her with Mrs. Murphy, explaining our plans."

"*Your* plans," Penny primly corrected. "And I hope to goodness you left out the part about us working on a baby brother or sister."

"Hmm. I can't remember if I did or not. But I'm sure you wouldn't want to disappoint her. So . . ." He lifted his brows suggestively, his blue eyes gleaming. "Why don't you put on that beautiful dress for me?"

Penny curled up on her tiptoes, kissed him—and he kissed her back—then whispered, "So you can take it off?"

"Oh, yes."

Epilogue

Two weeks later

Penny was in the process of slipping on a pair of butter-soft kid gloves, when she paused for a moment to admire her wedding ring. Splaying her fingers in front of her, she beamed proudly at the simple gold band Josh had given her almost a fortnight earlier. Although their honeymoon at San Francisco's famous Lick House had been more wonderful and more luxurious than anything Penny could ever have dreamed, she was nonetheless eager to return to Seattle. She was a wife now. And a mother. She had a home to tend.

"Ready, sweetheart?" Josh called from the open doorway of their suite as he checked the hour on his pocket watch.

Penny nodded, while counting again the numerous trunks to be loaded onto the steamer for their return trip home. Her new husband had proved to be an extravagant shopper, having purchased what Penny believed to be half the contents of San Francisco. China, clothing, furniture, books—she'd had to beg him to stop, warning that his excessive generosity was likely to sink the boat.

"Two, three, four . . ." She spun slowly around. "Wait a moment."

"Penny, we're already running late."

Penny pursed her lips and gave her husband a playfully reproving look. "And whose fault is that?" she asked, gesturing toward the enormous canopy bed, which Josh had refused to let her leave that morning.

He grinned wolfishly, not the least bit contrite.

"Josh, I don't see the old trunk from the attic. The one with the white gown?"

Josh leaned against the doorjamb, peering into the suite. "It must have already been taken to the ship with my luggage."

Penny frowned. "But it was here a few minutes ago."

Josh jingled his watch chain. "Darling . . ."

"Yes, yes, I'm ready." Gathering her bonnet and cloak, Penny cast one more curious glance around the hotel room. "Honestly, Josh, I would have sworn that trunk—"

"It's probably being loaded onto the steamer as we speak," he said, placing his hand upon her back to guide her out of the room.

"Of course." Penny smiled faintly at her own foolishness. Obviously the trunk hadn't simply vanished. "I must not have seen the porter collect it."

But the trunk did not make it onto the steamer that afternoon, nor did Penny ever again lay eyes on the ivory gown.

There was still magic to be done.

Casey Claybourne, an honors graduate in French literature from the University of California at Berkeley, is the author of nine novels and two novellas. She has earned a Romantic Times Career Achievement Award and a RITA nomination. Happily married, she is particularly proud of her two teenage children.

Beautiful Gifts

Catherine Anderson

Chapter One

No Name, Colorado
July 1887

*H*indsight is always better than foresight. Faith Randolph had heard that old adage since early childhood, but for the life of her, she couldn't see how it applied now. Though the decision she had made two months ago to flee Brooklyn had ended with her and her six-year-old daughter, Charity, sleeping behind the livery stable these last three nights and picking through trash bins for food, Faith wouldn't have gone back in time to do a single thing differently. Her daughter's survival had been at stake.

In retrospect, Faith did wish that she'd been less trusting of her fellow travelers. She'd never expected all her money to be stolen from her reticule while she napped at a way station. Now only a single penny stood between her child and starvation.

"Maman," Charity wailed, "I'm hungry."

Faith squeezed the child's grubby little hand as they trudged along the plank boardwalk for what seemed the hundredth time that morning. "I know, sweetness. Let's say a little prayer that Maman will find a position of employment soon."

Faith's feet hurt, and her throat burned with thirst. It was approaching noon, and the morning's coolness was fast giving way to sweltering afternoon heat. Soon she'd have to take Charity back to the livery stable so the child could have some water. Just the thought made Faith shudder. Back in Brooklyn, they would be lunching in the formal dining room, clad in fashionable day dresses. Here, they were reduced to wearing servant's clothing to disguise their identities, eating morsels of food others had tossed away, and drinking from a horse trough.

I will not cry, Faith assured herself as she stared across the unpaved street at the Golden Slipper, No Name's only saloon. Judging by the scantily clad women she'd glimpsed through the upper windows, she suspected the establishment also served as the town brothel. A sign posted outside the batwing doors read, DANCING GIRLS WANTED. It was the only job advertisement she had seen. Shoving a tendril of sable hair from her eyes, she thought, *Not that, please, God.* She'd do what was necessary to care for her daughter, but she sincerely hoped she could find something respectable.

"Maman, look!" Charity cried, her voice edged with more excitement than Faith had heard in two weeks. "That man is selling candy."

The peddler seemed to feel their eyes on him. After anchoring the doors of his wagon open, he waved them closer. "Come, madam. Have a look at my wares. I've a little of everything here, including a sweet for the child."

Faith would have ignored the hawker, but Charity started across the dusty thoroughfare, tugging her mother along behind her.

"And what would suit yer fancy, my fine little miss?" the peddler asked as Faith and Charity reached the wagon.

Taking in the display of candy, Faith could well imagine how Charity's mouth must be watering. "I'm sorry," she informed the man politely, "but I'm temporarily without coin."

"No worries. 'Tis a gift I'll be making of it." The peddler waved his hand over the collection of sweets. "What do ye fancy, lass?"

"Peppermint!" Charity cried. "I *love* peppermint."

The eager hunger in Charity's large brown eyes forced Faith to swallow her pride and say, "Thank you, sir. You're very kind."

The hawker handed Charity a striped stick of candy. While her daughter popped the sweet into her mouth, Faith took inventory of the other wares. It seemed only polite to feign some interest, given the fact that the peddler had just given her child a treat.

Faith's gaze snagged on a lovely dress, hanging toward the back of the displays on a rod crowded with garments far less fine. A wedding gown? For reasons beyond her, Faith couldn't stop staring at the dress.

"Ah, so it's an eye for silk and lace that ye have," the peddler said with a chuckle. Using a wooden drop-down step, he pushed himself up to take the gown from the rod. "Not that I can be blaming ye. 'Tis a fine piece of frippery." He swatted at the garment and sent a layer of dust flying. "Sadly, I've been packing it around for nigh on a year. Not much of a demand for fancy wedding dresses in these parts. It's taking up space I could put to more profitable use."

He pushed the dress at Faith.

"No, no," she protested, even though she'd never seen anything quite so lovely. The gown had simple, elegant lines, which had always been her preference. The ivory silk underlay was sleeveless with a scalloped, fitted bodice, a fitted waist, and a full skirt that fell in graceful folds. The lace overlay was long-sleeved and high-necked with a delicate band collar, fastening down the front with countless lace-covered buttons. The effect was modest, yet alluring as well. "I've no use for a wedding gown, I'm afraid."

The peddler shoved the dress closer, and Faith couldn't resist touching it. Her fingertips tingled oddly the instant they grazed the lace, and inexplicable warmth coursed up her arm.

"Oh, my," she said breathlessly.

"It's perfect for ye," the peddler said. "Take it, please."

Faith laughed and shook her head.

"Come, lass, humor a silly old man. Ye're meant to have this dress. I feel it in me bones."

The peddler was so charmingly insistent that Faith would have felt rude had she refused. The strange tingle of warmth suffused her entire body when she took the dress into her arms.

"Words fail me. It's lovely. Thank you, sir."

"Off with ye," the peddler said with a pleased smile. "Mayhap the dress will bring good fortune yer way. It's needin' a husband, ye are, lass, someone to care fer ye and the little one."

Faith shook her head. She had endured marital bliss for seven long years, enough to last her a lifetime.

Charity had a skip in her step as they continued along the boardwalk. Faith attributed the child's increased energy to the ingestion of sugar. Candy wasn't very nourishing, but at least it was something.

As she had countless times over the last three days, Faith scanned the shop windows for job advertisements as they walked. When they reached the mercantile, she chanced to see a small sign taped to the door glass. In block letters, it read, HOUSEKEEPER NEEDED. In smaller letters, it said, "Experience required. Apply at the O'Shannessy place."

Faith's heart felt as if it might leap from her chest. Charity gave her an inquiring glance. "Is something wrong, Maman?"

"It's a job posting," she managed to squeeze out. "Someone needs a housekeeper."

Charity squinted up at the sign. "Do you suppose you can be a housekeeper, Maman?"

"Of *course*." How difficult could it be to keep a house? Granted, Faith had grown up in a home fully staffed with servants, rarely turning her hand to do much of anything. But she had supervised the work of servants these last eight years, first in her father's household and later in her husband's. That qualified as experience, didn't it? "Anyone can be a housekeeper. There isn't much to it."

Charity flashed a sticky grin. "Wonderful, Maman. Now what do we do?"

Tucking the wedding dress under one arm, Faith bent to grasp her daughter's elbow and hurried into the store. "Excuse me, sir?" She pressed close to the counter, willing the burly, gray-haired shopkeeper to glance up from a list of figures that he was tallying. "I need a bit of assistance, if you please. Would you be so kind as to direct me to the O'Shannessy place?"

The shopkeeper finally looked up, his frown indicating that he resented the interruption.

Faith hastened to add, "I'm interested in the advertisement on your door window."

The man's gaze sharpened on hers. "That old posting? It's been hanging there for months. The position is probably filled."

"Months?" Faith repeated stupidly. "Oh, but, no, that can't be. I've been past your shop countless times over the last three days. I would have noticed the sign had it been there earlier."

"Trust me, lady, it was there. Patrick O'Shannessy put it up last August. He's probably not needing anyone now."

Faith's heart sank, but this was the only respectable job posting she'd seen. "I believe I shall check into it, anyway."

"It's your time you'll be wasting." He jabbed a beefy thumb in the direction she needed to go. "The O'Shannessy place is a handful of miles that way."

Tugging Charity along behind her, Faith exited the shop and turned in the direction that the shopkeeper had indicated. She and Charity had only just left the town proper when the child asked, "How far is it, Maman? When will we get there?"

"Soon," Faith replied, mustering as much cheerfulness as she could, given the fact that she was already footsore and weak with hunger.

Please, God, she prayed silently as she fixed her gaze on the dusty, forbidding horizon that danced in heat waves before them. *Don't let it be too far. And, please, please, let the position still be open. This is my last hope.*

Chapter Two

$\mathcal{F}$aith was stumbling over the hem of her dress, so exhausted she could barely keep going. Charity had long since fallen silent. Faith was grateful the questions had ceased, for she feared that they were lost. They had walked at least five miles on the rutted road, one plodding step after another, their shoes sending up clouds of dust that stained the hem of Faith's dress and Charity's stockings. *Lost.* The word circled endlessly in Faith's mind.

Though she looked in all directions for a rooftop, she saw nothing. Finally she stumbled to a stop, convinced that the shopkeeper had pointed them in the wrong direction. Charity drew up beside her and pushed at her dark, sweat-dampened hair. "Why are we stopping, Maman?"

Because I'm afraid we're lost, and I don't know what to do, Faith thought dismally. There were undoubtedly large predators in this godforsaken land. She had no weapon with which to defend her child and wouldn't have known how to use one anyway. Never in her life had she felt so inept and useless.

"I just need to rest a moment," Faith lied.

Charity plopped down on a rock at the side of the road. "I'm tired, Maman, and I'm so very hungry. Do you suppose the O'Shannessys will feed us?"

"Perhaps. People who can afford to hire household servants are usually well off, and it has been my experience that the wealthy are inclined to be generous to those less fortunate."

"Are we the less fortunate now, Maman?"

Speaking around a lump in her throat, Faith said, "We are, I'm afraid."

Sinking onto a rock near her daughter, she considered her options. They had been walking for two or three hours, making it midafternoon. In another three hours, the summer sun would start to set over the Rockies. What if they kept going and never came upon the O'Shannessy place? She and her daughter could be stranded out here all night.

Faith had about decided to turn back when Charity abandoned her rock and skipped a ways up the road. At the crest, she cried, "I can see a house!"

As Faith scrambled to her feet, a wave of dizziness washed over her. The wedding gown that she'd been carrying under one arm slipped from her grasp and fell in the dirt.

"Oh, no!" Charity cried as she raced back to her mother. "Oh, Maman!" The child picked up the dress and brushed uselessly at the dirt stains. "Do you suppose you can wash it?"

It took a great deal of know-how to clean fine silk. "No, sweetness, I'm afraid it's ruined."

Faith almost tossed the dress away, but something stopped her. It was madness, she knew. The last thing she needed right now was a wedding dress. But crazy or not, she tucked the gown back under her arm.

As she followed Charity up the incline, her limbs felt oddly numb and leaden. Over the last three days, most of the morsels of food she'd found in the trash barrels had gone to her daughter. That was only as it should be, but now exhaustion and lack of nourishment seemed to be taking their toll. She had to force her feet to keep moving.

When they finally crested the rise, she stared stupidly at a large, two-story house surrounded by outbuildings and fences.

"We're there, Maman," Charity cried. "This must be it."

Even from a distance, the house looked in sorry need of repairs and paint. It wasn't what Faith had pictured. "Perhaps it's the caretaker's residence," she mused aloud, "similar to our servant quarters at home."

"I just hope you get the job and they feed us."

A few minutes later, when they reached the house, Faith could only stare in hopeless dismay. There were no other dwellings in sight to indicate that this was a caretaker's quarters. The rickety picket fence surrounded a yard littered with all manner of equipment, everything from rusty old plow rakes to discarded washboards.

"Can I help you?"

Faith nearly parted company with her skin at the sound of the man's voice. She blinked against the slanting sun, brought him into focus, and then just gaped. The man rounding the corner of the house was tall and muscular, with dark auburn hair, countless freckles muted by a lifetime in the harsh sun, and startling blue eyes. He looked to be in his twenties, possibly twenty-three or twenty-four, her senior by only one or two years.

When he came to a halt about five feet from the fence, his stance was that of a dock ruffian, hands resting at his lean waist, one hip cocked, his opposite leg bent at the knee. He wore faded denim pants and a blue work shirt patched at the elbows. The washworn clothing hugged his body, displaying the powerful breadth of his shoulders and bulging upper arms. In a rough and very earthy way, he was extraordinarily handsome, the kind of man Faith might have admired at a distance in the recent past, but not someone to whom she ever would have spoken.

"I, um—" Angry with herself for losing her train of thought, she swallowed and started over. "I'm looking for Mr. O'Shannessy."

"You've found him." His brilliant blue eyes met

hers, the directness of his gaze unsettling. "I'm Patrick
O'Shannessy." He looked past her at the road. Then
he cut a quick glance at Charity, who had pressed
close to Faith's skirts. "How'd you get here?"

"We walked, sir."

"All the way from town?" Incredulity laced his
voice. "Jesus H. Christ. Are you out of your mind,
lady?"

Faith's spine snapped taut. Before caution could still
her tongue, she said, "My good sir, with all due respect I will remind you that a child is present."

He gave her a bewildered look, prompting Faith to
add, "Your language. Some phrases are inappropriate
in the presence of a little girl." Or in the presence of
a lady, for that matter.

"My apologies." His thick auburn brows arched
high. Then he swiped a hand over his mouth. "Sounds
to me like you hail from some place back east."

"Brooklyn." Faith immediately wanted to bite her
tongue. The less this man knew about them, the better. There was no doubt a large and very attractive
reward being offered by her father for information
about her and Charity's whereabouts.

"Brooklyn, New York?" When she nodded, he said,
"You're a long way from home. What exactly can I
do for you?"

"I saw your advertisement at the mercantile."

"I'll be damned. I had about given up on that. Are
you experienced?"

Faith felt confident that she could learn to do almost
anything. "I am, most certainly." It was only half a
lie. She had supervised housekeepers, after all.

"I was hoping to find someone older."

"What I lack in years I make up for in knowledge
and skill, Mr. O'Shannessy."

"It isn't that." He hooked a thumb over his shoulder at the house. "I'm a bachelor. I'm not sure how
it would work with you living here. I sure as hell don't
plan to sleep in the barn in order to keep tongues
from wagging."

Faith was encouraged to learn that he even recognized the impropriety of such an arrangement. His language was appalling. In Brooklyn, the gentlemen cursed only while in the company of other gentlemen.

Patrick took thoughtful measure of the woman and her kid. Ever since his sister, Caitlin, had married Ace Keegan two years ago and moved to the neighboring Paradise Ranch, he'd been in desperate need of a housekeeper. For several months after Caitlin's marriage, he'd convalesced from a bullet wound in his back, and then, after regaining his strength, he'd spent most of his waking hours trying to get his ranch back on its feet. In a nutshell, he was tired of working himself into an exhausted stupor only to come in at night to a dirty house and no food on the table.

He'd been advertising for help for almost a year, hoping that a stocky, no-nonsense widow might apply for the job. Never in his wildest dreams had he pictured a beautiful young woman like this. She had a wealth of curly dark hair, some of which had escaped from its pins to trail like dribbles of hot fudge over her slender shoulders. Even worse, she had large, pleading brown eyes that he found irresistibly appealing.

"I'm sorry," he said, trying to gentle the words with a smile, "but I don't think you're right for the job." She looked ready to drop in her tracks. He couldn't see her milking the cows of a morning or managing to carry the brimming five-gallon buckets back to the house. "I need someone with a little more bulk."

Her small chin came up. "I'm stronger than I look, Mr. O'Shannessy." A telltale quiver attacked one corner of her soft mouth. "You shan't regret hiring me."

Her fancy speech alone was enough to make him run in the opposite direction. *Shan't?* Nobody hereabouts talked like that.

"I'm sorry," he repeated, trying to avoid looking at the child. He felt terrible about turning them away. "I need an older woman."

She finally nodded. "Very well. I apologize for taking up your time."

Patrick was about to offer them a ride back to town when all the starch suddenly left the woman's spine. The next second, she crumpled like a rag doll, hitting the weed-pocked dirt in a limp sprawl.

Bracing a hand on the fence, Patrick vaulted over the pickets. "Lady?" He dropped to his knees beside her. The little girl started to cry, a shrill, broken wail that made his ears ring. "Jesus," he whispered as he felt the woman's wrist for a pulse. "It's okay," he told the child. "She's just fainted."

"Maman!" the child sobbed, tugging on her mother's sleeve. "Maman, wake up. Please, wake up!"

Maman? Mother and child were ducks out of water in a place like this. Patrick lightly tapped the woman's cheeks, hoping to revive her. Not even a flutter of lashes rewarded his efforts. "Get back," he ordered the child as he lifted the mother into his arms.

She weighed little more than a child herself, he thought. Her head lolled over his arm, exposing the delicate arch of her throat. He tried to shift his hold to support her neck, but it was like trying to juggle a limp rag, and no matter how hard he tried, his hands seemed to find feminine softness better left untouched.

Angling sideways to get through the gate, Patrick carried his burden toward the house, the child wailing at his heels. Once inside, he hurried up the hallway that bisected the first floor, his goal the kitchen at the rear.

Once there, he rested the woman's rump on the edge of the table and cleared the surface behind her with a sweep of one arm, sending his breakfast plate and coffee mug clattering to the bare planked floor.

"Quiet!" he barked at the child, his voice much harsher than he intended. He tipped the mother over onto her back and winced when her head struck the wood with a loud *thunk*. "She's going to be fine, sweetheart. She just fainted, is all."

"Maman never faints."

"It's a long way from town in the heat of the afternoon," he mused aloud. He'd seen strong men pass out in the fields when they worked too long under the hot summer sun. "We'll get some water down her. That'll probably bring her around."

"She's hungry, too," the little girl revealed brokenly. "She's been giving all the garbage she finds to me."

Patrick's heart caught. He gave the child a horrified look, hoping to God he'd misunderstood her. "Garbage, did you say?"

The child nodded, her dark curls bobbing. "Someone stole all our money while we were sleeping at a stage station. All Maman has left is a penny they missed at the bottom of her reticule. She's been trying to find a position of gainful employment ever since we arrived in No Name, but there are no jobs."

The child used words twice as big as she was, her eastern twang sounding strange to Patrick's ears. "Where on earth have you been staying?"

The little girl blinked her huge brown eyes and swallowed convulsively. "We've been sneaking into the livery stable to sleep in the hay. Maman hid our satchels under an overturned trough out back."

Patrick almost let fly with another "Jesus H. Christ." He managed to hold his tongue and said instead, "You'll find some corn bread in the warmer and some milk in the icebox, honey. Get yourself something to eat while I tend to your ma."

The child cast an anxious glance at her mother.

"She's going to be fine," Patrick assured her with far more confidence than he felt. "Before you've finished eating, she'll be awake and right as rain, I'll wager."

"Are you quite certain?" the child asked in a quivering voice.

The woman's pallor concerned Patrick, and her pulse felt weak and irregular. "I'm pretty certain. Mind what I say, now. You need to get some food in your belly. I can only care for one fainting lady at a time."

The child licked her lips and glanced hungrily around the kitchen. "Where's the warmer?"

The question brought Patrick's head up. Had she never seen a kitchen? "The top shelf of the stove."

She turned to stare at the old cooking range.

"There's a stool in the corner," Patrick told her as he unfastened the woman's collar. "You can use it to climb up. And mind you, don't go spilling the milk. You'll find a clean glass there in the cupboard to the right of the sink."

The little girl made short work of dragging the stool across the floor. While she fetched the corn bread, Patrick unfastened the woman's threadbare gown to mid-chest, trying his best to ignore the swell of her breasts above the lacy chemise and the flawless ivory of her skin. No luck. It wasn't every day that he found himself partly disrobing an unconscious female, after all. Suddenly all thumbs, he placed a cool, damp cloth at the base of her slender throat and pumped a glass of water to moisten her parched lips.

Her cheeks bulging with bread, the child asked, "And where, pray tell, is your icebox, sir?"

A recent addition to the outdated kitchen, the icebox sat in plain sight at the end of the counter. Patrick gave the little girl another wondering look. The drab and worn condition of her clothing indicated to Patrick that she and her mother were poor, not members of the pampered upper class who supped at fine tables on food prepared by servants.

After directing the child to the icebox, Patrick returned his attention to his patient. Her pallor alarmed him, and he wished now that he'd thought to ask her name. If the worst happened, he would have to contact her relatives back east and arrange for someone to come fetch the child.

"What's your name, honey?" he asked the little girl.

Her rosebud mouth ringed with milk, she stared at him with wary eyes. "Charity," she finally revealed.

Patrick offered her a smile. "My name is Patrick, Paddy to my friends. My last name is O'Shannessy." He let that hang there for a moment. Then he asked, "What's yours?"

She pursed her lips. "I'm not allowed to say, sir."

"Not allowed to tell me your last name?" He gave a low laugh. "Why not?"

"Because we've run away."

"Run away?" The phrase filled his mind with memories that he had tried very hard to forget. "Who are you running away from?"

"My grandfathers. My papa passed away two years ago, and they are trying to make Maman get married again to a perfectly awful man. He has a nasty disposition, and he quite dislikes me. When Maman discovered that he had enrolled me in a boarding school far away from Brooklyn and planned to keep me there all year long, she decided we had to leave." The child shrugged and nibbled her lower lip, the glass of milk clutched to her narrow chest. "One night when everyone was asleep, she sneaked me out of the house, and we embarked on our journey here."

"In servants' clothing," he guessed aloud.

Charity nodded. "It's not as if she *stole* the clothing. She replaced everything she took with garments of ours, which were much finer. I'm sure the upstairs maid and her little girl were delighted when they awakened the next morning."

"I imagine they were."

The picture forming in Patrick's mind wasn't pretty. In Colorado, a young woman was still occasionally coerced into marrying a man not of her choosing, but for the most part, such archaic marital arrangements were a thing of the past.

Charity dimpled her cheek in a mischievous grin. "I doubt that Grandfather Maxwell, Maman's papa, was very pleased, though. Maman emptied all his household coffers before we left."

Patrick chuckled, then returned his attention to his patient. When he trickled some water into her mouth, she choked and moaned.

"How on earth did you end up here?" he asked.

"We hoped to reach a place called San Francisco, but when our money was stolen, we couldn't go on."

San Francisco was the devil's lair for impoverished young women, especially beautiful ones. In Patrick's estimation, it was probably a blessing in disguise that they had been robbed and ended up stranded in No Name.

"Now," the little girl added forlornly, "we are without resources and have nowhere to go."

Patrick didn't consider himself to be an overly charitable man, but he wasn't so coldhearted that he could turn away an impoverished young mother and child. Tomorrow he'd go into No Name to retrieve their satchels. While he was there, he would visit the community church. Surely there was a respectable family in town that needed a housekeeper.

Chapter Three

*F*aith drifted slowly awake to the morning sunlight. After blinking her surroundings into focus, she was startled to discover that she was abed in a strange room. There were feminine touches—lace curtains at the windows, an ornate hurricane lamp on the bedside table, and tatted lace doilies on the battered surfaces of the dresser. An old, scarred armoire loomed like a dark specter in one corner of the room.

Faith pushed slowly to a sitting position. Her head spun sickeningly, and she pressed a trembling hand to her throat. Where was she? More important, where was her daughter?

Memory of the previous day came rushing back to her. *Patrick O'Shannessy.* She recalled his saying that she wouldn't suit for the housekeeping position. After that, she had no memory at all.

She trailed a hand from her throat to her upper chest and gasped in dismay. She wore only her chemise. Her gown, pantalets, and corset had vanished. Appalled, she pulled the faded coverlet taut over her bare legs and cast a frantic look around the room in search of her clothing.

The faint sound of a child's laughter drifted to her ears. She swung out of bed, pushed to her feet, and promptly almost fell on her face. Putting a hand on the wall to keep her balance, she went to the armoire, where she found her missing garments hanging inside on the rod. The ruined wedding gown was nowhere in sight, but Faith had more pressing concerns at the moment, namely getting some clothes on.

Making her precarious way back to the bed, she grasped the bedpost for support while she dressed. Then she sat on the edge of the mattress to lace her kid boots, which proved to be more of a challenge. She was so light-headed that every time she leaned over she almost pitched to the floor.

"What in God's name are you doing?"

Faith glanced up. Patrick O'Shannessy loomed in the open doorway. This morning he wore a fresh pair of faded denim trousers topped by a green work shirt. The neck of the shirt hung open, revealing burnished chest hair and more muscle than a woman cared to see when at the mercy of a stranger.

"I am *en dishabille,* sir," she said with as much hauteur as she could manage. "A gentleman would refrain from entering my bedchamber uninvited."

"You're on dissa what?"

"En dishabille," she repeated. "In an improper state of dress."

"Ah." The corner of his firm mouth twitched. He ran an unsettling blue gaze over her as he rested a brawny shoulder against the doorjamb. "One thing I've never claimed to be is a gentleman."

Faith had determined that for herself the previous afternoon.

"And, beggin' your pardon, ma'am, but this bedchamber happens to be mine, not yours. If I want to enter uninvited, I reckon I can."

Faith had no ready comeback for that, either. The bedchamber did indeed belong to him. It was she who was the interloper. "That being the case, I shall collect my daughter and relieve you of our presence, Mr. O'-Shannessy." She ran trembling fingers up the front of her bodice to be sure it was properly fastened, the thought not far from her mind that it had undoubtedly been his strong fingers that had last touched the buttons. "I appreciate your generous hospitality and apologize for the imposition." She pushed weakly to her feet. "I must have swooned from the heat."

"I'm glad to see that you found your things." He pointed to a trunk at the foot of the bed. "I stowed the wedding gown in there." His gaze moved slowly over her. "It's a real pretty dress. You plannin' on using it anytime soon?"

"Using it?"

"Yeah, you know, to get hitched."

Hitched? She could only surmise that he referred to the institution of marriage. "Most assuredly not." She recalled the dirt stains all over the skirt. "And even if I were, the dress is ruined."

He frowned slightly. "It looked fine to me."

Faith seriously doubted that the dress would ever look fine again, but she chose to let the comment pass and concentrate on more imminent concerns, namely getting out of there. Despite her announcement that she intended to leave, he remained in the doorway, much like a huge tree that had put down roots.

"Do you always talk like that?" he asked.

"Like what?"

"Like you've got a bad case of the highfalutins."

Faith swayed and grabbed the bedpost. O'Shannessy was across the room in a beat. Instead of grasping her elbow as a gentleman might, he cinched a strong arm around her waist, his big hand splayed familiarly over her side, his thumb resting in unacceptably close proximity to the underside of her breast.

"Please, Mr. O'Shannessy, unhand me."

"Damned if I will. You're so weak you can barely stand." If anything, he tightened his hold. "Let me help you downstairs. You'll feel better with some food in your belly."

"I must collect my daughter and go. It's no short distance back to town."

"You're not going anywhere," he informed her as he half carried her toward the door. "The way Charity tells it, you have no place to go and no money to get there. I'll check around in town today to see if I can come up with a more suitable arrangement. If not, there's no denying that I need a housekeeper, and you clearly need a job. We'll have to iron out the wrinkles somehow."

Wrinkles? His thumb had found a resting place in the hollow just under her breast, the touch seeming to burn through all three layers of her clothing.

"I fear that I cannot work for you after all, Mr. O'Shannessy. You've no wife. I'm a widow. Gossip about such an arrangement would abound."

At the top of the stairs, he pulled her closer to his side. "Watch your step, darlin'. It's a long way to the bottom."

Try as she might, Faith couldn't bring the treads into clear focus. Terrified of falling, she knotted her right fist on the front of his shirt.

"I've got you," he assured her huskily.

He had her, all right. A hysterical giggle bubbled at the back of Faith's throat. "I truly can't stay here," she told him again.

"If no one else in town needs a housekeeper, what're your options? There are very few jobs for decent young women in No Name."

"I shall manage, Mr. O'Shannessy."

"Right. You'll end up working on your back to keep food in your daughter's mouth. Somehow I don't think you're cut out for that particular profession."

"On my back?" They reached the bottom of the stairs, at which point Faith hoped he might release her. Only, of course, he didn't. "I'm sorry. To what sort of work are you referring?"

"You know damned well what I mean," he said huskily. "You didn't find that child under a cabbage plant."

Scalding heat rushed to Faith's cheeks. For a moment she yearned to kick him, and then in the next she wanted to kick herself for asking such a stupid question. She was no innocent, fresh from the schoolroom. She was simply too addlepated at the moment to make sense of what he was saying.

His steely arm still locked around her, he stopped outside a door at the end of the hallway. After giving her a direct, searing look that completely unnerved her, he lowered his voice and said, "Gossip will definitely *abound* if you're reduced to that. Seems to me you'll be a lot better off staying here, the impropriety of it be damned."

She'd never had the misfortune to meet anyone so plainspoken and crass.

"You wouldn't last one night at the Golden Slipper," he went on relentlessly. "A fair half of the men who frequent the place are prospectors—rough, filthy fellows with little or no regard for the unfortunate females who service them. And what of Charity? Will you tuck her away in the armoire while you're entertaining? That's no way to raise a child."

Little black spots danced before Faith's eyes. Yesterday when she'd looked across the street at the saloon, she hadn't allowed herself to think beyond the foul-smelling men who swilled liquor inside the establishment. Now Patrick O'Shannessy's words had drawn a brutally clear picture of what would surely transpire if she returned to No Name and pushed through those swinging doors to seek employment.

"No," she said shakily. "No, never that."

"I hope to hell not. Charity's a sweet little thing. I'll check around to see if someone else needs a housekeeper. If not, you and the child can stay here."

He opened the door onto a roomy kitchen that apparently served as the dining area as well.

"Maman!" Charity bounced up from a scarred, hand-hewn table. "Oh, Maman!" The child raced across the room to clamp her thin arms around Faith's skirts. "I was ever so worried. Paddy promised that you'd come perfectly to rights, but you were so white and still last night when he put you to bed. I was beside myself with worry."

"Careful, sweetheart," Patrick warned when Charity hugged Faith's legs more tightly and swayed to and fro. "Your ma is pretty unsteady on her feet. Did you eat all the flapjacks? I think she'll feel better once she gets some grub in her belly."

Charity reared back to beam a smile. "I only ate three."

"Only three?" Patrick led Faith to a chair and gently lowered her to the seat. Before he released her, he leaned low to search her face. "You steady on, darlin'? I don't want you toppling off onto the floor."

Faith grasped the edge of the table to support herself. "I'm fine," she said, even though her head was still swimming and all her limbs quivered with weakness. Now that she was sitting down, at least her vision had cleared.

He left her to rattle about at the stove. It was an antiquated monstrosity that required wood for fuel. At home, gas ranges were all the rage. *Thank goodness it's not my worry,* she thought with some relief. A housekeeper's duties did not extend into the kitchen, a fortunate thing given the fact that she couldn't cook.

"How do you take your coffee?" he asked.

Faith generally preferred a nice cup of tea, but at the moment anything hot and wet sounded utterly divine. "With cream and sugar, thank you."

He came to the table, poured some cream from a small pitcher into a large blue mug, and then set himself to the task of chipping sugar from a block. Faith watched the process with some interest. At home, the sugar arrived at table in a dainty bowl.

"Here you go." He slid the mug toward her, handed her a spoon for stirring, and presented her with his broad back again as he returned to the stove. "How many eggs?"

Her stomach growled. "One, please."

He sent her a scolding look over his shoulder. "Ah, come now. Charity tells me you haven't eaten in days. Two, at least. Don't worry about running me low. The chickens are laying over a dozen a day right now."

"Two, then."

"Flapjacks?" He sent her another inquiring look. "I made a heap. They may not compare to the fancy breakfast fare you're used to, but they're delicious drowned in butter and warm honey."

At home, the pancakes were the size of a silver dollar. And how did he know that she was accustomed to fancier fare? "Six, please."

His eyebrow shot up. "Six?"

"Yes, please, if you've plenty."

"Let's start with three," he suggested. "I know you're hungry, and I'm happy to feed you, but I don't want you busting a gut."

Busting a gut? The expression almost made her shudder. "Does everyone in this vicinity talk the way you do?"

"Mostly. Amazing, isn't it? We're from the same country, but we speak different languages." He retraced his steps to the table, carrying a plate fairly heaped with food. "Here you go. Honey and butter are right in front of you."

"Oh, *my*." Faith stared in startled amazement at the three pancakes, which were nearly the size of the plate and half an inch thick. "I shall never be able to eat all this. The cakes at home are quite small. I had no idea."

He flipped a chair around and straddled the seat. Folding his arms over the back, he flashed her a slow grin that reminded her of just how handsome he was. "No worries. If you can't get 'em down, they'll make great hog slop."

Hog slop? Back home, such a phrase never would have been uttered at the table. For the moment, however, Faith was far too hungry to mind. With her first bite of flapjack, she nearly moaned. The honey and butter melted over her tongue, warm and sweet. She closed her eyes and went, "Mmm."

Watching Faith eat made Patrick wish he could have her in his bed, making those low sounds of pleasure. He immediately banished the thought. If there were no other housekeeping positions in No Name, he would have to hire her himself. Being a bachelor, he had physical needs that were rarely satisfied, and Faith was a tempting little swatch of calico, fragilely made but sweetly rounded in all the right places. If he allowed himself to entertain improper thoughts about her, he might eventually find himself trying to charm her out of those fancy bloomers he'd glimpsed last night.

Chapter Four

*F*aith was too weak to work that first day. Even with the hearty breakfast to rebuild her strength, her head went a little dizzy every time she stood up. After she'd enjoyed her morning repast, Patrick O'Shannessy ushered her to an old horsehair settee in the sitting room and insisted that she stay there.

"I can't lie about all day, Mr. O'Shannessy," she protested. "I must make myself useful to repay you for your kindness."

"We'll worry about paybacks tomorrow."

In Faith's experience, a wise woman never allowed herself to be indebted to a stranger, especially not one so virile and masculine. There was a hungry look in Patrick O'Shannessy's eyes that made her uneasy whenever his gaze settled on her.

He stepped over to an old cherry bookshelf. While he rummaged through the dusty tomes, Faith took stock of the room. Before the door lay a colorful braided rug that looked handmade. Most of the wall hangings looked handmade as well, dried flowers under glass and pretty ovals of needlepoint. The only exceptions were some family portraits that hung above a table near the hallway door, one of a small, pretty woman and a brawny older man who bore a striking resemblance to her rough-mannered host.

"Your parents?" she ventured.

Patrick glanced over at the likenesses. "My mother, yes."

"She's lovely," Faith said. And then, "Who is the man?"

He took so long to reply that Faith wondered if he had heard her question. "That's Connor O'Shannessy, my biological sire."

The cold hatred in his voice sent a chill chasing up Faith's spine.

"If I had another portrait of my mother," he added, "I'd burn that one so I'd never have to look at his face again."

Patrick O'Shannessy would see his father's face for the rest of his life whenever he looked into a mirror, Faith thought sadly. She trailed her gaze lower, to a portrait of two children—a girl, who looked to be the older, and a little boy with an impish grin and freckles.

"Is the other portrait you and your sister?"

His expression softened. "Yes. I was seven, or thereabouts. Caitlin is two years my senior, so she was about nine, maybe ten."

The warmth in his voice told Faith that he loved his sister very much. He straightened from the book-shelf and returned to the settee with a thick tome. His stride, Faith noticed, was distinctly masculine, his lean hips and muscular legs working together in an easy, undulating harmony of power and grace.

"Caitlin used to read to me from this book." He winked at Charity. "Have you ever heard 'The Emperor's New Clothes' or 'The Ugly Duckling'?"

Charity sat primly on the edge of the settee, tugging at the hem of her borrowed dress to cover her knobby knees. "Yes, but I'd enjoy hearing both again."

"There you go," Patrick told Faith as he handed her the collection of fairy tales. "Your day's work is cut out for you."

Moments after Patrick left the sitting room, Faith heard him rattling around in the kitchen. She glanced at her daughter. "Was Mr. O'Shannessy kind to you last night?"

"Very kind, Maman. He fixed me fried chicken and

spuds for supper, and for dessert he made chocolate gravy over biscuits."

"The proper term is 'potatoes,' dear heart."

"Paddy calls them 'spuds.' "

"Yes, well, Mr. O'Shannessy speaks like a dock ruffian. And one other thing, sweetie. Proper young ladies don't address gentlemen outside their family by their given names—or by their nicknames."

"But, Maman, he asked me to call him Paddy. He says my calling him Mr. O'Shannessy makes him feel older than Methuselah."

"Nevertheless, it's improper. Just because we've come to Colorado is no sign that we must abandon all semblance of propriety. Do you understand?"

Charity scrunched her nose. "I understand, Maman. It's just—"

Faith opened the storybook. "It's just what?"

The child sighed and rolled her eyes. "We're not in Brooklyn anymore, Maman. People are different here. If we're going to stay, we must try to be like everyone else. Otherwise, we'll never fit in."

Although Faith saw the wisdom in her daughter's observation, she was not yet prepared to abandon all the social mores drilled into her since childhood.

"Humor me," she said with a smile. "Perhaps after I've been here for a while, I'll no longer find terms like 'hog slop' and 'busting a gut' so offensive."

Charity giggled. It was a wonderful sound to Faith's ears, one that she hadn't heard in months. "That's just the way he talks, Maman. He doesn't mean to be offensive."

"I'm sure he doesn't," Faith conceded.

"I like him," Charity added. "He was ever so nice to me last night, and he took very good care of you."

Her cheeks going warm with embarrassment, Faith ran nervous fingertips down the line of buttons on her bodice.

"I'm glad that we came here," Charity said fervently. "Not to No Name, but *here,* to Mr. O'Shannessy's house."

"It sounds as if the two of you have become fast friends." Faith smoothed the yellowed pages of the book. "I do hope you remembered the need for discretion. We'll be in a fine pickle if your grandfathers somehow learn of our presence here and come to fetch us home."

Charity bobbed her dark head. "Oh, yes, Maman, I was very discreet. When he asked my last name, I told him I wasn't allowed to say. He was very understanding when I explained our situation."

The hair at the nape of Faith's neck prickled. When she searched her daughter's big, guileless brown eyes, her heart sank. Unless she missed her guess, Patrick O'Shannessy now knew far too much about them. Faith couldn't really blame Charity for that. She was an extremely bright child, but she was still only six years old. Children her age trusted a bit too easily and had a tendency to be loose-tongued with adults. And in all fairness, Faith hadn't been the soul of discretion herself. Yesterday when O'Shannessy had asked where they were from, she should have fabricated a clever lie instead of blurting out the truth.

Faith could only pray that the man could be trusted. Judging by the condition of his home, he was barely scraping out a living on this patch of land. A large monetary reward for information about two runaways might be very attractive to him.

A half hour later, Patrick O'Shannessy returned to the sitting room. His wavy auburn hair looked damp and had been slicked back from his face. He wore what Faith surmised was a dress shirt in these parts, white linen and open at the collar, the cuffed sleeves folded back over his thick, tanned forearms.

"I'll be taking off for town now," he informed them. "I put on some stew for supper tonight. The fire is low, but it might be a good idea to keep an eye on it."

"Of course," Faith assured him.

He drew a gold watch from his pocket. "I'll be four hours or so. You feelin' all right?"

Faith nodded. "Just a bit weak, Mr. O'Shannessy."

When their host had left the house, Faith and Charity adjourned to the kitchen to stand at the stove. Faith stared nervously at the pot. "I've never watched over a stew before."

Charity lifted her thin shoulders in a bewildered shrug.

Using a dingy pad, Faith removed the lid from the pot and peered in at the slowly bubbling concoction. "Mm, it smells like Cook's Irish stew."

"I miss Cook's stew. Don't you?"

"I do." Faith missed many things from home. She resettled the lid on the pot. "It looks fine to me. Here in a bit, perhaps I'll give it a stir or two."

"Just so, Maman. I can remember Cook stirring the stew now and again."

Three and a half hours later, Patrick was headed for home. He had managed to find Faith and Charity's satchels, which now rode saddlebag fashion behind him over the rump of his horse, but his trip to town had been fruitless otherwise. He'd spoken to the pastor at the community church, and so far as the man knew, no one in No Name was in need of a housekeeper. There were no other respectable positions of employment available for a young woman, either.

It seemed that Patrick had himself a new housekeeper. And wasn't that a fine kettle of fish? Every time he looked at the woman, his mouth went to watering. She was a beautiful female, make no mistake— one of the prettiest that he'd ever seen. How in the hell was he going to rub elbows with her, day in and day out, and manage to keep his hands to himself?

In his thoughtless and drunken younger years, Patrick would have solved his dilemma with a Saturday-night visit to the upstairs rooms of the saloon, but now that he was older, his conscience bothered him if he even thought about it. That left him only one option: taking lots of midnight swims in the ice-cold creek near his house. Somehow that solution didn't strike him as being very appealing.

"I hope you fine ladies like stew," Patrick O'Shannessy said that evening as he ladled up servings from the cast-iron pot that Faith had watched over all afternoon. "It's one of the few things I can leave unattended for long stretches."

Faith was just relieved that the concoction wasn't ruined. She'd stirred it several times over the course of the afternoon, but beyond that, she hadn't known what to do. As a child, she'd always gotten a scolding when she ventured into the kitchen, and as an adult, she'd trespassed on Cook's domain only to discuss the weekly menu. As a result, the goings-on in a kitchen were completely beyond her ken.

At her host's insistence, Faith had taken a seat at the table with her daughter and was waiting to be served. She felt much stronger after resting for several hours. "We quite like Irish stew," she told him. "At home we often had stew for lunch on cold winter days."

He chuckled. "I can't be sayin' if it's Irish or not." With a shrug of his broad shoulders, he added, "Although I suppose that's a good bet. It's my grandmother's recipe, and she was about as Irish as they come." He sent them a twinkling glance. "Straight from the old country, with fiery red hair and a temper to match."

"Ah," Faith said with a smile, "now I know where you got your coloring, Mr. O'Shannessy. Have you her temper as well?"

"I do, I'm afraid. It was a curse in my younger years. Now that I'm older, I've learned to keep a lid on it. For the most part, anyway."

Faith was glad to hear it. A man of Patrick O'Shannessy's stature would be intimidating in a temper. His hands were large and calloused from hard work and every inch of his lofty frame looked to be roped with muscle.

"I threw together some corn bread, too. Nothing fancy, but at least it'll fill your hollow spots."

"Words cannot express my gratitude for your kind generosity, Mr. O'Shannessy."

"No need to say thank you. As of tomorrow, it looks as if you'll be taking over as housekeeper. I talked to the preacher and everyone else I could think of. There are no other positions available."

Faith wasn't surprised to hear that. She folded her hands tightly in her lap. "Are you certain that you wish to hire me? In the beginning, you didn't seem to think that I would suit."

As he came to the table with filled bowls for her and Charity, he said, "Like I said this morning, we'll iron out the wrinkles somehow." When he returned a moment later with a dish for himself and a pan of bread piping hot from the oven, he added, "I'll just be needing to know how many wrinkles we're likely to encounter."

Faith met his gaze. "Pardon me?"

He propped his elbows on the table, tented his forearms over his bowl, and rested his chin on his folded hands. His regard was searching and steady. "I get the impression that you and Charity come from pretty wealthy folks. That being the case, I can't help but wonder about your experience. You wouldn't be the first person to stretch the truth a little in order to land a job."

Faith raised her chin. "Are you accusing me of lying, Mr. O'Shannessy?"

He arched his burnished brows. "I'm asking if you have, no insult intended. If you don't know how to do something, you'd best tell me now."

Faith had every confidence that she could sweep floors, polish furniture, and change bed linen. "Keeping a house isn't that difficult. If you'll leave me a list of the tasks you wish done tomorrow, I shall endeavor to complete them to your satisfaction."

He studied her for a long moment. Then he nodded and began eating his meal. Faith had just taken her first bite of stew and was about to compliment him on its fine flavor when he said, "It's glad I'll be to have you take over. I'm damned tired of eating stew and fried chicken. I can make a few other things, but overall, those are my two specialties." Catching Faith's appalled expression, he paused with his spoon halfway to his mouth. "You do know how to cook? That's one of the main reasons I need a housekeeper. During fair weather, I work from dawn 'til dark. Any time I waste in here, trying to rustle up grub, is time I should spend outdoors."

Faith struggled to gulp down the bit of meat and potato in her mouth. She felt her daughter's startled gaze fixed on her face. Cheeks burning, she searched for something to say.

In Brooklyn, there had been a clear delineation between the duties of the cook, who reigned in the kitchen, and the housekeeper, who reigned over the rest of the household. "I'm rather surprised, Mr. O'-Shannessy. In my experience, a housekeeper need not be well versed in the culinary arts."

He smiled slightly. "What kind of arts?"

"Cooking, Mr. O'Shannessy. Housekeepers in Brooklyn are not expected to cook."

"You're having me on, right?"

"I am completely serious. When I applied for this position, I did so with the understanding that someone else would do the cooking."

"Does that mean you don't know how to cook?"

Faith's stomach felt as if it had dropped to the region of her ankles. She desperately needed this job. If Patrick O'Shannessy sent them packing, Charity would soon be eating from trash barrels again.

Surely, Faith reasoned, she could learn her way around a kitchen. At home, Cook had kept books filled with recipes in a cupboard. Patrick O'Shannessy must as well. Had he not said that the stew recipe was his Irish grandmother's? That had to mean that the ingredients and instructions for preparing the stew were recorded somewhere.

"Of course I can cook." Even to Faith's ears, her voice sounded strained and high-pitched. "It's a fairly simple thing. Is it not?"

"My sister, Caitlin, makes it look simple." He buttered a square of bread. "She can toss any old thing in a skillet, and it comes out tasting good."

Exactly so, Faith assured herself. Mankind had been preparing food for centuries. If others could master the art, she certainly could. All she needed were some recipe books to guide her.

They finished the meal in silence. Then Faith's new employer said, "I'll tidy up the kitchen. You have a long day ahead of you tomorrow. I normally eat breakfast at four thirty. You'll have to be up before then to get the meal on the table. You should turn in early and rest."

"I'm feeling much stronger tonight," Faith protested.

"Probably because you rested all day." He pushed to his feet, ruffled Charity's hair, and said, "Upstairs with the both of you. There isn't much of a mess. I'll take care of it."

Faith had been taking orders from men all her life. She rose and held out a hand to her daughter. "Will you make out a list of my duties for tomorrow, Mr. O'Shannessy?"

"No problem. I'll leave it here on the table."

Chapter Five

"*M*aman, why did you tell him you know how to cook?"

Faith tucked the faded quilt in around her daughter and sank onto the edge of the bed with an exhausted sigh. "You heard him, Charity. If he discovers I know nothing about cooking, he may send us away."

The child pursed her bow-shaped mouth. "But, Maman, what will you fix him for breakfast?"

"Eggs and flapjacks," Faith said brightly.

"Do you know how to make flapjacks?"

Faith bent to kiss the child's forehead. "How difficult can they be? There are surely recipe books somewhere in the kitchen. I'm quite capable of reading instructions. I shall manage well enough."

"He didn't look in a book when he made flapjacks this morning. And I saw no books when he was opening the cupboards."

A tingle of alarm raised goose bumps on Faith's skin. "You didn't?"

With a glum expression on her face, Charity shook her head. "Whatever shall you do, Maman?"

Faith thought for a moment. Then she drew a bracing breath, smoothed her daughter's hair, and forced a smile. "It's not for you to worry about. I shall manage, dear heart. Flapjacks are simple fare. I'm certain that I can throw some flour and milk together with a pleasing enough result."

Charity shook her head. "No, Maman, he put in a lot of other stuff."

"What kind of stuff?"

"An egg." Charity's brows drew together in a frown. "And some drippy stuff in a tin that he keeps on top of the warmer. I think it was grease."

"The warmer? Where, pray tell, is that?"

"The stove shelf above the burner plates. The heat from the oven keeps it warm up there. He heats his bread and stuff there."

Faith filed that information away for later. "Can you recall what else he used to make flapjacks?"

"Sugar. And some white powdery stuff he called saleratus."

"Saleratus?" Faith had never heard of it. "Oh, my. Flapjacks, it would seem, are going to be more difficult to make than I hoped."

Charity sat up and hugged her knees. Her white gown, fashioned of fine lawn, boasted delicate embroidery around the ruched collar and across the bodice. In order to disguise their identities, Faith had been forced to leave all their outer clothing behind, but she had felt it was safe for them to keep their own undergarments and nightgowns.

"I shall help you in the morning, Maman. Perhaps I can remember how he made the flapjacks."

As reluctant as Faith was to involve her daughter in this deception, she could see no alternative. Their survival hung in the balance. Patrick O'Shannessy was expecting a hearty breakfast the next day, and a hearty breakfast he would get. Once the first meal was behind her, she could search for his recipe books. They had to be somewhere. If not, she was in big trouble.

"We shall have to be up and about quite early," Faith mused aloud.

Charity nodded. "I can't imagine eating at four thirty. It'll still be dark."

Faith lifted her palms in a bewildered shrug. "It's a puzzle to me as well. But he was very clear about the time."

* * *

Faith slept fitfully and was fully awake at three o'clock in the morning. After she figured out how to light the infernal lantern in her bedchamber, she performed her morning ablutions, shivering in the chill air. Brooklyn summers could be unpleasantly warm at times, but there was seldom such a drastic drop in temperature at night. Here in Colorado, the sun baked the earth all afternoon, but the moment it dipped behind the Rockies, a frigid coldness took hold.

Once downstairs, Faith once again struggled to light a lantern. Then she set herself to the unfamiliar task of building a fire in the horrid old range. When she had finally nursed the flames to life, she was able to search the cupboards for recipe books. She found none.

Trepidation mounting, she advanced on the table to peruse the list of tasks that her employer had left for her. *Milking* headed the lot. Faith frowned. Surely he didn't expect her to milk his cows. She smiled at the absurdity and read on. The second duty was almost as bewildering. *Gather eggs.* Hmm. Any fool knew that chickens laid eggs. But where, precisely, did his domestic fowl deposit their offerings? Undoubtedly in one of the ramshackle outbuildings, she decided. She could surely locate the eggs without much difficulty.

Smiling with renewed confidence, she read on. *Breakfast.* She had already anticipated that edict. The next task set her to frowning, however. *Skim cream.* What exactly did he mean by that? *Make butter.* In parentheses, he'd noted that he liked his butter salted. *Slop hogs.* Faith suddenly felt a bit breathless. The words began to swim, and her head started to hurt.

Feeling cold all over, she sat in stunned disbelief for a full minute. He actually expected her to consort with barnyard beasts. He was out of his mind, she decided. And in her desperation, she was even crazier, because she was actually contemplating the possibility.

"Good morning, Maman."

Faith jumped so violently that she almost fell off

the chair. "Charity!" She clamped a hand over her heart. "Don't creep up on me like that."

"I'm sorry, Maman. I heard you get up. I thought I'd come down to help."

Faith had a bad feeling that she was going to need more help than her small daughter could provide.

"What's wrong, Maman?"

As a rule, Faith tried never to burden Charity with adult concerns, but she'd been caught in a decidedly weak moment. "I've been going over Mr. O'Shannessy's list. He expects me to milk the cows and feed the pigs."

Charity's eyes widened. "Surely not. Ladies don't do such things."

"It's different here, I'm afraid. I'm beginning to realize that learning to cook is the least of my concerns."

Charity stood at Faith's elbow and stared at the list. "What else does it say, Maman?"

Faith swallowed, hard. "After I milk the cows, I must skim the cream and make butter."

Charity's eyes grew even rounder. "How does one make butter?"

Faith had only ever just spread the stuff on hot bread. "I believe it's made in a churn."

"Out of what?"

"Cream." Which Patrick O'Shannessy expected her to collect from a cow.

"Perhaps we can find the churn."

First, Faith had to catch the cows and convince the huge beasts to give over their milk. In that moment, she accepted that she didn't have what it took to be Patrick O'Shannessy's housekeeper.

"It's no use, darling." Faith struggled to keep her mouth and chin from trembling. "Your maman is hopelessly inept, I'm afraid. That being the case, we shall have to leave. We cannot expect Mr. O'Shannessy to feed and shelter us out of the goodness of his heart."

"Where will we go, Maman?"

"Back to No Name. I shall apply for a job at the saloon."

"What sort of work will you do there?"

"I shall be a dancing girl," Faith replied shakily.

Charity beamed a smile. "That is *perfect,* Maman. You've always loved to dance."

Patrick half expected to find his housekeeper still abed when he got up the next morning. He was pleasantly surprised when he heard sounds of activity downstairs. He smiled at himself in the shaving mirror as he sloshed water from the pitcher into the bowl. *A housekeeper.* He was going to enjoy having hot meals on the table again. Yet another luxury would be clean clothes.

When Patrick hit the bottom of the stairs, he sniffed the air, expecting to smell breakfast cooking. *Nothing.* Frowning, he entered the kitchen and stopped dead in his tracks. Faith stood by the table. The two satchels that he'd fetched from town yesterday sat at her feet. Charity was nowhere to be seen.

"Mr. O'Shannessy," she said in that hoity-toity way of hers. In the space of twenty-four hours, her strange accent had started to grow on him. "I am tendering my resignation."

Patrick closed the door and leaned against it. Most times, folks in Colorado just threw down their hats and said they were quitting. How like her to find a fancy way to say it.

"What brought this on? As of last night I thought we had agreed that you'd be staying."

"I'm afraid I've misrepresented myself." She held up a hand to stop him from interrupting. "In my defense, I must say it was unintentional. In Brooklyn, housekeeping is a far different undertaking than it is here."

"I see." He had suspected as much. Faith had "fine lady" written all over her.

She pushed at her hair. Black soot streaked her delicate wrist. "I have never milked a cow or slopped hogs, I've never skimmed cream or made butter, and I don't really know how to cook. With recipe books, I'm sure I could learn, but I searched your kitchen, high and low, without finding any."

"I cook from memory, a little of this and a little of that."

She nodded regally. Then with a lift of her hands, she said, "So there you have it. Charity and I must be on our way. I am ever so grateful for your kindness. I only wish I had the experience you require in a housekeeper."

A strange, achy sensation filled Patrick's throat. From the first instant he'd clapped eyes on Faith, he'd felt attracted to her. Now the feeling had intensified and become something more, something that he couldn't readily define. He knew only that she was beautiful and that her sense of fair play touched him deeply.

"You can't leave, Faith. Where will you go? What will you do?"

"That is not your concern, Mr. O'Shannessy. I shall manage somehow."

It was sheer madness, but he couldn't let her go. He knew where she would end up. Five years from now, she'd be old before her time, the innocence in her eyes shattered by one awful experience after another. Even worse, Charity would suffer as well.

"I can't let you do this."

She brushed at her cheek. "You're very generous." Her eyes luminous in the lantern light, she searched his gaze for a moment. "You frightened me when I first saw you. You have the air of a dock ruffian about you."

"Do I, now?"

She smiled. "You do, Mr. O'Shannessy. Having met you and come to know you this little while, I shall never again judge a man's character by the outward trappings."

"Thank you. That's a fine compliment."

"Sincerely meant, I assure you."

Patrick pushed away from the door. "So how's about staying and letting this dock ruffian teach you how to cook and milk a cow?"

She shook her head. "I've far too much to learn. In order to remain here, I need to feel that I'm earning our keep. It wouldn't be fair to you otherwise."

"So you'll go back to No Name and end up at the Golden Slipper? You've no idea what awaits you there, Faith. Men will use you as if you're nothing, and they'll never look back. In exchange for a coin, you'll sell your soul, not once but a dozen times a night. The next morning, the saloon owner will take half your wages. You'll earn just enough to survive, but never enough to leave. And one day soon you'll feel so used up and exhausted you'll no longer care."

Her face drained of color. "Nevertheless, I cannot in good conscience prevail upon your kindness when I've nothing to give in return."

"You've everything to give. If you're going to prostitute yourself, damn it, do it here." Patrick had no idea where that had come from. He only knew that she was about to make the worst mistake of her life, and he couldn't allow it to happen. "I'll pay you a dollar a pop and take half your wages for your room and board. At least here, Charity will be safe."

"Are you asking me to become your paramour, Mr. O'Shannessy?"

That was a fancy term for it, and Patrick had no such intention. But for the moment, it was the only reason he could come up with to keep her there. "In the meantime, I can be teaching you all that you need to know about keeping my house. In time, after you've learned everything, we can renegotiate."

"So I'll only be your paramour temporarily?"

"Trust me, it's a better offer than you'll get at the Golden Slipper. And no one need ever know, either. When it comes time for you to leave, your reputation won't be in complete shreds, only a bit tarnished."

She nodded slightly, which gave Patrick reason to

hope. Then, her lovely eyes dark with shadows, she asked, "When you say no one need ever know, will that include Charity?" Her chin came up a notch. "I would very much like to maintain her high regard."

In that moment, Patrick almost leveled with her. She held herself so rigidly that he fancied she might shatter like fragile glass if he touched her. "Of course it will include Charity. She'll never know—or even guess that anything untoward is going on between us."

It was a promise Patrick felt he could keep, not because he considered himself to be the soul of discretion but because nothing untoward ever *would* occur between them. He'd told Faith yesterday morning that he'd never claimed to be a gentleman, and that was true. But he did have standards that he lived by, one of them being to treat women with respect. He'd broken that rule many times in his younger days, the crowning glory being two years ago when he had gotten too cozy with a whiskey jug. Carrying the guilt of that with him to the grave was, in his estimation, burden enough for any man to bear.

"I accept your proposal, Mr. O'Shannessy."

Acutely conscious of how greatly it pained her to say those words, Patrick searched her pale face, nodded, and moved away from the door. In as jovial a voice as he could muster, he rubbed his hands together and said, "Well, then!" She jumped as if he'd poked her with a pin. "Let's begin this arrangement with a cooking lesson, why don't we?"

All that day, Faith's stomach felt like a wet rag that gigantic hands were wringing out. While learning to mix flapjack batter, she could barely attend Patrick's instructions. Later, when he led her to the henhouse, she was so distracted that she barely even noticed the pecks of the chickens or the horrid green yuck on the eggs. When the hogs clambered into their trough as she poured slop from a bucket into their feeding chute, she didn't even flinch. In that moment, she al-

most wished the horrid beasts would break through
the wire and trample her to death.

Faith's employer kindly excused her from the milking that morning, saying she might be overwhelmed if
he threw too much at her the first day. As a result,
she was left to tidy the kitchen while he went to the
barn. She managed to heat water on the stove, and
then she and Charity experienced for the first time the
joys of washing, rinsing, and drying dishes.

"This isn't so bad, Maman."

Faith had to agree. Under any other circumstances,
she might have found the task relaxing. As it was, she
could think of little else but the coming night. Once
she visited Patrick's bedchamber, there would be no
turning back.

What have I done? In her wildest imaginings, Faith
had never dreamed she might come to this. She was
a *kept* woman now, the lowest of the low. Patrick O'-
Shannessy would expect her to warm his bed tonight,
and rightly so. That was their bargain, after all. And
no matter how she circled it, she knew she was extremely fortunate that he'd made the offer. Better to
suffer the attentions of one man than dozens.

I'm lucky, she kept telling herself. He was a handsome man, and he kept himself clean, donning fresh
clothes each morning and washing up several times a
day. His breath wouldn't smell of tobacco and whiskey, there was no grime under his fingernails, and for
all his rough manners, he seemed to be a kind man.

In her present circumstances, she should be grateful
that he even wanted her in his bed. She had it on
good authority from her late husband that she lacked
the voluptuous curves that pleased a man's eye. Harold had also given her poor marks as a lover, often
chiding her for an unsatisfactory performance. As
awful as that had been, she had lived through it.

And she would live through this as well, she assured
herself. After Charity fell asleep each night, she would
visit her employer's bedchamber, allow him to do his

business, and then creep back to her own room. Charity need never know, and perhaps one day, when Faith had put this place far behind her, she herself would be able to forget.

Chapter Six

*T*hat evening, after hearing Charity's prayers and reading the child to sleep, Faith crept down the hall to prepare for her last and most distasteful duty of the day. By the soft glow of a lantern and with shaking hands, she ran a cool cloth over her nude body. Waves of sick dread washed through her when she thought of Patrick O'Shannessy's hands following the path of the cloth, touching her in places only a husband should. *Oh, God.* She squeezed her eyes closed and prayed for strength.

It'll be over with quickly, she assured herself repeatedly as she pulled on a nightgown, spent an inordinate amount of time brushing out her hair, and dabbed perfume behind her ears. She would simply tap on his door, slip inside the dark room, and join him in his bed. When he'd grunted his last grunt and collapsed beside her in a pool of sweat, she would be able to return to her own room and hopefully find oblivion in sleep.

She could do this. For her daughter's sake, she *would* do this.

Patrick had just stripped off his shirt and loosened the top button of his Levi's when he heard a light tap on his bedroom door. Bewildered, he stepped across the room and cracked open the portal to find Faith in the hallway. Without a word, she pushed her way inside, cast a disgruntled look at the lighted lantern, and softly closed the door behind her.

In that moment, Patrick knew, beyond a shadow of doubt, that she was the most beautiful creature he'd ever clapped eyes on. Her hair fell almost to her waist in wavy ripples of sable. Her sleeveless shift, though modestly made, revealed just enough flawless ivory skin to make his heart pound like a sledgehammer.

Her lovely eyes almost black with shame, she whispered, "I am here."

For an instant, Patrick was sorely tempted to take what she offered. Only a strong sense of decency forestalled him. He retreated a step to put her beyond easy reach, rubbed a hand over his bare chest, and managed to choke out, "I'm sorry, honey, but I'm flat tuckered." He feigned a yawn. "Maybe tomorrow night."

She fixed him with an incredulous gaze. After staring up at him for several tense seconds, her eyes filled with tears. "It was never your intention to carry through with this, was it?"

"Shh," he countered. "Don't talk so loud. You'll be waking Charity."

Her chin started to quiver, and her mouth twisted. "It was a ruse to keep me here, nothing more."

The way Patrick saw it, he had two choices, either confessing the truth or taking her to bed. "You're not leaving," he warned, his voice still pitched low. "If that's what you're thinking, get it straight out of your head. If I have to tie you to the bedpost, you and that child are staying right here."

She cupped her slender hands over her face, and her shoulders started to jerk. For an instant, Patrick thought she was laughing. Then, to his horror, she dragged in a taut breath, making a sound like the shrill intake of a donkey right before it brayed. Awful sobs followed, the eruptions coming from so deep within her that he feared she would damage her insides.

"Faith," he tried. Then, "Sweetheart?" *Jesus H. Christ,* she was going to wake Charity. "Faith? Hey?"

She made the donkey sound again, more loudly this time.

"Shh," Patrick tried, to no avail. Not knowing what else to do, he gathered her into his arms and pressed her face against his chest to muffle the noise.

To his surprise, she went limp against him and continued to sob her heart out. Patrick had held his sister a few times while she cried, so he was no stranger to the ritual. He ran his hand into Faith's hair, tightened his hold on her, and whispered nonsensical words of comfort while swaying to and fro. She felt right in his arms, he realized, as if she'd been made to fit, her head hitting him at the hollow of his shoulder, her breasts nestling sweetly just under his ribs.

When she finally quieted, she gave an exhausted sigh, turned her head to press her damp cheek over his heart, and closed her eyes.

"You lied to me, Mr. O'Shannessy," she whispered.

"I'm sorry. It seemed like the thing to do at the time."

"No, no, I don't mean about that. You told me"— her voice went thin and shaky again—"that you weren't a gentleman."

Patrick mentally circled that. Before he could collect his thoughts to reply, she added, "You are, without question, a gentleman, sir—the finest that I've ever had the good fortune to meet."

Patrick didn't much care about how he stacked up as a gentleman. "Just say you'll stay here, Faith."

"It's unfair to you," she squeaked. "I'm completely useless, even"—broken sob—"at *this.*"

"At *this*?" Patrick wasn't sure what she meant.

"Yes. You know." She flapped a hand at the bed. "I'm not fleshy the way men like, and I am completely inept as a lover. Harold said so."

"Harold?"

"My late husband," she said with a sniff, prompting Patrick to fish in his pocket for a handkerchief.

"Here, sweetheart." When she took the square of cloth and gave it a peering look, he quickly added, "It's clean."

She blew her nose with far more daintiness than she had exhibited while crying, which made him smile. Of all the sounds he might have expected this lady to make, last on the list was the first half of a donkey bray.

After dabbing under her eyes, she hauled in a shaky breath, gulped, and cut him an embarrassed glance with tear-swollen eyes. "You must think me a complete flibbertigibbet."

"Nah." He thought she was far too beautiful for her own good, and possibly his as well. "I think you've been through a hell of a time and finally just sprang a leak. Everybody needs a good cry sometimes."

As he spoke, he led her over to sit on the edge of his bed. To his surprise, she slumped onto the mattress, let her head fall back, and sighed wearily as she closed her eyes. She was so lovely, even with swollen eyes and a puffy mouth, that it took all of his control not to touch her again.

"Everyone should have at least one talent," she whispered. "What is mine?"

Patrick curled his hands over his knees and bit down hard on his back teeth. He could think of several things she might be good at, but he refrained from naming them. "You helped make butter today. And you gathered eggs and slopped the hogs."

She smiled, straightened, and lifted her long, wet lashes to give him a wondering look that made his bones feel like pudding. "I did, didn't I?"

"Before you know it, you'll be a fine housekeeper." Forcing his mind to more practical concerns, Patrick considered the situation. "I'll tell you what. If you're really that concerned about this arrangement being fair to me, you can work without pay until you've learned how to do everything. In the meantime, you'll be helping out enough around here to earn your room and board."

Tears sprang to her eyes again.

"Don't cry." He'd always felt panicky when women cried. Why, he didn't know, but there it was.

She shook her head and blinked. "Normally I'm not given to weeping, Mr. O'Shannessy. It's just that you're such a surprise."

"Not a dock ruffian, after all?"

She smiled tremulously. "No, not a dock ruffian. How will I ever repay you for your kindness?"

Again, he could think of several ways, which he immediately banished from his mind. He had asked her to remain here to save her from lechery, not to subject her to it. "You can start by calling me Patrick. I don't much like my surname."

"Why ever not? It's a lovely surname."

The question sobered him and helped to get his mind off the way her breasts thrust against her shift. "It came from my father, and he was a bastard."

"There's so much pain in your voice when you speak of him. Whatever did he do to make you hate him so?"

Patrick chucked her under the chin and pushed up from the bed. "We can tell each other our life stories another time. It's late." He gave her a slow grin. "When there is time to talk, I'll be particularly interested to hear how you ended up married to a blind man."

"Harold wasn't blind."

"Oh, yes, he was, darlin', stone blind, and stupid to boot."

In the not so distant past, Faith never would have thought it possible for her to become friends with a man like Patrick O'Shannessy. But that was exactly what transpired over the next month. They met before dawn in the kitchen each morning to prepare breakfast, he the teacher, she the student, and always, always, the lessons were fun. Patrick showed her how to crack an egg using only one hand, a feat that she never mastered. He also tried to show her how to flip a flapjack high into the air. When Faith tried to do it, everyone dived for cover.

"Darlin'," he said after retrieving a half-cooked flapjack from the kitchen floor and tossing it into the slop bucket, "the idea is to land it in the skillet."

Faith wondered how he could expect her to learn much of anything when he always looked so distractingly wonderful. Freshly scrubbed and shaven, in clean jeans and a work shirt, with his wavy hair still damp from the washbasin, Patrick O'Shannessy was enough to make any female's heart skip beats. Sometimes when their hands accidentally touched, Faith's fingertips felt electrified. At other times, the husky timbre of his voice near her ear set her heart to pounding so loudly that she felt certain he might hear it.

After breakfast each morning, they adjourned outdoors, where Faith learned about the goings-on in a barnyard. Charity was not excluded during Faith's training.

"Someday, sweetheart, you'll need to know how to milk a cow," Patrick pronounced, and the next thing Faith knew, her little girl was sitting on a tripod. "Excellent!" Patrick said when Charity succeeded at the task. "I'll make a country girl out of you yet."

It was Faith who proved to be a slow learner. Unlike her daughter, city ways had been ingrained in her for a full twenty-two years. She trembled with fright the first few times she went near a cow. Eggs covered with green excrement made her gorge rise. The hogs intimidated her. And, after encountering a snake one afternoon, she ran into the house and refused to come out again.

"Honey, it was only a harmless garden snake," Patrick assured her.

"A snake is a snake is a *snake*!"

Faith couldn't gather the courage to go back outdoors until evening, whereupon Patrick schooled her in identifying serpents while they milked the cows. "The only dangerous snakes we have in these parts are rattlesnakes," he assured her, "and they're real good about warning you before they bite. Also bear in mind that they're more scared of you than you are of them."

Faith seriously doubted that. Even so, she found herself falling in love, not only with the man but with his ranch as well. Living with Patrick was like being released from prison. Back east, she'd had to concern herself with appearances her every waking moment. Ladies dressed in a certain way. Ladies walked in a certain way. Ladies spoke in a certain way. Rules governed every occasion.

In Colorado, Faith could forget all that, and she felt gloriously free for the first time in her life. She could go for long walks with her daughter to pick wildflowers in the heat of the day, unconcerned about the sweat that filmed her brow or the freckles that might appear on her nose. She could snort when she laughed. She could yell when she grew angry. She could even strip off her shoes and stockings to go wading in a stream without fear of reprisal.

To her surprise, she didn't mind the hard work that came with her newfound freedom. She felt a wonderful sense of accomplishment when each day was done. She actually liked to cook, once she got the hang of it. Making butter and cheese proved to be easy. She soon grew relaxed around the barnyard animals. And there was nothing so satisfying as to stand inside Patrick's home, feeling proud as punch because every room was sparkling clean.

That wasn't to say that she never made mistakes. One morning Patrick entered the kitchen in a shirt that hung from his torso in tatters. "Stub your toe when you were putting in the lye?" he asked.

Faith was horrified. She rushed across the kitchen, gathered some of the shirt material in her fingers, and gasped in dismay when it fell apart at her touch. "Oh, Patrick, I'm ever so sorry."

"No matter. I needed new shirts, anyway." He gave her a mischievous grin. "Tomorrow we'll go into town and buy some yardage." He glanced down at her

threadbare dress, his gaze lingering overlong on the
bodice. "It's high time that you and Charity had some
decent dresses, as well."

"But I can't sew!"

"You can learn."

True to his word, Patrick hitched up the wagon the
next afternoon, and off the three of them went to
town. En route, his arm frequently grazed Faith's,
scrambling her thoughts and making her acutely aware
of him on the seat beside her. Though she tried to
keep her gaze fixed straight ahead, she found herself
admiring his muscular forearms, displayed to best advantage by his rolled-back shirtsleeves, his thick, masculine wrists, and his large, capable hands.

What would it be like, she wondered, to have those
hands touching her?

"It's a gorgeous day, isn't it?"

Faith jumped with a guilty start and blinked the
countryside back into focus. "Yes, it's lovely," she
agreed.

He slipped her an amused glance that made her
wonder if he could somehow read her mind. The very
thought made her cheeks go hot with mortification.
Taking herself firmly in hand, she forced her mind
onto the shopping trip that lay ahead.

After purchasing the fabric, Patrick took Faith and
Charity for ice cream, a treat that Faith had despaired
of ever enjoying again.

"Yum!" Charity said as she licked her spoon. "I
could eat this all day."

Faith couldn't help but smile. "It is delicious. Thank
you, Patrick."

He glanced over just as she touched her tongue to
the ice cream perched on her spoon, and his eyes,
normally a deep, twinkling azure, went as hot as the
blue base of a flame. "You're welcome," he replied
in a gravelly voice.

Faith quickly broke visual contact, but not before

her hands went suddenly clumsy, causing her to drop her spoon on the floor. When she bent to retrieve it, Patrick did as well, and their heads bumped, making white stars flash before her eyes.

"Oh, damn, I'm sorry." He reached out to steady her, his hand curling over her upper arm. Faith jumped at his touch as if it had burned her. "Are you all right?"

Faith nodded, but in truth she was far from feeling all right. Being around this man wreaked havoc with her common sense. She wasn't a young girl, fresh out of short skirts and her hair still in pigtails. She'd been married for five long years and had hated every minute of it. The last thing she wanted was to be under a man's thumb again.

Only somehow she sensed it would be different with Patrick. The touch of Harold's hand had never set her heart to pounding. And to her recollection, he'd never made her laugh. More important, he never would have thought to buy her ice cream simply because she loved it.

"Let me get you a clean spoon."

Faith shook her head. "No, no. Thank you for offering, but I've had enough."

"But you've hardly touched it," he pointed out.

Faith felt a sudden need to escape the restaurant and get some fresh air. Luckily, Charity had gobbled down her ice cream with unbridled enthusiasm, and they were able to leave.

After paying their bill, Patrick joined them on the boardwalk. Her stomach jittery with nerves, Faith hurried Charity along in front of them, anxious to get back to the ranch where she might find some time alone to get her feelings sorted out. And sort them out she would. Her reactions to this man were beyond silly; they were downright ludicrous.

Up ahead of them, in front of the general store, there sat a large crate. As they drew closer, Faith saw that it contained puppies, darling little things with brown and white splotches and huge, floppy ears. A sign tacked to the side slats of the crate read, FREE TO A GOOD HOME.

"Oh, aren't they sweet?" Faith said.

Charity had long wanted a dog of her own. With a squeal of delight, she dropped to her knees and leaned over the crate. One of the puppies jumped up to lick the sticky remains of ice cream from the child's face. Charity laughed. "Oh, Maman!" she cried. "Please say I can have one. *Please?*"

"Oh, darling, I'm sorry. Perhaps one day soon."

Patrick gave Faith an inquiring look. "Why can't she have a pup now? There's plenty of running room out at my place. It'll give her a playmate."

Faith was stunned by the offer. "But a puppy must eat."

His lean cheek creased in a grin. "Yeah, I reckon so. Most dogs do."

"No, Patrick. You've already done so much."

Ignoring her protests, Patrick crouched beside Charity. "Which one do you want, sweet pea?"

"This one," Charity cried. "He likes ice cream."

Patrick nodded. "He's the boldest and friendliest, too. If I were doing the choosin', he's the one I'd pick. Gather him up."

"Truly?" Charity's eyes went wide with excitement and incredulity. She hugged the puppy close, beaming an adoring smile. "You mean he's mine?"

Patrick chuckled. "It'll be good to have a dog around the place. He'll be your responsibility, though. You'll have to bathe him and brush him and feed him. Dogs are a lot of work."

"I won't mind."

"Best go put him in the wagon, then," Patrick suggested.

As Charity scampered away, Faith blinked away tears.

"Don't cry," Patrick ordered. "I'd rather take a beating than watch you cry."

Faith gulped and wiped her cheek. "You've already

taken on two extra mouths to feed, Patrick." She almost added, *What are you trying to do, make me fall in love with you?* But she caught herself before the words escaped and settled for saying, "This is too much."

"Don't be silly. All kids should have a dog."

Three mornings later, Faith was upstairs putting fresh linen on the beds when she heard a feminine voice call out downstairs. "Hello? Faith? Hello? Is anyone home?"

By the time Faith got downstairs, Charity and her puppy, Spotty, were becoming fast friends with a lovely young woman who held a stack of papers and a wooden box clutched in her arms. The moment Faith saw the woman's red hair, she guessed her to be Patrick's sister, Caitlin.

"Hello," Faith said shyly as she entered the kitchen.

Caitlin set her burdens on the table and came across the room to grasp Faith's hands. "Ah, and now I understand! No wonder Patrick looks like a sick calf whenever he talks about you."

A sick calf? Faith smiled in bewilderment. In another twenty years, maybe she would understand all these people's odd sayings. "You must be Caitlin."

"I am." Placing a palm over her slightly swollen waist, she grinned impishly and added, "And this is Ace Junior. My husband says it's going to be a girl who looks just like me." She laughed and patted her tummy. "But we'll show him."

"Your husband wants a girl?"

"Ace says we need another female around the place," Caitlin said with a laugh. "Even my cat is a male."

After Charity's birth, Harold had entered the birthing chamber, given the baby only a cursory glance, and then informed Faith that she would be expected to do better the next time.

"Well, enough about the baby," Caitlin said with another chuckle. "Given half a chance, that's all I want to talk about. Patrick stopped by after your shopping trip the other day. I'm here to show you how to cut out shirt and dress patterns." She pointed to the stacks of folded paper on the table. "The latest fashions. Later today, my husband, Ace, or my brother-in-law, Joseph, will bring over my sewing machine. I'll teach you how to use it, and you can keep it here until you've replenished your wardrobes."

"Oh, I—" Faith gulped. "I've only ever done needlework. Seamstresses were hired to make our dresses."

Caitlin snapped her fingers. "Simple as pie. You'll see."

Faith wasn't so confident, but she was soon visiting with Caitlin around straight pins clenched between her teeth while they cut out pattern pieces on the kitchen table. It was Charity's job to lay table knives in strategic spots to hold the patterns and material anchored when Faith and Caitlin ran low on pins.

"I brought my recipes, too," Caitlin said as they worked. "I'll leave them here so you can copy them. There are extra cards in the box. Feel free to use as many as you like. When Patrick has a spare moment, you might ask him to make you a box to keep them organized. He made mine for me." Her eyes went soft with affection. "It was his birthday present to me one year. I've treasured it ever since. I never open it without thinking of him."

Faith smiled. "It was kind of you to come, Caitlin."

"Not at all. I've been *dying* to meet you." Caitlin glanced after Charity as the child scampered from the room with Spotty at her heels. "I wanted to see what sort of woman had finally managed to capture my brother's heart."

Faith stopped cutting to glance up. "Pardon me?"

"He's in love with you," Caitlin said simply. Her cheek dimpled in a smile. "Oh, he isn't quite sure about that yet," she said with a shrug. "Men never are, until it hits them square between the eyes."

"In love with me?"

Caitlin sobered and gave Faith a woman-to-woman look that spoke volumes. "My brother has suffered in ways you can't imagine," she said softly. "You can't force yourself to return his affection. I understand that. But I do hope you'll have a care for his feelings. He's seen enough hurt in his life."

Faith was so stunned by this revelation that it took her a moment to reply. "I am indebted to your brother in ways I can't begin to explain. I would never intentionally cause him pain."

Caitlin smiled and returned her attention to the patterns. "That's good enough for me." With a mercurial unpredictability that Faith was fast coming to realize was a part of Caitlin's personality, the pretty redhead launched into the story of how her marriage had come about. "The last man on earth I wanted to marry was Ace Keegan!" she said with a laugh. "It wasn't the best of beginnings."

"But you're happy now?"

"Deliriously happy," Caitlin said with another laugh. "I love him with my whole heart, and he loves me just as much. I honestly believe that Ace would lay his life down for me."

With a shrug, Caitlin changed subjects yet again and began giving Faith a summary on her recipes. "Just *don't*, under any circumstances, try the sauerbraten," she warned. "Right after Ace and I were married, I wanted to impress him and his brothers with something special. I can't remember who it was now, but one of them took a bite and spat the meat out on his plate, telling everyone else not to eat any more because it had gone bad."

Faith loved sauerbraten herself. She laughed until her sides hurt.

"I was crestfallen," Caitlin said with a sigh.

Ace arrived with the sewing machine right after they finished cutting out all the garments. When he entered the kitchen, Faith had cause to wonder if handsome men grew like weeds in Colorado. Keegan was as dark as Caitlin was fair, a tall, imposing figure of a man who wore a nickel-plated pistol on his hip and walked with a slight limp. He was, Faith decided, almost as handsome as Patrick.

"So you're the young woman who has my brother-in-law all moon-eyed," he said as he took Faith's hand in his. After giving her a bold once-over, he winked at his wife and said, "Pretty as a picture. That's one mystery solved."

Faith blushed. "You flatter me, sir."

Ace Keegan threw back his ebony head and laughed. "Not the first time, I'm sure, and it won't be the last." He encircled his wife's narrow shoulders with a strong arm. "How are you feeling, little mother?"

"I'm fine," Caitlin replied with a smile. "You worry too much. Pregnancy isn't a fatal disease, you know."

"I just don't want you to overdo."

"I won't." Caitlin shoved playfully at his chest. "Off with you now. Go pester Patrick while I show Faith how to operate my sewing machine."

That evening, Patrick invited Faith for a walk after supper. While Charity and her puppy raced off to explore, they walked in silence for a while, lost in their own thoughts. Faith's were centered on the man beside her. Was it true that he was developing an affection for her, as Caitlin had implied? And if so, was he thinking of asking her to marry him?

Faith had mixed emotions about the possibility. On the one hand, she was fearful of surrendering her life to someone again. But on the other hand, she had to admit that Patrick was like no other man she'd ever known. He seemed to genuinely enjoy her company, for one thing, and she truly enjoyed his. He had a way of making her laugh when she least expected it, and she looked forward to their suppertime conversations, which usually began over the meal and continued as they cleaned up the kitchen together after Charity was in bed.

"Do you remember that night when you came to my room, and I said we'd have to share the stories of our lives sometime?" he suddenly asked.

Jerked from her reverie, Faith sent him a bewildered look.

"I've grown very fond of you in the time you've been here," he said candidly. "At this point, I don't know where that may lead, or if it will even lead anywhere. But I think it's time for you to know a little more about me."

Faith felt she already knew all the things about Patrick that really mattered—that he was good and kind and generous.

His voice thick with emotion and sometimes taut with anger, he began by telling her about his father. "Wasn't a day went by that Caitlin or I didn't get the back of Connor O'Shannessy's hand," he said gruffly. "And when a cuffing was the worst of it, we felt damned lucky. All during my childhood, he was workin' his way toward the bottom of a bottle. He wasn't a happy drunk, to put it mildly. Mean as a snake, more like."

"Oh, Patrick."

He shrugged and gazed off at the darkening horizon as they walked along. "Many was the time that I crept out from my hiding place when he was tearing hell out of the house in search of Caitlin. For reasons I've never to this day come to understand, he preferred to beat on her rather than me."

"You took the beatings in her stead?"

"Don't go growin' a halo around my head. After he died, I adopted his ways. Started drinking myself stupid and flying into rages. The last time I got drunk, I struck my sister. Slapped her across the face and knocked her clear off her feet."

Faith saw the aching regret in his eyes.

"Caitlin has forgiven me, and I pray that God has, but I'll never forgive myself. All she ever did to deserve it was love me."

Driven by compassion and a need to offer comfort, Faith reached to grasp his hand. "We all do things that we regret," she assured him.

His throat convulsed as he struggled to swallow. Then he hung his head, saying nothing for several paces. "Things went wrong in my head for a while, Faith. That's no excuse, but it's the only way I know to explain so you can understand."

He fell quiet again, as if trying to sort his thoughts. When he finally resumed speaking, his voice had gone hollow. "When I was only a little tyke, a family named Paxton came west and settled on a tract of land that adjoined ours. The man, Joseph Paxton, Senior, had paid good money for the parcel and had the papers to prove it. My father and others refused to recognize the validity of Paxton's deed and ordered him off the land. Paxton was a peaceful man, not given to fighting. He started packing his family up to leave.

"It was a swindle, plain and simple, perpetrated by my father and his friends. When one of them got shot in the back, they accused Paxton of the murder, and then, without a trial, they hanged him."

Faith's heart twisted at the pain she saw on his face.

"That wasn't the worst of it. I won't get into all the horrible details. Suffice it to say that they hanged the poor man in front of his family. I like to think that my father believed Paxton was guilty." His mouth twisted in a bitter smile. "Why, I don't know. He was a terrible man who did terrible things. But there's still a part of me that wishes there had been a little bit of good in him somewhere. You know what I'm saying?"

Faith understood better than he could realize. She often caught herself making excuses for her father, wanting to believe he had a few saving graces.

"Ace Keegan, Caitlin's husband, was Joseph Paxton's stepson."

She gasped. "And he married the daughter of his stepfather's murderer?"

Patrick sighed. "That's another story. But, yes, in answer to your question. He married the daughter of his stepfather's killer. How he has made his peace with it I'll never know, but somehow he has."

Faith recalled Caitlin's saying that her marriage had had bad beginnings. Now she understood why.

"Ace was only eleven years old the night Joseph Paxton was hanged. I'm sure you noticed the scar on his cheek and the way he limps. That's because my father, Connor O'Shannessy, bashed him in the face with the butt of a rifle and then shattered his hip with a kick of his boot."

Faith knew she should say something, but words eluded her.

"After my father died, Ace Keegan returned to No Name, hell-bent on clearing his stepfather's name. In the process, he made some terrible accusations, all of them directed at my father in one way or another." Patrick dragged in a shaky breath. "Deep down, I suspected that the accusations were true, but that didn't make the truth any easier to swallow, and I detested Ace Keegan for forcing it down my throat. Came to a point where I was ashamed to hold my head up when I went into town because my last name was O'Shannessy."

"Your father's actions were no reflection on you."

"Oh, yes. You've seen the portrait of him. I'm a dead ringer for my old man. 'Just like your daddy,' people used to say. 'A regular chip off the old block.' You can't know how those words haunted me. I didn't *want* to be like him, but I knew I was. I saw the resemblance when I looked in a mirror, and more times than I wanted to count, I caught myself acting like him. Talking like he did, walking like he did, laughing like he did. As time wore on, and Ace Keegan's accusations became common knowledge, the shame I felt became intolerable. I found numbness in a bottle. I wasn't thinking of Caitlin or how my drinking might affect her. For a while there, I was bent on becoming just like my father and proving everyone right."

"You're *nothing* like him," Faith protested. "Noth-

ing like him, do you hear? There's a physical resemblance, yes. But inside, where it truly counts, you're
as different from him as night is from day, Patrick.''

"Do you really think so?''

"I know so.'' Faith gave his hand a hard squeeze.
"You're a good man, Patrick, a *fine* man.''

He curled his fingers warmly around hers. "So was
my father at some point in his life. I don't know what
made him turn bad. Maybe the death of our mother.
Who knows? But turn he did. When my sister was
only sixteen, he sold her favors to a friend for six
cases of whiskey.''

A picture of Caitlin's lovely countenance moved
through Faith's mind. *"No,"* she whispered. "Oh, dear
God, Patrick, no.''

"It wasn't like he did it when he was crazy drunk
and not thinkin' straight. He planned it. Sent me away
on a cattle drive to get me out of the way, then sat
at his desk, swilling whiskey, while a man brutally
raped my sister.'' Patrick's mouth thinned and drew
back from his teeth. "Try living with that,'' he said
tautly. "Knowing a man like that sired you, that his
blood flows in your veins.''

Faith could only shake her head.

"I needed for you to know,'' he told her. "Like I
said when I started, I've grown very fond of you,
Faith, and of your daughter as well. That being the
case, it doesn't seem smart to keep secrets. We inherit
certain traits from our parents. Bloodlines are the
making of a man. Mine are nothing to be proud of.''

"And you think mine are?'' Faith thought of her
father again, and the awful sick feeling returned to
her stomach. "Think again, Patrick O'Shannessy.
Bloodlines can determine our appearance, but they
have nothing to do with who we are inside.''

He gave her a searching look. "I'll bet you have a
pedigree that would put a champion racehorse to
shame.''

Faith laughed. "Oh, yes, I come from a long line of

Maxwells, all of them very fine and upstanding on the surface. Just don't look too closely."

Patrick leaned around to search her gaze. "You can't tell me that your father ever did anything as despicable as mine did."

"I doubt he's ever killed anyone. That isn't to say he may not have been responsible for someone's wrongful death. He probably just hired it done." She lifted her shoulders in a helpless shrug. "Fathers back east do despicable things to make money, too, Patrick. The swindles are prettied up to make them seem respectable, but they're swindles all the same. They also sell their daughters. The asking price is just a good deal higher, and it's all made legal with marriage."

"Meaning that you were sold to Harold?"

"Essentially."

His jaw muscle started to tick. In that moment, Faith knew that he was in love with her. Not so very long ago, she might have recoiled at the very thought, but she'd come to know Patrick O'Shannessy now. On the outside he appeared to be a rough, common man, but on the inside there was nothing common about him.

"Did the bastard hurt you?" he asked with a dangerous edge to his voice.

Under Harold's tutelage, she had learned that there were many different kinds of pain, but for now, she chose not to go into that. "No, not in the way you mean. Most of the pain in my marriage was more emotional than physical. I was born and raised a Maxwell. From early childhood, I was expected to comport myself with pride and dignity and grace. And then, in marriage, I was stripped of all three." She felt her chin tremble and swallowed hard to steady her voice. "It wasn't a conventional union, if indeed such a thing exists. My father was in textiles. My father-in-law owned a shipping line. When Harold and I married, the two enterprises merged."

Patrick stopped walking and turned to search her

expression. "Don't make light of it, Faith. Six cases of whiskey or a fleet of ships, it doesn't matter a damn. You were sold all the same. It must have been bad for you."

Faith seldom let herself recall that period of her life precisely for that reason, because it had been so hurtful.

Peering through the twilight gloom to check on her daughter, she haltingly recounted to Patrick the pertinent details of her life, specifically that her mother had died when she was quite young, leaving her to be raised by a father who resented her because she hadn't been born a boy.

"Shortly after my mother's death, my father remarried. Sadly, his new wife miscarried late in her first pregnancy and then died of childbed fever. My father's hopes for a son seemed to die with her. After living my whole life being virtually ignored by him, I suddenly became the center of his attention."

Patrick gripped her hand more tightly. "Were you glad about that?"

Faith considered the question. "In the beginning, I suppose I was, yes. It was wonderful to be noticed, even when his attention grew obsessive. He began hiring tutors to teach me French and give me music lessons. If I forgot to stand straight or walk like a lady, the punishments he meted out could be quite severe." Faith's throat went thick at the memories. "As I mentioned, I was very young, about ten or so when the worst of it began—and having lost my mother, I was a desperately needy child. In the beginning, I think I mistook my father's absolute focus on me as a sign that he loved me after all. I didn't even suspect his motives when he sent me away to a finishing school at far too young an age."

Patrick gazed solemnly at her. "Why do I get this feeling that Harold is about to enter the picture?"

"Because you're so very astute?" Faith forced another humorless laugh. "If only I had been so intuitive. Perhaps then it wouldn't have hurt so deeply when I figured out my father's plan."

"Tell me," Patrick said simply.

"It truly isn't a very interesting story." Faith turned her hands to stare at the lines on her palms. "Sad, perhaps, but not interesting."

"Humor me."

"When I was polished to my father's satisfaction, he began to seek a suitable husband for me. Harold and his father were invited to supper. I was put through my paces. They liked what they saw. After the meal, the three men adjourned to the library and began negotiating the marriage contract over cigars and brandy. On my wedding day, I had just barely turned fifteen and had never been alone with my husband."

"Oh, honey."

The understanding in his tone gave Faith the courage to continue. "It wasn't so bad, Patrick. Not that part, anyway. Unbeknownst to me, Harold was gravely ill with consumption and not expected to live out the year. Even with his father pressuring him to get me with child to provide him with another heir, Harold was too weak to bother me on a regular basis, and when he did, more times than not, he failed to accomplish the deed."

"Sweet Christ. And he blamed you for his failures?"

Faith frowned in bewilderment. "How did you—?"

"Never mind. I spoke out of turn. Go on with your tale."

Faith took a deep, cleansing breath. "That's pretty much it, the sordid little story of my life. In the short while we've been here, you've been more of a father to Charity than mine ever was to me."

"I've done precious little for your daughter," he protested.

"Say what you like. Before we came here, it had been months since I'd heard her laugh. Just listen to her now." Her daughter's laughter and the barking of the dog drifted lightly to them on the wind. "Thank you so much for allowing her to have the puppy. She's wanted one for a long while, but neither of her grandfathers would hear of it."

"I'm sorry about your marriage, Faith. It shouldn't happen that way, you know. Two people should love each other when they're joined in holy matrimony."

There had been nothing holy about Faith's marriage.

"It isn't always sordid," he went on. "The physical side of marriage is a beautiful thing when two people love each other."

He spoke with such conviction that Faith could almost believe it. "Perhaps," she settled for saying.

"Trust me. It's beautiful."

She hugged her waist. "I'll have to take your word for it. Nothing between Harold and me was beautiful, not even the birth of our daughter. He was so infuriated when he learned that I'd brought forth a girl that he didn't even look at her when he entered the birthing chamber. He came directly to my bedside and began ranting at me about the fine mess I had made of things. He was growing sicker by the day, time was running out, and his father was absolutely livid that our child was a useless female."

"How old was Charity when Harold died?"

"Four, and it wasn't a day too soon." Faith caught the inside of her cheek between her teeth and bit down until it stung. "Forgive me, Patrick. I shouldn't talk that way. But, God forgive me, it was how I felt. When I wasn't daydreaming about grabbing Charity and running far away, I was wishing the disease might kill him more quickly."

"Don't apologize for being honest. If I had been there, I might have done more than wish him gone. Any man who chastises a woman for giving him a beautiful little girl instead of a son isn't worth the powder it'd take to blow him to hell. You and your daughter are well rid of him."

Faith could only wish that everything else in her life could be so easily resolved. She'd gotten her first taste of freedom here on this ranch, but if her father had anything to say about it, that wouldn't last for long.

"Somehow I have this bad feeling that I haven't heard all of the story," he said gently. "Something prompted you to leave Brooklyn. Charity said your father was trying to make you remarry, but that makes no sense. You're what, twenty-two?" At her nod, he added, "And a widow, to boot. Your father can't pick and choose your husband for you now. You're free to make your own choice."

Faith gazed off through the dimness at her daughter for a long moment. "After Harold died, things were complicated," she confessed. "Considering his wealth, he left me only a paltry sum, but it would have been enough for Charity and me to live in modest comfort, had I ever received the money. Unfortunately, my father convinced Harold that I was financially inept, and the bequeathal was put into a trust, with my father appointed as trustee. After my husband died, I was penniless except for the small monthly stipend Papa allowed me, and even that was conditional. If I behaved and did as I was told, he was generous. If I balked and kicked up a fuss, he withheld all funds and threatened to toss me and my daughter out in the street."

"Surely he never would have done it."

"Perhaps not, but knowing him as I did, I was afraid to put him to the test."

"So he held you in financial bondage."

"More or less. My father is a powerful, ruthless, and relentless man who's accustomed to having his own way. If one tactic fails him, he quickly tries another. He's fond of saying that everyone has an Achilles' heel. At that point in time, Charity was mine, and I didn't protest overmuch when he found me another husband."

Even though Faith had long since come to accept that her father had never loved her, it still hurt to tell Patrick the rest. "His name is Bernard Fielding. He's an old man who may still have it in him to sire a son but will surely die soon after, leaving me to play the bereaved widow again." Tears leaped into her eyes, and she blinked rapidly to chase them away. "When I met Bernard, the truth smacked me right between the eyes. It was no accident that my father had chosen a dying young man to be my first husband. It was never his plan for me to marry happily and raise a family. The plan was for Harold to get me with child and then conveniently die, leaving my father to do the childrearing."

A stricken, horrified look drew Patrick's face taut. "He deliberately chose husbands for you that had one foot in the grave?"

"That's an interesting way of putting it." Faith's neck had grown so stiff that it hurt to nod her head. "But you're absolutely correct. First Harold, and then Bernard. All Papa cared about—all he has ever cared about—is acquiring a male heir to take over the enterprises and possibly even carry on the Maxwell name if he plays his hand right. I was and still am only a means to that end. He doesn't care if I'm miserably unhappy. He doesn't care if I'm mistreated. He doesn't even care what may happen to Charity because of his evil scheming. We mean nothing to him."

"My God, if he had his way, you'd be nothing but a broodmare."

Again, Faith was momentarily taken aback by his choice of words, but she'd been around Patrick long enough now to shake it off. "A broodmare, yes. That describes it, exactly."

He slowly closed the distance between them, his eyes holding hers with somber intensity. Lifting one hand, he lightly smoothed a tendril of hair from her cheek, his fingertips setting her skin afire wherever they touched. "You deserve more than that, Faith. You deserve a father to love you, and a husband to cherish you."

"We don't always get what we deserve," she whispered.

He bent closer, so close that she could feel the

warmth of his breath on her lips, and she realized that
he was going to kiss her. Even more surprising, she
wanted him to. Oh, how she wanted him to. The air
between them went electrical, and an eerie hush
seemed to surround them. She leaned toward him, as
helpless to resist his lure as a hapless moth diving at
a candle flame. Her lips parted. Her breath started
coming in shallow, uneven pants that left her lungs
aching for oxygen. He slipped his hand under her chin,
grasped her jaw, and lifted her face to his.

"Maman!"

Faith jerked, and Patrick stepped quickly away as
he turned toward the approaching child. "What have
you got there?" he asked, his smile revealing no trace
of irritation as he crouched to look into Charity's
cupped hands. "Ah, a rock."

Faith almost giggled. She stifled the urge and
stepped closer to admire her daughter's grimy treasure. "Oh, my, it has sparkly ribbons all through it
that look like gold. You don't suppose it is, do you?"

Patrick lifted the rock in the fading light, turned it
this way and that, and then nodded. "You may have
something here, sweet pea. Are there any more like
this one lying about?"

Charity fairly bubbled over with delight. "Oh, *yes*.
Lots and lots of them, Paddy! Are we going to be
rich?"

"Maybe so." He cast a glance at the darkening sky.
"Run collect as many as you can. When we get back
to the house, I'll take a closer look in the light."

Charity was off like a shot. Patrick grinned after
her. "Fool's gold," he said softly as he turned back
toward Faith. "It's so thick in some parts of this country that Ace Keegan decorated his fireplace with the
stuff."

"Too bad. I could do with a windfall."

"Couldn't we all? That isn't to say there isn't gold
in this country. No Name was originally a gold rush
town that went bust so quickly no one ever got around
to christening it."

Faith chuckled at the revelation. "Ah, well."

"Easy for you to say. I've been wanting to steal a kiss from you for over a month, and then when I finally work up my courage, I get interrupted."

A flush crept hotly up her neck.

"It's just as well, I suppose," he added. "I distracted you from your story."

"That's it. When I discovered that Bernard meant to farm Charity out to a boarding school directly after our nuptials, we left Brooklyn. When our money was stolen, we could go no farther and ended up stranded in No Name."

"I, for one, am mighty glad you did."

Faith shared that sentiment. If they hadn't stayed in No Name, she might never have met Patrick.

"All's well that ends well," he observed, his eyes trailing slowly over her face as though he meant to commit each feature to memory. "You're here now. It's time to look forward and put the bad memories behind you."

"I wish it were so simple."

"What's complicated about it? You're over twenty-one. You have a job to support your daughter. Your father's hold on you is broken."

"You don't know my father."

The haunted look in Faith's eyes made Patrick's heart catch.

"If he finds me—and there's strong possibility that he may—he will stop at nothing to have his way. Even more frightening, I know he won't come after me alone. He'll bring a small army of hired guns with him." She toed the weeds that grew between them, then sighed and closed her eyes. "Perhaps we'll be lucky," she whispered, "and he'll never find us."

In an entirely different way, Patrick had experienced the long reach of a powerful man during the early years of his life. On countless occasions, he and Caitlin had tried to run away, only to be caught by well-meaning neighbors or townsfolk and carted back to their father. To this day, he could remember the fear that had nipped at their heels after they made good an escape, how they'd both jumped at shadows and kept looking over their shoulders, terrified of seeing their father towering behind them.

"I honestly don't believe he'll ever think to look for you in Colorado."

"My father might not, but he won't be doing the looking. He'll hire paid bloodhounds, the best investigators in the country. I want to believe they'll never track us down, but realistically, what are the chances that a woman and little girl, traveling so far by themselves, drew no one's attention along the way?"

In that moment, as he searched Faith's eyes, Patrick knew that this was no irrational, feminine fear, but spine-chilling terror based on fact. Her father was searching for her even as they spoke, and eventually he would find her.

Chapter Seven

*T*he following morning, Patrick strapped on his gun. Then he saddled his gelding and rode over to the Paradise Ranch to seek the advice of his brother-in-law, Ace Keegan. Joseph, Ace's younger half brother, joined them out by the corral. Patrick would have preferred to see Ace alone, but he'd long since come to understand that Ace and his brothers were as thick as thieves. When there was trouble, they faced it together, and Patrick had definitely come to them this morning with trouble riding double behind him. He guessed that showed on his face.

"That's a hell of a note," Ace said when Patrick had recounted Faith's story to them.

"Sure is. What kind of father is this Maxwell fellow?" Joseph spat on the ground. He wasn't a tall individual, but for a short man, he packed one hell of a wallop, in Patrick's estimation. Only a fool would tangle with him. "Give me ten minutes alone with the son of a bitch," he said. "Sounds to me like he needs a boot planted up his highfalutin ass."

Patrick had to smile. He and Joseph Paxton talked the same language.

"Jesus, Joseph, get a rein on that temper," Ace inserted. "Patrick's here for advice, not to rally a mob."

Joseph leaned over to spit again. He gave his older brother a narrow-eyed look. "Time was when you were as quick to get riled as I am. Has marriage turned you soft, big brother?"

"There's nothing soft about me, you cocky little bastard. Any time you get to wonderin', hop on it like a frog."

Patrick couldn't help himself. He had to laugh. He quickly sobered when both men glared at him. He coughed and rubbed his nose. How Caitlin managed to rule her household with such a small fist, he'd never know. There wasn't a man in her new family who dared to enter her home without wiping his boots clean first.

"Back to your problem," Ace said to Patrick, with a warning look at his brother. "And just for the record, I don't think a boot up her father's ass is the answer."

"What is the answer?" Patrick asked.

"Marry her," Joseph said. "Only way I see."

Ace rolled his eyes. "That isn't the answer, Joseph. How do you know if he even has feelings for the woman?"

"By lookin' at him," Joseph replied. "He's got that same sick-calf look that you used to have when you were chasing your tail over Caitlin."

"I never chased my tail over Caitlin."

Joseph chuckled. "You sure as hell did, and had me chasin' mine, too. Snarlin' at everybody, ornery as a badger with a thorn in its paw. Hell, big brother, she's still got you chasin' your tail. You love that girl beyond all reason."

Ace parted his lips to argue, and then snapped his teeth closed. "I'm going to remember this when you finally get hitched."

"Never happen," Joseph replied confidently. "I'm a grazer. Fence me in on one pasture, and first thing you know, I'll be stretchin' my neck to nibble the grass on the far side of the wire."

Ace rolled his eyes again. Then he settled a thoughtful gaze on Patrick. "Is Joseph right? Do you have feelings for this woman?"

Patrick almost said no, but as the word tried to

creep up his throat, he swallowed it back, recognizing
it as a lie. He'd been in over his head with Faith
almost from the first, and he'd been struggling to stay
afloat ever since. He loved the woman; that was the
long and short of it. He'd also come to love her daughter as if she were his own. The thought of marriage
still sort of alarmed him, but not nearly as much as
the thought of losing them did. When he tried to imagine his life without Faith and Charity in it, his blood
ran cold and his chest hurt.

"I love her," he confessed. Once the words were
out, he wondered why he'd been so reluctant to say
them.

"Enough to put your bacon on the plate?" Ace
asked.

Patrick straightened his shoulders and nodded.

"Well, marry her, then," Ace said. "That'll put a
hitch in Mr. Maxwell's get-along like nothing else will.
Man sounds like a bully to me, and bullies only push
people around when they can get away with it. Faith
won't be so easily intimidated by the arrogant bastard
if she has a husband who won't hesitate to push back."

That made sense. Patrick had known a bully personally, and for a goodly number of years. In all that
time, he'd never once seen Connor O'Shannessy whale
the tar out of a man bigger than he was. His father's
victims had always been unable to fight back.

"What about Charity?" Patrick asked. "If I marry
Faith, she'll be safe enough, but what of the child? Is
there any way Maxwell could get custody?"

Ace scowled thoughtfully. "I think you'll automati-
cally become the child's legal guardian, but to be on
the safe side, go straight from the justice of the peace
to the courthouse and file for adoption."

Faith was struggling to dismember a plucked
chicken when Patrick returned to the house. Charity
sat at the table, building a house of cards, the puppy
asleep by her chair. Patrick moved in close behind

Faith where she stood at the sink and bent to nibble the nape of her neck. She missed her aim with the butcher knife and nearly relieved herself of a thumb.

"What are you about?" she asked breathlessly.

"Trying to get your attention."

He had definitely succeeded. Fiery heat swirled in her belly, and her nipples had gone as hard and sharp as screw shafts. "A simple hello would suffice. I'm trying to make chicken and dumplings."

Patrick latched on to her earlobe and did fascinating things to it with flicks of his tongue. "I love chicken and dumplings. But right now, I've got other things on my mind."

Faith's knees almost buckled. "Like what?"

He glanced at Charity. "Can you tear yourself away from that hen and take a turn around the yard with me?"

"Can I come?" Charity asked.

"May I come," Faith corrected, wondering when her daughter had started to talk like a Coloradoan.

"Not this morning," Patrick told the child. "I need to speak to your ma in private."

Patrick seldom denied Charity anything. Of late, Faith had even begun to worry that her daughter would become spoiled and willful if he had his way. She gave Patrick another wondering look. He only smiled, handed her a towel to wipe her hands, and then grasped her by the arm to lead her outside. Once there, he stalked in a circle around her for a moment, then stopped, planted his hands on his hips, and said, "I love you."

Faith was so startled that she cocked her head. "I beg your pardon?"

"Damn it, Faith, you heard me the first time. Don't make me say it again until you're ready to say it back."

"You love me?"

"That's what I said, isn't it?"

He didn't seem to be very happy about it. In Faith's

estimation, it was marvelous news. She started tapping her toe. "May I ask what brought this on?"

"Your father. If he finds you now, he may find a way to make you go home. He could claim you're emotionally unbalanced—or that you abuse your daughter. God only knows. If you marry me, nothing he says or does will hold any sway. I'll be able to tell him to go whistle Dixie."

"That isn't enough reason for us to marry, Patrick."

"I love you. Isn't that reason enough?" He winced and turned his gaze toward the sky. "Damn it. You made me say it twice." He leveled a burning look at her. "Out with it. I want an answer right now. Do you feel the same way or not?"

"You are cursing at me, sir."

He winced again. Then he threw up his hands and turned a full circle. When he faced her again, he leaned forward to get nose to nose with her. "'Damn' is a byword. It's not a curse word by my definition. All the same, I apologize. I don't reckon I should say it while I'm proposing to you."

"Is that what you're doing, proposing?"

The glint in his eyes intensified. "What? Do you want me on my knees? Is that it?"

"No. It's just that you seem so upset!"

"If you felt like this, you'd be upset, too."

An odd, tight sensation closed around Faith's throat. "How is it that you're feeling, Patrick?"

"Scared."

She searched his sky blue eyes, trying to understand. "Scared of what?"

"Scared to death that you don't love me back."

Tears stung her eyes. The next instant she was in his arms. She wasn't sure if he'd grabbed her, or if she had jumped. And it didn't really matter. She was in his arms, right where she belonged.

"I'm not a good lover," she whispered against his neck.

He laughed and spun in a circle with her clasped

against his hard chest. "You will be, darlin'. Leave it to me."

He had taught her so many things, how to milk cows, how to make butter and cheese, how to slop hogs, and how to do laundry. She was also becoming a halfway decent cook. Perhaps he could teach her how to make love as well.

Faith prayed so. She wanted to please this man. She wanted that more than almost anything.

"Oh, Patrick," she whispered fervently, "I love you, too. I love you so very much."

"It's a damned good thing. Otherwise I'd be in a hell of a fix."

At Patrick's insistence, Faith stood at the center of her room an hour later, draped head to toe in ivory silk and lace. To say she was bewildered was an understatement. Patrick was right; the dress that he had stowed in the trunk that first afternoon bore no dirt stains. It was as spotless and perfect as new. There was just no explaining it. Faith clearly remembered dropping the gown in the dirt and despairing afterward that it was ruined. And yet, by some miracle, it wasn't. Even stranger, it fit her like a glove. It was almost as if the dress had been made especially for her.

Faith closed her eyes and ran a hand down the front of the gown, marveling at the tingling warmth that ribboned through her body. She'd felt it the instant she slipped into the dress, and the heat had intensified with each button that she fastened. It was almost as if the dress were imbued with some inexplicable magic. She remembered how she'd felt drawn to it the first time she'd seen it and then how she'd felt when she touched it. Even stranger, directly afterward, she had spotted Patrick's advertisement taped to the door window of the mercantile. How was it that she'd passed that store a fair hundred times and never seen the sign until she'd been holding this dress in her arms?

"Knock, knock. You about ready?"

Patrick shoved his head through the crack of the door. Faith felt suddenly self-conscious as she faced him.

"Dear God," he whispered.

"Is it too fancy?" she asked.

He stepped into the room, his expression stunned. He wore a white shirt and black dress slacks. He was, in Faith's estimation, the handsomest man who'd ever drawn breath.

"Too fancy? No. It's gorgeous. *You're* gorgeous. You look so beautiful, I can't believe you're real."

Faith's stomach was churning with nerves. She wanted to become Patrick's wife more than she'd ever wanted anything, but she couldn't shake the feeling that something terrible might happen to spoil their happiness together.

"Oh, Patrick, I'm scared."

"Of me?"

She gave a startled laugh and then found herself blinking away tears. "No, never that. I'm just—oh, I don't know." She glanced at the window. "It's probably stupid, but ever since you asked me to marry you, I've had this feeling that my father will appear at any moment."

He stepped across the room and drew her into his arms. "All the more reason to get this done. Once you're my wife, you can stop being afraid. If he comes around, I'll draw him a map in the dirt to guide him out of here and give him a boot up the ass to help him on his way."

Faith wanted to believe that. She needed to believe it. But she couldn't shake the feeling that something dark and sinister awaited them just around the corner.

It was to be a simple ceremony before a justice of the peace. And by all rights, it should have been the plainest, simplest wedding on record. The JP performed all nuptial ceremonies in his sitting room, the walls of which were papered in a pattern of ancient roses, long since turned brown from the smoke of his cigars. His wife was a stout, unadorned woman who nodded and seldom spoke. Faith had barely recovered from the shock of finding goats on the people's doorstep when she and Patrick were saying "I do."

Nevertheless, she felt thoroughly and wonderfully married afterward. Caitlin and Ace were there to witness their vows, along with all of Ace's brothers. Charity preceded Faith into the sitting room, sprinkling rose blossoms from Caitlin's flower garden on the worn carpet. All in all, it was, in Faith's opinion, the most beautiful wedding ever.

After the brief ceremony, Faith nearly swooned when Patrick kissed her. It was not only their first kiss but also a startling revelation. She actually *liked* it. He encircled her waist with one strong arm, drew her snugly against him, and tasted her mouth as if she were a succulent piece of fruit.

"My turn," Joseph Paxton said with a laugh. The next thing Faith knew, she was draped over his muscular arm, expecting to feel his mouth on hers at any moment. Instead, he winked at Patrick and bussed her cheek.

After that, Faith received more kisses on the cheek, the first delivered by Ace, the second by Caitlin, followed by quick kisses from the rest of the Paxton men. Esa was a quiet, gentle-mannered man with a kindly smile. David had a tough, wiry look about him, and he wore a silver star on his shirt, leading Faith to believe he must be a lawman.

With congratulations ringing in her ears, Faith signed the necessary papers to record her marriage to Patrick O'Shannessy. When those particulars had been completed, Patrick led her and Charity to the courthouse, where he filed more papers to adopt Faith's daughter. Then Caitlin arrived to collect the child.

"Your daughter and her puppy will be spending the night at our place," she cheerfully informed Faith. "It's your wedding night, after all." Ruffling Charity's hair, Caitlin winked at Patrick and smiled. "Charity has kindly offered to help me make cookies tonight."

Faith had never been apart from her daughter overnight. As though attached to the child by an invisible string, she followed Caitlin and Charity from the courthouse. Never leaving her side, Patrick gave her elbow a reassuring squeeze as Ace swung Charity up into his wagon.

"They'll take good care of her, honey. No need to worry."

Faith was about to agree when she spotted a well-dressed gentleman entering the hotel farther up the street. Her heart gave a nasty lurch.

"What is it?" Patrick asked.

Faith blinked and shook her head. The man had already entered the building. "Nothing. It's just—" She shook her head again and reached blindly for her husband's hand. "Nothing. I just thought for a moment that I saw my father."

Patrick curled an arm around her. "And so what if you did? I told you once how that will go. Do I need to say it again? From this moment forward, the only man you need to worry about is me."

Faith dragged her gaze from the hotel and forced herself to look up at Patrick's dark countenance. His deep blue gaze gave her the strength to dredge up a smile. "You're right. Absolutely right. I'm just being silly."

Faith went up on her tiptoes to kiss her daughter good-bye and then surrendered happily to the circle of Patrick's arm as Ace drove the family wagon away from the boardwalk. When the dust had settled, Patrick bent to kiss her forehead.

"Well, Mrs. O'Shannessy, are you about ready to go home?"

Home. The word had such a lovely, final ring to it. With a last worried glance at the hotel, Faith relaxed and laughed. "I am, sir. Lead the way. I'll follow you anywhere."

"You'll never walk behind me," he whispered huskily. "Only beside me."

In truth, Faith didn't care if she led or trailed behind, only so long as she could spend the rest of her life with him.

It had been a hectic day, packed with varying emotions. By the time Patrick reined in the team of horses in front of his house, Faith was thoroughly drained. After he helped her from the wagon, she went inside and stood at the sink in her wedding dress, wondering stupidly what she should fix for supper. The chicken she'd left in the icebox, she guessed.

"We'll have eggs and bacon," Patrick said when he came in from the barn a few moments later. "It's late. We're both tired. That'll make less mess to clean up after."

Faith jerked back to awareness, wondering how long she had been staring blankly at nothing. "I'm sorry. What did you say?"

He came to wrap her in his strong arms. "Why the worried frown? Are you thinking about your father again?"

Faith wanted to deny it, but when she looked into her husband's eyes, she couldn't bring herself to lie. "That man going into the hotel. He truly did look like Papa. I know it's unlikely, but I can't shake the feeling that it may have been him."

Patrick's embrace tightened. "Given the fact that it's our wedding day, I sincerely hope not. But if he's here, we'll deal with him."

"He isn't easily dealt with."

Patrick's mouth thinned. "You can't live the rest of your life terrified that he may show up, Faith. Have some trust in me. You're my wife now. His hold on you is forever broken. From this moment forward, you have nothing more to fear from him."

She closed her eyes and pressed her face to his shirt. After drawing in the scent of him, she sighed shakily.

"You're right. No more worrying." She let her head fall back and smiled. "Eggs and bacon sound lovely."

"I'll cook." He bent to kiss her and set her head to spinning. Then, his voice husky with desire, he gently nipped her lower lip and said, "Why don't you go upstairs and get into something more comfortable while I'm tossing together some grub?"

Faith felt perfectly comfortable in the wedding dress, but she might dribble food on the bodice if she didn't change into something else. She went upstairs, rifled through her armoire, and selected Patrick's favorite, a pale blue dress that had seen better days. After stepping out of the wedding gown, she carefully folded it and laid it at the foot of the bed until she could put it away in the trunk.

When she'd finished dressing, she turned to pick up the wedding gown. It no longer lay on the mattress. Bewildered, she got on her knees to look under the bed. Then she checked inside the trunk, thinking she might have put the gown away without thinking. *Nothing.* It had vanished into thin air.

Patrick found Faith at the foot of the bed. "What's wrong, sweetheart?"

When she told him that the wedding dress had disappeared, he executed a search as well. Finally, he gave up, shrugged in bewilderment, and scratched his head. "I'll be damned. Where on earth could it have gotten off to?"

Faith swallowed, hard. "I think it was charmed," she whispered.

"You think it was what?"

"Charmed." Afraid he might think she was crazy, Faith told him about the tingle of warmth that she'd felt the first time she touched the dress, and how, afterward, she'd seen his advertisement for the first time, even though she'd walked past the mercantile on countless occasions. "When I dropped the gown along the road, I felt sure that it was ruined. But when I got it out of the trunk earlier today, there wasn't a dirt stain to be seen. How could that happen? You didn't clean it, did you?"

"No. I just folded it up and stuffed it in the trunk." He frowned slightly. "I don't remember there being any dirt stains on the skirt, though. I just remember thinking how pretty it was."

"It was ruined, I'm telling you." Faith gave the room another appraisal, half expecting to see the dress somewhere. "I can't help but wonder if it wasn't charmed, Patrick."

He didn't laugh, just gazed wonderingly at the trunk. "Maybe it was charmed," he agreed. "You ended up here, didn't you? That's all I care about, that you found your way to me."

Tears of happiness stung Faith's eyes. "That's what truly matters," she agreed. "That we're together."

He sighed, smiled slightly, and said, "Supper's done. You hungry?"

Faith felt hungry, but not for eggs. "Not really. Are you?"

He moved slowly toward her. "I'm starving."

Moments later, Faith giggled. "I just fastened all these buttons, Patrick O'Shannessy. Now I can only wonder why I bothered."

He nibbled at her throat, sending tingles of heat spilling into her belly. "Beautiful gifts must always be unwrapped," he whispered.

Faith let her head fall back, trusting him as she'd never trusted anyone. "Love me, Patrick," she whispered.

He slipped the sleeves of her dress down her arms, kissed her deeply, and then granted her request, loving her as every woman yearns all her life to be loved. He began with a deep kiss that made her toes curl. Then he lifted her into his arms and carried her to the bed. Her chemise and bloomers soon followed her dress into a puddle on the floor.

"Oh, *yes*," Faith cried when his wonderful mouth trailed to her breasts. "Oh, *yes*!"

Faith floated on a dizzying rush of sensation, surrendering all that she was to him. When at last he entered her, she felt complete as she never had in her life.

Bracing his muscular arms, he suspended himself over her, not moving, barely breathing. "I love you," he whispered raggedly. "Ah, Faith, my sweet, I love you so much."

Before she could respond in kind, he plunged deeply within her and took her with him to paradise.

The next morning, Faith felt content in a way that only a well-loved woman can. She and Patrick had made love several times during the night, each time sweeter and more fulfilling than the last, until they'd collapsed with exhaustion in each other's arms just before dawn. As a result, they had awakened late, and both of them were scrambling to complete their morning chores before the day was half gone. After gathering the eggs, Faith blew her husband a kiss from the back stoop. Then later, just after she finished the milking, he caught her as she exited the stall and led her to the hayloft, where he gave her good reason to wish the day were over so they could make love all night again.

"For a woman who had no taste for this, you're sure warming to the experience mighty fast," he said as he fastened her bodice with deft fingers.

Faith giggled and plucked straw from her hair. "I must look a sight."

"You look beautiful," he whispered and kissed her again.

Before she knew quite how it happened, she was prone in the hay again, her body quivering with yearnings that only he could slake. And, oh, how wonderfully right that felt. For the first time in her life, she felt really and truly loved, just for herself.

That was such a fabulous feeling.

Some time later, Faith was gathering carrots from the kitchen garden for a stew for supper when she heard the sound of horses approaching. She cautiously circled the house, her heart pounding with unreasoning dread. She wasn't really surprised when she reached the front yard and saw her father sitting astride a galloping horse, flanked by at least a dozen riders, all wearing sidearms.

Faith almost bolted, but then she remembered that she was legally married. Legs trembling, she walked resolutely to the front fence and rested a hand on one of the pickets. The men who rode with her father ran hard, glittering gazes over her as they came to a halt in a long line. When Faith looked at them individually, they stared back unflinchingly. The stench of their bodies drifted to her on the warm summer air—a sickening mix of soured sweat, whiskey, and another smell she felt certain was pure meanness. They were mercenaries, the kind of men who regularly sold their souls for a dollar. Faith had seen men like them before in Brooklyn, only there they'd worn suits and postured as gentlemen.

Saddle leather creaked as the men shifted in their seats. A horse snuffled and pawed the dirt, sending up puffs of dust that quickly vanished in the breeze. Faith tried to speak, couldn't, and swallowed hard to find her voice.

"Papa," she finally pushed out by way of greeting. "Whatever are you doing here?"

"I've come to fetch you and my granddaughter home. What do you suppose I'm doing here?"

The harsh clip of his voice propelled her back through time to her childhood, when his every command had been her edict and disobedience had earned her an unpleasant punishment. A shiver of icy fear coursed through her body. She dug her nails into the wood. "I shan't ever return to Brooklyn, Papa. I've remarried. You've no control over me now."

Her father leaned forward in the saddle, his face turning almost purple with rage. "You dare to defy me? Collect your daughter. You shall return home. The marriage can be annulled easily enough."

Faith had no doubt that her father could do it.

There was always a way to bend the law if a man was wealthy and determined. "I have the right to make my own choices now, Papa, and I've chosen Patrick O'Shannessy as my husband."

"Don't argue with me, girl. You'll come home if I have to drag you."

Faith feared that her father would try to do just that, his plan undoubtedly to browbeat her into submission once they were back in Brooklyn. There was just one problem; she had a husband now who would object very strongly to her being forcefully removed from the premises.

Fleetingly, Faith wondered where Patrick was. When last she'd seen him, he'd been mending the door of the henhouse. "I'm not going back with you, Papa."

"You will do as you're told!"

One of her father's henchmen wrapped his horse's reins around the saddle horn, as if he meant to dismount and collect her. Faith fell back a step, prepared to run. But before the command from her brain could reach her legs, the smell of smoke surrounded her. Horrified, she glanced over her shoulder. To her dismay, she saw a black cloud billowing up from somewhere behind the house. For an awful moment, her heart froze. Then she rounded on her father.

"What have you *done*?" she cried.

"Nothing!" Her father narrowed his gaze on the sooty plume. "There's a fire, apparently. I didn't start it."

Faith didn't believe him. Her father could be ruthless when he wanted something, and right now, he wanted her married to Bernard Fielding. After being with Patrick, the very thought sickened her. If she ever had a son, and she prayed that she would, the child would be Patrick's, conceived in love.

She ran a frightened gaze over the ruffians her father had hired. They all sat relaxed in the saddle now, their hands close to their guns. They were the sort who could kill without blinking an eye.

"What have you done to my husband?" she cried.

"Nothing," a deep voice said from behind her.

Faith sagged with relief. "Patrick!"

His hand came to rest at the small of her back. His touch soothed her as nothing else could. "Go in the house, sweetheart."

Faith threw him a terrified look. When she saw the tick of his jaw, she cried, "No, Patrick. You're one man against a dozen."

Patrick settled a fiery blue gaze on her father and smiled calmly. "No worries. Your father knows he'll be the first to go down if bullets start to fly. We'll just talk and reach an understanding."

Faith didn't want to leave him. In that moment, as she looked up at his burnished face, she knew that she'd never loved anyone as much she loved him. She loved her daughter, of course, but that was an entirely different kind of love.

"No, Patrick. Please, if you make me go, come with me."

"Faith, do as you're told," he said evenly. "Go into the house. And don't come out until I say it's all right."

She started to argue. But then Patrick glanced down at her. "Trust me," he whispered. "It's going to be fine."

After sending her father a pleading look, Faith turned to go inside. Leaving the front door ajar so she could monitor the exchanges between her father and husband, she went only as far as the sitting room. There, she stood with her nose flattened against the window glass, whispering disjointed prayers for Patrick's safety. *Foolish man.* Feet planted wide apart, arms held out to his sides, he stood alone against a small army, his right hand poised over his gun. Did he have no sense at all?

Nevertheless, Faith felt proud to be his wife, fiercely proud. By comparison, her father was a pale figure of a man, courageous only when the odds were heavily in his favor.

In the distance, Faith saw a cloud of dust fast approaching. Soon she could make out riders. Her heart lifted with hope. Seconds later, Joseph Paxton brought his stallion skidding to a stop in the yard. He was out of the saddle before the horse had come to a complete stop. Shortly after, Esa and David rode in. They dismounted from their horses and went to flank their older brother.

Faith's father shifted nervously in the saddle. "Don't push me, mister," he warned Patrick. "My men are expert marksmen and fast at the draw. You and your friends here are going to die if you get in my way."

Patrick kept his hand over his gun. "You've got a lot of men riding with you," he agreed, "but sadly for you, Mr. Maxwell, their loyalty is rented." Patrick slowly turned his head to look each hired gun directly in the eye. "I may go down, just like he says, and maybe my friends will go down as well. But we're going to take some of you with us. Which of you falls remains to be seen, but mark my words, at least half of you aren't going to be sitting down for breakfast tomorrow." He looked back at Faith's father. "Are they willing to die for you, Mr. Maxwell? Seems to me that money sort of loses its shine when a man's facing possible death. Can't spend a paycheck from six feet under. Another thought for you to ponder on is that you'll be our first target. No matter how fast your men are, they can't get all of us before one of our bullets finds you."

Joseph flexed his fingers over the butt of his Colt. "You'd best perk up your ears, Mr. Maxwell. Your boys may be fast, but we're faster." Narrowing his eyes against the sun, Joseph scanned the group of hired guns. "If you boys are fast draws, then you've surely heard of Ace Keegan."

"What if we have?" a swarthy man asked.

"Ace is our brother," Joseph replied. "He taught all of us boys how to handle a gun. Maybe we aren't as fast as he is. Maybe we are. Carry on with this madness, and you'll soon find out."

The dark man shifted uneasily in the saddle. He

sent Faith's father an angry glare. "You said this would be easy. I didn't bargain on facing fast guns. If I've got to put my life at risk, I want more money."

"He's bluffing," Faith's father cried.

"Am I?" Joseph flashed a dangerous smile. "Proof's in the pudding, boys. Let's slap some leather and see who meets his Maker."

Faith's father had started to sweat. "There's no need for violence. I've just come to collect my daughter and granddaughter."

"You mean my wife and child," Patrick corrected. "Sorry, old man, but that ain't happenin'."

"The marriage is invalid!!" Faith's father shouted. "Faith is betrothed to another man. She cannot be married while she's contractually obligated to someone else."

David stepped forward, thumbing his badge. "By whose law? You're in Colorado now, not Brooklyn, and I'm the marshal hereabouts. Your daughter's marriage to my brother-in-law is legal. Unless you want to ride out of here slung over the back of a horse, I suggest you accept that and make fast tracks."

Carlton Maxwell sent Faith a burning look through the window glass. "This isn't finished, young lady," he called. "Mark my words, this isn't finished by a long shot."

"Oh, it's finished," Patrick corrected evenly. "If I see you on my property again, the time for talking will be over. I'll shoot you on sight."

"Do you hear that, Faith? This no-account piece of trash that you married just threatened to shoot me." Her father jabbed a finger in her direction. "You'll rue the day you formed this alliance. When the time comes that you realize your mistake, don't come whining to me. From this moment on, I don't have a daughter. Do you hear me?"

Faith was still trembling when her father and his men wheeled their horses and rode from sight. She raced from the house. Patrick held out an arm to encircle her shoulders and draw her close to his side. He bent to kiss her hair. "Hey, darlin', you're shakin' like a leaf."

Faith turned her face against his shirt. "Oh, Patrick, never in my life have I been so sick with fright."

"All's well that ends well." Patrick drew his wife closer and met Joseph Paxton's gaze over the top of her dark head. "I owe you one."

Joseph dusted his hat on his trouser leg. "You don't owe us nothin'. If the tables were turned, you'd do the same for one of us."

"That may be, but I still appreciate that you came so fast."

Joseph's cheeks creased in a grin. "Of course we came fast. You're family now. We Paxtons look after our own. Besides, it appeared to me like you were handlin' them well enough on your own." He clamped a hand on Esa's shoulder. "We just evened up the odds a bit. Right, little brother?"

Esa nodded. "Ace is gonna be flat pissed that he missed out on all the fun."

David spat in the dirt, then toed away the evidence. "Nah. He's got more important fish to fry this morning." With a twinkling look at Faith, he added, "He took Caitlin and Charity into town to shop for baby stuff."

Joseph settled his tan Stetson back on his blond head. The wind kicked up just then, lifting golden hair straight as a bullet to trail the strands across his chiseled face. "Well, boys?" He narrowed an eye at the sun. "Looks to me like it's near about noon, and my belly's sayin' it's lunchtime."

"Won't you stay and have the noonday meal with us?" Faith asked. "We've plenty, and we'd love to have you."

"What're you fixin'?" Esa asked with a hungry glint in his eyes.

Joseph gave his brother a sharp jab in the ribs. "Thanks for the invite, but we'd best mosey on home. Chores to do, and all that."

"What chores?" Esa asked.

"Afternoon chores." Joseph grasped his younger brother's elbow and turned him toward their horses. "Do I need to make out a damned list?"

As the three brothers mounted up, Patrick could hear Esa muttering under his breath that all the chores were done. Joseph and David ignored his protests, waved farewell, and herded the youngest Paxton's horse from the yard.

"I think they refused the invitation to lunch because we were married only yesterday," Faith observed.

Patrick nodded. "I think you're right."

When the Paxton brothers had ridden out of sight, he tightened his hold on his bride and turned her into his arms. "Are you all right?"

She nodded and went up on her tiptoes to hug his neck. "Just a little rattled. When I came around the house and saw my father, my heart almost stopped beating." She leaned her head back to look up at him. "Whatever will we do if he comes back?"

"He won't," Patrick assured her. "I got my message across to him, loud and clear, and Joseph let him know that I'll always have their backing. Men like your father are too fond of their hides to risk getting shot. They only throw their weight around if they think they can get away with it. I can almost guarantee that we've seen the last of him, and good riddance."

A troubled expression entered her eyes. "That bothers you, doesn't it?"

"That men like your father are too fond of their hides to risk getting shot?"

"No, that you'll always have the Paxton brothers' backing."

Patrick bent his head to rest his forehead against hers. "I suppose it does in a way. I reckon it always will."

"Why, Patrick? Your sister is married to Ace. Soon she'll have a child, binding your families together. It's time to put the past behind you."

His throat went tight. "My father killed theirs. Two

years ago, we all buried the hatchet, and on the surface it's all but forgotten. But down deep, I can't believe they don't still hate me, at least a little."

"Why? Because down deep, you'll always hate yourself?" Faith leaned back to take his face between her hands. "Oh, Patrick. You aren't your father. You're a kind, wonderful man, and I love you with all my heart. I'm so proud to bear the O'Shannessy name. Don't you think it's time that you felt proud of it again yourself?"

"My father—"

"Enough about your father. It isn't about him anymore, Patrick. It's about *you*. It's about *us*. We can spend the rest of our lives looking back, but to what end? I don't want our future to be tainted by bad memories, neither yours nor mine. I want Charity and our other children to hold their heads high when they go into town, proud to be O'Shannessys."

Faith held her breath as she waited for Patrick's response. When his eyes went suspiciously bright, she knew that she had reached him.

"You're right," he whispered huskily. Then, grabbing her hand, he led her to the barn. "Stand right here," he ordered.

Faith did as he asked, frowning in bewilderment as he rummaged around inside the building. After a few minutes, he emerged into the sunlight, dragging a huge wooden sign behind him. Faith stepped around to read the carved letters. Then she laughed.

"Will you help me hang it back up?" he asked.

"I'd love to."

And so it was that Faith stood on the tailgate of Patrick's decrepit old wagon, holding up one end of the sign while Patrick nailed the other end to the side of the barn. When the task was completed, they linked arms and stood back to admire their work.

The sign read, THE O'SHANNESSY RANCH. Faith nodded in approval, and in that moment, she knew she would never again yearn for all that she'd left behind in Brooklyn. Everything that she'd ever wanted or needed was right here. She turned to hug Patrick's waist with a deep sense of rightness and belonging.

As their lips met, she thought of the wedding dress, wondering once again where it might be. After making the bed that morning, she'd searched the room a final time and found nothing, which had convinced her, for once and for all, that the gown had vanished. She had no explanation for that, other than the one she'd whispered to Patrick last evening, that the dress was magical.

It was a fanciful, crazy answer, Faith knew. Or was it? As her husband deepened their kiss and her blood began thrumming with desire, she couldn't deny that sometimes, when a woman least expected it, truly magical things could happen to forever change her life.

Catherine Anderson lives in the pristine wood-lands of Central Oregon. She is married to her high school sweetheart, Sid, and is the author of more than twenty best-selling and award-winning historical and contemporary romances.

Epilogue

❧◆❧

Catherine Anderson

Charlotte Hamilton almost walked past the boutique without stopping, but a vintage wedding gown in the window display caught her attention. She pressed close to the ice-frosted glass, her gaze fixed on the ivory silk and lace, so mesmerized by their beauty that the sound of the traffic behind her was momentarily snuffed out. *Gorgeous,* she thought, and then, *But so totally what I don't need.*

To say that Charlotte had no marriage prospects would have been an understatement. It had been more than a year since she'd even been asked out on a date. Nevertheless, the dress drew her out of the cold air into the warm shop like a magnet attracting metal shavings.

"Isn't it lovely?" a slender older woman asked when Charlotte went directly to the window display. "For reasons beyond me, I haven't been able to sell it. It's marked down, if you're interested."

Charlotte reached out to touch the dress. The instant her fingertips grazed the lace, a tingle of warmth shot up her arm. In that moment, she wanted to buy that dress more than she'd ever wanted to buy anything. *Madness.* She had just been laid off from her job. She was living with her mother and had a four-year-old son with leukemia to support. She couldn't afford to squander her money on a dress that she'd probably never have an opportunity to wear.

"It is beautiful," Charlotte agreed. "But I'm afraid

fifty dollars is more than I can afford to spend. My little boy is sick." She shrugged and smiled at the clerk. "I just wanted a closer look."

The older woman raised her elegantly drawn brows. "It would look lovely on you. If I reduce the price to twenty-five, can you afford it?"

"You can't sell it for so little," Charlotte protested. Then, with a roll of her eyes, she added, "And even twenty-five is too much, I'm afraid. I was laid off last week. Unemployment benefits don't stretch very far when a child is gravely ill."

The woman tipped her gray head. "I'll let you buy it in installments. If you can't pay for some reason, just give me a call." Her smile deepened. "Maybe I'm a silly old woman, but I can't shake the feeling that the dress is meant for you. All that glorious red hair and those fabulous blue eyes." She shook her head. "You must have that dress. You'll be a vision in it."

Somehow Charlotte found herself leaving the boutique with the boxed wedding gown clutched in her arms. She was so excited as she stepped back out on the sidewalk that she didn't think to look both ways. The next instant, she felt as if she'd been sideswiped by a speeding train. The box flew in one direction, she in another.

"Oh, *God*! I am *so* sorry. Are you all right?"

Charlotte blinked to clear her vision and discovered that she lay sprawled on her back. Snowflakes landed softly on her cheeks. *Was* she all right? She couldn't honestly say. Dimly she was aware of the sounds of passing traffic, plowing through the slush on the asphalt. Nothing seemed to hurt, but she felt decidedly dazed. She found herself looking into eyes the color of melted chocolate— warm, concerned, beautiful eyes ensconced in a chiseled, incredibly handsome face capped with curly black hair.

"I'm fine, I think."

"I didn't see you," he said. "I'm so sorry."

"It was my fault. I stepped out onto the sidewalk without looking."

"No way. It was totally *my* fault," he countered.

They argued the point for a moment, and then the absurdity of it struck them both and they started to laugh. He grasped her by the shoulders and helped her to sit up, then gently massaged her arms to check for injuries. Even through her wool coat, the touch of his hands made her heart miss a beat. A steady stream of people walked around them, but Charlotte barely noticed them, and she had the strangest feeling that he didn't either.

"Let's settle this debate over coffee," he suggested. Inclining his head toward a nearby shop, he flashed a crooked grin that didn't help to slow her racing pulse.

"Oh, I couldn't," she said.

"Please. I can't let you go until I'm sure you're all right."

With his help, Charlotte managed to regain her feet and collect her package. Then, after glancing at her watch, she said. "I'd love to have a cup of coffee. Really, I would. But I have a very sick little boy waiting for me at home." She felt in her pocket to make sure the prescription for chemo nausea that she'd just filled hadn't been broken by her fall. "Mark is looking forward to watching the new *Shrek* release tonight. I still need to stop by the video store to pick it up, and then I have to pick up some Chinese takeout. Ginger chicken. The chemo makes him horribly nauseated, and the ginger seems to help settle his stomach."

His smile dimmed. "Chemo?"

Charlotte nodded. *Too bad, so sad.* This was where all men made polite excuses and ran in the opposite direction. "Yes. He has leukemia."

"Ah." He nodded and gave her a searching look. "You're married, then."

He sounded disappointed. Charlotte laughed. "If only. I could use a husband's paycheck right now." Sobering, she added, "No, I'm a single mother. My husband did a vanishing act shortly after my son was born."

"It must be hard, going through the illness of a child all alone."

Hard didn't describe it by half. She cried herself to sleep some nights, terrified that her son might die. "I really need to go. I'm sorry. It's just—"

"Name and phone number." He reached inside his overcoat and drew a pen from under the lapel of what looked like a very expensive suit. Pen to his palm, he gave her an expectant look. "Please. I swear I'm not a serial killer."

Charlotte laughed again. It felt good, she realized. For her son's sake, she had to wear a cheerful face, but she seldom actually felt cheerful. "I wasn't thinking that.

"So what were you thinking?"

A taxi honked just then, making her jump. "It's just that—"

"I want to see you again," he pressed. "Call me crazy, but I have to see you again. I've got this feeling. I saw your face, and bang. I can't explain it. I never ignore my feelings. If I let you walk away, I'll always regret it."

Charlotte searched his brown eyes. She saw nothing sinister in their depths. Bemused, she gave him her name and phone number, watching as he wrote the information on the palm of his hand. Then she asked, "Are you slightly hard of hearing? My son is very ill. He has leukemia."

"I got that." He reached into his coat pocket and withdrew a business card. "Leukemia is no longer a death sentence for children, Charlotte. And I'm accustomed to dealing with sick little boys."

He handed her the card and retreated a step. "I'll call tonight to make sure you're all right."

She nodded stupidly.

"And be prepared with good excuses if you don't want to see me again. I know this great Chinese place that has the best ginger chicken on the planet. You, me, and your son. We'll make it a threesome. If his white count is down, we'll eat in while we watch movies."

Charlotte wondered how he knew that chemo could

wipe out a patient's white count, making it imperative to avoid public places. She was still staring after him when he disappeared behind the curtain of falling snow. She looked down at the business card. STEWART REDENHAFF. A string of letters followed his name. Stunned, Charlotte read on and realized that he was a pediatric oncologist who specialized in treating leukemia.

An inexplicable warmth ran through her as she clutched the dress box closer to her chest. She was smiling as she turned in the opposite direction. Maybe, she thought nonsensically, she'd been meant to step out of the shop without looking. Maybe, just maybe, she'd just had a head-on collision with fate.

New York Times bestselling author
Catherine Anderson

Morning Light

Born with second sight, Loni MacEwen
must warn the handsome rancher Clint
Harrigan that his son is in danger—
except he doesn't even have a son.
Then the drama Loni predicted unfolds
on the news: an orphaned boy is lost in
the wilderness. As Loni and Clint help in
the search for the boy, they begin to
form a bond of their own...

CONNIE BROCKWAY

HOT DISH

Here she is...

Years ago, Jenn Lind's family's dynasty crashed, forcing them to move out of their Raleigh penthouse and into a cabin in Fawn Creek, Minnesota. But Jenn saw a way out: She'd win the Buttercup Pageant, grab the scholarship, and run far, far away. The plan almost worked too, until some conniving townspeople cheated her out of her tiara. Still, she swore she'd make it out someday...

Miss Minnesota?

Twenty years later, she's on the cusp of real stardom. She's about to leave for New York to be crowned queen of daytime TV when Fawn Creek asks her to be grand marshal of the town's sesquicentennial. Her network accepts, delighted over the potential PR, especially since she'll be sharing the "honor" with international celebrity Steve Jaax, a man she got tangled up with once long ago. Between the all too attractive Steve, the townspeople, and a hundred-pound butter sculpture, Jenn may never escape Fawn Creek.
Or even worse, she might.

**Available wherever books are sold or at
penguin.com**

BARBARA METZGER
Truly Yours

Alone in the world, Amanda Carville has
no dowry, no reputation left, and no one
who believes her to be innocent of murder,
since she was found holding the gun that
killed her stepfather. Viscount Rexford also
has his troubles. He's scarred by war, and
cursed—or blessed–with the family trait of
knowing the truth when he hears it, and his
success at extracting the truth from military
prisoners has left many doubting his honor
and his methods. When Amanda tells him
she didn't do it, he believes her. Tired of
the truth business, Rex refuses to get
involved...until his heart leaves him
no choice.

**Available wherever books are sold or at
penguin.com**